To JANE

ENJOY!

BILOXI

By R. J. Bonett

R. J. Bonett
7-27-2022

Credits

Grateful appreciation to Marie Bonett and Charlene Lewis for their immediate assistance.

Editors

Rachel Heitzenrater – Managing Editor of the Canton Independent Sentinel

> *"Readers will appreciate the hard work the author put into each character's back story and life throughout the novel, as well as the stories that unfold when their worlds collide. You become attached to the characters and really enjoy seeing their stories unfold. You laugh, cry, and get excited reading what each of them does and has to say."*

Joseph Carreon – Owner of Carreon Publishing and the Canton Independent Sentinel

> *"Biloxi is an exhilarating story of success, failure and interpersonal growth within societal changes. The story and its characters hook you until the end."*

Marty Hufnagle – RN, PSU Clinton County Certified Master Gardener and avid reader

> *"The cover of Biloxi intrigued me... What would it be like to be transported back to the Antebellum South? I immediately was transported to the places, the people, the joys and sorrows of the characters, and was impressed with the historical correctness of the story."*

Cover credits

R. J. Bonett and Todd Heckler

Special thanks to Charlene Lewis & Sherman T. Eberhardt for their review of this work.

Charlene Lewis

> *"Biloxi is a book about the behind the scenes relationships of a painful era written from a different prospective. It is enlightening, thought provoking, and emotionally moving. It left me wanting more."*

Sherman T. Eberhardt

> *"I thoroughly enjoyed the read. Every chapter was on point. I particularly enjoyed reading about Myrna the dressmaker. It was characters such as hers that really pulled this novel together."*

On a side note: Biloxi, although taking place in a difficult period of America's history, is but one story of a nation striving for perfection.
– *The author.*

Fall 2021
First Edition

Chapters

Introduction

For Tom Stewart 1850 was the year his dream of owning a plantation came to fruition. With the financial help of his older brother David, he was able to buy at auction, Cliveden, a 600-acre property on the edge of the Mississippi Delta. Not fully understanding the depth of responsibility that goes with owning and operating a plantation, he has financial difficulties, which leave him no alternative but to seek further financial assistance from David.

David, wealthy in his own right, owns a shipping dock in Biloxi, and half interest in a dock in New Orleans. His primary business is shipping and trade, but occasionally dips into the institution of the slave trade, a necessity for keeping a plantation going. Realizing Tom's disadvantage, David barters for the beautiful black girl, Elizabeth, who works in the kitchen at Cliveden. Wealthy enough to possess any woman freely, what was the underlying force fueling his overwhelming desire for her? Was taking her to his home in Biloxi worth the scrutiny he was put through that almost cost him his life in a duel? Why did her sworn hatred for David change after being offered her freedom?

With the impending Civil War over abolishing slavery, both plantation owners and shippers realize there would be a devastating effect on their businesses of growing cotton and tobacco.

With the collapse of plantations and the blockade of southern ports eminent, David turns to Edward Atchison for advice. Edward, his future father-in-law, a prominent figure in New Orleans and wealthy sugar plantation owner in Cuba, advises him to seek the help of an unassuming character in Havana, by the name of Frank. Little did he realize, Frank wielded such immense international connections, stretching from New York, Washington, D.C., Cuba, and beyond. Could he be the solution to one of David's biggest problems?

Chapter 1
Cliveden

The rich history of Cliveden can be traced back throughout its 150 year Dubois family dynasty. Augustus Dubois, the last connection to the plantation had just died. His wife Joan died childless 10 years ago and without siblings to pass it down to, the old mansion was auctioned off.

Cliveden, a 600-acre cotton plantation, is situated at the edge of the Mississippi Delta, 55 miles northwest of the city of Biloxi. It's bordered by a swamp on one side, and 100 acres of forest on the other.

The main house stands like a white monument, with its wide front porch roof supported by four white columns. Two wrought iron gates at the entrance of the main road were secured by two brick columns that stood like sentries guarding the old plantation.

The road coming in is lined on both sides with 100-year-old oak trees, their thick branches extending across the road almost touching, made it appear as though they were holding hands. Spanish-Moss, an air plant that's a muted olive green and gray in color, hangs from the branches like a shroud, moving gently at the slightest breeze. A section of the road has a split rail fence to keep the horses from straying, and beyond the fence just over the rim of the hill, are the quarters. Fifteen two-room wooden cabins with roofs made of cedar shakes fashioned from trees harvested in the swamp, were aligned on a secondary road leading to the fields.

James and Luke were two 12-year-old boys that lived in the quarter with their parents. After their morning chores, it was like every other summer day, too hot to do much besides fighting boredom.

"Betcha can't walk the top rail of this here fence!" James said, slapping his hand against the top rail.

"Betcha I can!" Luke replied.

Accepting the challenge, Luke climbed to the top rail, and with out-stretched arms for balance, began the slow walk. Successfully reaching the other end, he jumped down and slung the upper part of his body over the second rail, letting his feet come off the ground.

"See, told ya I can," Luke said mockingly.

"Look, Luke! Here come the flat wagon. Old Mr. Moses, Adam and George, they be in it. Where they be goin'?" James asked inquisitively.

Still swinging his feet off the ground, Luke looked up replying, "My daddy say they dun been sold to Master Henry at Five Oaks."

"You think they be mean to them?" James asked.

"Na... they just probably make Old Moses do the garden. You know, like he be doin' here," thinking for a moment, "'Dat, and maybe sittn' 'round by the fire at the old oak tree at night. Like he be doin' here. You know, tellin' stories."

"They have an oak tree like us?" James asked.

"Yeah dummy!" pausing for a moment, "I'm sure gonna miss his stories," Luke said.

"Me too! Look, he's crying. Why he be doin' 'dat?" James asked.

"I heard my daddy tell my momma he was crying when he came to our cabin to say goodbye last night."

"Why?" James asked.

"I heard him tell momma he been here at Cliveden all his life. We the only family he know. I use to see him bring wild flowers from the meadow every Sunday and put 'dem on his wife's grave. He puts 'dem on his two little girl's graves too," Luke said.

"He had two little girls? I never knew dat'. I guess he be alright when he gets to tellin' 'dem stories over there," James replied.

"Look James, he's wavin' to us."

Swinging on the bottom rail as the wagon past, Luke said as he looked up, "Sure hope I don't never be sold. I hope Master Tom don't sell us."

"Why he sellin' everybody?" James asked.

"My daddy say he ain't never owned a plantation. He don't know how many people he be needin'."

The boys sat in reverence that sunny afternoon as the flat wagon slowly passed, realizing they would probably never see them again.

Old Moses was a deeply religious man, always having a kind word for everyone. No one really knew for sure how old he was, not even him. He had been here the longest, and always wore a tattered old straw hat that looked like it could have complimented a scarecrow in any cornfield. It was sort of an identity with Old Moses that somehow fit his personality. With his sleeves rolled up, the signs of old age couldn't mask the hard work he had done throughout the years. In the evening when he set the fire by the old oak tree, he would tell stories or start humming gospel songs. This would always generate a reaction from at least one or two people, and before long, everyone was participating. The strong voices of the baritone men mixed with the sopranos' repetitive responses, were inspiring enough to compete with any professional church choir. With the coolness of the night air, it seemed to be a much needed relief from a hard day in the fields.

Slaves that were born here, like Moses, and fortunate enough not to have been sold, actually lived their entire life without identity. If it wasn't for the bill of sale, no one would have ever known Old Moses or the other two were alive, for the exception of the people here at Cliveden, and the people where they were bound.

Master Tom only owned the plantation for a year, and your dependence on whether you lived out your life as a slave in one place had everything to do with the owners. Most plantations were handed down from generation to generation, and that sort of secured your future. Since there was less acreage sold to Master Tom from the original plantation, he felt he had to sell some slaves to adjust economically.

Luke's mother, Flora, worried constantly for the past year, wondering whether they would be sold. They didn't know the new owner well enough to feel free to ask. Flora, as well as Luke's father Daniel were born here, and both their parents were buried out back of the quarter.

Master Tom, not wanting to get familiar with the slaves that were still here, realized he would probably have to sell more, but was waiting for the cotton season to end, to see how many he would keep.

Flora begged Daniel almost daily to ask, but he kept telling her, "We be better not to bring attention to ourselves. Just do your chores as best you can, and pray every night we don't be separated. Master Tom, he don't seem to be the type 'dat ain't fair."

Tom Stewart, a man in his late 30's, is tall and muscular, with brown curly hair. You could tell he too, was used to doing some manual labor.

The only one in Luke's family they feared for was Luke's sister Elizabeth. Being 22, she would have brought a fair price at any auction. With a fair complexion, she was well built with long black wavy hair, and didn't possess one visible flaw.

Miss Bertha was the cook at Cliveden, and although she was no blood relation to Flora, Flora's family always looked on Bertha as their grand-mother. Through Miss Bertha, Flora hoped Elizabeth would eventually get recognized with her cooking skills; Bertha had been patiently teaching her for the last year and a half. She would often visit at the end of the day, and teach Elizabeth how to prepare certain foods the new Master liked. If Elizabeth had any chance at all of staying, it would be through Bertha and her relationship to the family.

Everyone loved Bertha. She was a heavy set woman in her late 50s, with dark skin. In the kitchen, she always wore a bright yellow flowered bandana around her head knotted at the front. When someone said or did something funny, she had a laugh that was contagious.

Daniel was a better field hand than anyone else on the plantation, and didn't fear Elizabeth being sold as much as Flora. They lived in the best cabin in the quarter, and unlike some of the other cabins, they had a wood floor. There weren't many cold days on the delta, and the cook stove was more than adequate to make the cabin comfortable on chilly days.

Master Tom knew Daniel was his best field hand, and would work much better if his family stayed intact. To separate the family might have a negative effect, so in Daniel's eyes, they had several things going for them.

Luke and James were like the other young slaves in the quarter, relegated to the easier duties, like caring for live stock, and other chores they could handle. When they finished their chores, they would sometimes go down by the swamp and sit at their favorite spot, a hollow log next to the water's edge. There, they did what they liked to do best -fish. Trying to catch a catfish or snare a snapping turtle when it raised its head above the surface of the water isn't easy. You have to be quick, as only a young person's reflexes are, but success was always rewarding. Sometime, they would get real lucky and catch a big catfish.

The only thing you had to look out for was snakes. Water moccasins in particular were their main concern. Black in color with a cotton white lining inside their mouth, they're capable of pumping poison through their fangs potent enough to kill a person. On occasion, they would have to jump back when they saw one gliding by on the surface of the water.

Luke recalled Miss Bertha telling his mother, "Master Tom's favorite dish be turtle soup. Maybe I can teach Elizabeth how to make it the way Master Tom likes."

That was the quest today, as it was the last few times they visited the swamp. Today, they would be successful catching a fair sized one, and ran to the cabin with their prize.

When Bertha found out, she came down to the cabin to instruct Elizabeth on how to make it. After it was finished, Bertha sampled the broth. Hugging Elizabeth she said, "Child, it sho' is perfect. I 'spect Master Tom would surely appreciate this." Putting the lid on the pot, Bertha carried the mixture up to the big house kitchen.

A few minutes after she returned, Master Tom opened the door slightly to the kitchen.

"Bertha! I'm having a guest for dinner. Make something special," he said.

He began to close the door, when he was drawn in by the tempting odor of the soup. Going to the stove, he raised the lid of the pot and took a deep breath to savor the aroma. "This smells delicious," he said. It was too tempting not to try. Picking up a spoon, he carefully dipped it into the mixture. Putting it to his lips he blew on the hot liquid before sampling it. "Ah! Turtle soup! That's my favorite. Bertha, you sure know how to make it. It's perfect."

"Master Tom, I didn't make it, Elizabeth did."

"Who's she?" he asked.

"That be Flora's daughter. Her brother, Luke, and James, they catched it down in the swamp this afternoon. She made it."

"Isn't Flora married to Daniel, Daniel the head field hand?"

"Yes sir."

Thinking for a moment, "Do you think Elizabeth would like to help in the kitchen?"

"Yes sir, she surely would," Bertha excitedly replied.

"Well, go down to the quarter and tell Elizabeth to come on up here. I want to speak with her."

After Master Tom left the room, Bertha ran out the back door and down the path that wound through the herb garden as fast as she could. When she got to Flora's door, she knocked then stepped in without waiting. Flora was at the kitchen fireplace with Elizabeth stirring a pot of catfish stew, when Bertha told her the good news.

"Praise Jesus! I was hoping for a miracle," Flora said. Throwing her arms around Elizabeth, she hugged her as though Elizabeth was being rescued from a terrible fate.

"Master Tom! He wants to see you. Better put on yo' best dress and get on up to the big house as fast as you can. If he likes you, I think you be in the big house kitchen from now on," Bertha said before returning to the big house.

Doing what Miss Bertha asked, Elizabeth put on a clean dress then hurried up the hill and knocked at the kitchen door.

"Come on in honey," Bertha said, "Master Tom's in the living room waitin' to speak to you."

After running her hands over the front of her dress to make sure she was presentable as possible, Elizabeth pushed open the swinging door from the kitchen, entering the main hallway. She had never been inside the house, and was amazed at the big rooms, with high ceilings and fine furniture. Something she could have never imagined.

Master Tom came into the hall and paused when he saw her looking around. Realizing she was in awe taking in the site of the big rooms and fine furniture he asked, "Haven't you ever been in the house before?"

"No, Master Tom, I ain't never seen it," she said pausing as she looked around, "It sure is beautiful."

"Did Bertha tell you you're going to be in the kitchen helping her from now on? I sampled some of your soup, and it's something I like. You made it to perfection."

After thanking him, Elizabeth returned to the kitchen. "Miss Bertha, Master Tom said I'll be in the kitchen from now on," she excitedly said.

"That's good honey. You go on down and get your clothes and whatever else you have. Bring it on up to the house. From now on you be stayin' here."

Elizabeth paused for a moment asking, "You mean I can't stay at the quarter?"

"No, honey," Bertha replied, pointing to a small room just off the kitchen. "There's where you sleep."

"Couldn't I just stay at the quarter and come up each morning?" she asked.

"No. If Master Tom wants something during the night, he won't want to be running on down to the quarter to get you," Bertha replied.

Elizabeth didn't care for the idea of leaving her family, but had no choice. She slowly walked back to her cabin to get the few possessions she had. After saying goodbye to her mother, she came back to the big house.

The 8 x 10 room she would use had a bare wood floor with a small window high on the wall. The room was sparsely furnished with a bed, a chair, and an old dresser, where she put her few things neatly in a drawer.

Coming out to the kitchen Bertha said, "You learn everything I teaches you as fast as you can. I'm gettin' on in years, and I been feelin' right poorly now and again. I think that's why Master Tom wants a helper in the kitchen, somebody he can trust after I'm too old to do it."

"What kind of master is he?" Elizabeth asked.

"Master Tom, he don't seem to be easy goin' like Master Augustus, but I ain't really know him that long to tell. I never heard him speak bad on anyone, and not hiring an overseer, well, that's a good thing."

"What about the slaves he already sold? Luke told me Old Moses was crying when he was leaving," Elizabeth said.

Pausing for a moment while stirring a cake mixture, Miss Bertha stopped and looked up, "Well honey, seems like Master Tom's trying to place them where they won't be mistreated. People like Old Moses, well, they always gonna feel bad about leaving the place they knows. He dun' been here all his life."

Thinking about what Bertha said, Elizabeth helped clean up the kitchen, washed a few dishes, then went to bed.

As she lay there looking at her new surroundings, she thought, *It isn't at the quarter, but it's my own room,* realizing for the first time in her life she had privacy. With that thought in mind, she drifted off to sleep.

***

The sun wasn't up when Miss Bertha knocked on Elizabeth's door. After waking, she sat up, wiped her eyes then stretched. She didn't sleep well on a bed she wasn't accustomed to, tossing and turning through the night. Her bed at the quarter was stuffed with straw, but her new bed was stuffed with cotton.

"You got's to get use to going to bed early, child," Bertha soundly remarked. "The kitchen be the first place the day begins. You even got's to get up befo' that old rooster out in the yard starts a crowin'."

The cooking area was a separate small building from the house just outside the back door and Miss Bertha took her outside to show her all there was to know about the hearth.

"When you needs more wood chopped, you hangs a towel on the line outside just like this," she said demonstrating, "John will chop some more." Looking at Elizabeth with a smile she added, "I 'spect you know him the way you two always be lookin' at each other," after saying it, Miss Bertha held her stomach while letting out a hardy laugh. Elizabeth smiled.

Bertha was right; Elizabeth already knew John. He came from another plantation about five years ago when he was 17. Over the last five years, he developed into a solid man, over 6' feet tall and very muscular. Whenever they met, he would comment on how beautiful Elizabeth looked or have some other compliment.

Luke awoke that morning expecting to see his sister helping his mother make breakfast for him and his father as usual, but something was different. There wasn't the sound of conversation between his mother and sister. Suddenly he remembered; Elizabeth no longer lived in their cabin. There seemed to be an empty feeling in his stomach, and he wasn't sure he liked the idea of her no longer being home.

"Sure gonna' miss Elizabeth 'round here!" Luke said.

"She ain't under the same roof, but she still be on the same plantation. Just you be thankful fo' dat'," Daniel replied, sitting on a chair while putting on his shoes.

When breakfast was over, Daniel went outside to join the other field hands and headed for the fields. Luke went to the stable where James and two other boys from the quarter always began their day.

The stable was a building about four or five times the size of a cabin, and made of brick, with thick oak boards separating the stalls. Each stall was topped with fancy wrought iron rails, and a large, round iron ball dressed the top of each post. The floor being brick made the stable easy to clean. Luke never minded the smell of the horse barn. Unlike the cow barn, it didn't have a foul odor. They started the day by cleaning the stalls, putting down new straw and feeding the horses. After that, they rubbed down the harnesses and saddles with wax. When they finished in the horse barn they fed the rest of the livestock.

It was always fun feeding the chickens. When Luke or James picked up the sack of feed, about 30 chickens would gather around them. James would take a hand full of feed and pretend to throw it just to watch the chickens scatter in that direction. When the chickens realized it wasn't thrown, they came right back, surrounding them clucking in anticipation of being fed.

James didn't act like his usual self today. Normally, he was happy and doing crazy things that made them both laugh like hanging upside down by his legs over a hitching rail, or make crazy noises, or jumping into the hay pile.

"What's wrong with you? You sick?" Luke asked.

"No. I think my cousin Solomon," James said and paused for a moment looking down at the floor.

Luke looked at him, impatiently waiting for James to tell him what was wrong, he said, "Yo' cousin Solomon, what?"

James looking at Luke finally replied, "He's suppos' to get sold."

Luke was surprised. It was almost a year since Old Moses left, and everyone thought Master Tom was done selling people.

"My daddy, he heard Master Tom say he wants to sell off some slaves he's got to get rid of, 'fore' his new wife come. He ain't want her to be here if he had to sell anybody else," James said.

Luke suddenly realized the feeling he had when Elizabeth left, was probably what James was feeling now having a relative possibly sold.

When Luke got home, his parents were weeding their own garden out back of their cabin. Like the other people that lived in the quarter everyone had their own. He pitched in with weeding and told his father what James said about Solomon being sold. Looking up, Daniel said, "Yes, I dun heard someone was supposed to be sold. But I don't rightly know who. I dun told Master Tom, 'Solomon, he be one of the best workers here. Selling him only makes things harder when cotton harvest time comes'."

Looking over the garden, Daniel said as he put his arm around Flora's shoulder, "I thinks "dat be it for the weedin'. It looks mighty fine." Flora put her arm around his waist replying, "I thinks you're right Daniel. It be 'bout bed time."

Before Luke stepped into the cabin something caught his eye. Looking toward the woods, he saw what looked like a shadow of a person running. Thinking it was his imagination he dismissed it and went inside.

***

Early the next morning, James came running into the cabin excitedly saying, "My cousin Solomon! My cousin Solomon! he dun up and run away last night."

Daniel got up from his chair. Putting on his shirt he said, "Even if he do be a good field hand, runnin' away don't make things no better. Master Tom's sure to sell him now."

Dumont was a plantation about 40 miles away that paid the most for slaves like Solomon. A place everyone feared being sold to. The owners didn't live on the plantation; it was strictly a business -a business run by two brutal overseers. They were always looking to buy the younger, healthier slaves, and would pay the best prices for them. Sometimes, when a female that looked desirable came up for auction, they would buy her for the house duties, cooking, cleaning and sometimes for their own personal pleasure.

"My cousin, Clarence, told my daddy he was supposed to be sold to Dumont, 'dat's why he cut and run," James excitedly said.

"After I dun talked to Master Tom bout how good Solomon works, I don't think he would have sold him. Whered' you hear 'dat he be sold?" Daniel asked.

"Clarence told me," James replied.

Flora attentively listening said, "Solomon and Ester were gonna jump the broom after the harvest. Ezekiel always wanted Ester. I thinks he might be the one startin' trouble."

Thinking for a moment Daniel replied, "Dat's right! I bet 'dat no account Ezekiel, he be the one."

When James and Luke got to the stable, there were two men talking to Master Tom getting a description of Solomon. The men had a few hounds with them that had to be restrained. The dogs, pulling at their leashes, were anxious to get started obviously knowing their purpose. Looking at the men, Luke noticed their hair was uncombed and they were unshaven. They had on soiled clothes and both were completely disheveled. One of the men speaking with Master Tom was chewing tobacco, and during the conversation, turned his head and spit out a hefty amount of tobacco juice. It landed close to Luke's feet and Tom looked at the slave catcher with disgust. Turning away he said, "Luke, saddle my horse. I want to go with them."

"Yes sir, Master Tom," he replied heading into the stable.

After mounting his horse they left. About 20 minutes later, the hounds picked up the scent where Luke saw the shadow along the wood line the night before. As he and James began their work, they could hear the sound of the baying hounds fade into the distance.

It was almost noon when Master Tom came back alone. "Here Luke, unsaddle my horse. After you brush him down, put him in the stable. I won't be going out again today."

"Yes Sir, Master Tom."

At nightfall there was a commotion near the quarter. The slave catchers and their dogs had run Solomon to ground and were returning.

Lights were turned on in the cabins, and everyone came out to see what was going to happen. Gathering together, they watched as Solomon was being led to the quarter at the end of a long rope tied around his waist. His hands were tied behind his back and he kept falling down, being dragged most of the way. His shirt and pants were torn to shreds, and you could see small cuts and scratches from being drug through the woods and dense swamp. After the slave catchers dismounted, they tied Solomon to a tree and stripped what remained of his shirt from his back.

Master Tom, hearing the commotion, came out of the big house. By that time, most of the quarter was already gathered around the tree, watching to see what was going to happen.

"Solomon, why did you run away? Daniel said you're one of the best field hands on the plantation. Why did you do it?" Master Tom asked.

"Master Tom, I... I... I heared I was gettin' sold to Dumont, where they whip they slaves for no good reason," he said, nervously shaking with the uncertainty of his punishment.

"I don't know who told you that. It isn't true. Why didn't you ask me first? You leave me no alternative but to punish you," turning to Daniel he said, "Daniel, fetch a whip."

Stepping forward Daniel replied, "Excuse me, Master Tom. I don't thinks we have one. Ifn' we do, I ain't never seen it. We ain't never had a whippin' here at Cliveden, as I can 'member."

One of the slave catchers spit tobacco juice, and with a grin, took a whip from his saddle bag. Taking a position about eight feet away from Solomon, he twirled the coiled whip in his hand, anxious to begin the punishment. Before Master Tom gave the go ahead, he said in a loud voice looking over the group, "If anyone else hears they're being sold, ask me first before you go running off."

Ester, Solomon's intended, came over pleading, "Please, Master Tom. Have mercy. Sell me, but don't whip Solomon. Please don't whip him."

Flora and Daniel grabbed Ester, holding her away. Tom gave the slave catcher a nod, and with that, the punishment began. The whip cut through the night air, and you could hear it snap when it hit Solomon's back. Each time it struck, Ester reacted, flinching with every stroke as if she was the one being whipped. The catcher doing the whipping paused briefly to spit tobacco juice, and smiled as he recoiled the whip.

Luke glanced up at an almost full moon with clouds racing by its face. The breeze of the night air made the Spanish-Moss hanging heavy from the trees, sway in the wind, as though it was restless at what was taking place. After the 6 lashes were administered, some of the field hands, as well as Daniel, untied Solomon and took him to his cabin. Ester and Flora went in, and immediately began treating his wounds.

Daniel said as Solomon lay motionless on the bed, "Solomon, you won't be able to work for a couple days. You just rest easy like." Solomon's only reply was a groan as his wounds were being treated.

Daniel, not able to contain his rage, went to Ezekiel's cabin. After knocking, he stepped in uninvited. Addressing Ezekiel, he said. "Since you be the one 'dat started 'dat rumor what caused Solomon to get whipped, you gonna do twice the work to make up for him," he angrily said.

Ezekiel was about to deny it, when Daniel grabbed him by the shirt, "Don't you be a lyin' on me. You knows you be the one 'dat be doin' it. 'Dat's why you weren't there for the whippin'."

After all the excitement, everyone returned to their cabins and quiet fell on their world once again.

**

Ezekiel was always a little slower than the rest, even when Master Augustus owned the place. He didn't give much concern for being lax, he realized without concern, everyone else had to work a little harder to compensate. Daniel, understanding that fact, went straight to Ezekiel's cabin in the morning. He wanted to make sure he heeded his threat from the night before, and after knocking, entered without being admitted. Daniel wasn't going to tolerate him doing less than his share and was rough with Ezekiel. He grabbed him behind the neck, and flung him out of the cabin before he was fully dressed. As Ezekiel was trying to tuck in his shirt, Daniel kept pushing him along, making him walk with the rest of the field hands and not lag behind.

When Luke and James finished their work that afternoon, they were going to the swamp for some fishing. Passing Luke's cabin, they saw Flora standing in the doorway. As they walked by, she warned, "You be careful of 'dem snakes!"

"We will momma!" Luke replied as they waved goodbye.

As they passed by the cotton and corn fields that would soon be harvested in a few weeks, they could hear the field hands singing. Harvest time marked the end of the field work that consumed most of the labor on a plantation. Everyone knew when it was finished it would be a good time. With the two couples jumping the broom and the harvest being as good as last year, Master Tom seemed happy, and he'd let everyone have a couple days to relax. The corn was as high as Luke had ever seen, and the cotton fields were pure white.

Corn is relatively easy picking, but when the cotton fields were ready, everyone pitched in and harvested, even the youngest children that could reach the tops of the plants. Walking between the rows with burlap bags strung over their shoulder, they put the cotton bolls inside as they went. Luke, always wanting to be as big and strong as his father and Solomon, filled his sack as heavy as possible, before bringing it back to the flat wagon. The flat wagon was where they emptied their cotton into larger burlap bags. When that was filled, it was taken to the cotton barn where the older men packed it in bales, stomping it down with their bare feet to compact it. When there were enough bales made, it was taken to the cotton market in a town 10 miles away. For now, Luke and James had something else on their minds, and couldn't wait to get to their favorite spot.

They had already passed the fields and were in the marshes when they heard a shot. Quickly stopping, they ducked down and became wide eyed. "What's 'dat Luke?" James anxiously asked.

"I don't know, but somebody be shootin'. We best stay here in the tall grass," Luke said.

They had a strong urge to go back home, but were afraid to move. Curious at what the shooting was about, they slowly raised their heads just high enough to see over the tall grass.

A few hundred feet away, they saw one of the slave catchers that whipped Solomon, chasing a runaway heading into the swamp. The slave catcher not wanting to follow on foot fired another shot in the air instead. Luke could see other men on horseback in the chase, and eventually caught the runaway. He was about 25-years-old. Bleeding from the leg, he pleaded for mercy, and as he got to his feet, one of the men hit him with a club knocking him to the ground. When the runaway got to his feet again, James and Luke were shocked. It was George, one of the slaves that had been sold with Adam and Old Moses the year before.

Amongst the commotion, one of the men on horseback said, "Why don't we hang him here and take his body back? We won't get as much money, but we won't have the trouble. Dumont's 40 miles from here."

Luke wondered, *George was supposed to have been sold to a plantation called Five Oaks, five miles away. How did he wind up at Dumont?*

They watched from the safety of the tall grass as the men tied him over a horse leading him out of the swamp. Luke knew whatever George did his punishment would be as bad, or worse, than Solomon's.

The boys stayed hidden until almost dark, and when they were sure the slave catchers were gone, they ran back to the quarter.

"Where you been Luke? I just told your daddy to go on out and look for you. How come you all out of breath?" Flora upsettingly demanded.

Excitedly he replied, "Me and James! Me and James! We seen 'dem slave catchers 'dat dun whipped Solomon down by the swamp. They be there with some other mens chasing George."

"What! You mean George, George from here?" Daniel attentively asked.

"Yeah daddy, I thinks they dun shot him in the leg. We heard 'dem say, 'We should hang him here and just take his body on back to Dumont.'"

"You mean Five Oaks?" Daniel asked.

"No daddy. They say Dumont."

"I wonder how George wound up there?" Daniel said with a curious look on his face. "When I goes to the cotton market in two weeks, I try and find out."

***

A week passed, and the corn was being harvested. In spite of his whipping, Solomon seemed to be happy being back in the fields. He was in better spirits knowing he wasn't going to be the one sold, and about to be married to Ester.

Everyone was still buzzing about what Luke and James seen in the swamp, but still, no one knew why George had run away, or how he wound up at Dumont.

The corn was harvested in record time, and was finished on a Saturday evening. On Sunday, the only thing to be done, were chores necessary at the plantation. Monday was picking cotton, and Daniel wanting to get an early start, had all the equipment necessary, ready to go.

Before the sun came up on Monday, lanterns were already lit in all the cabins, and the smell of cornmeal being stirred on the cook stoves filled the air.

The weather had been warm, but it started to cool off at night, and wasn't too hot in the fields early on in the day. Flora packed a basket of food for the field, and a goat skin filled with water. Even she and the rest of the women would help with the harvest, getting it in prior to any unsuspected rain storm.

About midday, the first wagon was loaded and sent to the cotton barn. Everyone stopped picking about noon to eat, then began again until just before dark. The flat wagon was loaded again for the third trip, but wasn't quite full, and some of the women with young babies hitched a ride back to the quarter.

The whole week was pretty much the same, and the fields were finished in record time.

Daniel and some of the older slaves said, 'One reason was because Solomon and Sam, the third top hand, were getting married, and were anxious to jump the broom.' They all laughed and Luke, being too young to understand, wondered why.

There were about 20 bales that had to be taken to the cotton market 10 miles away, and would require several trips. No one was ever allowed to venture off the plantation on their own without a pass, and the only way to get news from other plantations, was when someone went to the cotton market, or when Master Tom's coachman took him to another plantation.

While Daniel was waiting to get his bales weighed, he noticed Adam. He was sold with George and Old Moses to Five Oaks, and Daniel was anxious to hear about George and the reason he ran away.

Asking Adam, he found out George had been involved in a fight with another slave over a girl. When the owner of Five Oaks went to break it up, George struck him by accident. After being warned about his fighting a few times, the master of Five Oaks sold him to Dumont. George ran away trying to get back to Five Oaks to the woman he fought over. That's why he was in the swamp.

At the time, Luke never thought a girl could be such a temptation to go through all that, but eventually with maturity, he would discover hormones take over and the whip would seem secondary. For now, the thought of being sold to Dumont was a deterrent from making a fuss over any woman. When Daniel got back from the cotton market, he told everyone the story about George.

Everyone knew there were still several more people to be sold, and were anxious to see who it may be before Master Tom left to pick up his intended. Finally hearing it was Ezekiel's family, no one seemed to feel bad about it, and within the week, they were sold to Southport Plantation. The owner of Southport was a long time friend of Master Augustus when he owned Cliveden, and like here, they didn't have a whipping post or an overseer, so Ezekiel's family was fortunate in that respect.

Before Ezekiel left, he barged into Daniel's cabin, "Daniel, I knows you be the one 'dat had my family sold. Someday, someday, I gonna' pay you back," he screamed then stormed out of the cabin.

***

After the harvest was in, Master Tom was getting ready to leave to pick up his intended Miss Sharon. She was from a wealthy family that owned Bellevue, a large plantation just outside Charleston, South Carolina. At present, she was staying with Tom's older brother David and his younger sister Anne in Biloxi.

David owned a shipping dock in Biloxi, and had a part interest of another dock in New Orleans. His main business was shipping, but occasionally dipped into the institution of slave trading.

Before leaving for Biloxi, Tom said, "Daniel, tell Solomon and Sam they'll have to wait till I return with Miss Sharon before they jump the broom. She might like to be here when they do it. I'll only be gone a week."

"Yes Sir, Master Tom, I tell 'em," Daniel replied.

The coach was already packed for the trip and as it was pulling away, Tom stuck his head out the window saying, "Daniel, I'm counting on you to see everything gets done! Now don't you let me down, you here?"

"Don't you be worrin' none, Master Tom, I see to it," Daniel replied as he waved goodbye.

For now, they were all secure with the threat of being sold gone, and everyone was looking forward to the celebration. It seemed as though they had forgotten they were owned on Master Tom's Plantation. Slaves were pretty much on their own to tend their gardens or anything else within the confines of the plantation in their spare time. As long as the field work was done, and the maintenance on the place was kept up, Master Tom wasn't unhappy. Without an overseer, they were on their honor not to run away, and with the thought of being shipped to Dumont, Master Tom really didn't need one.

***

While he was gone, Elizabeth was able to come down to the quarter and stay with her parents for a few days which made her mother happy. Flora asked, "What it be like, livin' in the big house? Do Master Tom treat you good?"

"It's fine Momma. I'm learnin' a lot from Miss Bertha. Master Tom, he just treats everbody in the house real good. He don't be askin' for too much."

"I'm glad fo' dat," Flora replied.

Elizabeth staying at the quarter for the few days made Flora happy. She couldn't have been happier, being able to make a fuss over her family being together again. Luke was just as glad, it was the same feeling he had before she moved up to the big house. Elizabeth was home again.

Chapter 2
Jumping the Broom

Within a few days, Master Tom and his wife Miss Sharon returned, and the whole quarter came out to greet them. Miss Sharon stepped from the carriage, and looking over the group she said, "I'm just so glad to be here at Cliveden. At Bellevue, my parents' home, I always looked in on the people that lived in the quarter when they were sick. I want you to know, I'm going to do the same here. I'm looking forward to getting to know each one of you, and be able to call you by name. Who are the two men that are going to jump the broom?" she asked.

Solomon and Sam stepped forward. Nodding, they removed their hats. "It be us, Miss Sharon, me and Sam here," Solomon said.

"That's fine. I want you to know, on my father's plantation we never sold anyone, and I don't want any of you to fear that."

To Luke, she seemed sincere, and he realized why Master Tom wanted to sell the slaves before she arrived. If they were still here, she would have probably objected. It was Friday, and the wedding ceremonies were to be held the next day.

***

Saturday morning at first light, you could hear Solomon's deep voice, partly singing, and partly humming, as he washed up in a basin out front of his cabin. Sam, who was also awake, could be heard humming in his deep voice the same tune.

As Flora was cooking breakfast, Daniel, hearing them humming, walked up behind her and put his arms around her waist. "Flora, you 'member if I was 'dat tuneful on our weddin' day?"

"Humph," she replied looking over her shoulder, "You sang louder, 'cause you knew you was gettin' somethin' special."

"And I knows 'dat for a fact," he said as he smiled, giving her a kiss on the side of the neck.

Looking over her shoulder with an approving smile, she said jokingly, "Get away from me, old man. I have too much to do today." They both laughed. Sometimes they jousted with words, but it was always, "Just funnin'," as Daniel put it.

Luke didn't know how his mother was able to find time to do everything during the course of the day, but they never had to wait on supper, and always had clean clothes and a clean cabin. Her primary duty was working in the herb garden, and doing the wash for the big house, or any visitors that may be there. Sometimes Master Tom had guests for several days, sometimes as long as a week. When his brother David and sister Anne visited, it was always more than a week. There were already several guests here with more expected today, some coming from as far as Biloxi, 55 miles. They were coming for a dual purpose, wanting to meet Tom's bride, and celebrate a good crop year. Solomon and Sam jumping the broom was a side treat.

Solomon was Daniel's best friend, and was knocking on Daniel's door before Daniel finished breakfast. When Solomon came in, you could tell he was anxiously awaiting the ceremony; he couldn't sit still in his chair.

"Settle down! Yo' wife ain't goin' nowhere. 'Dat weddin', it be gonna take place soon enough," Daniel said.

Flora, standing by the stove with her back to them, put her hand to her mouth, trying to stifle her laughter.

Solomon asked, "Daniel, I ain't never seen no weddin', what I'm supposed to do?"

"Well, they puts a broom on the ground, held up a little bit by a piece of kindlin' at each end. After the preacher say the words, you got's to jump over the broom backwards. If one of ya'll knocks the broom off, the other one 'dat don't, has to listen to the one 'dat didn't."

"You means for life?" Solomon asked.

Daniel turned around, looking at Flora with a smile he said, "Yeah, but it ain't all 'dat bad."

Flora looking over her shoulder smiled.

Luke listened, but still not understanding their conversation, excused himself and went outside to where James and some of the other boys from the quarter were. They had already watched a pig being butchered and put on a long rod with a handle at one end. It was placed over the barbeque pit, where embers of burnt hickory were already aglow. James, Luke, and the other boys would be taking turns during the day turning the spit, until the pig was golden brown. The aroma of hickory smoke blending with the smell of drippings from the pork on the hot embers, made the task of turning it easier. They knew when it was done they would enjoy the fruits of their labor.

A large black kettle was hanging over another fire with boiling water for the ears of corn, and another pit of embers was for potatoes. The potatoes were already wrapped in large wet burdock leaves, waiting to be baked. The drink Miss Bertha made for the occasion had the flavor of mint, with a piece of sugarcane.

When everything was ready, the brides came out of their cabins, wearing their finest clothes. Atop their heads, they wore a wreath of wild flowers woven into a crown. Solomon and Sam looked as nervous as two frightened cats, and had on their best clothes with the least amount of patches for the ceremony.

When everything was ready, Miss Bertha went to the big house to tell Master Tom and his guests. Filing out of the house in quiet conversation about the successful crop year, they gathered where the ceremony was to take place. There hadn't been a wedding here in several years, and Luke never remembered seeing one. After everyone was gathered around, an elder slave that came along with Master Henry from Five Oaks performed what was a short ceremony. There were no formal vows as there were with white folk. It was more or less for their benefit, some sort of recognition between husbands and wives.

The ceremony began with placing a broom on the ground behind the couples to be wed. The elder then said, "Is anyone here that could find reason these people shouldn't be united in marriage?" After looking over the group he continued, "With no objection, hold hands and jump over the broom into the world of holy matrimony."

Both couples held hands and did as he asked, then everyone clapped, even the white folk.

The barbeque was spread on the table outside for Master Tom, his wife, and their guests, while several servants from the big house stood by to serve their food. Everyone else went back to the quarter where a few tables had been set outside of Solomon and Ester's cabin.

Everyone enjoyed the feast, and sat up until way after dark by the fire at the old oak tree where they used to gather when Old Moses was here. The people from the quarter seemed to be content humming tunes, but for Luke, something was missing. Without Old Moses, the fire beside the tree somehow didn't seem as warm. There were flames, and they were hot, but the cozy feeling somehow wasn't there, and Luke was certain it was because Old Moses was absent.

Several hours after dark, the younger children were told to go to bed, and the adults only stayed a short while before joining them.

Lying in the darkness of his bed, Luke heard his father ask his mother, "Flora, do you 'member the day we jumped the broom?" he said pausing for a moment before she had a chance to reply, "Yo' daddy, he just kept a lookin' at me?"

"He sure did give you a look, didn't he," she replied with a chuckle, "Seems like it was just yesterday. Twenty five years went by so fast Daniel, where'd it go?" Flora asked.

"It was good seein' Elizabeth workin' in the Master's house," Daniel said.

"I know, Miss Bertha said he was pleased with her cookin'," Flora replied continuing with a concerned voice, "I heard Master Tom's brother David, he dun asked if Elizabeth could be brought to Biloxi for awhile. Master Tom told him no. Miss Sharon, she say, 'Elizabeth done has a place in her kitchen right here.'

"I wonder if Miss Sharon wasn't here, would he have let her go?" Daniel asked.

"I thinks Miss Sharon, she be growin' fond of Elizabeth, not like Master Augustus' wife Miss Joan. Miss Sharon, she wants to know more 'bout cookin' and sewin'. Elizabeth been teachin' her a little. Miss Sharon don't seem like she wants to be pampered, least ways, not like Master Augustus' wife," Flora laughed then continued, "Miss Joan, she sure didn't wanna' do much."

When their room fell quiet, Luke went to sleep.

***

Time seemed to pass quickly that winter, and the spring air was filled with the smell of Honeysuckle and Magnolia. There had been a few sicknesses in the quarter during the winter, and Miss Sharon kept true to her word, coming to the quarter when anyone was ill. Miss Bertha was down with a weakness in her arm the whole month of February, and Miss Sharon, Flora, and Elizabeth, were there every day looking in on her until she passed.

Flora took the death particularly hard, even more so than the others.

Miss Bertha was always like a mother to her, and Luke suspected there was more to their relationship than he knew. Curiosity getting to him one day he asked his father, "Daddy, did Miss Bertha always live here?"

"No, Miss Bertha and yo' grand momma were the same age when they come here from a plantation called Boone Hall, 'bout 60 miles away. They were married 'bout the same time, and had babies within 3 weeks of each other. Miss Bertha had a son 'dat died just after he was born, and yo' grand momma died within two weeks after your momma was born."

"What she die from, havin' babies?" Luke asked.

"No, the lung disease was real bad 'dat winter. Miss Bertha was still able to nurse a baby, so she raised your momma like she was her own. Dat's why your momma always looked on Miss Bertha as her natural momma."

Finally understanding the connection, Luke hugged his mother.

The fields were turned and the crops were planted, just in time for the gentle spring rains; a warm rain which would bring life to the seed, coaxing it up through the soil to bask in the warm southern sun.

After the crops were sown, the only field work was hoeing between the rows, and weed control, a monumental task with the acreage being farmed. It was also a time for building a needed shed, or doing maintenance on the quarter.

Cliveden had its own small sawmill, and cutting trees on the property was economical. Sometimes they would saw extra boards to sell to neighboring plantations.

Tom found Daniel repairing a fence and asked, "Daniel, I was thinking about clearing another field and raising a tobacco crop. What do you think?"

Looking up from his work, Daniel adjusted his hat replying, "Master Tom, 'dat be a heap to do. It's gonna' take all us to get it ready for the plantin'. Would been better if we dun' started clearin' the land in February, when the ground weren't so wet."

"Well, I'm thinking on it. Maybe I can borrow a pair of oxen from Master Henry at Five Oaks? That should help."

The end of March had rain almost every day, and so had the beginning of April. Master Tom was able to borrow a pair of oxen from Five Oaks to clear the heavy trees and brush. As Daniel explained, it took every male strong enough to handle a pick or shovel to help clear the two fields.

Luke and James were 14 now, and able to help with the heavier work. It was hard for about two weeks, until most of the tree stumps and heavy brush was cleared, and put in a pile ready to burn. A tool shed was built at the site, so equipment wouldn't have to be carried every day from the plantation.

Solomon was next in charge after Daniel, and one day while they were working, he told James, "Go on up to the tool shed and brings me back a chain. I wants to hook up the team and pull this old stump outa' here," he said quietly muttering to himself, "It's mighty stubborn. Just like my wife's momma."

James ran down the hill to the tool shed and went in. A few minutes later, there was a scream, and he came running out of the shed holding his hand, and fell to the ground. Everyone ran to see what was wrong and he screamed again.

"What be wrong James?" Solomon excitedly asked.

"Mr. Solomon, de'z a snake in dare. It dun bit me on da hand. He be behind the chain."

Sam looked in, and in a darkened corner, saw a rattlesnake among the shovels. Picking up a shovel, he cut off the snakes head. The rattler was about three feet long and its fangs had sunk deep into James's hand. Grabbing a knife, Solomon cut two X's on the fang marks, and began sucking out the poison, spitting it on the ground. James was shaking and sweating, while Solomon was treating him, and after Solomon finished, Solomon told Luke, "Walk on down to the quarter with James. Tell Master Tom what happened. Go on James, go with Luke," Solomon said.

On the way back to the quarter, James nervously asked, "Luke, you 'member when Lewis got snake bit? He died a few days later."

"I 'member when 'dat happened," Luke replied.

"You thinks I'm gonna die? If'n I do, what you think's it's gonna be like?"

"Don't worry 'bout 'dat. Solomon dun' got out the poison," he said with a shrug of his shoulders, "You be fine in a few days."

Of all the times in the swamp, they were always cautious of snakes and seen quite a few, but never expected one to be in the tool shed. James heard what Luke said about being fine, but wasn't completely reassured he would survive the bite. When they got back to the quarter, Luke ran to James' cabin, and told his mother what happened.

She screamed, "Oh good lord. Not my baby! Luke, run on up the hill to the big house. Tells Miss Sharon and Master Tom what happened. Ask if they's any way they can help."

"Yes Ma'am. I tell 'em," Luke said, as he hurried out the door.

Getting to the big house kitchen he excitedly knocked hard on the door.

"What's wrong Luke, why you making so much fuss?" Elizabeth asked.

"James... James, dun' got bit by a snake. His momma ask if Miss Sharon or Master Tom can do somthin' to help?"

Miss Sharon was entering the kitchen just as Luke was telling Elizabeth and said, "Luke, I'll tell Master Tom. You go on down to the quarter. Tell James' mother we'll be down directly."

"Yes, Ma'am," Luke replied, before hurrying out the back door to deliver the message.

Within a few minutes, Miss Sharon and Master Tom went down. After examining the bite, Master Tom said, "Solomon didn't cut the fang marks deep enough. I'll have to open them a little more," he told James' mother. She began to cry hysterically and Master Tom turned to her saying, "Being upset isn't doing James any good. It's only making him more upset, go on outside. For now, he has to stay settled so the poison that was missed; doesn't travel as fast through his system. Luke, stay here with James, don't you go back to the field today."

Looking over Master Tom's shoulder at James, he replied, "I won't Master Tom. I'z stay right here."

From all the excitement and the rush of adrenalin, James became tired and fell asleep.

"Master Tom, is James dead?" Luke asked, looking over Master Tom's shoulder.

"No Luke, he's not dead. He's just tired from all the excitement."

With nothing else to be done, Master Tom returned to the big house. Luke did as he was told and stayed with James the rest of the day.

It was almost dark when everyone else returned from the field. People, especially in bondage, sometimes have a greater sense of loyalty to one another than the best of friends. In their situation, permanence in being there depended on the Master and everyone realized that could change at any time. You may not have enjoyed being with a person, or may not have chosen a particular person as a friend, but being there together seemed to create a bond, something almost as strong as blood relations. Everyone coming in from the field stopped by James' cabin to see how he was doing. Luke's father and mother came to visit, and when they left, Luke went home with them.

***

The next day as the sun came up, Luke quickly put on his clothes and ran to see how James was doing. James' mother and father were sitting beside his bed, and his mother was putting a damp cloth on his eyes. Luke saw James' eyes were swollen shut, and James could barely open them.

"How's James be doin' this mornin'?" he asked.

Hearing Luke's voice, James forced his eyes open. "Is 'dat you Luke? I had a dream 'bout us catching the biggest snappin' turtle," he said pausing for a moment. "He dun' pulled us both in the swamp where an alligator swallowed us."

"Boy, James, 'dat's sure some bad dream," he replied, as he watched a tear coming from the corner of James' eye running down his cheek.

A little further on in the morning, Miss Sharon came to the cabin to look in on James. Taking his mother by the hand, she led her outside to talk to her. Luke had already imagined she was telling her James was going to die, and by the look of him, Luke knew it wouldn't be long.

"Luke, stay here with James and his mother today. Come up to the big house to let us know if anything happens," Miss Sharon said.

"Yes, Ma'am, I surely will," Luke replied.

In a few hours, it seemed like James was breathing slower and wasn't able to open his eyes at all. In late afternoon, James suddenly called out, "Momma! Momma!" then stopped breathing. She started crying, kissing his face saying aloud "My baby! My poor-poor, baby."

"Luke, go on up to the big house. Tell Master Tom and Miss Sharon 'dat James passed," James' father said.

"Yes Sir!"

As Luke walked up the path to the big house, he could smell the aroma of cornbread Elizabeth made coming from the open kitchen window. When he got there, he knocked on the door. Elizabeth opened it and

Luke saw her eyes were red and teary. James was like a second brother to her, and she knew Luke was bringing bad news. Hugging him she asked, "Did James pass?"

"Yeah, he just died. His Momma told me to tell Master Tom and Miss Sharon."

"Wait here Luke, I'll tell them," she said.

After she left the room, Luke sat on a kitchen stool. When she returned, she wiped the tears from her eyes with the corner of her apron and sat down with him.

"How's James' momma?" Elizabeth asked.

"She be just a wailin' and a wailin'," he replied.

"Let me get you a cookie; I made them last night," Elizabeth said.

Looking around the big room he asked, "How it's like, workin' in the big house for Master Tom and Miss Sharon?"

"They real easy to please, not bad at all," pausing for a moment she said, "The only thing I worry about is Master Tom's brother, Master David. He's from Biloxi, and wants to buy me, but Master Tom say Miss Sharon won't let him. Every time Master David comes to visit, he always be stayin' around the kitchen. I'm kind of afraid of him."

Several men in the quarter were interested in Elizabeth, but she didn't care for any as potential suitors for the exception of John. He was the one she would ask to chop wood for the kitchen when she needed it.

Being light-skinned too, like Elizabeth, it was suspected his blood line was white from either the plantation's owner, or an overseer. When John came to the kitchen door, Elizabeth's face lit up.

"Come in John, I have something for you," she said.

Removing his hat as he entered the kitchen, he replied, "Mornin' Miss Elizabeth, Luke. Mighty fine smell commin' from this kitchen," he said.

Turning with an approving smile at his comment, she cut a generous piece from the loaf and handed it to him. She only offered Luke a cookie, and Luke saw there was a special reason. She didn't want to cut into the full loaf until John got the first piece.

John looking a little nervous with Luke there, fumbled for words. Finally he said, "Miss Elizabeth, you makes the best cornbread I ever did taste. And you sure keeps a beautiful kitchen too," he added looking around the room. Luke, realizing they wouldn't have much time together, didn't want to spoil the moment and stood up to leave. He could tell John was grateful, and as Luke was about to go out the door John said, "Luke, I sorry your friend James died. I see you at the funeral tonight."

Waving goodbye, Luke took another cookie from the jar then left. For the short time he was with Elizabeth, it somehow lifted his spirits, and the thought that James died, temporarily left his mind.

Returning to the quarter, he passed James' cabin. He could hear James' mother weeping, moaning the loss of her only child. Looking in, he saw his mother and two other women trying to comfort her.

Going to the barn, he watched as James' father, Daniel, Sam, and Solomon, were busy building the coffin James would be laid to rest in.

That evening when everyone was around James' cabin paying their respects, Master Tom, Miss Sharon, and everyone who worked in the big house came down. Miss Sharon embraced James' mother as if she was part of her family, and Luke honestly believed Miss Sharon felt that way. Some people were singing gospel tunes, and the ones that weren't, hummed in unison. It was a lamenting sound of souls trying to lift the burden of a most tragic event, a woman burying her child, her only child.

When Luke looked in the coffin at James, it brought tears to his eyes that a friend who was like a brother was gone. They would never again get to sit at their favorite spot to fish, or do any of the other things they did together.

Around midnight, most of the people returned to their cabins, and Luke went back with his parents. In the darkness of his room, he lay awake wondering if James' spirit could see him, or was he in some glorious place in heaven. Today, everyone was able to look at James, but tomorrow he would be buried out back of the quarter with Old Moses' wife, daughters, and Miss Bertha. Luke didn't think James could have been with better company. It was some consolation that allowed him to get over the idea James was no more, and finally drifted off to sleep.

The next day after the burial, Master Tom put his hand on Luke's shoulder. Always seeing them together he asked, "Luke, will you be alright?"

Looking sullenly up at him, Luke replied, "Yes Master Tom, I be alright."

***

A week passed, and everything went back to normal. For the first few days after James died, Luke would come out of his cabin thinking the funeral of his best friend was a dream, and reality would take over. Jobe, another boy his age from the quarter, took over James' chores.

Summer was coming on strong, and the planting was already done. The new field was ready and tobacco was planted for the first time. It required more work than the rest of the crops due to the plant's size. As it grew, the ground had to be pilled high against its base to keep the plant upright, which made for a much longer day. With tobacco being a lot more work, Master Tom regretted selling some of the slaves like George and Adam who were good workers. Luke didn't think anyone missed Ezekiel's family, and their contribution to work wouldn't have made all that much of a difference. Daniel would say, 'Ezekiel could lie down next to work all day long, and won't never bother him at all.' For now, there was more work to be done and everyone pitched in, even the women folk.

Master Tom, realizing he sold off too many people, knew he would have to find more help or risk losing both the cotton and tobacco fields. Miss Sharon asked, "Why not write to my father and ask for a loan?"

"No, I'll wait and see whether I can borrow some people from another plantation," he replied.

He went to his neighbors at Five Oaks and South Port Plantations but was turned down. Everyone harvests at the same time, and the owners of both plantations said they would like to help, but couldn't spare their people. They knew Tom's brother had a connection with slave traders in New Orleans, and that alone was part of their decision. Realizing he couldn't get the help he needed from neighbors, felt he had no recourse but to ask David. He was reluctant to do so because David helped finance the purchase of Cliveden, but there didn't seem to be an alternative.

"Why don't you write to my father and ask him for a loan until after the harvest?" Sharon repeated.

"No, that would be like admitting to him I'm a failure, someone you shouldn't have married."

"Well, it wouldn't hurt to ask," she replied.

"South Carolinians seem to have a lower opinion for people in other southern states. I'll just have to wait and see if the people we already have can handle it," Tom said.

Chapter 3

Mourning the Dead

Daniel and Solomon would work in the hot sun setting an example, encouraging everyone to work a little harder. One day when it was excessively hot and humid, Daniel was working in the middle of the field. Stopping for a moment, he took his handkerchief from his pocket and wiped his brow. He stood for a moment glaring up at the sun then suddenly looked unsteady on his feet and fell to his knees. Luke, Solomon and Sam rushed to his side.

"What's wrong daddy?" Luke excitedly asked.

"Don't know Luke. I just all of a sudden got weak in my legs. I can't stand. I be all right though. Just let me have some water, and lets me sit in the shade for a bit... I be alright."

Solomon helped him to the shade of a tree, where he sat Daniel down. "You think you be alright Daniel? I lets Luke stay with you," Solomon said.

"No, go on back to the field. You too, Luke! I be fine in just a bit. Just let me rest here."

Luke reluctantly went back to the field, but returned several times to look at his father. After about two hours, Solomon thought it was unusual Daniel didn't feel better and sent Luke to check on him again. When Luke got there, he found his father slumped to one side unable to speak plainly.

"Daddy what's wrong? What's wrong?" Luke frantically asked.

Realizing something was desperately wrong, Luke yelled for Solomon and Sam to join him. When they got there, Solomon asked, "Daniel, what be wrong?"

With slurred speech Daniel said, "Solomon, I tried, but I can't stand up or move my arm. Feels like it be dead."

After Solomon and Sam carried him to the wagon, they drove him back to his cabin and put him on his bed. Flora was in the herb garden when she looked up and saw them. She frantically rushed down to the cabin saying, "What's wrong with Daniel? What's wrong with my husband?" she screamed anxiously demanding.

"We don't know Miss Flora, it be powerful hot today. He just stopped to wipe the sweat off his head then just fell down."

"Luke, go to the big house and tell Master Tom what happened," Flora excitedly said.

"Yes, Ma'am!" he replied hurrying out the door.

Running as fast as he could, he went straight into the kitchen. Without knocking he stepped in. "Elizabeth, momma dun told me to tell Master Tom and Miss Sharon daddy be sick. She wants to know if they be able to do somethin' to help."

"What's wrong with him?" Elizabeth excitedly replied, putting down the pot she was using.

"We don't rightly know. He be workin' in the field, den just fell down."

"Go back home and help Momma. I'll tell Master Tom," Elizabeth said.

Luke ran back to the cabin, and in a little while, Master Tom, Miss Sharon, and Elizabeth came in. After Master Tom looked at Daniel, he realized something was very wrong and said,

"Flora, I sent for the doctor. He'll be here in about an hour."

"Thank you, Master Tom," she replied, as she put a cool wet wash cloth on Daniel's forehead.

"Luke, stay here with your mother until the doctor arrives. Come up and tell me when he gets here," Master Tom said.

"Yes Sir, Master Tom."

Within the hour, the doctor arrived, and Luke ran to the big house to tell them. After the doctor's examination, he told Flora, "It looks like he has apoplexy. The best thing for him would be bed rest. Here, when he wakes, give him some of this powder in some water."

"Doctor, will he get the feeling back in his arm and leg?" Flora asked.

Packing his bag to leave, he looked up replying, "That's something no one can tell."

At the end of the day, everyone came to the cabin to look in on Daniel. He was awake when Solomon and Sam came in. They wanted to ask him if they should speak to Master Tom about getting a few more people. Daniel at this point, wasn't able to speak at all, and could only nod in agreement. They realized they needed to get the help as fast as they could, so they wouldn't lose both the cotton and tobacco fields. With Daniel reassuring them they were making the right decision, they left.

During the night, Luke heard his mother awake calling Daniel's name. Looking in, he saw her shaking him trying to get him to open his eyes. She soon became hysterical beating him on the chest, trying to get him to respond, but it was no use. Daniel died peacefully in his sleep, and Luke's heart sunk knowing he was gone. Daniel was the cornerstone of the family, and Luke suddenly realized he would have to try and fill his shoes, a monumental task.

When Luke went to tell Elizabeth, Miss Sharon was standing at the kitchen doorway.

"Elizabeth, daddy passed during the night. Miss Sharon, can Elizabeth come home and be with Momma? She surely be needin' her for a spell."

"Yes. Elizabeth, he's right. Your mother's going to need you for a few days. I can manage."

Untying her apron, Elizabeth hung it up and went out the back door to the quarter with Luke.

Going into the cabin, they saw their mother sitting at Daniel's side holding his hand humming a sorrowful tune. *"Wade in the Water"* was one of Daniel's favorite gospel songs, and at funerals when slaves sang or hummed it, it expresses more sadness than any other hymn. *"Wade in the water, wade in the water, to wash all my sins away,"* Luke thought, *"Daniel never had any sins."*

Solomon and Sam made the coffin for Daniel, and within two days, he was buried in the cemetery behind the quarter.

Master Tom, arriving late that afternoon, went straight to Daniel's cabin to console Flora.

"Master Tom, what I gonna' do without my Daniel? I just feels so empty inside," she said.

"Flora, you still have Luke and Elizabeth to be thinking about. We'll all miss Daniel. He was the best man at Cliveden," Master Tom said.

"Thank you for 'dat Master Tom. I guess you be right. I have to look after Luke now."

***

Several weeks passed after the funeral, and Master Tom went to Flora's cabin once again. After knocking, he stepped in.

"Flora, how are you feeling now?" he asked.

"I'm fine Master Tom. I be gettin' over it. I guess you be wantin' to speak with me 'bout changin' cabins?"

"Yes. That's what I've come to talk about," he said, pausing for a moment with his head down he continued, "I want you and Luke to take the cabin at the end of the quarter?"

"Yes Master Tom. I see to it," she replied.

With Daniel gone, the certainty of the same cabin was always in doubt. Flora knew at some point after the funeral when the grieving was over, they'd be asked to move. She realized either Sam or Solomon would probably get the better cabin, just as Daniel, when the head field hand before him died. That's the reality of life on a plantation, and although Master Tom, or Master Augustus were good to them, in the end, it came down to keeping everyone content as far as their usefulness. It seemed strange that in just a few weeks after Daniel passed, things had turned around, and they were now at the end of the line.

Without Daniel in Flora's life, she seemed lost, and only went through the motions of living. She made Luke's meals, and still did the wash for the big house along with keeping up the herb garden, but you could see her heart wasn't in it.

The old fear of Luke being sold was coming back to haunt Flora. She realized, when Daniel was alive there was a need for keeping the family together. With Daniel gone, that need was no longer there. Luke still wasn't to the point he could handle the heavy work, and Master Tom needed immediate help.

***

Two days after Master Tom came back from South Port Plantation, he told Luke and Jobe, "Get your things and meet me at the wagon."

They were supposed to be going with Master Tom to Biloxi for some unknown reason, but Flora suspected they were going there to be traded or sold. She ran to the wagon screaming, "Please, Master Tom. Be kind. Don't do this to him. Don't break up the family. I do anything you ask, but please don't break us up," she begged. Sharon, hearing the commotion, came out of the house, and was shocked to see Flora and Jobe's mother groveling on the ground at Tom's feet, begging him not to take the boy's away.

The funeral for Daniel delayed working the crops, and Tom knew he had to move quickly to get more help in the fields.

"Tom, I've never witnessed a family broken up; this is terrible. We never did this at Bellevue; it's horrible. I refuse to allow it. You'll just have to find another way," Sharon sternly said.

"Sharon, we won't have the money until the cotton and tobacco crops are harvested. If I don't get immediate help, both crops could fail or be poor and worthless," he frustratingly replied.

"Write to my father, and ask him for a loan, but I implore you. Don't break up these families," she said adamant in her demand.

"I can't ask your father. The only other alternative would be to ask David. I really don't want to do that, I'm already in his debt. You're just making things more difficult," he forcefully said.

"Well, ask David then. If you leave now, you should be back by the end of the week."

Finally relenting, Tom left for Biloxi alone.

As Sharon started walking back to the house, Flora and Jobe's mother being grateful, threw themselves to the ground, clinging to the hem of Sharon's dress.

Flora said, "We thanks you, Miss Sharon. We thanks..."

Cutting them short, Sharon said, "Get up! I've never seen the like of this at Bellevue, and I don't want to see it here again, ever!"

***

Tom arrived in Biloxi two days later, and stayed with his brother and sister. The evening after Tom arrived he was sitting with David on the veranda after dinner. Thelma, David's house maid poured them a julep. Tom looked at his glass for a few moments realizing he was only postponing the inevitable. Getting up enough courage he asked bluntly, "David, I'm in need of a few slaves. If you could loan me a few, I'll pay you back after the harvest."

"I assumed that's why you're here. There's no other reason you would leave Cliveden during this part of the growing season," David candidly said. Thinking for a few moments, he slowly stirred his drink then looked up, "Tom, I can help, but I want a favor in return."

"If it's about Elizabeth, Sharon created such a fuss when I was going to bring Luke and Jobe to the auction, I couldn't do it. She wanted me to borrow the money from her father which I won't do either. You're my last hope David," Tom implored.

"Look, I'll lend you the few slaves that come in on Tuesday, if you'll let Elizabeth come here until the harvest is in. This way, it will be just a swap of people without losing Luke and Jobe. You wouldn't have to worry about getting money from anyone else. I'll lend you whatever you need."

"I'm not sure I can convince Sharon to let Elizabeth go. I'll tell her it will only be temporary until you find another cook," Tom said.

***

Tuesday came, and they went to the dock to see the slaves coming in. There were agents bidding for the owners of Dumont, and other plantations David knew from prior sales. As the slaves came off the ship, they were herded into a holding cell. After everyone that was purchasing looked over the group, they were brought out one at a time to be bid on. They weren't directly from Africa, and most had been living in the country since birth. They were from plantations that didn't need as many slaves with the invention of the cotton gin years earlier, so slaves were cheaper than they had been in years past.

Several younger slaves the buyers wanted for Dumont were brought out first. The buyers gave David a nod, and he had them separated from the rest. David was always looking to make an extra dollar, and the people from Dumont always paid him more for putting the better ones aside. There were three people that looked to be in their mid to late 40's and two of them didn't look to be in the best physical condition, but Tom had no choice other than take them. Half-heartedly satisfied with the acquisition of the three people, the next morning he left for home.

***

Arriving at Cliveden at dusk two days later, he pulled up directly to the barn. Opening the barn door he told them to go inside, then called for Solomon to join him.

"Solomon, here's the new people. I hope they'll be enough help. They're your responsibility now. Bed them down in the barn tonight. I'm going up to the main house, I'm tired."

"Yes Sir, Master Tom, I takes good care of 'dem," Solomon replied.

Looking over the three new people Solomon asked, "Have any of ya'll ever worked a tobacco field?"

"I have. It be on a plantation in Norf' Calina'," one of the men named Ezra replied. They weren't the help Solomon thought he would get, but was happy they appeared to be able to do at least a little work. When Ezra took off his shirt, his back was laced with whip scars, and a few looked to be recent. Solomon, seeing the scars commented, "They ain't no whippin' post here at Cliveden, and we don't be havin' an overseer. Master Tom, and Miss Sharon, they ain't hard as some, but the thought of you bein' sent to Dumont, should be 'nough to keep you from runnin' away."

"I heard 'bout 'dat Dumont place. I saw some peoples at the dock sold to them. What's 'dat Dumont place be anyway?" one of the men asked.

"Just be glad it wan't you. Bed down here for the night, and come by my cabin in the mornin'. My Missus will feed you. Then ya'll get ready to work the tobacco fields."

When Tom went into the house Sharon asked, "How was your trip to Biloxi?"

"David gave me some more money, and let me have three people. They look to be in their mid to late 40's, and two of them don't look all that healthy," he replied unenthusiastically.

"What did he charge for them?" she asked.

"He didn't. They're only on loan until the tobacco crop is sold."

Not wanting to begin an unpleasant conversation, he tactfully avoided mentioning David wanting Elizabeth.

"Do you think the new people are enough to do the work?" she asked.

Taking off his boots he replied, "I'll find out from Solomon tomorrow night when they come back from the field. Sharon, I've had a long day. I'm going to bed."

She watched as he climbed the stairs wondering why he was so blunt with his answers. Tom still didn't know what to do about his brother's agreement, and upon entering the bedroom he put it out of his mind.

***

In the morning, Tom went to the quarter to speak to Solomon about the new people.

"Well Solomon, what do you think?" he asked.

"Master Tom, one of them, he say he worked tobacco fields in Norf' Calina, wherever 'dat be, and I sure it grows there, just the same as it do right here. He should be some help. The other two, I can't rightly say. They be able to at least do the hoein' and gathering cotton when the crops ready."

"Ok, remember what I said; they're your responsibility."

Everyone gathered outside where Solomon was standing, and together they began to head toward the tobacco fields. Tom went back to the house, still trying to decide how he was going to convince Sharon about the swap to his brother for Elizabeth, and at the breakfast table he finally got up enough courage to ask.

"Sharon, part of the deal with David was allowing Elizabeth to go to Biloxi for a few weeks until he can find a new cook. I said she could. It's only going to be for a few weeks."

Putting down her fork, she gave him a stern look saying, "I wouldn't part with Elizabeth for any amount of people you got from David. Not now! Not ever!"

As adamant as she was, he didn't press the issue, and went outside wondering what to do about his commitment with David, when he didn't show up in Biloxi with Elizabeth.

That evening when Solomon and the rest returned from the field, Tom asked, "Solomon, how did the new people work?"

"Master Tom, they not the best I ever did see, but they be some help I suppose. Ezra, the one 'dat worked tobacco befo' gave me an idea. He said he never did see tobacco plants 'dat big. He must knowed what he talks 'bout, he know it was a first plantin' on new ground. He say the plantation he was on, de' wheel barrowed dirt from the edge of the field into the rows. 'Dat way, it cuts down the hoein' time."

"That's good, what about the other two?"

Solomon, removing his hat, wiped the sweat from the inside band. "Master Tom, Ezra was teachin' them a little 'bout fieldwork. I thinks they be better field hands in a little bit."

***

Two weeks went by and the field work seemed easier with the extra help. One day, Sharon was sitting on the front porch when David unsuspectingly came to visit. When the coach pulled up, he got out.

"Good afternoon Sharon, where's Tom?"

"He's down at the tobacco barn. Would you like a cool drink?"

Joining her on the front porch he replied as he sat down, "I sure would after that dusty ride."

Sharon opened the door to the house, and called for Elizabeth to bring out two glasses of lemonade. When she brought them out, David asked, "Sharon, did Tom mention anything to you about Elizabeth staying with me for awhile?"

Putting down her glass of lemonade, she replied, "Yes, but that's out of the question. I'll never part with Elizabeth's talent in the kitchen, not for any amount of people."

David's eyes followed Elizabeth as she was serving them, and could see her shapely figure as she bent down to pick up a napkin that fell from the table. Sharon caught his eyes looking at her realizing immediately, it wasn't for the cooking he wanted her at his home. Hearing what Sharon told him, Elizabeth gave her an endearing smile then returned to the kitchen.

When Tom came up to the porch he was surprised to see David. Fearing what David might say to open a sore point with Sharon he said, "Come on David. I want to show you the new tobacco drying barn we're building," attempting to hide the fact he was embarrassed at David's visit. Something he wasn't looking forward too, but expected. David got up, put down his glass, and followed him off the porch. On their walk to the barn, David tactfully asked, "How are the new people working out for you?"

"Fine, David, just fine," he replied.

Stopping for a moment, David took Tom by the arm. Looking at him he asked in a demanding tone, "Well, why haven't you fulfilled your part of the bargain?"

Tom looked at the ground then began toeing the dust with his foot, replying in a frustrated voice, "Sharon was so upset at the suggestion; she said there would have to be another way to repay you. How am I supposed to get around that kind of attitude David?" he said pausing for a moment, "How long are you staying?"

"I have a week until the next ship comes in. Tom, you realize you depend on my dock for giving you the lowest price for anything you ship, don't you?"

"Yes, you're my older brother, and I appreciate any help you give me until I get through this financial squeeze," Tom replied.

"Yes, we're brothers, but the saw cuts both ways, and I expect you to fulfill your end of the bargain," David demanded.

***

During the week, David spent quite a bit of time at the kitchen doorway talking to, and watching Elizabeth. Sitting on a kitchen stool one afternoon he asked, "Elizabeth, how would you feel about going home with me for a few weeks?"

Turning to look at him she replied, "I don't think Miss Sharon will let me."

Knowing how Sharon objected, he didn't press the issue and left the kitchen.

***

One day, when David was standing in the doorway of the kitchen watching her. John came to the back door. He saw the towel Elizabeth hung on the post, and entering the kitchen he said,"I see you needs more wood chopped, Miss Elizabeth."

Usually she acted friendly, offering him a cool drink of water or a piece of cornbread, something she knew was his favorite. Not getting a favorable response he continued, "Sure is a hot one today Missy, I surely could use a drink of cool water from 'dat there jug."

It seemed as though she didn't want to speak to him, and he wondered why. Feeling slighted, he pressed, "Did I do somethin' to makes you mad Missy?"

"No! I'm just busy today. Go on, get yourself on outta' here. Fetch me some wood," she said sternly.

With David standing there, she was trying her best not to look like she cared for John. Feeling as though he was scolded, John left the kitchen shaking his head, mumbling to himself as he closed the door and slowly walked down the back steps, *"I don't know what I did, but she sure seems mad at me today!"*

David, remembering seeing them talking several times, suddenly realized the connection between them was deeper than John just chopping wood. Being reassured with his new found knowledge, he smiled at Elizabeth then walked through the kitchen to the back door. Standing in the doorway looking out, he watched until John was out of site.

Pushing the screen door open he said aloud, "I think I'll see what Tom's doing." Looking over his shoulder, he smiled at Elizabeth once more then slowly walked down the back steps. She suddenly felt anxious, and held her clenched fist to her chest realizing David discovered the reason she didn't want to go to Biloxi.

Finding Tom at the tobacco barn, David said, "Tom, I was thinking.

There's another way you can repay me."

"What do you mean David? What way?"

"You have a man here name John. He's not married is he?"

"No. He's not married. Why?" Tom replied, looking up at the roof of the tobacco barn being finished. Without looking at David he said, "John has no family here."

"He's the kind of buck I want for helping load the ships at the dock, I'll take him for the three I gave you. How does that sound?"

Tom thought for a moment then replied, "That sounds reasonable. I'm sure Sharon won't mind that arrangement."

Going to the house to draw up papers, Tom told Sharon about the agreement.

"Sharon, David agreed to take John in place of the three he lent me. He said he could use him at the dock. How's that arrangement?"

"Since he's not married and doesn't have any other family here, that will be fine," she replied.

That evening after everyone came back from the field, David walked down to the quarter. Seeing John he said, "You'll be leaving with me for Biloxi when I leave day after tomorrow. You'll be working on the docks there."

Shocked at what he was hearing, it was as though John was in a bad dream wanting to wake up to find it wasn't really happening. He wanted desperately to tell Elizabeth the bad news, but had to wait till morning.

***

In the morning before going to the fields, he saw Elizabeth at the cook house door and ran to tell her. "Missy, I'm sold to Master David. He be takin' me to Biloxi when he leaves out tomorrow. I don't knows if I ever get's to see you again," he said helplessly.

She hadn't yet heard and was shocked to hear it.

"I always wanted to jump the broom with you Missy, now it's too late. Now I don't thinks I ever be able to, and might not never see you again. Miss Elizabeth, Miss Elizabeth," he said filled with emotion trying to express himself. Unable to find the words, he seized her by both arms lifting her off the ground with ease. After kissing her on the lips, he said, "I loves you Miss Elizabeth, you always 'member 'dat. You see me again, 'dat's fo' sure. I promise."

By being silent and not telling Sharon she wanted to marry John, she missed her chance and now it seemed to be too late. Her fears were right, when David heard John ask if she was angry with him, David realized the connection.

After John left she went into the cook house. In a few minutes David came to the door. Leaning on the doorframe he said, "You know, I traded for John. He's leaving with me for Biloxi tomorrow."

Turning to look at him, she replied frustratingly wringing her hands together, "Yes, Master David. He just told me. Can I do something to change your mind?"

"Yes, you can ask Miss Sharon if you could go to Biloxi with me for a few weeks."

Looking down at the small hearth she was using, she replied, "I'll try. But I don't think she'll let me."

That afternoon, she saw Miss Sharon sitting at a small table under the magnolia tree writing a letter and asked, "Miss Sharon, I hate to be botherin' you. But can I go with Master David to Biloxi when he leaves out tomorrow?"

Pausing momentarily, Sharon was surprised at the request and looked up from the letter. "I can't let you go. There's no one else to take your place in the kitchen," she said.

With her head down feeling dejected, Elizabeth slowly walked away.

That evening while she was in the kitchen David came in, "I already heard you aren't allowed to go, but things could be easier for John if your attitude towards me were different the next time I visit."

Looking down, understanding his meaning she replied, "I'll try to be more friendly, Master David," she said pausing for a moment pleading, "Please don't let any harm come to my John."

Smiling, he put his hands around her slim waist. Pulling her close he kissed her gently on the side of the neck. She froze at his touch, but made no attempt to pull away. With confidence of being successful, he walked out of the kitchen.

Elizabeth worked in the cook house long after dark that evening, and the aroma of fresh cornbread being baked could be smelled all the way down to the quarter.

***

Early next morning as the coach was about to leave, she ran to it. Looking up at John seated next to the driver she handed him two loaves of cornbread to take with him. Looking down at her, he was puzzled, wondering why all of a sudden she was so concerned, when it appeared to be too late. David, seeing her, leaned out the coach window and said, "Remember your promise on my next visit Elizabeth," then told his coachman, "You can start out now Arthur."

***

Within two days they were in Biloxi. John had never been to a city, and kept looking around in awe. Arthur asked, "Why are you looking around so much, ain't you ever seen a city before?"

Continuing to take it all in, John replied, "The only town I ever did see, is where the cotton market be, and 'dat be only a few houses and a store. I ain't never see so many darkies livin' together in one place. They be free?" he asked.

"Well, some are, and some ain't. I lived on a plantation before Master David brought me here. You probably be workin' on the dock Master David owns," he said looking John up and down examining his physique. Arthur continued, "By the size of you, he probably gonna make you the headman some day," then chuckled.

Arthur had been Master David's driver for almost 15 years. David got him from a debt he was owed when Arthur was about 40. He was 5'9", thin, with white hair, and was always dependable for getting David wherever he had to be on time.

With all the new scenery, John temporarily forgot about Elizabeth, and his thoughts turned to what his new life might be like. Stopping first at David's home, John surveyed David's house and grounds asking, "Arthur, how long Master David dun lived here?"

"The house was owned by his daddy. It was handed down to Master David, Master Tom, and they sister, Miss Anne. Master David and Miss Anne, they still lives here."

Pulling up to the front steps, several servants came out to carry the baggage.

"Arthur, take John down to the dock and introduce him to Jeremiah. Have Jeremiah show him where he'll sleep, and tell Jeremiah I'll be at the dock in the morning. There's a ship due in, and I want to be there when it arrives," David said.

"Yes, Master David. I'll tell him."

Turning the coach around, Arthur headed for the dock. He knew John was wondering how all this was like a dream he couldn't imagine. Arthur knew, John like him, would soon realize it was hidden by only being allowed to inhabit the small world he lived in at Cliveden.

Arriving at the dock, there were several Negro's moving bales and boxes that were to be shipped out the next day. Climbing down from the coach, Arthur gathered the men around and said, "This is John. He was bought by Master David. He be workin' with you from now on," turning to Jeremiah he continued, "Jeremiah, Master David wants you to show him where he sleeps, and where he gets his food. You can 'spect to see Master David in the mornin'. After patting John on the shoulder, Arthur walked back to the carriage.

By the dock hand's silence, it was obvious to John he wasn't taken kindly to. Being bigger and stronger, they kept their feelings silent and returned to what they were doing. Jeremiah, looking him up and down said, "Come on with me. I shows you where you be beddin' down tonight."

Going to the end of the dock, Jeremiah pointed to a shack, "There it be! You sleeps there," he said.

Going in, there was a strong odor of hemp rope and burlap sacks, and it brought back memories of Farnsworth to John, the first plantation he was brought up on. This shack wasn't much better than the one he had there, but at least he didn't have to share it with anyone. His family of four lived in a space at Farnsworth about this same size. The boards on the side of the shack were spaced, and as he lay on the temporary bed he fashioned from the pile of rope and burlap sacks, he could see the sunlight fading into dusk.

Thinking about Elizabeth, he consumed the last piece of cornbread, wondering whether he would ever see her again. He had a lot on his mind, and couldn't understand why the other slaves on the dock didn't seem as friendly as they were at Cliveden. He thought, *They were owned like me,* but there seemed to be resentfulness, something he wasn't used to. After tossing it around in his mind, he wondered what his new life would be like. Pushing it to the back of his mind, in a half hour he fell asleep.

In the morning he awoke to the sound of men shouting orders, "Hey down there! Tie the ships ropes to the bollards on the pier," someone on the ship yelled. Quickly coming out of the shack, he wiped the crust from his eyes. A large sailing vessel was being secured to the dock, and he hurried over to the other men, grabbing the line to help. After securing the ship, he was told by one of the dock hands, "Get the boarding plank and fasten it to the ships side, so's the captn' can walk off."

Confused, not knowing what a boarding plank looked like, he picked up a loose board lying on the pier and began to fasten it to the ship.

"No dummy, the ship's gang plank is over there," the person that gave him the order said pointing to it.

After tying it on, one of the dock hands took him aboard. "You climbs down in the ship's hold, down there," he pointed, "When the winch and rope come down, you helps the other two men's that be down there, tie up the cargo. After it be tied up, we lift it out and set it down here on the dock."

Given the order, John quickly did as he was told.

He hadn't had anything to eat or drink all morning, and after a few hours of working in the ships hold on a hot day, made him lightheaded. The other hands woke earlier but didn't wake him, so he missed eating. By their attitude, he soon realized they didn't like the idea of him being there. They considered him to be a dirt farmer, a dumb field hand who was very much beneath them.

About 10 o'clock, David came to the ship. "Jeremiah, where's John working?" he asked.

"Master David, he be in the hold on the ship, he be loadin' cargo in the winch net."

Going aboard David looked down in the hold. He watched for a few minutes and it appeared to him John was working a little slow. Realizing there was something wrong, he yelled down, "John, come up out of there for awhile. Have a drink of water."

Coming up on deck, John wiped the sweat from his face then picked up the dipper next to a bucket of water. He downed the first one in three gulps then proceeded to have two more. Noticing his unsteadiness David asked, "Did you have anything to eat today?"

"No Master David. When I woke up this monin', they was already pulling the ship to the dock. I just started helpin', I didn't have a chance for nothin'."

"Come with me," David said.

Walking off the ship together, David called to Jeremiah, "Jeremiah, replace John with another dock hand," he angrily ordered.

"Who you wants me to replace him with, Master David?"

"Noah there, he'll do. You're in charge of this dock. Why didn't you wake John and let him eat with the rest of you?"

"I sorry Master David, but with the ship commin' in, I dun fogot all about him bein' in the storeroom."

"Don't let it happen again, or you'll be in the hold working," David threatened.

"Yes Sir, Master David. It surely won't never happen again -ever!"

"I'm making you responsible for teaching John everything he has to know about being in charge," David commanded.

"Yes sir, I surely will," Jeremiah replied.

Without having any personal contact with the rest, John realized he was already on their bad side. He never experienced this division amongst slaves, and being put in this position made him uncomfortable. Time would prove him right.

***

The next few weeks were testy dealing with the other dock hands. On occasion, he would hear them grumble about, why a dumb field hand was brought in by Master David, when there were other people available, more familiar with dock work. A quick learner, John was attentive to everything Jeremiah was teaching for the next several weeks, and became familiar with the use of different ropes, pulleys, and how to tie different knots for hoisting cargo.

Arthur had taken a liking to John, coming from a plantation the same as him, and knew the difficulties of getting used to a new way of life. Trying to make things easier for him to be accepted, Arthur would speak with the dock crew occasionally, imploring them to accept him.

Eventually, by working hard and having something funny to say now and again, he was finally able to fit in. Although John found it easier to be in their company, he chose to stay bedded down in the shack on the pier. It was small, but it gave him the privacy he wanted to think about

Elizabeth. Most nights he lay awake listening to the water lapping gently against the pilings holding up the pier. It seemed as though the relaxing sound let his mind wander back to Cliveden, and the conversation with Elizabeth in the cook house, the day before he left. The kiss he so boldly gave her that day, even after a hard day's work, made him feel good thinking about it. He thought, *"I wonder if Miss Elizabeth still be thinkin' 'bout me?"* His mind never stopped wondering what life would have been like married to her, and most nights with that thought in mind, he would drift off to sleep.

Chapter 4
Return to Cliveden

David stayed in Biloxi for a few weeks until the ships finished coming in and transferred their cargo. It seemed like every time David spoke to John, like a thief in the night, the thought of possessing Elizabeth came back to haunt his mind. His desire to have her was becoming burdensome and being unable to quench that desire, forced him to take a trip back to Cliveden with his sister Anne. With the harvest of tobacco underway, he would use that as an excuse to collect on some advance monies he loaned Tom.

Anne would accompany David as often as possible. She liked the idea of living a life on a plantation rather than a home in Biloxi. She was 22 years old, and around 5' 3", thin, with brown curly hair. Being a premature birth, she was sickly most of her young life.

He and Anne arrived at Cliveden in late afternoon, and were met by Sharon who always enjoyed Anne's company. David asked, "Where's Tom?"

"He's at the tobacco barn watching the harvest being put up. Would you like a drink after that long dusty ride?" Sharon asked.

"I don't know whether David does, but I do," Anne replied.

Sharon opened the door and called to Elizabeth to bring three glasses of lemonade. Not knowing who the other two glasses were for, she was surprised when she came out to see David and Anne sitting there.

"Hello Elizabeth," David said. "I guess you're wondering how John's doing? I'll have to speak to you later about him."

Looking at her, he knew her temptation to say something was great, but although she didn't answer, he realized he succeeded in arousing her interest. With his glass of lemonade in hand he looked at her again then excused himself and headed for the tobacco barn. When Tom saw him he said, "David, the harvest is a better crop than I expected. Some of it was due to Ezra, one of the slaves I brought from Biloxi. He had some experience raising tobacco and proved to be a big help. Did Anne come with you?"

"Yes, she did. I'll only be here for a few days, but I think Anne wants to visit for a few weeks."

"I won't be able to spend much time with you or Anne until after the tobacco and cotton's been picked. I'll be too busy," Tom said.

"Tom, did you ever think about hiring an overseer for the place?"

With a shrug of his shoulders, Tom replied, "I hardly had the money for the help I got from you let alone an overseer."

Tom called to Solomon who was standing on a platform putting up slats filled with large tobacco leaves to dry and said, "Solomon, I'm going back to the house and have dinner with Miss Anne and David. You take over."

Looking down from the platform where he was working, Solomon replied, "Yes Sir, Master Tom. I knows what to do."

Before dinner was served, David went to the kitchen to speak with Elizabeth. She was putting the dinner meal on serving trays when he said, "I sure missed your cooking Elizabeth. I'm looking forward to some fine meals while I'm here."

Not smiling at his remark, she realized the time she dreaded had come. Knowing she would have to fulfill her commitment, she wondered to what degree he expected her to cooperate.

The kitchen was busy with servants getting the meal ready to serve, but again, David couldn't keep his eyes off her. Looking forward to something he desired for a long time, like a hungry wolf, he realized that time was near. Without actually saying it, by his look he made his point known and Elizabeth clearly understood.

After returning to the table where everyone was seated, he began talking about events of the last several weeks. As one of the servants was going back to the kitchen, Elizabeth heard Tom ask, "David, how's John working out for you?" The timing of the question couldn't have been more perfect. Wanting to hear what was being said; Elizabeth put her ear to the door.

Realizing that might be the case, David spoke in a louder tone, "John's doing fine right now, but I want to wait awhile to see how he progresses. You know -see how he'll work out for the future." It wasn't general conversation, it was to let Elizabeth know he still had control over the person she cared for, and depending on how she fulfilled her commitment, she ultimately controlled John's fate. Sharon, noticing his louder tone of voice, looked toward the swinging kitchen door as one of the servants was bringing desert to the table. She saw Elizabeth standing by the door and realized she was right with her assumption. Elizabeth was in fact, standing near the door listening.

After dinner, everyone went out on the veranda to enjoy a julep, while feeling the cool breeze of the night air. Within a half hour, Tom and David went back to the tobacco barn to watch Solomon and the other hands put up the last wagon load of tobacco. It had been cloudy all day and you could smell the rain coming. Looking around Tom said, "You did a good job Solomon. Go on back to your cabins now and rest."

After looking over the work again, Tom nodded with approval, "Mighty fine work Solomon, mighty fine."

Looking up at the sky David said, "It looks like they made it just in time Tom. Here comes the rain."

"Yes, just in time. Let's get back to the house before it comes down hard," Tom said, as they hastily retreated to the shelter of the front porch. After some discussion about the success of the crops, Tom said, "David, I'll have some money for you before you leave."

"You don't have to worry about that right now. I'm here for a few days," he replied.

"Well, I just wanted you to know. I appreciate what you've done for me."

Looking out at the horizon, Tom could see faint flashes of lightening in the distance, followed by a roll of thunder. David took a seat as the rain began to come down a little harder and said, "Tom, why don't you sit and talk for awhile?"

Looking at David he replied, "Sharon and Anne have already retired for the night. I had a long day. I think I'll do the same. Goodnight, David."

"Goodnight Tom. I'm not tired. I'm just going to sit for awhile and enjoy this cool breeze and watch the rain fall."

After everyone went to bed, David waited for about 15 minutes to insure everyone was in their rooms before visiting Elizabeth. With the thought of finally possessing her he didn't want to be disturbed. Going into the kitchen he noticed the door to her room was slightly open. Was she anticipating him coming? Pushing it open a little further he saw her lying on the bed. She wasn't asleep as he expected wanting to hear more about John. After lighting the lamp, he turned the flame down as low as he could. She sat up, and he could see her long hair draped over her upper body, and the fullness of her breasts beneath her night shirt.

Sitting on the edge of the bed he quietly asked, "Are you ready to fill your part of the bargain?"

"Yes, Master David," she replied in a nervous tone.

Like many other plantation owners or overseers, he could have just taken her, but wanted it to be mutual; something she could never consider. Realizing he had total control, and she would do anything to keep John safe from harm he said, "Take off your night shirt."

Understanding her position she did as he asked. He could see the outline of her beautiful body in the dimly-lit room, a body he always wanted to possess. She lay back on the bed again and he took off his trousers laying them neatly over a chair. Getting in bed beside her, he began running his hands over her smooth skin. Caressing her breasts, he sensed immediately she was nervous and afraid.

"Is this your first time?" he asked quietly.

"Yes, Master David, I ain't never did this before."

Hearing her words he stopped, compassion took over. When a flash of lightning illuminated the room, it revealed the extreme fear in her eyes. He thought, *What am I doing?* The overwhelming desire for her clouded his judgment. He never took a woman before without their full consent. Sliding out of bed, he put on his trousers and headed for the door. Not looking back fearing her naked body might weaken his resolve to leave, he said in a disappointing voice, "Go to sleep!"

After leaving the room, she was relieved he didn't take her, but worried how her reaction would affect John. Rolling over on her side still shaking from the experience, she pulled the blanket up to her neck and began to cry. After calming down, she rolled over on her stomach and within the hour fell asleep.

After leaving the room, David went to the liquor cabinet and retrieved a half bottle of brandy. Slowly climbing the stairs to his bedroom, he realized the only remedy to tonight's frustration was the grasp he had on the drinking glass, and the bottle he was carrying. The more he drank, the more he kept telling himself, *I can take her as many times as I want, if I can only get her to Biloxi,* although he knew in his heart, it wasn't his nature. As he finished the bottle, something in his innermost conscious came to him, *Elizabeth isn't her. Elizabeth isn't her.*

***

In the morning, Sharon encountered David coming down the stairs. By his appearance she could tell he had been drinking heavily. Realizing he must have been awake after everyone had gone to bed, she immediately went to Elizabeth's room. Opening the door, Elizabeth quickly sat up. Sharon noticed her eyes were red and puffy obviously from crying, and quickly surmised David had visited her room after everyone had gone to bed.

"Are you alright Elizabeth? Are you sick?" she asked.

"No. Miss Sharon, I'll be up in a hurry to start breakfast. I just couldn't sleep last night."

"No, Elizabeth, stay in your room today. I'll get your mother to help with the cooking."

When Tom opened the door to the kitchen, he saw Sharon standing at Elizabeth's doorway and asked, "Elizabeth, when will breakfast be ready? I wanted to get an early start today. I want to make sure Solomon's finished putting up the tobacco and getting things ready to harvest the cotton."

Sharon looked at him with contempt for what she thought David had done replying, "Elizabeth's not feeling well today. We'll have to survive this morning with cold food."

"I hope she's feeling better by suppertime," he replied.

"If it wasn't for David being here, you would have your breakfast," Sharon angrily exclaimed.

With the hostility of Sharon's words, he glanced towards Elizabeth's door again quickly surmising her intent. Going to the cabinet he took out a piece of bread. Hastily consuming a few bites, he hurriedly walked out the back door towards the quarter.

Sharon was still in the kitchen when David came in, and she asked in a loud hostile tone, "How long were you downstairs last night after everyone went to bed?"

He got the message she knew he visited Elizabeth, and wasn't pleased with what she assumed he had done. Not answering immediately, he looked at her with contempt for her pre-judgment of him. Elizabeth's silence only made Sharon's opinion of the incident worse than it was, and when David didn't respond, Sharon continued, "You're a guest here David. We treat our people like family."

Taken aback with her words, he hurried out the back door to find Tom. Although David knew the real facts about the visit with Elizabeth, he wasn't going to be lectured by his sister-in-law. Finding Tom at the tobacco barn, he sternly said, "Tom, I visited Elizabeth last night and Sharon didn't take kindly to it. She reminded me that I was a guest. Well, you remind your wife that I'm more than a guest or a brother; I'm also your financier. You could easily remedy the situation by letting Elizabeth come to Biloxi when I leave tomorrow."

Surprised at the unprovoked tongue lashing, Tom realized his assumption why breakfast wasn't served was correct; it did have something to do with David visiting Elizabeth. Looking at David he said, "I'm sorry. I'll speak to Sharon again. I'll let her know until the crops are sold in another month, I'm still in your debt."

Tom went back to the house and saw Sharon in the hall. Seeing him, she quickly told him what she thought David had done.

"You know, Sharon, you're making things difficult by standing in the way of David wanting to take Elizabeth back to Biloxi. It would only be for a few weeks."

She turned to walk away, when he grabbed her by the arm and said, "David already experienced her. Why don't you try being patient?"

Elizabeth, hearing what they were saying, remained in the kitchen until Sharon came in. Fearing John would be punished for her not going with David she said, "Miss Sharon, my mother would be glad to cook for you while I'm gone. She's a better cook than me."

"Are you sure you want to go with him?" Sharon replied.

"Yes!" she exclaimed, almost pleading to let her go.

When Flora heard the news Elizabeth was leaving, she didn't care for it, but the thought it would only be temporary eased her mind. That night after dinner, Tom quietly told David, "Sharon finally agreed to let Elizabeth go with you."

"That's fine, Tom. Thank you."

After everyone had gone to bed, David went to the kitchen to look in on Elizabeth. Opening the door slightly, to his surprise, Flora was lying there. She had brought her things up to the big house to take over the cooking, and told Elizabeth to go back to the quarter until morning when she was supposed to leave.

The next morning everyone was already up when David came down-stairs.

"Flora, would you get me a cup of coffee?" he asked, before joining Tom, Sharon and Anne sitting at the dining room table.

"Anne, are you ready to go home?" David asked.

"If you wouldn't mind David, I'd like to stay for a while longer," she replied.

"Well, I have two ships coming in. I can't stay. I'll be back in several weeks to bring you home, how does that sound?"

Tom said, "That will be good. The cotton and tobacco will be ready for market, and I'll be able to pay you the rest of the money I borrowed."

As Elizabeth served David's coffee, she said, "Master David, I'll be ready to go whenever you and Miss Anne are ready."

"Miss Anne won't be going with us. Have you seen my driver, Arthur?"

"Yes, he's in the kitchen eating his breakfast."

"Good. Tell him to load your things, and let him know we'll be leaving in about an hour."

After telling Arthur, Elizabeth went back to the quarter to pack her clothes in a travel bag Miss Sharon gave her. When she got back to the house, Sharon quietly took her aside and asked, "Are you sure you really want to go?"

"Yes, Miss Sharon. Thank you for helping me."

She embraced Elizabeth as if she was her own, realizing what might possibly be in store for her saying. "I'll miss you. I hope the time passes quickly until you return."

Within the hour, Arthur pulled the coach up to the front of the house. David said goodbye to Tom, Sharon and Anne, then held the door open until Elizabeth said goodbye to her mother and got in. After closing the door they departed.

The trip back to Biloxi would take two days and require an overnight stay. David thought the trip would be on a friendlier basis, but Elizabeth remained silent for the first few hours. He was beginning to be disap-pointed, when she finally spoke. Not looking directly at him, but looking out the coach window she asked, "Will I be able to see John when we get there Master David?"

"That depends on you!" he replied. The rest of the day she remained silent.

Near dusk, they stopped at an inn for the evening. Traveling slaves had separate quarters, but after checking in, he asked the proprietor, "Would you see to it she's made comfortable with her accommodations," handing the proprietor a few extra dollars.

After accepting it the proprietor replied, "Yes, Sir. I'll see to it."

Before going upstairs to his room David said, "Goodnight Elizabeth, I hope you sleep well. I'll see you in the morning."

Retiring to where she was to sleep, she thought it would be some makeshift room much like the one she had at Cliveden. When the proprietor opened the door, it was much better than she anticipated. After getting undressed, she climbed into bed. Staring at the ceiling she wondered about the change in David's personality, and why he was all of a sudden concerned with her comfort? She didn't know, but was confused by his actions. With the thought of what her life might be like for the next several weeks, she drifted off to sleep.

Chapter 5

The Concubine

Late afternoon the second day, they arrived in Biloxi. Elizabeth, like John, had never been to a town, not even the nearby town with the cotton market. In fact, she had never been away from Cliveden. Surveying all the people walking around she asked, "Master David, I never seen so many darkie women walking around. Are they free?"

Turning his focus from her to look out the coach window, he replied, "Well, some are, and some aren't."

After a few minutes of silence, she asked, "How do they know which ones are?"

"That's a good question. I guess they know it themselves."

"Is John able to walk around like that?"

"Yes, as long as he goes back to the dock and does his work, I don't mind."

Taking it all in, she realized it was something she never knew existed, and like John, it opened her eyes from the narrow world she too was only allowed to inhabit. When Arthur pulled up to David's house, several servants came out to greet them. They took the baggage and David introduced Elizabeth.

"Elizabeth, this is Thelma, she runs the house. Markus here, he's the butler. You already know Arthur, and the woman in the kitchen, her name is Sarah. Markus, take Elizabeth's bag to her room," David said.

Elizabeth noticed Thelma looked remarkably like Miss Bertha at Cliveden. For the exception of the yellow bandana Miss Bertha wore, Thelma could have been her double.

Markus was extremely dark skinned and looked to be in his early 50's. Tall and balding, his white hair rimmed the side of his head.

"Which room, sir?" Markus asked.

Thelma quickly replied, "Markus, you just carry the bag on up to the hall outside Master David's room. Come on honey, I'll shows you."

Getting to the second floor, Thelma opened the door to the bedroom Elizabeth would occupy, "Here honey, here's where you sleeps."

Looking in the room, Elizabeth asked suspiciously, "Miss Thelma, does Master David always have the cook sleeping on the second floor across from where he sleeps?"

Thelma looking at her replied, "Since Master David's wife died, he always keeps a woman at hand so he could be satisfied in the night if'n he gets the urge."

Elizabeth knew she was there to perform a function like that, but was surprised she was there explicitly for that purpose. She said warily, "I'm supposed to be the cook until he finds another one."

Thelma laughed, "Master David dun had the same cook for 10 years. You ain't got but one purpose child, being here when he needs it. The last one that was here, he treated her real good. She had finer clothes than anybody else, and was free to go to the market to buy whatever she wanted, or go anywhere she wanted. You're lucky, the plantation I lived on when I was a young girl, the owner or overseer did what they wanted, when they wanted, and you ain't get nothin' exceptin' maybe bein' pregnant, ifn' you wasn't careful."

Elizabeth stood for a moment in the doorway looking around the room in awe. It reminded her of the first time she was in the big house at Cliveden. Slowly opening the door the rest of the way, she got a better look at a room she never dreamed of living in. It was bright with yellow and green flowered wallpaper, and sheer white curtains on the windows. The furniture was polished to a high shine, and gleamed with the late afternoon sun coming through the window. At Cliveden, her room in the kitchen only had a wood floor. But here, she not only had hardwood floors, these were hardwood floors with carpeting, just like the big house. The bed was made up with a white flowered spread, and had a white canopy over it. Against the wall was a dressing table with a large mirror and cushioned bench seat. On the dressing table, there were several fancy perfume bottles. Carefully picking up one, she examined it removing the ornate glass stopper to sniff the contents. It was a familiar fragrance, a fragrance she had a whiff of before. Suddenly remembering, *That's it! It was when Miss Sharon's friend walked by. Yes, that's the very same fragrance.*

She wondered, *"Why is he doing this? Is it to make me feel better about the commitment I agreed to? He didn't have to go to this extreme. He could have had his way at Cliveden. He had the opportunity, why didn't he take it?*

Looking around the room, she was surprised at her innermost thoughts, *If I accept the fact I can't change my situation, at least I'll be in a position to live a life for a few weeks I could have never imagined.* Pushing that thought from her mind, she focused on John, the real reason she came here. In a half hour, David came upstairs to Elizabeth's room. After knocking lightly on the door, he opened it. Seeing her sitting at the dressing table with a bottle of perfume in her hand, he quietly asked, "Can I come in?"

Startled by his voice, she looked up. Seeing his reflection in the mirror, she quickly turned when he stepped into the room. Not knowing his intention, she rose to her feet unsure of what was going to happen.

"You don't have to be afraid of me," he said. "Do you think you'll be comfortable here?" motioning with his hand around the room.

"Yes, Master David," she cautiously replied.

Smiling, he said, "I have business to take care of. I'll see you later at dinner. Did Thelma mention anything about what your duties would be?"

Slowly turning away embarrassed, she quietly replied, "Yes, Master David. Miss Thelma said I wasn't going to be the cook. You already have one."

"That's right! I really want you for myself," he passively admitted. "We'll talk about it later."

Drawing close to her, she nervously stared into his eyes, wondering what he was going to do. Putting his hands around her slender waist he pulled her close. She drew back apprehensive at his touch, but instead of continuing his advancement, he gave her a gentle embrace then left the room. She stood for a few moments wondering why she didn't seem to feel completely repulsed at his gesture, or as cold toward him. Was it because of what happened at Cliveden, when he entered her room, then saw how frightened she was and left? After he walked away, she followed him downstairs.

"Thelma, tell Arthur I want to go to the dock this evening to get ready for the ship arriving in the morning. Have the coach ready after dinner -at 6."

"Yes, Master David, I'll tell him," she replied.

Going into the study, he sat at his desk reading the correspondence he received while he was away.

Elizabeth wandered through the house going into each room down-stairs, getting familiar with her surroundings. Entering the kitchen, she saw Thelma and Sarah sitting at the table sipping tea. Sarah was a light skinned woman in her early 40's. Heavy set, she too wore a head scarf just as Miss Bertha. Sarah looked at Elizabeth studying her for a few moments, as if she was seeing an apparition of someone from the past. Eyeing her up and down, Sarah laughed.

"You thought you was gonna be the cook!" Sarah said.

"I was the cook at Cliveden. I been the cook there for the last few years," Elizabeth said, proud of her accomplishment.

Putting her tea cup down, Sarah replied, "Get use to bein' served for awhile honey. The woman in Master David's service, they only does light work, and very little of that. The hardest thing you be doin' is go to the market," pausing for a moment, "And as pretty as you are, you be in some new clothes and may not have to do anything at all."

Suddenly feeling uncomfortable in their company she left the kitchen. She was wandering through the hall when David opened the door of the study. Looking up from the letter he was reading, he looked at her.

"Are the clothes you're wearing the best you have?" he asked.

Looking down at her dress, she suddenly felt embarrassed at her appearance.

"Yes, Master David. I only have two dresses; this one is best of the two."

"Follow me," he said.

Going back into the study he rang for Thelma. Entering the room, she asked, "Did you want me, Master David?"

Looking up from reading his letter he gave her a nonchalant hand gesture. "Yes, make sure you have time to take Elizabeth to town to-morrow. Get her some new clothes. You know -dresses and things." Still reading the letter he was intent on finishing, he continued, "That's all I wanted."

Elizabeth suddenly felt embarrassed thinking again, *Why is he doing all this? With what he's offering, any woman would be more than happy to be in his service, Why me?*

When the dinner bell rang, Elizabeth felt awkward. Not knowing what to do, she started for the kitchen.

"Where are you going?" he asked.

"I was going back to the kitchen, Master David."

"No, go to the cabinet and get another plate. Sit at the table with me."

Surprised, she paused for a moment. Seeing the plates in the china cabinet, she got one and reluctantly put it down at the far end of the table.

"You don't have to sit so far away. Come down to this end of the table and sit beside me."

She thought, *At Cliveden, I may have been a favorite of Miss Sharon, but when it came to eating, I stood by while Master Tom and Miss Sharon ate dinner. After they finished, I went to the kitchen and ate with the rest of the servants.*

She wasn't used to this rapid change, and it made her uncomfortable. The thought came back to her, *"I wonder what kind of price he'll expect in return? He hasn't mentioned anything."*

Jarring her from her private assessment of the situation, she was startled when he said, "You'll have a place set here every night unless I have someone here for business."

When Thelma came to the dining room with the food, Elizabeth felt awkward being served and suddenly grew silent. After a few moments of trying to understand her silence, David said, "You're allowed to speak without being spoken to."

Looking up from her dinner plate, she said, "It's not that, Master David. I've never eaten at the table with the Master of the house before. I don't know what to do."

Smiling, he replied, "Well, you can start by telling me what you think about all the changes from being at Cliveden."

Beginning to describe what she'd seen so far was like opening a flood gate. She went on and on about what she saw, and after what seemed like a 5 minute nonstop description, she suddenly realized she might be talking too much. Apologizing, she said "I'm sorry, Master David, I've just seen so much today."

Enjoying her conversation, he looked at her, "Well, maybe you should eat a few bites of dinner before it gets cold."

Going completely silent again for about five minutes, David looked up at her, "I didn't want you to stop talking. Go on, I'm enjoying it."

Slowly moving a morsel of food around her plate with a fork, she looked at him. After staring at him for a few moments, she asked, "Master David, why are you doin' all this?"

Putting down his glass, he replied, "To be quite frank, I find you extremely attractive and wanted to make love to you from the first moment I saw you. I realized the day John came to the kitchen, it was him you were interested in, and I had to scheme a way to get you here. I thought once you were away from Cliveden and saw how different things were, you might be more agreeable to do what I want. After seeing your fear of me the night I came to your room, I decided I wouldn't force myself on you. That's not the way I want it."

When he stopped speaking, she looked at him and realized she was right as to why he left her room that night. He was legitimately concerned she was frightened.

After finishing dinner, she rose from the table, and began to gather the dishes.

"Don't do that! Thelma will take care of it," he said. Going to the sash, he pulled it twice then left the room.

At 6 o'clock, Arthur brought the coach around to the front of the house, and David left for the dock. After he was gone, Thelma came in to clear away the dishes. Elizabeth asked, "Thelma, I'd like to wash off the dust from the coach ride. Where can I get some soap and water, and maybe a towel to dry with?"

"Come on honey, I shows you where everything's at."

After showing her where she could get what she needed, Thelma said, "You can draw water from the pump in the kitchen. The last woman Master David had used to keep fresh water in a pitcher in his bedroom. That's one of the things Master David liked for her to do."

Going into the kitchen, Elizabeth began drawing water into a bucket. Thelma and Sarah looked at her then laughed.

"What on earth are you doin' child? Draw the water into a pitcher. You ain't at some farm, or back at Cliveden," Sarah said.

For a minute she felt embarrassed, realizing just how unsophisticated she was. Thelma, seeing it in her face, took pity on her saying, "Don't you be ashamed now. You learns everything soon enough."

After taking the pitcher to her room, she washed then sat at the dressing table. Looking in the mirror, she began brushing out her long black wavy hair. After exploring the rest of the bottles of perfume on the dresser, she carefully lifted the stoppers sniffing the scent of each one, trying to decide which one to use. Selecting the one she liked, she splashed it on herself not realizing you only needed a few drops. The scent was overpowering. Taking the wash cloth, she tried to get the heavy scent off, when she heard Thelma downstairs greeting David.

She heard him say, "Where's Elizabeth?"

"She's up in her room, Master David, been there for some time now."

Elizabeth could hear him coming up the stairs, and walk toward her room. She could see his shadow from under the door pause for a moment, but didn't knock. Still frantically trying to get the strong scent of perfume off -she heard him open the door to his room, then close it. It was too late to go back to the kitchen for more water to wash. If he came in now, she would just have to bear the embarrassment. Standing silently at the door, she strained to hear any sound of his movements. In about five minutes, she slowly opened it. Looking across the hall to his bedroom, she could see the light go out. Realizing he wasn't going to pay her a visit, she was relieved, but surprised at the same time. Quietly going back to the kitchen, she refilled the pitcher and went back to her room. After washing the remaining perfume off, she retired to bed.

Laying there looking around the room, reminded her of the first time she was in her small room at Cliveden. It was a big change from the quarter then, but this change was unbelievable. She thought, *Maybe he'll come tomorrow. If he does, how will I feel? Will I respond to him the way he expects?* She tried but couldn't get the idea out of her mind she no longer totally hated him after expressing his feelings, and couldn't say she would be absolutely repulsed by his touch. Still wondering about everything that had taken place that day, she fell asleep.

***

Sunshine was coming through the window when she opened her eyes. Hopping out of bed, she hurriedly dressed and headed for the kitchen.

"Good morning, Thelma. Is Master David up yet?" she asked.

"Yes. He's not only up -he's already gone for the day. He has two ships coming in -one today -and one tomorrow."

"Did he say what I'm supposed to do?"

"Yes, have your breakfast then go with me to get you some new clothes," Thelma said, as she was setting out silverware for Elizabeth.

After Elizabeth finished eating, Arthur pulled the carriage around and they headed for town. When they got there, Elizabeth was over-whelmed by all the shops with fine things in the windows. Pulling up in front of a dress shop, they went in. The woman's name who owned the establishment was Jennifer Cole, a very attractive woman in her mid 30's. Knowing David was a widower, she seemed to have an interest in him after his wife died. The last time she saw him was a few years ago when he came in with another woman. She also remembered Thelma from coming in before, and knowing she worked for him she said, "Hello Thelma, what can I do for you today?"

"This here is Elizabeth. Master David say he wants for her to have some new clothes. He wants for you to pick them out." Thelma replied.

Looking at Elizabeth, eyeing her size Jennifer said, "Step this way. You're a beautiful young lady," pausing for a moment she asked, "What's your favorite color?"

Elizabeth wasn't used to hearing compliments about her beauty by white folk, but getting past her embarrassment, she looked around the shop. Without speaking, she pointed to a light blue dress on a hanger. Jennifer took it off the rack and handed it to her saying, "Hold this in front of you. I'd like to see if it's your size."

Holding the dress in front of herself -she looked in the full length mirror. "I like this one," she said.

"It goes well with your long black hair too," Jennifer replied. "Now let's see," she said as she thumbed through the dress rack. Finding another Elizabeth's size, she took it off the hanger, "Here, hold this peach color one in front of you."

Looking at the color contrast of Elizabeth's black hair and olive skin, Jennifer said, "That's perfect! Thelma what do you think?"

After giving Elizabeth a glance, she replied, "I thinks it sure looks fine. I think Master David will be pleased."

"Did David say how many he wanted her to have?" Jennifer asked.

"No, but I thinks a few more would be good, she be needin' some night clothes too."

"I'll fix her up. Why don't you go into the backroom and have some tea while you're waiting," Jennifer suggested.

In about a half hour, she called Thelma to the front of the store and said, "I think this about does what David asked. Tell him I said hello."

"I surely will, Miss Jennifer." Looking at Elizabeth, Thelma smiled as they were leaving the shop and said, "I thinks you already goin' to like bein' in Master David's service. Come on now, we have to get you some shoes and a few other things."

Arthur carefully carried the boxed dresses to the carriage, and they continued shopping until she had a full wardrobe. Returning to the house, Elizabeth took her treasured possessions to the privacy of her room where she tried each one on. After taking stock in her appearance, she carefully hung each one in her closet. Running her hand over the six, she quietly exclaimed, "These are mine -really mine!"

Around 5:30, she could hear David come in.

"Thelma, where's Elizabeth?" he asked.

"Master David, she's been in her room all afternoon. I 'spect she be trying on all them new dresses. You wants for me to tell her to come down?"

"Not just yet. Let her know I'd like her to wear her favorite one to dinner tonight."

"I surely will, Master David. What time would you be wantin' dinner?"

"Around 7 will be fine. I'd like to go upstairs and freshen up."

Opening the door to his room, he saw the pitcher was full and a fresh towel lying neatly on the bed. He thought, *I wonder if Thelma did this.* Just then, Thelma came up the stairs to tell Elizabeth about dinner. Before she knocked on her door, David quietly asked pointing to the basin and towel, "Thelma did you do this?"

"No, Master David, I just mentioned to Elizabeth that's what you liked. I didn't see her, but she must have done it after we came back from shopping."

Smiling he said, "That's fine, that's just fine."

After freshening up, he went down to dinner. When he entered the room, Elizabeth was already there wearing her blue dress.

"Elizabeth, you look stunning. Stand up and let me look at you," he asked.

She felt embarrassed to be showcased, but did as he asked.

After a look of approval he said smiling, "Come, sit down and tell me all about your day."

Cautiously avoiding the idea she was excited about her new clothes she said, "I have six new dresses, this is my favorite color," pausing for a moment. "I want to thank you Master David for buying them for me."

Still not feeling comfortable being waited on she pushed her feelings aside and sat down.

After Thelma set the food on the table, she left the room. Again, after they were alone, they discussed the changes in Elizabeth's life.

After a few minutes of silence, he said, "Elizabeth, you knew I was at the dock today, but you didn't ask whether I spoke to John. Is there something wrong?"

Suddenly feeling embarrassed, she didn't know what to say. Although she still didn't trust David's intention, she realized her inner feelings for John were changing. She wasn't sure whether John meant the same as when they were back at Cliveden. Her new life was beginning to crowd out the idea of being happy jumping the broom and living in the quarter, doing the bidding of Master Tom and Miss Sharon.

"I don't know what to say, Master David. I felt different back at Cliveden. Here, everything's different, I'm confused."

"Well, I won't embarrass you again. I won't ask."

After dinner, David retired to his study to read, and Elizabeth went to her room. She prepared herself in case he wanted to visit, and around 10 o'clock, she could hear him coming down the hall. Nervously watching his shadow from under the door, she saw him pause briefly outside her room. Holding her breath, she felt a lump in her throat anticipating his entry. She watched the door knob closely expecting it to turn but when it didn't, she went to the door to listen. A few moments later, she saw his shadow from under the door disappear. Hearing his door open, then close again, she realized he wasn't going to knock, and once again felt relieved.

***

Each day they were in conversation at the table made her feel more at ease in his company. Each night, she anticipated his coming to her room, but he only paused briefly; then went to his own room. After the sixth night, she thought, *Why isn't he bothering? Should I have told him John wasn't what I wanted any longer? Maybe he's waiting for me to make the first move?* Surprised at her feelings, she thought, *Tomorrow night might be different.*

Just when she thought the night was over, she heard a quiet tapping on her door. Quickly sitting up, she saw David slowly opening it. In a whispered tone he asked, "Elizabeth, are you awake?"

"Yes, Master David, I am."

"Would you please join me in my room tonight?" he quietly asked.

Without hesitation she replied, "Yes," then suddenly thought, *"Did I really say that so quickly?"* Until he responded, she wasn't really sure.

"Please, come over in about 15 minutes," he said before closing the door.

Was she hearing things right? He said "Please!" Getting out of bed, she put on some of her favorite perfume and nightgown. Walking across the hall, she slowly opened the door. Entering the room, she saw him lying on the bed. The lamp was turned down low and he asked, "Would you please stand near the lamp and undress. I want to watch you."

She couldn't believe what she heard. He said *'please'* again. She was beginning to realize this wasn't a show, he really meant what he said about the way he treated her at Cliveden. Slowly doing as he asked, she still felt uncomfortable, but wanted to try pleasing him for the new life she was about to have. His eyes seemed to study her every move as she slowly walked across the room, then slipped under the blanket beside him. He caressed her and she temporarily froze as she did before, not really knowing what to expect. David was in his early 40's, a handsome man -over six feet tall, with thick brown wavy hair. Feeling her tenseness he said, "Relax, take your time getting use to me."

After a few moments he leaned up on his elbow. Studying her eyes, he leaned over giving her a passionate kiss. Unlike the first time he ran his hands over her naked body feeling the fullness of her well developed breasts, she didn't seem repulsed by his actions. He realized how much more she was responding to his touch. How long had he been waiting for just this moment?

Slowly, his powerful body descended upon her, and with much care, he passionately made love to her. Being her first time, she wanted to please him, and to her surprise, with every stroke it began to feel better.

Never having experienced another man, she reached several climaxes before he let out a groan, followed by a rush of warmth within her. For the first time in her life she felt like she reached maturity, and with a white-man she thought she hated, was something she could have never imagined. After laying there for a time talking, he began again. This time she was more passionate, anxious to feel the same sensations. After being satisfied a second time, he ran his hands over her naked body until they both fell asleep.

***

In the morning she awoke with him still asleep beside her. Slipping out of bed, she quickly picked up her robe and returned to her room. After washing her face, and combing her hair, she looked in the mirror. Seeing her reflection in the glass, she tried justifying hating David for what they did by being under his control. Realizing she was voluntarily responsive to him the second time, she couldn't make such a claim, she enjoyed it. She began to realize just how immature she was. A person who just the night before, was a young girl that didn't really know much about life. The short walk across the hall and the experience she had, seemed to transform her into a woman, and she was looking forward to their next encounter.

Still in her robe, she went back to David's room and got the pitcher to fill before he awoke. After filling it, she returned to his room and found him sitting on the edge of the bed. He quietly said, "You really pleased me last night. It's something I haven't enjoyed for a very long time."

Feeling good about his comment, she didn't respond immediately to it. Thinking she should say something, she only smiled replying, "Is there anything else I can do for you Master David?"

"No, thank you," he replied.

Returning to her room, she dressed then went downstairs.

"Miss Thelma, what am I supposed to do now?" she asked.

"If Master David wants for you to do anything, he'd tell you," she replied.

David was coming down the stairs, when he heard the conversation. By their inner action, Thelma realized Elizabeth must have pleased him, and after going into the dining room, Thelma brought his breakfast.

"Elizabeth, have you eaten?" David asked.

"No, Master David, but I'm not hungry."

"I'm going to the dock. I'll be gone most of the day. Thelma, I want you to show Elizabeth where the market is."

"Do you wants for us to wait till Arthur comes back?" she asked.

"No, you can go with us. I'm not in a hurry."

After getting in the coach, Arthur headed for the dock. After dropping David off, Arthur was turning the coach around, when Elizabeth caught a glimpse of John standing on the dock. To avoid him seeing her she slunk down in the seat. She suddenly couldn't believe her action. This was the man she was supposed to be in love with, the man she was willing to spend the rest of her life being married to.

John was coming in the direction of the coach to speak to Arthur, but after David got out, Arthur quickly turned the coach around and headed for town. He wanted to spare John the hurt feeling knowing Elizabeth was servicing David.

Chapter 6
The Hurricane

When they arrived at the dock, the ship was being unloaded, and David went aboard to speak with the captain. Captain Jarvis was a man in his late 50's with a full head of white hair, and a neatly-trimmed beard to match. A salty old mariner, you could tell by his appearance, he had plenty of sea miles under keels of ships he commanded over the years as his credentials.

"Captain, the ship's supposed to return to New Orleans to get another group of slaves to be auctioned," David said.

"I know, David," Jarvis remarked looking up at storm clouds building, "October isn't the most reliable month for good weather," Captain Jarvis said.

Seeing Master David standing on deck, John went aboard.

"Master David, we be runnin' out of dock space to store cargo. With tobacco comin' soon, they won't be enough room for it," he said.

"We'll have to find another storage building, John. I don't want the holding cells torn down just yet."

John had never witnessed a slave auction, and didn't know what to expect or how he would feel seeing one.

"Get your clothes John, and come aboard. I'm taking you with me to New Orleans."

Doing as David asked, he returned to the ship. John had never been on a sea voyage. It was a new experience, and something he wasn't sure of.

"Master David, did you gets to see Miss Elizabeth when you was at Cliveden?"

"Yes, John," tactfully avoiding telling him she was staying at his home, he didn't comment any further.

***

After several days at sea, they arrived in New Orleans. John was amazed the city was so much larger than Biloxi. After tying up to the dock, David left the ship to speak to his partner Charles, who was half owner in the shipping business.

"Hello David, what brings you to New Orleans, business, or pleasure?" Charles asked.

"Business, Charles. I wasn't satisfied with the group of slaves we had the last trip. They were mainly old men. We'll have to do a better job. If it wasn't for my brother being desperate for help, we wouldn't have had a buyer at all. I'll be here until tomorrow. Can I impose on you for lodging tonight?"

"Yes. My driver's at the end of the pier. I'm almost ready to leave. If you'll wait for about 15 minutes, I'll go with you. I'd like to get these slaves situated aboard first," he said.

John was on the dock looking at the 15 people being brought aboard, and remembered how it was at Cliveden when he was sent there. The sullen look on their faces as they boarded, was as if their only worry was where their journey would finally end. Would it be in another plantation that had a harsh overseer? Would they be there for the rest of their lives? Their future as bleak as it was, would be in the hands of their new owner, whoever that may be.

As they passed, John looked at each person, and amongst them was a face he thought he remembered. *That face looks familiar. Yes, I know him, that's Adam* he thought. *I remember when he was sold with Old Moses and George.*

Calling his name as he passed, Adam looked up, "Adam, it's me, John. Don't you be 'memberin' me? We be at Cliveden together."

"I 'member. You be a dock hand here?" Adam asked.

"No, I be a dock hand in Biloxi. I works for Master David. He be Master Tom's older brother. He owns half the dock here and the one in Biloxi. That be where we be headin'?"

"When we suppose' to leave?" Adam nervously asked.

"We be leavin' in the mornin'; I got's to go fetch ya'll some food, I be right back," John said, hurrying away.

After returning with the cornmeal, John asked, "How comes you got traded from Five Oaks?"

"Master Henry, he owed some money and he dun sold off three of us. I don't think Five Oaks be doin' too good. Master Henry's son Beau, he don't seem to take no intrest in the place. Sure takes the heart out of Master Henry; he's getting on in years. I don't 'spect they be at it too long. What be the news at Cliveden? Is Daniel still head-man?"

"No, he died last year. Solomon, he be the boss now. I had a real sweet eye for Daniel's daughter Miss Elizabeth. Oh, and Miss Bertha died two years ago too," John said.

"How's Daniel's boy, Luke? How he be doin'? Him and James, they be walkin' the top of the fence when we left out from the place. Those two be like two peas in a pod. They always be together," Adam said.

"Yeah, they saw George being caught by the slave catchers down in the swamp. How comes he got traded?" John asked.

"Don't you 'member, he dun always had a bad temper and be fightin'. Master Henry dun told him 'bout it once, but he ain't pay him no mind. One day he was fightin' over a girl, and accidently hit Master Beau trying to break it up, dat's when he got sold," Adam said.

John recalled, "Oh, I just remembered, one more thing dun happened. James got snake bit and died too. Sure was hard on his Mammy and Pappy. Luke sure took it hard too. Dat's bout all the changes I can thinks on, exceptin' Ezekiel's family got sold to South Port," continuing with a light laugh, "And guess what? Before he left out, he told Daniel he knowed he was the one 'dat got him sold. He say he was gonna' pay him back one day. Can you imagine on 'dat happenin'?" Knowing the threat couldn't possibly be real, they both laughed.

Adam replied, after taking a spoon full of cornmeal, "Well, him or his family was no account anyway," pausing for a moment he looked hopefully at John, "You thinks Master Tom can use me back at the place?" he asked.

"I don't rightly know. He was sure sorry he let you and George go though. He ain't really know how many people he be needin'; he ain't know tobacco was 'dat much work. When we started the tobacco field, I dun heard him speak on it to Daniel."

"They be raisin' tobacco now?" Adam asked.

"Yeah, Master Tom had to get a few more people from Master David, that's why I be here. Master David traded me to pay for them."

Adam, not knowing what his future was going to be, asked again, "You thinks Master Tom could use me back there?"

"I don't rightly know. I got's to leave now," pausing for a moment collecting the now empty food bowls, "We talks on it some more later," John said.

Adam felt a little better after talking to John. Seeing a familiar face somehow made him feel he was no longer alone. After securing them onboard, for some reason John suddenly felt uncomfortable being in their company. Not wanting to be near the group, he found a place to sleep in a small shed on the dock.

Lying there he wondered, *Why did he suddenly feel uneasy being with someone he knew. Was it because he was confused? Or just saddened to see someone he knew in that position? Did he realize he was fortunate it wasn't his fate? Should he be grateful to Master David for the better life he now leads? On the other hand, should he be angry with the thought, if something goes wrong, he could be just as easily cast out like Adam?* Those were questions for now that would go unanswered.

Awaken by dock hands putting more cargo aboard, he came out of the shed and pitched in to help. After the cargo was loaded, he went to the ships galley and brought the food to the hold for Adam and the others.

"John, we fixin' to go now?" Adam asked.

"Pretty soon now, I heard the capt'n say after Master David comes aboard."

"I ain't never been out on no ocean; I'm kinda scared," Adam said.

"I wasn't neither. Comin' here was my first time. You be alright though."

After David came aboard the ship departed.

The few hours it took for the 70 -mile downriver trip between the city and the Gulf had a notable change in the sky. The cloud cover seemed to be condensing, and the stillness of the hot humid air seemed to give a concerned look to the captain's face. As they left the river entering the Gulf, the stillness began to give way to increasing winds stirring ever heightening waves. As the clouds thickened, the ocean appeared to be a pea green in color. The farther out to sea, the rougher and more violent the wind and waves became. Under normal sailing conditions the ship wouldn't venture very far from shore, but with the hurricane, Captain Jarvis decided it would be safer further out to sea.

Just before dark, the crew battened down the hatches locking every-one not necessary to the ship's function in the hold. They only had a few lanterns to see by below deck, and with the motion of the ship and stuffy conditions, seasickness began to take affect almost immediately. Some of the men began to heave as the storm grew stronger, and the stench of vomit didn't help. Before long everyone was sick. David was in a cabin next to the captain's above deck, and was feeling it as well.

Close to midnight, the storm became so violent the captain ordered the crew to shorten sail, surrendering his ship to the elements. With the wind shrieking through the rigging, the ship was tossed around like a corked bottle, literally at the mercy of the sea. During the night, the main yardarm broke, and half of it came crashing down penetrating the deck, injuring two sailors and killing one. After assessing the damage, Captain Jarvis called down to the slaves in the hold, "A few of you darkies come up here and help."

John, and Adam, along with two others, hesitatingly came out of the safety of the hold. With fear in their eyes, they looked around then helped take the two sailors who were injured to the crew's quarters. Going back on deck, they saw the broken yardarm that caused their injuries. It had broken through to the hold, like a hot knife through butter and sea water was gushing into the cargo-hold every time a wave washed over the deck. The ropes still attached to the yardarm, trailed in the ships wake on the starboard side, and Captain Jarvis, recognizing the danger of the ropes possibly wrapping around the rudder, gave the order to the first mate.

"Take axes and cut the ropes. -Hurry!"

The chief boatswain turned to John, Adam and the other two. He shouted in a commanding voice trying to be heard over a howling wind, "Here! Take these axes and start cutting them ropes."

John and the others looked in fear as the waves pummeled the ship, washing over the deck. With the flashes of lightning, they could see at times the waves were higher than the ship's sides. After the ropes were cut, the boatswain yelled, "Here, help pull up this broken piece of yardarm so we can plug this hole with canvas. Try not to get washed overboard. If you do, you're a lost soul. We can't save you."

Adam was helping John and the others pull up the yardarm, when a wave suddenly rolled over the side. The boatswain yelled, "Hold on tight! Here comes a big one." The wave hit John catching him off guard, and knocked him off his feet. It began to wash him toward the ship's rail when Adam quickly grabbed him by the arm just in time to pull him back to safety.

Wide-eyed Adam said, "Here John, tie this rope round yo' middle so's you don't get washed over."

"I thanks you, Adam. I'm sho' glad you be here. I sho' enough would'a been a lost soul."

After removing the yardarm, they helped some of the crew cover the hole with canvas. After finishing, they returned to the hold with the rest of the slaves who were too frightened to go above deck. When John and Adam were helping, they lost their sea sickness probably out of fear. Returning to the hold, the stench of vomit filled their nostrils once again bringing them back to reality, and before long, they were just as sick as they were before going up.

When David heard the crash of the yardarm hitting the deck, he came out of his cabin and stood in the passageway watching. Seeing what John, Adam and the other two men were doing to save the ship, he knew the only right thing to do was to take them off the auction block as a reward. Knowing other dock owners, he could probably find someone that might have need of them. If not, he decided he would keep them himself, or find a place for them on his dock in New Orleans, or Biloxi.

The morning brought with it clear weather and calmer seas, and the cargo hold was opened once more to fresh air and sunshine. With the storm and broken yardarm, it took an extra two days to get back to Biloxi.

Captain Jarvis said during a dinner prior to their arrival, "David, you know if it wasn't for the four men that helped during the storm, we just might have lost the ship. If I were you, I'd give some serious consideration to them before they get to the auction block. One of my men is dead, and two others will be laid up for a considerable amount of time. I'll need the help, and the ship can't wait on the injured to get well. I was impressed how they risked their own lives to save the ship from possible disaster, even knowing their fate."

"I saw what they did, and I wouldn't mind them going to sea with you, but John is one of my best dock hands. I can't afford to lose him," David replied.

Arriving in Biloxi that evening, the ship was tied up for the night. Surveying the devastation of the port, it was obvious the storm must have been severe. David's dock was damaged, but not as bad as he anticipated.

The storm had damaged some of the freight on the dock, and the roof of one of the storage sheds had partially blown off, but the damage was minimal. Compared to some of the other docks, his wouldn't take long to repair.

Taking the men from the hold, they were being escorted to their holding cells, when John pulled Adam and the two men who helped during the storm from the line.

"Adam, for helpin' during the storm, you and the other two are gonna be part of the ship's crew. Get back on board," John said.

"John, I'll be back in the morning in time for the auction," David said as he left the ship.

When he arrived home, everyone was happy, especially Elizabeth. They hadn't seen him for almost a week, and didn't know what happened.

Arthur said, "Master David, I went back to the dock that evening. They told me you boarded a ship with John and went to New Orleans. When the storm hit, we didn't know if you was at sea or just stayin' in New Orleans till the storm passed."

When Elizabeth heard Arthur mention John's name, it brought her back to the day he left Cliveden, and her handing him the loaves of cornbread. She thought about what she had seen and done since then, and felt guilty desiring the person who separated them. It was true, she had a new life, but with the thought of the woman that was here before her, she wondered how long it would be before David tired of her too. For now, he was back and safe, and that's all that mattered. After David went into the dining room, Elizabeth brought him some tea from the kitchen.

"Elizabeth, get another cup from the cabinet and sit with me," he asked.

After pouring her a cup, he said, "I missed you, and thought about you during the trip. You look beautiful in your new clothes."

"Thank you for getting them Master David. I hope you like what I picked?"

"Stand up! Let me see," he asked.

Getting up from the table, she turned in a full circle for him to approve. Wearing her peach colored dress, her long black hair swayed slowly behind her, and the contrast was perfect.

David, yearning to feel the closeness of her again, asked, "I'd like you to come to my room tonight."

Without hesitation she replied, "I'd like that."

"I'll knock when I'm ready, about 10 o'clock," he said.

After getting caught up with some of his correspondence and ledgers, he looked up not realizing the time had slipped by so quickly. It was already 9:30. Closing the ledger, he climbed the stairs to get ready for bed.

Elizabeth wanting to experience more of what she felt the first night, laid on her bed in her night robe, anxiously waiting for him to tap on the door. After hearing it, she crossed the hall to his room. Turning the knob, she slowly pushed open the door. The lamp had already been dimmed, and she disrobed slower than she did the first night. Leaning up on his elbow, he said, "Elizabeth, turn slowly so I can appreciate your beauty."

Doing what he asked, she turned slowly then walked across the room, and slipped in bed beside him. She no longer felt shy, and found herself making the first move. The experience was better than the first time and not long after they climaxed they began again. After it was over, being completely satisfied, he fell asleep.

Quietly picking up her robe, she returned to her room and climbed into bed. Unlike the warmth she felt across the hall, it felt cold and empty. Feeling the comfort, the warmth, and security of a man next to her was truly satisfying, and she tried to imagine what it would be like on a full-time basis.

The next morning she slept late, and when she awoke, she hurriedly got dressed and went downstairs. David was already having breakfast when she entered the room.

"I'm going back to Cliveden in two days to bring Anne home. Do you want to go along?" he asked.

The words pierced her ears, and she thought the fantasy world she was allowed to put her feet in for awhile, was in peril of being taken away. This was where she wanted to be, and she replied, "I would like to see my mother and brother, but I'm afraid Miss Sharon would want me to stay."

Realizing he won her over, he smiled. Getting up from the table he said, "Think about it." then left for the dock.

When he got there, a group of about 10 people had already looked over the slaves to be auctioned. There were the usual two men that would bid for the interest of Dumont, and spoke to David about the ones they wanted before the auction began. John had never seen an auction, and stood silent, waiting to see what it was like. The first few brought out were people he spoke to during the storm at sea. He knew if they were going to Dumont, from what he heard, their lives would be a living hell. Being in their company for only a few short days, had a profound effect on him. Somehow, it felt personal they were about to be sold. Was it because he helped bring them from New Orleans? It was another question in his mind that would go unanswered.

David looked carefully over the group then spoke to one of the men from Dumont. After he handed David an envelope, the first few were taken away, and John's heart sunk from what he was witnessing. He thought again about how fortunate he was, chosen to work for Master David, and how Adam too, was fortunate putting his fear behind him during the storm. The rest of the auction went well, and David became richer by several thousand dollars.

Before leaving, David spoke to John and Jeremiah, "Watch out for the dock while I'm gone. I have to go back to Cliveden and pick up Miss Anne. I'll be back in about a week."

John quickly asked, "Master David, could you look in on Miss Elizabeth while you be there? Tell her I misses her, and some of that fine cookin'?"

"I'll be sure to tell her, John," David said before leaving for home.

Elizabeth, not knowing what was going to happen at Cliveden, visited David's room both nights before leaving.

The morning they were to leave, Elizabeth packed the same dresses she brought with her in the travel bag Miss Sharon gave her when she left.

"Why don't you wear one of your new dresses?" David asked.

Looking down at the floor she replied, "I wouldn't feel right dressed like that around the people I grew up with. Wearing this dress, they would know I was someone you took to satisfy your needs instead of being the cook. I don't want my momma seeing me dressed like this."

Putting his hands on her shoulders he looked into her eyes, "I understand, but they wouldn't expect you to be wearing the same old clothes in the city. If you change your mind about wearing one, you could always change in the coach just before we get there. I don't think it's inappropriate. If it bothers you, I'll hide the dress in my bag."

At 9 o'clock, Arthur pulled the coach up in front of the house and they left. During the trip, David held her close and kissed her several times. Although he didn't say one way or the other about her staying at Cliveden, she desperately wanted him to reassure her he wanted her to return.

***

The two days it took to get there were the longest days of her life. She thought, *Would I be able to leave again with David and Anne? How would I tell my mother I want to go back with them?* The questions seemed to haunt her mind constantly. David not bringing the subject up during most of the trip, only heightened her fears. Would she be able to return to Biloxi?

The second day of the trip, when they were still several miles from Cliveden, David looked at her and said, "Elizabeth," then hesitated for a few moments looking out the window of the coach. She feared by him not facing her, his words would end her fantasy, and she waited impatiently for him to finish what he began to say. Turning to look at her he continued, "I'd like very much if you could return to Biloxi, but that's in Miss Sharon's hands. All I can do is wait and see."

His words were a relief. It was what she wanted to hear, but realized he was right. Her fate was still in Miss Sharon's hands. She thought, *I'll have to find a way. There's got to be a way.*

As the coach pulled up to the front steps of Cliveden, Miss Sharon was sitting on the veranda and leapt to her feet, excitedly saying aloud, "Anne, Flora, come outside. Come quick! Elizabeth's back. Elizabeth's back."

Flora hurried out of the house, embracing Elizabeth as soon as she stepped from the coach. Elizabeth threw her arms around her mother, but although it was Flora, the feeling somehow wasn't the same. The whole trip, she was trying to figure a way she could swap being the cook at Cliveden with her, but for the moment she put it out of her mind. Everyone seemed to be speaking all at once, excited at their unexpected arrival.

"Where's Tom?" David asked.

"He's at the cotton barn; the crops are very good this year," she replied.

"I'll see you later," he said, heading in the direction of the cotton barn.

When he got there, Tom was surprised. "Hello David, did you come to collect Anne? She's been anxious for your arrival," then turned his attention to Solomon saying, "Solomon. Take charge of bailing the cotton, me and David are going back to the house."

"Yes sir, Master Tom," Solomon replied.

Walking back, Tom said, "David, I'll have the rest of the money to pay you when they take the cotton to market day after tomorrow."

"I'm not in any rush to leave. I'll wait until you have it," David replied.

"How did Elizabeth work out for you?" Tom asked.

"She worked out well. It's a shame she has to come back," he paused, "I don't think she really wants to."

Tom gave him a strange look, but didn't answer.

Getting back to the house, Flora stepped out on the front porch to tell them dinner was almost ready. After they washed and dressed, they seated themselves at the table.

"How did you weather the hurricane in Biloxi? I hear it was pretty bad," Tom asked.

"I wasn't in Biloxi, Tom. I was at sea returning from New Orleans when it happened. The ship spent three extra days at sea because of a broken yardarm."

After describing how violent the storm was he said, "Remember Adam, he was sold with Moses and George."

"Yes, I remember them. I was sorry I ever let them go. They were good workers," Tom said.

"Well, Adam was one of the slaves we picked up in New Orleans. It was John, Adam, and two others that helped during the storm. The ship was getting beat up pretty bad, and without their help, we might have lost it."

"I knew Five Oaks sold some people to pay debts, but I didn't know Adam was one of them. If I had, I would have bought him back. He didn't go to auction did he?" Tom asked.

"No, I gave Adam and the two who helped during the storm to the captain of the vessel as deck hands. During the storm, one of his crew was killed, and two others were badly injured. Adam and the two others were the replacements."

Tom, present when David was given money by the people from Dumont said, "I'm glad Adam didn't have to go back and cast his lot with the others. He might have wound up at Dumont."

David looked at him as though he didn't approve of his insinuation, and Tom sensing David knew what he was referring to, decided to change the subject. He asked, "How much damage did your dock have?"

"Biloxi didn't have much. Oh, I lost the roof on a storage shed, but that was minor compared to some of the damage to the other docks. I don't know what happened in New Orleans."

Elizabeth and Flora were in the kitchen listening about the storm, and didn't know John was so instrumental during it.

"Did you see John while you was in Biloxi?" Flora asked.

"No, I didn't mother." Quickly changing the subject, "How would you like being the cook here instead of doing laundry and keeping up the herb garden?" Elizabeth asked.

"I like it fine, but I don't wants to be takin' your job," Flora replied.

Just then, Luke came into the kitchen. He had been working in the cotton barn bailing. After the cotton was bailed, he ran to the house to let Master Tom know. Seeing Elizabeth he excitedly asked, "Did you see John when you was in Biloxi?"

Hugging her little brother she replied, "No, I was very busy and didn't get to see him."

Luke asked, "If you be goin' back to the quarter, where you gonna stay? I lives with Jobe's family, and they ain't no empty cabins left."

"I don't know. For now, I'm just glad to see you," she replied.

"Luke, fetch a bed that ain't bein' used from one of the cabins. Set it up in the room I sleeps in. I wants to visit with Elizabeth for awhile. Go on now, you get's to see her when you get back," Flora instructed.

Luke ran down the hill to the quarter doing what his mother asked, while Elizabeth helped Flora clear the dishes from the table, wash them, and put them away. While they were in the kitchen, Miss Sharon came in, "Are you ready to come back to the kitchen Elizabeth?" she asked.

After a few minutes of silence Elizabeth said, "What would my momma do? She's a better cook than me."

Looking at Flora for a moment, Sharon replied, "Don't worry, I'll make some other arrangements for her."

After everyone went to bed, Elizabeth and her mother went into their room. The beds that Elizabeth and her mother would sleep on, reminded her of how much she didn't want to be back. After Flora drifted off to sleep, Elizabeth stared at the ceiling, remembering the first night

David came to her room. She hated him at the time, when he threatened her with the possibility of being taken against her will using John to accomplish it. She would have never believed she would feel the way she does about him now. She felt good in his company, and although she did things that were embarrassing at times like splashing too much perfume on herself, he never embarrassed her by laughing. She no longer wanted the life she left here, and was determined somehow to go back with him.

In the morning she awoke to a familiar sound, her mother opening and closing cabinet doors. After washing her face, she hurriedly dressed and began helping with breakfast. Going outside to the cook house, she remembered how uncomfortable it was working there, especially on hot days. She didn't want her mother to go back to the hard work of being the laundress because of her age, but was that really the reason? All of a sudden she felt selfish and cheap. She remembered when her father died from working so hard and wondered, *how would I feel if mother passed having to do the heavy work laundering? Was that the reason? Or was it an excuse to justify in her mind what she was trying to do, go back with David?*

After they finished cooking and served breakfast to everyone in the dining room, Elizabeth heard Anne say, "Sharon, I'm happy you're going to have a baby."

David looked up from his plate and said, "Tom, I didn't know. Congratulations!"

"Thanks, David. We just found out last week."

Sharon quickly added, "I'm due in about 7 months, but I'm worried about who's going to help with the birthing if the local doctor isn't available. Being here in the country isn't like being at my parent's home in Charleston. There are plenty of doctors there, one need not worry."

Elizabeth returning to the kitchen asked her mother, "Did you know Miss Sharon was pregnant?"

"Yes, and Miss Sharon, she be worried about who be here to help when it's time," Flora answered.

Elizabeth thought for a moment, "Is Miss Mary at the quarter still birthin' babies?" she asked.

"She's gettin' old, and hasn't been doin' it for a few years now. Miss Mary's feelin' poorly. She can't hardly get round anymore," Flora replied.

"I remember you helping Miss Mary birthin' a few. Would you be the one that delivers if Miss Mary can't?" Elizabeth asked.

"I 'spect I could, if they ain't no doctor, or if Miss Mary ain't able."

During the day, she saw David and quietly told him, "There might be a way I can go back with you. My mother might have to do the birthing when Miss Sharon's baby comes. She should be close by when it's time."

"You should ask. Make sure your mother will do it," David replied.

Returning to the kitchen Elizabeth said, "Momma, why don't you tell Miss Sharon about helping Miss Mary birthin' babies? I'd like to go back to Biloxi and see if I could marry up with John."

Flora, knowing he was someone she always cared for, was reluctant, but didn't want to stand in her way.

"I'll tell Miss Sharon that I dun helped Miss Mary do it. I don't know whether she trusts me all that much, seem she's dead set on a doctor, but I'll try."

Just then, Sharon entered the kitchen, "Ask me about what? I heard someone say, 'I'll ask Miss Sharon...'"

Elizabeth quickly replied, "Miss Sharon, did you know my mother use to help Miss Mary with the birthin' at Cliveden?"

"No, I didn't. Flora, do you think you could do it alone if there's no doctor?"

"I could, I knows somebody else in the quarter that can help. Miss Mary's old, but she can watch and sees that we does it the right way," continuing, "Miss Sharon, Elizabeth was thinking on going back to Biloxi so she could marry up with John. They was always plannin' to jump the broom when he was here."

Sharon remembered John, but didn't know Elizabeth cared for him and wanted to be where he is. Reluctantly, not wanting to stand in Elizabeth's way, she gave her permission.

Happy with the decision, Elizabeth was anxious to tell David. Later in the day, she found him alone outside and told him the good news. His response wasn't as excited as she thought, but he seemed pleased, and she couldn't wait until tomorrow.

When Luke came in from the field every day, he would go straight to the kitchen to ask his mother if she needed more wood cut. Although he was only 17, he took over when John left and was strong enough to handle an axe with ease. Flora generally had a cookie or some other snack to give him, and it gave her a chance to see the only family she had left at Cliveden.

Flora said, "Luke, your sister wants to go back to Biloxi and ask Master David if she could marry up with John."

Arthur, sitting in the kitchen when she said it, quickly turned in Flora's direction knowing it was a lie.

Luke said, "I 'member when James died, I came to the kitchen to tell Elizabeth, and John was here. She be so nervous all the time when he be 'round. I'll miss her, but bein' in Master David's house, and Master Tom bein' his brother, won't be like bein' separated at all. We sees each other once in awhile, and if'n we don't, we be able to know how she be doin'."

Flora, surprised at the maturity of his statement, looked at him and gave him a hug. He was every bit the adult in thought his father was. Flora recalled the day Daniel told her when Elizabeth moved up to the big house, 'Elizabeth might not be in the same house, but she be still on the same plantation. Just be thankful fo 'dat,' those word's still echoing in Flora's memory.

Elizabeth walked across the room and hugged Luke tightly, "You're growin' up fast as a weed," feeling his arm she continued, "Building muscle like a grown man, too."

"You gonna marry up with John when you get back?" he asked.

"I guess, sometime after I get back."

Again, Arthur looked at her knowing it wasn't true.

She felt bad lying to her mother and brother, but even with the bad feeling it gave her, she was still anxious to leave.

The following morning Arthur brought the coach around, and after saying goodbye to Sharon and Tom they left. As they were driving away, Elizabeth looked back and saw her mother wiping the tears from her eyes with the corner of her apron. Flora hated to see her go, but realized that was the cycle of life. As Daniel used to say, 'New flowers have to replace the old, dat's god's way of things.'

Chapter 7
The Orphanage

The two day travel to Biloxi was quiet. Anne didn't have much to say to Elizabeth. She knew Elizabeth's purpose in Biloxi, and thought she may only be in the way of David's lifestyle. Anne became very close with Violet, the first woman David was with for five years after his wife passed away. She knew if Elizabeth's attachment grew stronger, her future would probably end up the same.

Arriving home, Thelma and Markus came out to the coach to help bring their baggage inside. Thelma remarked, "Miss Anne, being at Cliveden must have done you a whole lot a good. Your face ain't as pale, and your cheeks have a rosy color."

Hugging Thelma she replied, "Thelma, I just don't know how I got along without you this month."

Picking up Miss Anne's bag, Thelma said, "Master David, while you was gone you got a few letters, I puts them on your desk in the study. One came by special messenger."

Being concerned, David hurried to the study and closed the door. Opening the letter he discovered it was from the orphanage where he placed Violet's baby. The note read that the administrator wanted to speak to him as soon as he returned. Immediately rising from his chair he rang for Thelma. Opening the door he said, "Thelma, let Arthur know I'll be going out again right away."

"Yes Sir, Master David, anything wrong?"

He didn't answer. Whatever was in the letter had his mind transfixed on what he read. Just then, Elizabeth knocked before stepping in the room. Before the door was fully open Elizabeth said, "Master David is there anything..."

She didn't get to finish the statement. He motioned with his hand for her to leave replying sharply, "No, I'll be out in a minute."

Hurrying to the front door he stopped abruptly saying, "Thelma, I won't be here for dinner this evening," then quickly left.

For the first time in their relationship he was short with Elizabeth, whatever was in the letter disturbed him. Elizabeth stood at the door watching for a few moments as he got in the carriage. With hurt feelings not knowing what to do, she watched from the window as the carriage pulled away. She was looking forward to being with him after two weeks at Cliveden, and thought he would be anxious too. *Did I do something to bring on that kind of attitude?* She thought, *Maybe it was something about the dock? Yes, that's what it has to be.* Justifying his mood she went to the kitchen to join Thelma and Sarah.

"Thelma, do you know why Master David's angry?" she asked.

"No child, but whatever it is, it sure be botherin' him."

They looked at one another trying to find a reason for his sudden change in attitude. Failing to understand, they laid it aside until his return. A half hour later Elizabeth said goodnight, retiring to her room.

Arriving at the orphanage David went directly to the administrator's office. Being a large contributor to the institution, he was given special privilege. The administrator came into the room sadly informing him, "David, Violet was allowed to come by the orphanage every few days to see her baby as you requested," pausing for a moment, "On her visit a week ago she found out her baby died."

"Died! Died from what?" David shockingly asked.

The administrator replied, "The doctor didn't know. But after she left, instead of going home, she went to the dock. We think she may have been looking for you. When she discovered you weren't there, she either threw herself off the dock, or fell off. Either way, she drowned."

With the words piercing his ears, David's face quickly grew sullen. It was as though his heart was just ripped from his chest. He was to blame, and he realized it. As a veil of guilt descended on him, his eyes began to well up with tears. Turning his face away from the administrator he slapped down at the arms of the chair thinking, *If I only let her raise her baby. I'm rich enough. I could have bought her a small house to live in and raise the child. If I had, she probably wouldn't have killed herself.* He spent five years with her and she meant more to him than just someone for his pleasure. After thanking the administrator for telling him, he left. On the way home, he thought about Violet and all the things they laughed about together. In any other circumstance he could have been happily married to her, but here, in this time and place, it was impossible. Socially unacceptable, he couldn't afford to do it, and hoped Elizabeth wouldn't make the same mistake as Violet -fall in love.

When he got home Thelma greeted him at the door.

"Where's Anne?" he asked.

"Miss Anne already went to bed."

"You can go to bed too Thelma, I won't need anything," he said then slowly went into the study and closed the door. After pouring himself a drink, he sat at his desk sipping it remembering how Violet filled his world with something that had been missing since his wife died. David married when he was 30, and his wife passed away in child birth two years later. He spent a long time getting over it, and it was Violet the maid who worked here, that turned his life around.

As he sat sipping his drink, he looked at the door remembering how a few years after his wife died, Violet came into the study. Like a mirage, he actually visualized how she came in the door that evening convincing him to go upstairs with her. It was what he needed at the time, and neither he, nor Violet, had any idea it would lead to an affair that lasted five years.

The thought of her being dead was the same experience he went through with the loss of his wife. He felt guiltier than ever he forced her to place the baby in the orphanage then sent her away.

Distain for what he caused, he thought, *some loyalty. The person who got me out of a depressing time, I turned around and put that same burden on her shoulders.*

He knew she loved him, but didn't realize how deeply until now. Looking up at the ceiling, he thought about Elizabeth upstairs. *If it wasn't for the color difference in their eyes, she was the image of Violet.* By bringing her here, was he subconsciously trying to recapture the years he had with Violet?

With Anne back home, it would be a little different for him, but the urge of wanting Elizabeth was strong. After finishing his drink, he went upstairs.

Elizabeth could hear him in the hall, but he didn't tap on her door as she expected. Instead, he went to his own room and closed the door. She wondered what had happened to upset him, but whatever it was would have to wait until morning for an answer.

She was up earlier than David or Anne and went directly to the kitchen. Thelma was there with Sarah sipping tea, talking about Master

David when she came in. After pouring a cup of tea for herself, Elizabeth she sat down with them.

"Thelma, why do you think Master David was so upset?" she asked.

"A woman that worked here died while Master David was away. Miss Anne went to the study after Master David left and read us the letter bout Violet and the baby. They was very close. Miss Anne felt so bad; she ran up to her room crying."

"Who was it?" Elizabeth asked.

"Her name was Violet. If it wasn't fo your age difference child, she could have been your twin sister. She looked just like you."

Sarah, looking over her cup of tea added, "Fo' fact. If I didn't knows better, I would have thought you were her when you first come in this kitchen. Seein' you, sent a chill right up my spine."

"What happened to her?" Elizabeth asked.

"You best ask Master David that question. But I wouldn't do that for awhile. I knows he's feeling bad, mighty bad."

"Has Master David ever been married?" Elizabeth asked.

Thelma replied, "That painting in the study; that be Master David's wife Miss Estella. She died two years after they got married," pausing to sip the hot tea she continued, "When the baby come."

Elizabeth, hearing David come downstairs, quickly poured him a cup of tea and brought it to him. Looking up as she entered the room he said, "Thank you Elizabeth. I..." he began to say something but stopped, thanking her again. He seemed to be in a calmer mood than when he walked out last night, and she found the courage to ask, "Master David, did I do something to upset you?"

"No. I'm sorry for being angry. It was just the shock of the letter I received. A very close friend died, and I felt guilty for not being here," he said. Looking up at her, his next statement sent shock waves to her ears, "Do you want to go to the dock with me today and see John?"

Against her true feelings she replied, "Yes," *wondering why he had a sudden change of heart towards her. It seemed as though the desire for her was no longer there.*

After Anne came down, they went to the dining room to have breakfast.

"Elizabeth, get a plate and sit down with us," pausing for a moment

David continued, "Anne, I'm taking Elizabeth to the dock today to see John."

Surprised but happy, Anne realized it was a decision he made because of what happened with Violet. Around 9 o'clock, Arthur pulled the coach around to the front of the house. After helping Elizabeth in, they left. Most of the way, Elizabeth gazed out the carriage window, avoiding eye contact with him. After a few minutes, she couldn't hold back what she wanted to express, "Do you still want me to come to your room?" she asked.

Not answering, she could tell his mind was still elsewhere. Thelma was right -she should have waited to ask. She didn't wear anything fancy for meeting John, and wasn't sure how she would react seeing him. In about 20 minutes they arrived at the dock. Before David got out of the coach, John was already heading in his direction.

"John, I have a surprise for you," David said, motioning for Elizabeth to step out. Could it be? Could it possibly be? The person he thought he may never see again was standing before him. Forgetting himself for a moment, he rushed to her giving her a hug. She responded with a hug in kind, but there was nothing there. She realized her feelings had definitely changed.

"Master David," John said, "Two ships come in and we loaded them full up with tobacco and cotton, and sent them out again. Me, Jeremiah and the other dock hands, we was able to handle them fine."

Purposely wanting to give them time together, David said, "John, talk with Elizabeth for awhile. I want to speak to Jeremiah."

"Yes, Master David, I surely will like that!"

In her presence John fumbled for words then became silent. She asked a question she already had an answer to, "How do you like working for Master David? He seems like a fair man," she said.

"He treats me and the other dock hands real good. What do you thinks of this place away from Cliveden?" looking around he motioned with his hand, "Did you ever? Could you ever knowed life was so different?"

Trying to act as if it was all new to her she replied, "Yes, it sure is different."

John related, "Late one evenin' 'bout a week ago, they was a girl 'dat looked like you. Fo' fact, in the dim light for a minute I thought it was you. She come to the dock askin' if Master David was here. Jeremiah dun told her, 'Master David went to Cliveden to get Miss Anne,' then she walked away, sad like. In the mornin' we found her floatin' next to the dock. She probably lost her footin' in the dark and fell off." Changing the subject he asked, "Did you come to work for Master David to be near me?"

"I'm working for Master David because he needs a cook. My Momma took over as cook at Cliveden."

Hesitating for a few moments he said, "Ask Master David if he be willing to let you come to the dock to see me sometime."

David returned to the coach, and John thanked him for letting Elizabeth come for the visit.

"Master David, would it... would it be alright if Miss Elizabeth could come back again sometime?"

"It would be fine John. I'll have Arthur bring her. You best get back to the dock now, they're getting ready for another ship coming in this afternoon."

"Yes Sir, Master David, and thank you again," John said, retreating back to the dock with a renewed spirit. Turning several times, he waved as the carriage pulled away.

On the way home Elizabeth said, "John told me about a girl that drowned here last week. He said she looked like me. Did you know her?"

Looking out the window and not at her he replied in a low voice, "Yes, Jeremiah told me. It was someone that had been a maid in my home. She became pregnant, and I had her place the baby in an orphanage, then sent her to a friend's house to maid for them."

After a few moments of silence she asked, "Do you want me to stay in my room across the hall?"

Turning to study her for a few moments he replied, "You don't realize what the consequences may be," but still desiring her he said, "Yes."

When they got home, Miss Anne was sitting on the front porch with her intended Steven Watson. They were to be married in the spring. His father owned a dock close to David's and although they weren't close friends, they had a few business encounters together. When Elizabeth and David stepped down from the coach, Elizabeth mentioned in a very unenthusiastic voice, "Miss Anne, I had a chance to see John."

"Oh! That's fine. How's he doing? I'll bet he was surprised," Anne said.

Without stopping, Elizabeth continued into the house answering, "Yes, he was."

Anne followed realizing she was distressed, but by the time she got in the door, Elizabeth had already run upstairs to her room. Closing the door, she paced the floor wringing her hands, hoping David wouldn't force her back into John's company. Not sure whether he would have a change of heart about his decision, she sat down at her bench-seat and began to cry.

***

Two weeks passed and David kept his distance. One evening after everyone had gone to bed, Elizabeth got up enough courage to go down to the study. After knocking lightly at the door, she stepped in just as David was closing his ledger. When he looked up, to his surprise, Elizabeth was standing there in the night gown he seemed to like best. She slowly crossed the room, not really knowing how he would react, but when he smiled she was happy. Staring at her, it brought him back more than eight years when Violet did the same. She brought him out of the shell he was in from his wife's death, and maybe it's what he needed now to get over his feeling of guilt.

Staring at her, he stood up and came around the desk. She drew close putting her arms around his waist, and he lifted her chin to look into her eyes. "I'm sorry for being so distant these last couple weeks. I had a lot on my mind," he said. Realizing he needed her more than ever he asked, "Would you go back upstairs to my room? I'll be up shortly."

Anxiously leaving, she thought as she climbed the stairs, *how glad she was for taking a chance by coming down*. She went into his room, and within a few minutes he came in.

She had already turned the lamp down and was fully undressed lying on the bed. David took off his clothes and lay down beside her. She began running her hands over his hairy chest and moved closer. Covering his mouth with hers, he responded by pulling her on top of him, a position new to her and they made love well into the night.

They awoke next to each other in the morning, and she quietly slid out of bed and returned to her room. After dressing she went downstairs to the kitchen. Thelma and Sarah were there, and she joined them after pouring a cup of tea for herself.

Thelma said, "I heard you come downstairs last night to see Master David. It was the right thing for you to do. Violet always knows just how to pull him up from his misery, and you probably be able to do the same," she said with an approving smile.

"When we were at the dock last week, John told me about a woman that came by asking for Master David. He said they found her floatin' next to the dock the next mornin', she was drowned."

"We know. It was Violet," Thelma replied.

Elizabeth wondered, *if she killed herself, what happened to make her choose such a fateful end? If it was because she had a baby, I'll make sure it won't happen to me. I won't get pregnant.*

In a short time David came to the dining room and rang for Thelma.

"Where's Elizabeth?" he asked.

"She's in the kitchen with Sarah and me. Shall I tell her you wants her?"

"Yes, have her come in and have breakfast with me."

"Should I puts out another plate for Miss Anne too?"

"Yes, please do."

With his request, Thelma realized Elizabeth's actions last night temporarily lifted the burden of guilt from his shoulders. For his sake, Thelma was happy.

Chapter 8
Fire at the Dock

As Thelma was serving breakfast David remarked, "I received a letter yesterday. Tom and Miss Sharon are coming for a visit. They'll be here for a few days."

"That's fine. I see to it they have a room ready," Thelma replied.

After Thelma left the room, Elizabeth nervously looked at David then asked, "Master David, what should I say to Miss Sharon when she comes? She'll know Sarah's really the cook, not me?"

"I'll tell her Sarah's been ill and just returned. You're awaiting the time you'll be able to marry John," Looking at her with a reassuring smile he said, "Don't worry. I'll make up something."

***

When they arrived several days later Sharon was happy to see Elizabeth. Embracing her she said, "Elizabeth, your mother wanted me to tell you she's doing fine."

"Thank you, Miss Sharon."

David and Tom went into the study and talked about how well the crops had done. Tom said as he opened a satchel emptying forty thousand dollars on David's desk, "I brought you the rest of the money I owe. Here it is."

David looked down at the pile of money then reached across the desk shaking Tom's hand.

"Tom, this calls for a drink, how about a brandy?"

"That sounds good David."

After pouring them they toasted the occasion and remained in the study talking. In about an hour they came out and left for the dock.

Before getting there they could see a column of smoke in that direction. Arthur pulled the carriage to the curb letting the horse drawn fire wagon race by. The horses were at a full gallop and the driver was furiously ringing the alarm bell to clear his path.

Getting closer to the waterfront they could see a dock was on fire, but which one? Several more fire wagons rushed by heading in the same direction.

When they got closer they could see it was David's dock. Pulling up close as possible, they saw a line of men with buckets dipping water from the river, passing it down the line tossing the water on the flames trying to extinguish the blaze.

John, Jeremiah and the rest of the dock crew were fighting the heat and heavy smoke as well, trying to move the undamaged cotton bales out of harms-way. When Jeremiah saw the coach he ran to Master David excitedly saying, "Master David, Master David, the fire dun started while we were loadin' the ship. We don't know how; weren't nobody over there at the time. The captain dun told us, 'We gots to push the ship away from the dock, so's it wasn't in any danger of catchin' fire. He anchored it on down yonder at another dock," he said, pointing down river. "We doing everything we can to save the rest of the cotton."

David saw there was extensive damage already and the fire was still out of control. The cotton bales smoldering were ruined and to keep the fire from spreading to the ones that hadn't been affected, the dock crew was using long poles to push the burning ones off the pier. The heat and smoke was so intense, they had to retreat several times to get away from the flames and heavy smoke for their own safety. Although the extent of the damage couldn't be ascertained until the fire was out, it appeared the damage was significant to the dock and cargo. David realized the expense financially, would probably absorb most of the money he just received from Tom.

After the blaze was extinguished, they stayed to survey the damage to see what could be salvaged. After examining the dock it was just as David suspected. The damage was severe and the dock would have to be shut down for repairs.

Leaving for home, it was after dark when they arrived. They were met at the door by Anne and Sharon who already knew about the fire from Anne's fiancé, Steven. He was at his father's dock when the fire broke out. David and Tom, smelling heavily of smoke wanted to get cleaned up before eating the dinner they missed hours ago. Elizabeth, not caring what Miss Sharon would think, followed David upstairs. As he was washing he said, "I'll be busy for the next several weeks. Since Tom can't do anything to help, he decided they should return to Cliveden tomorrow."

Suddenly realizing he was confiding in her the same as he did at times with his wife then Violet, it gave him a good feeling. After washing, he dressed and went downstairs to dinner.

"Tom, you're leaving tomorrow. I'll get in touch with you after everything's back to normal."

"Fine David, if there's anything I can do, let me know."

The following morning before they left Sharon asked, "Elizabeth, do you want to return to Cliveden?"

Hesitating she replied, "If I'm not needed Miss Sharon, I'd like to stay. John asked me to marry him and Master David gave us permission. He said we can be married soon."

"It's up to David whether he needs you," Tom said.

David was coming out on the porch when he heard them talking and answered, "It would be alright with me if she stays, an extra pair of hands are always welcome. They'll be a heap to do."

"Then that's settled, she can stay," Tom replied.

After saying goodbye they departed.

David left for the dock shortly after they were gone. Getting there he surveyed the fire damage. Looking at the decking he was right about being a lot to do concerning the damage. Work on reconstructing the pier was already underway. Jeremiah, John, and the dock crew had a stack of new planks from the lumber yard and already began pulling up the damaged ones, replacing them. After removing some of the burnt planks, David was able to get a better look at the pilings supporting the dock. They didn't appear to be as badly damaged as he first thought, and was relieved to know the dock would be ready to accept cargo again in about three weeks.

In the meantime temporary buildings would have to be constructed to warehouse some of the cotton until the buildings were completed, but that could easily be remedied by renting storage space.

The work was hard repairing the dock and every day at noon, Elizabeth would have Arthur take her to the pier with food and drink. David and Tom were raised to appreciate what it's like to work and unlike most other wealthy people in Biloxi, they weren't afraid of it. Other dock owners seeing him working with his shirt off alongside slaves was something they weren't accustomed to. Steven, Miss Anne's intended, seemed to be embarrassed more so than anyone else and expressed his opinion more than once to Anne.

John looked forward to seeing Elizabeth daily, and she tried hard not to show she favored David. Seeing David with his shirt off working alongside people he basically owned, only made her feelings for him that much stronger. She looked forward to taking care of him every day when he returned home, and would have clean clothes and a warm tub ready. Sometimes she would remain in his room until he was dressed and go downstairs to dinner with him fantasizing they were married. As time went on she realized she was getting further and further away from the idea of a marriage to John.

One day while they were working John got up enough courage to ask, "Master David, would you allow me and Miss Elizabeth to marry up?"

Looking up at a question he feared would come sooner or later he replied, "That's something she has to decide John. If she agrees, I won't object."

When he went home, he went upstairs to wash the same as he would every evening. Elizabeth had his water already drawn and clean clothes laid out on the bed.

"David, you sure got dirty today!" she said. Pausing for a moment she thought, *did he notice? I never said Master David.*

Realizing what she said he didn't mind. He already had her in the role of Violet. Trying to back away again he said, "John asked me today if you would be willing to marry him."

Gathering his soiled clothes she froze listening to his words. Turning in his direction, she slowly looked up at him without giving him an immediate answer, and thought, *Was he angry I didn't say Master David? No, it couldn't be. Maybe I'm acting too much like Violet. If I try to be a little distant, maybe he would want me more.*

"Elizabeth, did you hear what I said? John asked if you would marry him," he repeated.

Turning with a half forced smile she replied, "If that's what you really want, that's what I'll do," then quietly left the room.

After closing the door, she leaned against it trying hard to digest the bitter words she was forced to say. It tore her heart out to say it, but David's happiness meant more to her than her own. After having washed and dressed he went downstairs to have dinner with Anne.

After dinner, he went into the study to open his mail and do his ledger. About an hour into doing it, he heard a loud knock at the front door. He could hear Steven's voice in the hall, and heard Anne excitedly saying, "Steven! Steven! Come into the parlor. Come in the parlor. Please! We'll talk about it."

David heard Steven say in a loud voice, "No, thank you, Anne. I have no choice but to break our engagement."

"Why on earth would you do that?" she pleaded.

Replying sharply, "It's over what people have been saying about David working alongside his niggers at the dock!"

Hearing his words David quickly got up from his chair. Coming out of the study he saw Steven about to walk out the front door. Anne tried to block Steven's exit, but with ease he pushed her aside. David, adamant to confront him, tried catching him before he left and was about to open the door when Anne blocked his path. She was crying hysterically and David asked, "What happened to start this?"

She screamed, "It's your fault! It's your fault Steven's broken our engagement!"

"Why is it my fault?" David annoyingly shouted back.

"By working alongside your niggers at the dock, that's why!"

Hearing the commotion, everyone in the house came into the hall. Elizabeth took Anne by the arm trying to console her, but Anne angrily pulled away shouting, "It's your fault too this whole thing happened. Running to the dock every day with food, as if everyone didn't know it isn't for John, it's for David," then ran up the steps to her room slamming the door shut.

David quickly followed, and banged hard on the door with his fist, "I think there's an apology in order toward the people in this house!" he shouted, "Do you hear me, Anne!" banging harder he shouted again, "Anne! Did you hear me?"

Not getting a response, he could hear her crying,

"Go away and leave me alone!" she screamed.

"Do you want me to talk to Steven?" he asked.

Without opening the door she shouted, "Steven told me there are rumors you treat your slaves like you do because we have Negro blood in us. Is that true?"

He couldn't believe what he was hearing. Elizabeth had run up the steps behind David and grabbed his arm as he was about to pound again at the door.

"David, she didn't mean it, she's just upset," Elizabeth pleaded.

Still angry at what Anne said he turned to Elizabeth, "That's no excuse. You didn't deserve the insult you were given. Neither did anyone else in this house," turning his attention back to Anne yelling, "Anne, open the damn door this instant!"

"David, leave her be for awhile; she'll calm down. I think everyone here realizes she didn't mean it."

Realizing she spoke again without saying Master David for the second time he didn't seem to mind.

Coming downstairs to the hall where the house servants were gathered, David said, "I'm very sorry for what Anne said. She's completely out of line. I sincerely hope you don't think she expresses what I feel for everyone in this house. Arthur, bring the carriage around front. I'm going to pay Steven a visit before these rumors get out of hand."

When he got to Steven's residence, he knocked hard at the door. Expecting David, Steven answered it. Pushing his way in, David angrily began, "Anne was upset at what you said. Where did you hear that rumor?"

"It's been circulating for awhile. I don't know the origin sir, but I no longer want any part of Miss Anne or her family. The way you work at the dock and your relationship with Violet, and now Elizabeth, you look like you enjoy their company more than your own kind," Steven replied.

Grabbing Steven by the collar David pushed him against the wall and said, "You insulted my family and my sister by breaking your engagement over an unsubstantiated rumor. If you were any kind of gentleman, whoever told you that should have been challenged!" he angrily said.

"Get out of my house! Get out now! You'll be hearing from my second," Steven said as he straightened his collar.

When David returned home, Anne was downstairs anxiously awaiting his arrival.

"What happened? What did he say?" she quickly asked.

Looking at her with disappointment about the way she addressed the house servants he replied, "Steven's less than a man for not confronting the person who told him that rumor. I'm glad the engagement is broken.

He proved himself not to be much of a man, let alone a gentleman. He said I'll hear from his second in the morning."

With those words Anne ran up to her room crying again, slamming the door shut.

David went back to the study to finish the ledger he was working on before the disruption, and Elizabeth followed. After entering the room, Elizabeth closed the door and leaned against it. "Did it have to come to this, you possibly dying because of me?" she frustratingly asked.

Looking up he replied, "It's not your fault. It's a matter of family honor. Someone started that rumor and I'm going to find out who it was."

Seeing he was still visibly shaken she asked, "Should I pour you a brandy?"

Looking up at her, he put down his pen. Amused, he replied, "I'd like one, and after what Anne said to you, I think you should have one too."

After pouring them she handed one to David, "It's not Miss Anne's fault. She was just upset and didn't really mean it."

David raised his glass to acknowledge the fact Elizabeth wasn't angry with Anne's cutting words. Putting the glass to her mouth she took a healthy swallow as if it was water. Coughing, she couldn't catch her breath, and David was forced to come around the desk to tap her on the back. As she was slowly recovering he asked, "Haven't you ever had a drink?"

In a raspy voice she replied, "No! And I don't think I want another, it burned all the way down."

He laughed at the incident, and it seemed to snap him out of his anger for the moment.

Knowing there was going to be a duel that would possibly kill him she asked, "I'm afraid you'll be killed. Can I come to your room tonight?"

"I think I'd like that," he replied.

Putting down his glass, they both left the room. As they passed Anne's room, they could hear her still crying. David stopped outside her door for a moment wondering whether he should knock. Realizing what he was thinking, Elizabeth grabbed his hand. Shaking her head *NO,* they proceeded down the hall to his room.

He thought, *Losing my temper only made things worse. I should have waited till morning.*

Continuing to his room, he was anxious to feel the comfort of Elizabeth next to him. She had a way of taking the burden of a hard day's troubles off his shoulders, and after the events tonight, he realized she would be just what he needed. Stopping before entering his room, he remembered he forgot to turn off the kerosene lamp in the study and went back downstairs. After turning out the lamp, he returned to the second floor. Approaching his room, he could hear crying. Pausing for a moment outside Anne's door, he realized it wasn't coming from her room. No, it was coming from his room. Slowly opening the door, he saw Elizabeth completely undressed standing near the dimly lit lamp. When he entered, she quickly turned away. He realized it was her that was crying. Unable to contain her feelings, she rushed at him throwing her arms around his neck. She didn't care whether he knew it -she was deeply in love with him.

"David, I'm so sorry for what's happened. I should have never gone to the dock every day. If anything happens to you, I'll..., I'll..., I'll just die!"

Airing her true feelings, she didn't care about the consequences. If he should happen to die, she didn't want him not knowing how she felt. Gently taking her arms from around his neck he looked deeply into her eyes, "I don't know whether you know it, I assume you do. Ever since I saw you at Cliveden, you reminded me of Violet a woman that lived here. I fell in love with her just as I've fallen in love with you. Unfortunately, it can't go any further than this small world under this roof. It's not fair for you not to have a life with someone that can give you more. I don't mean the material things you have," he said gesturing with his hand at the comforts of her room "Something more, like a family. I wouldn't want to deny you of anything by just living across the hall."

Frustratingly raising her voice she said, "I know about Violet, and I don't care about only living across the hall. It's my life, and I don't mind living it like that."

"You're only 24, and haven't really lived long enough to make that decision. You'll feel differently once you get away from me. I'm doing what I think is best for you."

She shot back, "Do you really think I want to go back and jump the broom with John? I made that decision awhile ago. The only way I'll do that, is if you tell me to. Maybe if we make love tonight you'll feel different in the morning."

Helping him unbutton his shirt, in a few minutes they were lying in bed next to one another. She was bound and determined to make him change his mind at any cost. Deciding to try the best way she knew how, she initiated the love making and it lasted way into the night. She never returned to her room wanting to feel the warmth and comfort of him lying next to her, possibly for the last time.

Chapter 9
The Duel

In the morning as expected a friend of Steven's came to the house. Markus took him to the study where David was seated at his desk. Nervously, the visitor began to speak.

"Sir, I'm Allen Jenkins, Steven's friend, as well as his second. I'm instructed to formally challenge you to a duel. The appointed place is Willows Meadow. If it's acceptable to you, the appointed time will be tomorrow at 10 o'clock in the morning?"

The place chosen was a grove of willow trees surrounding a meadow just outside of Biloxi. David stood up replying, "Yes, that's agreeable to me."

"Then Sir, what's the weapon of your choice?" the challenger asked.

Thinking for a moment David replied, "The rapier!"

The rapier is a small sword used for dueling. David at one time was proficient with fencing, but hadn't done it for a long time, and hadn't really practiced for several years. He knew Steven attended the same fencing school more recently, and swords would be a more even match. David was the better shot with pistols and had proven it several times in the past.

After Allen left, David went to the dock to survey the work being done. While there, he was approached by Steven's father Aaron Watson, "David, I'm sorry for what happened. My son acted too hastily. I'm grateful you chose fencing for the duel. I know your reputation and success with a pistol. Is there any way I can persuade you to deny the challenge?"

"I appreciate what you said Aaron, and thank you for the compliment. It's out of my hands; I have to uphold his challenge."

Before taking his leave, Aaron said in a disappointing voice, "Well David, I'm sorry it has to happen. I truly am."

David told Jeremiah and John about the duel, and explained to them no matter what the outcome, continue with the dock repairs.

Returning home, he entered the study to straighten out a few affairs and write his last will and testament, something he had done several times in the past. As he was writing, there was a gentle knock at the door. Looking up, Anne was entering the room. In a nervous voice she asked,

"David, are you and Steven going to have a duel?"

"Yes, tomorrow morning at 10 a.m. If I happen to be killed, go to Cliveden and tell Tom to take over the business. Where's Elizabeth?"

"She's in her room crying. She's been there all morning. Shall I get her?"

"No, I'll go up. I want to speak to her too."

After finishing his will, he folded the paper neatly and put it in an envelope. After writing *Last Will and Testament* boldly across the front, he sealed it, and propped it against a picture of his wife on the desk. Looking around with a sigh, he left the room and climbed the stairs to console Elizabeth. When he opened the door to her room, she was sitting at her dressing mirror toying with one of her perfume bottles. After stepping in, he closed the door.

"Elizabeth I'm going downstairs to write documents for you and John's freedom. I'm going to send both of you to New Orleans where John can take over as the head dock foreman. You'll have less of a problem living free there, than here in Biloxi."

Turning to look at him he could tell she must have been crying for a long time; her eyes were bloodshot. With his words, her eyes began welling up again and tears ran down her cheeks. Desperate to find a way out of the danger she put him in, she couldn't contain her emotions any longer. Running to him, she threw her arms around his waist hugging him tightly. Looking up at his face, she put her arms around his neck, forcing his head down to her waiting lips. After a long pause gazing into his eyes she pleaded, "I had a life here, even as short as it was. I'm in love with you and nothing or no freedom paper will ever -ever take that away from me." His words were cutting, and she feared the worst -he was already talking as if he was going to die.

"Can I come to your room tonight?" she asked.

"I don't think so. I won't be in the right mood," he replied.

"I won't mind. I just want to be near you," pausing, "Maybe for the last time."

He didn't answer, leaving the question open.

Not having a relative close at hand to act as his second, he went to the fencing school where he had been a student years ago. Franz Chamberlain was the owner of the well renown fencing school, and they remained friends over the years. Franz was a well-spoken man, with a light French accent. In his early 50's, he was slender with graying hair, and had a razor thin mustache which added to his professional appearance. If one had to judge what a fencing-master looked like, Franz was a perfect candidate.

"Good afternoon, David. What brings you back to school?"

"Franz, I've been challenged to a duel. It's to take place tomorrow at Willows Meadow. Tom isn't here, and I have no second. Would you, or rather could you, oblige me?"

"I'll be your second of course. May I bring a few students with me?"

"Yes, feel free. I'll see you in the morning. The appointed time is 10 a.m."

"Then I'll be there at 9:45," Franz replied.

After the meeting David went home to continue straightening his affairs.

Later in the day when Thelma rang the bell for dinner, David entered the dining room. To his dismay, he was alone. Both Anne and Elizabeth were too distraught to join him.

"Thelma, where is Anne and Elizabeth?" he asked.

"Excuse me for sayin' Master David, but I don't thinks anybody's thinkin' on being hungry tonight. They both be up in they rooms cryin'."

With a teary eye she too left the room.

After dinner, he went back to the study for a few hours, and at the stroke of 10, he climbed the stairs retiring to bed.

Restless in his sleep, he had quite a bit on his mind. Instead of focusing on his possible demise, his thoughts were about Elizabeth's claim on his affections, and began to realize she took precedent over the duel he was about to have.

About 2 a.m., there was a knock at his door. Leaning up on one elbow he saw Elizabeth slowly open the door to see if he was asleep. No matter what was going to happen in the morning, she was determined to spend the last night by his side. Realizing he was still awake, she slowly crossed the room and slid into bed beside him. Although he wasn't in the mood for love making, she was eager just to be with him. The warmth of his body reminded her of the warm feeling she had the first night she spent with him. Like a sleeping potion, content, they both fell asleep.

In the morning she was still savoring the night while he was dressing.

"I didn't want to wake you, you looked so content," he said.

"Thank you for letting me stay," she replied.

"No, it's just what I needed. Come down and have breakfast with me. Please?"

Hurrying across the hall, she quickly dressed and went down to the dining room.

"Thelma, tell Arthur to have the carriage ready at 9:15; that's when I'll be leaving."

"Yes Sir. Master David, I'll tell him," she replied sniffling.

Looking at Thelma he said, "There seems to be an air of foreboding in this house. What's wrong with everybody? I'm not dead yet!"

Thelma quickly replied before leaving the room, "We know Master David, but last time you dueled, you come mighty close. Mighty close!"

Elizabeth raised her head listening intently. She had seen the scar on his body and wondered what it was from, but never asked.

"David, you've been hurt in a duel before?" she asked.

Again, Elizabeth spoke without saying Master David, and once again it went unnoticed. Before he could answer, Thelma replied, "He surely was, and it was nip and tuck till he got better."

"Where's Miss Anne this morning?" he asked.

Thelma replied, "I went to her room and she say she wasn't comin' down. She didn't want no breakfast," hesitating for a moment she looked at David, "And she say she didn't want to see you either!"

Looking disappointed he left the table.

Arthur pulled the carriage around front at 9:15, and just before David went out the door, Elizabeth embraced him again; holding on tight until he had to pry her away.

"Elizabeth, I have to leave," he said, forcing his way out the door.

Anne ran down from her room to say she was sorry, but he was already gone.

At 9:45, the carriage pulled up at the appointed place, and David saw Franz already there with his students. David, noting his presence, nodded to him after getting out of the carriage. Walking over to him, Franz introduced his students. Steven and two friends were there as well, and a physician was present laying out his instruments that were needed to treat wounds, or pronounce whoever lost, dead.

After taking off his coat and handing it to Arthur, David stood in the clearing flexing his legs leaning forward bending them, then turning his upper body to limber up. He was practicing parrying, which is a move to ward off a thrust from an opponent. Steven was doing the same and at exactly 10 o'clock Franz called them together.

"Gentlemen, I don't think I have to remind you of the rules you were taught in fencing school. I won't tolerate any deviation from them, and I carry a small pistol to insure it's done properly."

They acknowledged with a nod, then at each other. Holding their swords at a 45 degree angle, they pointed to each side before crossing blades. Franz gave the command, "En Garde," and the joust began.

They tested each other to start with a few lunges and parries then disengaged. David was beginning to get his footing again where he felt comfortable. Being younger by 15 years, it was obvious Steven was the fresher student with his agility and swordsmanship.

They attacked and counter attacked for about 10 minutes. David knew if he was to succeed, he would have to attack then feint, which is a tactic used to pretend a retreat to draw your opponent closer. With the distance between them closed he began his attack. The ruse worked, and Steven came in for the final lunge. David counter attacked but lost his footing in the wet grass falling to the ground.

Franz quickly shouted, "Wait until he recovers!"

Instead of abiding the command Steven lunged forward, aiming at David's heart. His point missed its mark and penetrated David's right side. At the same time, David rolled to one side and thrust his tip at Steven striking him in the heart, and death came to him instantly. The physician first looked at Steven who was obviously dead, then went to David who was unconscious and appeared to be severely wounded. Arthur and Franz rushed to his side and removed his shirt. The wound was deep, and although it had happened only minutes ago, the loss of blood was significant. Arthur and Franz, with the help of the students carried him to the coach, and after the physician got in, they quickly headed for home. On the trip, the doctor applied pressure to the wound trying to stop the bleeding.

The carriage horses were at a gallop coming down the street, and pulled up abruptly in front of the house. Everyone suspected the worst and when Arthur opened the carriage door, their fear was confirmed.

Seeing all the blood, Anne, Elizabeth and the rest of the house staff ran down the front steps wanting to see how badly he was injured. After carrying him up to his room, the doctor commanded, "Get some warm water and some bandages!"

After taking his vital signs the doctor said, "I don't think any major organs were damaged but there's a great loss of blood. Sarah, go to the kitchen and make some hot broth. When he wakes, feed it to him in small amounts."

When Sarah left the room, Elizabeth quickly followed. Entering the kitchen Elizabeth said, "I'll make it Sarah."

Seeing Elizabeth's concern, Sarah stood aside without saying a word.

In a few minutes Anne came to the kitchen and said, "The doctor just left. He said he'll be back in the morning. David seems to be resting comfortable now; he'll probably sleep through the night."

Elizabeth went to his room and had Thelma help her move a small sofa next to his bed. She was going to be by his side that night in case he needed anything. During the night she was awaken by David talking incoherently in his sleep. It was something about Violet, but she couldn't make out what he was saying. After caressing his face, he fell back to sleep.

When he awoke in the morning, he saw her asleep on the couch next to him, and laid there watching her. She was awakened by him stirring in bed and when she opened her eyes he had already propped himself up.

He asked, "Could you get me a drink of water please?"

"I have something better than that, I made it last night. The doctor said you should drink it."

Going to the kitchen she returned with the broth and sat beside the bed to feed him. Trying to pull himself up he said, "I can feed myself."

"The doctor didn't want you to be moving around too much. He didn't want that wound to reopen. You've already lost a lot of blood."

Smiling, he abided her command and lie back down.

"Where's Anne?" he asked.

"Miss Anne's in her room crying. She just found out this morning Steven was killed."

"Tell her to come in. I want to talk to her."

She left the room and in a few minutes returned with Anne. Her eyes were red from crying most of the morning over Steven, but she knew there was nothing David could have done, short of dying himself.

"Anne, get the envelope on my desk marked *Last Will and Testament.* Bring it to me."

She did as he asked, then opened it so she could read the instructions as if he was killed. The note instructed her to return to Cliveden until whoever started these rumors could be dealt with. It also mentioned she would be a great comfort to Sharon during Sharon's pregnancy.

"Ask Tom if he could come to Biloxi for awhile to take charge of the business for me."

"If you don't think you'll need me David, I'll leave in the morning," she replied.

"That will be fine."

Later that afternoon Elizabeth looked in on him, "Do you want me to go to the dock and tell Jeremiah and John what happened?" she asked.

"Yes, I want you to go now and bring one of them back so I can tell them what I want them to do."

Leaving the room, she found Arthur in the carriage house still trying to clean the blood stains from the carriage seat.

"Master David wants you to go to the dock and bring back either Jeremiah or John. He wants to speak with them," she said.

Arthur left, and within an hour returned with Jeremiah, and Elizabeth escorted him to David's room.

"Jeremiah is the work on the dock almost finished?" he asked.

"Master David, it be 'bout done. We be ready to ship tobacco in a few days."

"I'll be laid up for at least two weeks. I won't be able to help," grunting as he tried to raise himself up in bed.

"We see it gets done, me and John." Jeremiah seemed reluctant to continue and David asked, "Jeremiah, what's on your mind?"

"Excuse me for sayin' Master David. The other dock owners, they never did like the idea of you workin' with us. They be jealous 'dat yo' dock didn't have as much damage as they's after the storm too. Now 'dat Master Steven was killed, it may get worse ifn' somebody from the family don't be with us."

"Miss Anne's leaving in the morning for Cliveden. She'll ask Tom to come here for a few weeks until I get well."

As Jeremiah was walking out of the room he turned, "Don't you be a worryin' none. Me and John, we looks out for things 'till Master Tom gets here."

David tried getting to his feet but the pain was too great and he decided not to try.

After Jeremiah left, Elizabeth came in and said, "Thelma and I are helping Miss Anne get packed for the trip. Do you need any help?"

Overhearing what Jeremiah said about possible trouble Elizabeth said, "David, the trip to Cliveden is two days or longer by coach. It could be done a lot faster by a messenger on horseback."

Thinking for a moment he replied, "You're right. Get me a paper and ink from my study. I want to write a message."

David remembered one of the students at the duel's father raised thoroughbreds. He wanted to buy one and try to find a rider that could carry a message today. After finishing the note he asked Arthur to deliver it. Within an hour, a man came to the door from the stable. He had the papers for a beautiful thoroughbred, and the name of a person that would carry his message.

David asked, "Elizabeth, get the money from my safe to pay the messenger and give him the note with the directions to Cliveden."

"Okay, David," she said, then went downstairs to retrieve the money to pay the messenger. She watched from the front porch as the messenger rode away at a gallop. She thought, *it's late afternoon, and the trip is a little over 55 miles. Pushing it, he should be there day after tomorrow. If all goes well, Tom should be here by the end of the week.*

Miss Anne left the following morning, and while she was gone, Elizabeth happily continued to support David on his road to recovery.

When the messenger reached Cliveden, Tom and Sharon not expecting a visitor, were surprised when they read the letter. The note contained the basics of what happened and Tom wanted to leave immediately. Seeing Solomon at the barn he said, "Solomon, I have to go to Biloxi. I don't know how long I'll be there but I'm leaving you in charge."

Within an hour he was ready, and at a gallop, headed out to aid David. Clouds were on the horizon and Tom knew at some point on the trip, it would begin to rain slowing his travel. He rode until nightfall, stopping at an inn a little farther than their usual stop on the trip. There were no beds available that late, so he slept in the barn on a pile of straw.

As he suspected, during the night a light rain began to fall. When he woke, he was able to secure a fresh horse to continue his journey. In 20 minutes he was soaked from the rain, but pushed on, knowing there were only about 15 miles or a little more to go. Arriving at the house, he quickly ran up the steps to David's room. Throwing open the door he frantically asked, "David, what happened?"

David told him what happened, and about the rumor that started it. He said, "Tom, go to the dock and make sure things are okay. Jeremiah thinks there might be trouble if someone in the family isn't there. I don't want to have any problems with ships coming in or going out."

"I'll leave immediately," Tom replied.

As he turned to leave Thelma said in a commanding tone, "Before you go runnin' out Master Tom, you best get out of those wet clothes and have somethin' to warm you, else you be commin' down with the mizzery and be layin' right here alongside Master David!"

After agreeing, Thelma and Elizabeth drew water for a warm bath and brought him some brandy from the study. Comfortable again, he left immediately.

Arriving at the dock, he saw Jeremiah and John supervising the loading of a ship, and asked Jeremiah to step under an eave out of the rain. He asked, "Jeremiah, how did this rumor start?"

Shaking the rain off his wet cap Jeremiah replied, "Master Tom, I don't rightly know. The talk 'dat be goin' 'round, ain't start at Master Steven's father's dock. It started from a dock further on down the row." After telling Tom what he knew, he returned to his work.

Tom stood by watching until they finished loading the ship, and it pulled away from the dock. After it left, Tom said, "Jeremiah, I'll be here until David's able to come back. If there's any trouble, let me know."

"Master Tom, me and John, we be thinkin', 'dat fire was over yonder where none of us was at," pointing in that direction, "How it started, we still don't rightly know."

Tom, thinking about what he said walked away wondering whether the rumor and the fire could somehow be connected. On the way home, Arthur was driving past other docks in the row when Tom happened to see a familiar face. He thought, *I know that face from somewhere; now where have I seen it before?* It finally came to him, *that's right! It's Ezekiel, the slave I sold to South Port Plantation several years ago."*

After watching Ezekiel for a few minutes, he had Arthur turn back to the dock wanting to ask John a few questions.

Returning he asked, "John, do you remember Ezekiel?"

"Yes, Sir. I 'member him from Cliveden. Why you askin'?"

"I just saw him at another dock down the row. Have you ever seen him around here?"

"I never did see him 'round here, but I 'member him telling Daniel... 'dat be Miss Elizabeth's daddy. 'He knew Daniel be the one 'dat done had his family sold and someday he was gonna' pay him back.' Maybe he sees Miss Elizabeth here bringin' food every day. Maybe 'dat's what it be!"

Tom left, wanting to get back to the house and tell David where he suspected the rumor started. Entering his room he said, "David, I think I know where the rumor came from and who may have started it."

David sat up, anxious to hear what Tom had to say.

"I saw a slave that I sold from Cliveden a few years ago. He's working on another dock down the row. His name's Ezekiel. He knew we're brothers and thought maybe through you, it was revenge against me for selling him. He also knows Elizabeth was Daniel's daughter, and he thought Daniel was the one behind me selling them. Seeing her bringing lunch every day when you were working on the dock, may have given him the idea of getting even," pausing for a moment, he continued, "Jeremiah said the fire on the dock started where no one was working. Maybe Ezekiel's responsible for that too."

"Where did the idea of Negro blood in us come from?" David asked.

"Probably the same place. Jeremiah told me the other dock owners never liked you working like one of your people, so the rumor wouldn't have been hard to start."

"I know how to fix the problem, Tom. I know the owner of that dock. Send him and Steven's father a note asking them to come here for a meeting."

Going to the study, Tom wrote the notes as David asked, and had Arthur deliver them.

After returning to David's room, Elizabeth knocked lightly on the door then stepped in.

"Master Tom, I overheard what you and Master David were talking about. Would it help any if I come to the meeting and let them know the reason for me going to the dock every day was my interest in John?"

Tom looking at her inquisitively said, "I didn't realize there was any other interest, but it would help David's reputation."

The notes were delivered instructing the recipients the meeting was to be held the following afternoon at David's residence.

The next day, Tom helped David down to the study and sat him in his chair behind the desk. When the other dock owners arrived, they were escorted into the room. David offered them a glass of Sherry Wine, and began by telling Steven's father, "Aaron, I'm sorry for how things turned out with your son, but again... I had no choice."

Aaron replied sternly, "I'm a friend of Franz the fencing master, David. He told me my son violated the code. Franz would have had to do what was expected of him and shoot Steven. He embarrassed the family. You sir, did what you had to do."

After clearing the air, they got down to the discussion of Ezekiel, who was more than likely the origin of the rumor.

Tom began by saying, "I sold his family and what happened here was probably revenge. Elizabeth's father, Daniel, was the head field hand at Cliveden. When Ezekiel and his family were sold, he blamed Daniel. He threatened to pay him back some day, and seeing Elizabeth bringing the lunch every day to the dock was probably the perfect opportunity."

Getting up from his chair, Tom rang for Elizabeth. After entering the room, Tom asked her about her relationship with John. She said, "My only interest in coming to Biloxi, Sir, was to marry John who was traded by Master Tom to his brother. We were getting ready to jump the broom at Cliveden when he was traded."

Tom looked at Elizabeth, then at the visitors saying, "Gentlemen, that's true. Being busy running the plantation, I never knew they had plans."

David looked at Elizabeth realizing she was protecting his reputation, and without further comment she left the room.

Ezekiel's owner said, "Gentlemen, when the next group of slaves come in; I'll make sure Ezekiel will be sold to Dumont."

The meeting ended and David rose from his chair to acknowledge their departure.

Still obviously in pain, he quickly sat back down and blood became visible on his shirt. He knew he had reopened the wound, and after the visitors left, he rang for Thelma.

When she entered the room Tom said, "Quick, help me get him to his room. Tell Arthur to bring the doctor."

Elizabeth, hearing the commotion came out of her room and helped get David back to bed.

"Tom, would you mind stepping out of the room for a minute? I'd like to speak to Elizabeth alone," David asked.

"Certainly David," he replied before stepping into the hallway closing the door.

Elizabeth began to say, "The doctor..." when David interrupted.

"I know why you told them you came here to be with John; you were just trying to protect my reputation."

"David, I've been thinking about what you said, I realize you were right. It wouldn't have worked out between us even if I hadn't told them. I understand now, you're trying to get the life back you had with Violet, but we both been chasing a dream."

Looking at his bandage she said, "You're bleeding again. Those bandages have to be changed. All this moving around," frustratingly she continued in a low tone, "Why didn't you have them come up here?"

Smiling, he sat up while she un-wrapped his blood soaked bandage.

Tom opened the door to enter the room then suddenly stopped, "Looks like you're in good hands. I'm going downstairs and write a letter to Sharon."

As Elizabeth was washing the wound and applying disinfectant, David asked, "Do you want to go to the dock tomorrow?"

She didn't reply and David knew she was ignoring his question on purpose. As she was wrapping the wide bandage around his waist, he grasped her hand. Looking deep into her eyes he forced her to answer. She froze for a moment then said, "David, no matter what happens, I'll always love you, and that's something you can never take away."

He replied, "I want to give you and John your freedom. I'll see to it my partner Charles in New Orleans can use John. There, you'll be able to live easier; there's more tolerance toward Negro's in New Orleans."

Looking up after finishing wrapping the bandage she said, "Then I better tell Arthur to drive me to him tomorrow," Turning, she left the room slowly closing the door.

David lay awake for the next hour wondering how his normally regimented life had gotten so far out of hand. From his affair with Elizabeth, the fire on the dock, Violet drowning, the duel, the rumor that caused it; and it all happened in a span of several months.

After the doctor arrived, he examined the wound again, "You better stay off your feet for awhile, there's no reason to get up. Your brother can handle things," the doctor demanded.

After he left David fell asleep.

He woke at day-break to the sound of Elizabeth in the hall, talking to Thelma. He heard her say, "Thelma, I'm going to the dock today to see John."

"Does Master David know?" Thelma replied.

"Yes, he wants it that way."

After a few moments of silence David heard Thelma say, "I dun' told you. It would have been wiser not to show your feelin's. I made that same mistake once."

"I remember you telling me that, and I should have listened, but it's too late now," Elizabeth replied.

David felt good she was abiding his wishes, and could hear their voices fade as they went downstairs.

Chapter 10
New Orleans

Arthur pulled the coach up about mid day, and Elizabeth got in with a large basket of food for John and the rest of the dock crew. On the way she thought about what Thelma said about making her feelings known, and wished she had done things differently. Would she be able to fake an emotion with John something she only envisioned with David? Would John notice the change in feelings she had toward him? To keep from hurting his feelings it was something she knew she would have to overcome.

Arriving at the dock John came out to greet her. Opening the carriage door he took the basket and held her hand as she stepped down. She seemed more attentive today and it reminded him of the way she was the day he left Cliveden.

After setting up the food she brought she called the men to the table. There were no ships coming in or going out and John thought it would be a good time to ask her to marry him. Before he had a chance to speak, Elizabeth said, "I heard Master David say, since you were so good at the dock here, he wants you to help run the dock in New Orleans."

Fearing they would be separated again he anxiously asked, "When you thinks 'dat's gonna happen Miss Elizabeth?"

"I don't know, but I'll ask," she replied.

Looking at her he said, "'Member the day we were on the dock and I asked Master David if we could be married? He said, 'I'd have to ask you?' Well ifn' you please Miss Elizabeth," he said pausing for a moment, "I'm askin' now."

Looking at him she hesitated, and John thought she was either searching her memory, or getting ready to give him a sound rejection. After a brief moment he thought was an eternity, she replied, "I remember."

"Well, Miss Elizabeth, I'm askin' you again. Would you marry up with me?"

"Yes, but that depends on what Master David says."

Happy with her decision he replied, "That's just fine. How long do you thinks it be befo' he be well enough to come here?"

"About two or three weeks," she replied, "When I get back to the house, I'll ask."

Already knowing the answer, she still hoped David would somehow change his mind. For the second time in her life she lied and didn't feel good about it.

Returning home, she saw David in the study.

"You should still be in bed. You're not strong enough to be walking around. You want that to open up again?" she commanded.

Searching his desk drawer for stationary he said. "I'm writing papers for you and John's freedom. The other paperwork will be for you to give to my partner Charles in New Orleans."

Finding the stationary, he began to write. Looking at him she realized he had no intention of changing his mind, and she said, "John asked if we could be married before he goes."

Looking up from writing he replied, "That's what I want, and I want both of you to go on the next ship."

She thought, *Was it only to rid himself of a bad situation?* Little did she realize as time would prove, it wasn't for himself he was doing it, it was for her. Leaving the room she said in a low tone, "Then I'll go back tomorrow and let him know."

Going to her room she took out the old travel bag Miss Sharon gave her when she left Cliveden, and packed the few clothes she had when she came. She also packed two of the less fancy dresses David bought while she was here. Sitting at her dressing table brushing out her long hair probably for the last time, she remembered the day she arrived. The several months she'd been here were like awakening from a dream. She didn't know how she would handle her new life in New Orleans, but for David's sake, she was willing to try. He avoided her the rest of the day, and she decided not to continue pursuing the fantasy.

The next morning he handed her the papers they would need and said, "Tell John to be on the ship that docks today. It's bound for New Orleans."

She thanked him for their freedom and told him while tightly holding his hand, "David, you know I would have rather remained your servant than be free."

Looking at her he smiled and said, "Elizabeth, it's the right thing to do."

After she said goodbye to Thelma, Sarah, and a few other house staff, she left.

Arriving at the dock, there was a ship being unloaded. Seeing John she said trying her best to act excited, "Look!" holding up the papers, "Master David gave us our freedom."

Separating them she continued, "He gave me these papers for you to give the Captain. They're for Master Charles in New Orleans. He told me Master Charles is going to make you head foreman there and we're supposed to leave on this ship."

Excited, John took Elizabeth aboard and gave Captain Jarvis the paperwork relaying her message.

"Take Elizabeth and her bag to the passenger's cabin," Captain Jarvis said.

"Yes Sir, Captain," John anxiously replied.

Hesitating to walk away, Jarvis asked, "Is there something else you wanted to ask John?"

"Yes, Sir, Captain. Excuse me Sir for the askin', but could you find somebody to marry me and my Elizabeth before we leave?"

Realizing John didn't know he could perform the ceremony Captain Jarvis replied, "I don't think so," then looked down at the paperwork to keep from laughing. Glancing up, as he suspected, John looked disappointed and began to slowly walk away. Captain Jarvis, seeing his reaction said, "Don't worry John. I'll be able to do it while we're at sea tomorrow."

Hearing those words were like magic, and John went back to work with a rejuvenated spirit. Elizabeth could see by the way the captain treated and spoke to him; he was more than just someone David owned. John had built a reputation on hard work and people respected him for it. After putting her travel bag in the cabin, he told her he would return when they finished loading the ship.

With all the clamor of the ship being loaded, she went out on deck to watch. She had never been on a ship, and watched the activity in amazement. Wandering to the rail, she saw a person wearing a white apron. His back was toward her, and she gently tapped him lightly on the shoulder. Quickly turning around he asked, "You be a passenger on ship?"

He was a short, thin man with slanted eyes, and had a strange accent. Elizabeth asked, "Are you the cook?"

"Yes. My name's Ming; I'm cook on board ship," repeating his question, "You be a passenger?"

"Yes. I'm going to New Orleans. My name's Elizabeth. I used to be the cook at Cliveden."

"Me never heard of that ship. Where it sail to?" he asked.

Laughing she replied, "It's not a ship, it's a plantation Master David's brother, Master Tom owns."

Ming looking confused at her statement asked, "You want see galley?"

Looking puzzled at the word, Ming realized her bewilderment then clarified himself, "I mean kitchen."

She followed, and as they got closer she could smell food cooking. Much to her surprise, when they reached the galley, it was smaller than anything she had ever seen, even smaller than the cook house at Cliveden. Wondering how he could get anything done in such a small area she asked, "Mister Ming, I'd like to help you make dinner."

After he agreed, she tied on an apron and began cooking. She turned out a dish that could be smelled all the way down to the cargo hold and the dock. After the ship was loaded, the captain and crew sat down at the table in the galley. Elizabeth served them a meal they were obviously enjoying, when she saw Adam.

She said, "Adam, John told me you were here. He told me about the storm and what you did. You weren't afraid?"

"Yes, it was powerful rough that night Miss Elizabeth, but we got it done."

The captain interrupted their conversation saying, "Elizabeth, go down to the dock and tell John to come aboard."

After he came aboard Captain Jarvis said, "Your Missus sure knows how to turn out a great meal," looking at Ming Captain Jarvis continued, "We were thinking about leaving Ming here and making her ship's cook."

Ming excitedly replied, "She no be able to cook in galley. She say too small."

Everyone laughed. Elizabeth looking embarrassed at the compliment, said, "I don't know captain, that kitchen is kind of small."

"Thank you Miss Elizabeth," Ming said, smiling at the reprieve.

John remarked, "She was the cook at Cliveden Captain. She can turn out some of the best cornbread you ever did eat."

Adam remembering, agreed adding, "Dat's sure enough the truth!"

as he took another bite of his dinner. After everyone finished eating Captain Jarvis told the first mate, "I'm going to town for awhile. I'll only be several hours."

After the crew went to their quarters, Elizabeth and John went to her cabin. They talked for awhile and the whole time John was speaking about their future, she wasn't really listening. She was trying her best to fake a mood that wasn't there; something was missing. She no longer loved him and realized it.

Thinking her feelings might change, she decided to make love to him. The bunk was nothing like the spacious bed she shared with David, and for the most part was uncomfortable. They made love several times and although John was happy, Elizabeth was never really fulfilled. After he left the cabin, she lay there wondering whether her feelings would ever change. Putting it out of her mind she finally drifted off to sleep.

She awoke the next morning to men yelling, "Pull in the ropes from the bollards on the dock. Set the top sail."

Quickly dressing, she came out on deck to watch the ship as it slowly moved away from the pier. As the city faded from view she thought, *It's my last opportunity to see the place where my life as a woman really began.*

Several hours later they were well into the Gulf, on their way to New Orleans.

Captain Jarvis told the first mate, "Get John, I'm ready to perform his wedding ceremony."

John wasn't hard to find. Overhearing what the captain said, he was already on his way to Elizabeth's cabin. A few of the crew stood by as Jarvis read the marriage passage from his book, and after it was over, the crew clapped then patted John on the back congratulating him. Elizabeth too, felt good that the marriage was finally legal.

John, noticing Elizabeth looked a little seasick, escorted her to her cabin. After she lay down, he said as he covered her with a blanket, "You just lie still. It'll pass."

"How long will the trip be?" she asked.

"Three maybe two days, ifn' the weather's good."

Closing her eyes, she tried to sleep, but the motion of the ship was too much, and she was forced to get up several times. During the day he checked to see how she was feeling from time to time, and it made her feel good he was so attentive. Ming also checked in on her bringing a few dry crackers to help make her feel better. That evening John returned to her cabin, and since she was still seasick, he slept upright in a chair feeling content just being by her side. Thinking as he watched her sleep, *Could this be real? She's lying here in front of me, my wife!*

Coming out of the cabin after the first night, she enjoyed looking out on the water. The morning of the third day, she was able to see land which made her feel better, and by late afternoon they were tied to the dock. Anxious to get off the ship, she had her bag ready to go as soon as the gangplank was in place. Holding the papers David had given her for their freedom, she saw Adam and asked, "Adam, which one is Master Charles?" as she pointed to a group of men on the dock.

"Dat be him over there, the one in the blue shirt," he replied.

Elizabeth anxiously approached him and said, "Master Charles, Master David gave me these papers. He wanted me to give them to you."

Looking up from the manifest he was holding he took them and without looking, shoved them in his pocket. "I'll look at them later," he said.

Feeling as though what she handed him wasn't important, she said, "Excuse me, Master Charles. The papers were to let you know John and me were free."

Looking up from his manifest again as if he was annoyed, he replied in a gruff voice, "I'll read them later."

She began to walk away feeling slighted that he considered cargo more important than the document making her free. Noticing her disappointment, he looked up apologetically saying, "I already knew what they were. Captain Jarvis told me."

Ten minutes later, John came off the ship and began helping unload the cargo the same as he would back in Biloxi.

Charles called to him, "John, come here. You're going to be the foreman on this dock. I already knew that's what David wanted. You two will live in a small house not far from here. His instructions were for you to take Elizabeth there."

After giving them directions to it, Elizabeth and John excitedly picked up their belongings and hurried in search of their house. Finding it two streets away, it was at the end of a row of small houses David and Charles owned. It had a porch with a wooden picket fence and a small front yard. Staring in awe at their new possession, they opened the door and went in.

There were a few pieces of furniture in some of the rooms, probably left by the previous owner. The house had three rooms downstairs, and three bed rooms upstairs. The wood stove in the kitchen was in need of a good cleaning, and Elizabeth was anxious to get started. After examining the house, John said, "I best get back to the dock."

Walking John to the front door they kissed before he left. Closing the door she turned around and leaned against it looking into the room. Putting her hands to her face, she was amazed at what they were given to start their lives together. Suddenly thinking about David, she wondered, *Did he do this trying to erase the terrible wrong he did to Violet?*

After putting away their personal belongings she began cleaning the house. Starting upstairs, she worked her way down to the kitchen. After spending several hours cleaning the wood stove she explored the neighborhood in search of a grocer. Finding one several streets away, she bought some supplies for the next few days then quickly returned home. It was already late, and she immediately began cooking. When John came in, he sat down to a meal with his feet under his own table, in his own house, something neither one of them had ever dreamed of.

***

John went to work every day at the break of dawn, and Charles enjoyed the fact John was capable of running things. He was given a small salary that would allow him to have a life like several other former slaves living on the same row.

Life went on for Elizabeth, and time has a way of erasing hurt feelings. As time passed, she became accustomed to being a good wife, and within two years they began a family of their own, a baby girl. John never knew why, but Elizabeth named the baby Violet as a remembrance of the life she once had. It was the failed relationship between Violet and David which allowed Elizabeth and John to have the life they now enjoy.

One day she asked, "John, do you think Master Charles can get us back to Biloxi? I'd sure like to see Momma and Luke. It's been over two years since we been there," she said looking down at the baby she held in her arms, "I'd sure like to show momma and Luke this sweet little thing. Violet needs to see her grandmother."

John Laughed, "The baby's not three months old yet. I don't rightly thinks she's gonna hardly know what to say," then laughed again, "Anyway, I'll ask, but I don't thinks I be able to go. Right now they's harvestin' goin' on. We be sending out ships 'bout every day."

***

Several days later John went to the dock and asked, "Master Charles, do you think it be all right if my missus can get passage back to Cliveden to visit with her momma?"

Laughing Charles said, "Trying to get rid of her John?"

"No, Sir, but it be 'most two years since she been back. She likes to show off the baby."

"I'll get her passage on the next ship day after tomorrow. Will that be soon enough?"

"Yes Sir. She be mighty glad to get that news when I get's home."

That evening he gave Elizabeth the good news. She didn't care for the idea of traveling without him, but was determined to make the trip.

***

Two days later she arrived at the dock in time for John to carry the baby and the travel bag aboard. With the cargo already loaded, they said goodbye to each other then the ship departed. She stood on deck watching as John waved goodbye.

Remembering her first day at sea coming to New Orleans when she was sick, without John, she hoped it wouldn't be repeated. Getting into the Gulf she was thankful the weather was clear and the sea was calm.

***

Arriving in Biloxi, she walked down the gangway with the baby in one arm, and her travel bag in the other. Jeremiah seeing her quickly took her bag.

"I takes the travel bag, Miss Elizabeth. How's you and John be doin' in New Orleans?"

"We're doing just fine, Jeremiah."

Just then she noticed Arthur bringing David to the dock. Elizabeth, wanting to thank David for the life her and John were able to have due to his generosity, went to speak with him. David was happy to see her and the baby. After embracing Elizabeth, he took the baby in his arms and looked at her, "What name did you give the baby?" he asked.

Hesitating, not knowing what his response would be, she quietly said, "Violet."

Looking at her, he paused for a moment then looked down at the baby. Smiling he said, "Thank you, Elizabeth. That was mighty kind of you. What kind of arrangement did you make for going back to Cliveden?" he asked.

"I thought if Miss Anne was going, I'd like to go with her," she replied.

"I'll make sure you have transportation. Arthur, take them to the house and return for me in about two hours. Tell Thelma to set her up in the room across the hall from mine, and tell Sarah to make something special for dinner tonight."

"I certainly will Master David. Come on Elizabeth, I'll carry your bag," Arthur said escorting her to the coach.

As they passed through town, she recalled how she was able to shop for clothes, and how well she lived in David's house. Thinking about the changes in her life since then with the baby she bore, she realized David was right forcing her away from him. Everything she thought she wanted here, all of a sudden didn't mean very much. Although her life in New Orleans was harder, it was fulfilling.

When the carriage turned into the tree lined street, it all came back as if it was the first time she saw it. When they pulled up in front of the house, Anne and Thelma hastily came down the steps to greet her. As soon as Elizabeth stepped from the coach, Thelma took the baby and began rocking Violet in her arms as if she was her own. Sarah and several other house servants quickly joined them, and made more fuss over the baby than Elizabeth.

"I'm happy you're going with me to Cliveden. I want to get an early start in the morning," Anne said.

They talked the whole afternoon, and during the conversation Anne told Elizabeth Sharon had a baby girl too, and Flora was the one that delivered it.

When David got home, he went to the study to write a letter to Tom bringing him up to date on the business. After Tom's initial financial squeeze, he had extra money to invest, and let David use it to build a partnership. When he was finished, he gave the letter to Anne to deliver then sat down to dinner.

Elizabeth was in the kitchen talking to Sarah, who was still making a fuss over the baby. When Thelma entered the dining room, David asked, "Thelma where's Elizabeth?"

"She's in the kitchen Master David. She's looking in on the baby and wants to get some supper."

"Tell Elizabeth to come in and sit down with Anne and me."

Returning to the kitchen Thelma said, "Elizabeth, Master David wants for you to eat in the dining room with him and Miss Anne."

Elizabeth reluctantly handing the baby to Thelma did as he asked. When she entered the room, David got up from the table. Taking a plate from the china cabinet he set it down for her. A strange feeling came over her and she wondered, *Would he want a visit to his room tonight?* not sure how to act if he asked, she quickly dismissed it. She thought, *If that's what he wanted, he would have never sent me away.*

The conversation at dinner was more like bringing each other up to date, and they talked until Elizabeth heard the baby crying. After leaving the room to attend her, Anne went to her room to finish packing.

When Elizabeth came back to find Anne had retired for the night, she waited for David to speak. He spoke mildly of how he missed her, and how it took a long time to get over their relationship. He told her why he sent her away and knew for her sake, it was the right thing to do.

They talked for awhile and he began to sense nervousness in her voice. Relieving any thought he might want her to visit him he said, "By the way, there's a crib in your room. I had Arthur bring it down from the attic. It's the crib I had made for my baby that died."

All of a sudden she felt like a burden had been lifted off her shoulders. He spoke in a way that reassured her she didn't have to pay him a visit during the night. She thought, *A moment ago you were worried he would ask; now you're sorry he didn't. Best leave it aside for now. It was some-thing that was there in the past, and better stored to memory.*

The next morning while they were at breakfast, the bags were being loaded for the trip. David came downstairs and saw them to the front door, and said aloud as they were getting in the coach, "Anne, if I can get away, I'll join you in a few days.

Chapter 11
The Visit with Flora

Arriving at Cliveden, Miss Sharon, her 2-year old daughter Roselyn, along with Flora and the house-staff greeted them. After Flora opened the coach door, Elizabeth handed her the baby. Taking Violet in her arms Flora began rocking her.

After going inside, Elizabeth went straight to the kitchen with her mother and the baby. Elizabeth, noticing her mother had a helper just as she was to Miss Bertha when she was ailing asked, "Is there anything wrong momma?"

"I haven't been feeling well here lately, but now that you be here I be fine. Elizabeth, this here is Trisha. She came here from South Port just 'bout the time you left. I 'spect your brother Luke has a special eye for her, they be in each other's company whenever they gets a chance. Just the same way you and John used to be."

Trisha was dark complected, about 5'1, and on the heavy side. Embarrassed by what Flora said when Elizabeth asked her mother where Luke was, Trisha boldly answered before Flora could speak. "He be in the fields with' the other hands," looking out the window she continued, "They be back 'bout dusk." Turning to look at Elizabeth she continued, "He ain't the little brother you had when you left out, he's a man now." Elizabeth and Flora looked at each other, then looked at Trisha and began to laugh. They remembered how Elizabeth knew where John was every minute when they were here.

"David and Charles his partner in New Orleans bought us a small house. John runs the dock there for Charles and gets paid for it," Elizabeth said.

Flora quietly remarked, "Saying David and Charles might be fine in New Orleans, but as long as you at Cliveden, its Master David, and Master Charles. Since the war talk started again, Master Tom and Miss Sharon, they act's a little different. Your brother Luke was gettin' kind of free with his talk about freedom up north and almost got whipped for it when Master Tom heard him speak on it."

Looking up from attending Violet, Elizabeth asked, "They changed that much?"

"Seems so, I was hopin' Luke and Trisha might want to jump the broom and start a family just so's they can be together and have a life here."

Elizabeth, turning her attention towards Violet said, "I can hardly believe it! Master Tom and his Missus would change like that, but I'll watch my words while I'm here."

She told them how different Biloxi was compared to Cliveden, and how much better New Orleans was over both places. It was about dinner time when Flora handed Elizabeth a tray of food to be brought into the dining room. She felt as though time had stood still since she left then restarted again. When she brought the tray in no one asked her to take a seat to join them. Remembering what Flora said, she left the room returning to the kitchen where the three of them sat down to eat.

A half hour later, there was a knock on the kitchen door. Trisha hurriedly got up from her chair, knowing at this time of day it could only be one person, Luke. When she opened the door, Luke saw Elizabeth with the baby and hugged her.

"Luke, don't squeeze me to death," Elizabeth said, turning her attention to Trisha, "You're right! He's every bit of a man and not the little brother I saw the day I left."

Luke sat down to hear all about Elizabeth's new life, and was interested in hearing more about how the Negros lived in Biloxi and New Orleans.

"I hear you and John be free; what dat be like?" he excitedly asked.

"After I help clean up the dishes I can tell you all about it," she replied.

"I'll do all the cleaning just so's the three of you can be together," Trisha said.

Elizabeth gave her a look of approval for being considerate and went outside with Flora and Luke.

Walking toward the quarters, Elizabeth said, "Luke, the one thing I miss the most after you and momma, is sittin' around the fire at the old oak tree. Would you light one for me?"

Sitting on the make shift benches, Elizabeth watched as Luke gathered kindling carefully stacking it against the tree. Putting the lighted match to his creation, the flames quickly began to spread along the wood fibers. They watched as the crackling embers periodically sent a column of sparks upward through the branches, and the warmth from the flames took away the chill of the night air. It brought back a lot of memories of when Elizabeth was little, and how they would sit around and listen to Old Moses tell stories. She remembered when her father was alive, how strong he was for his family, and the comfortable feeling of security that only a child knows.

She began telling Luke about her trip to Biloxi, and how slaves walked around free, and the more she spoke, the more attentive he became. Flora becoming concerned that what he was hearing wasn't just an interest in his sister's life, he was hearing something he desperately wanted to be a part of, but for now, that was dangerous.

Elizabeth, intent on telling them what she'd done since leaving Cliveden, temporarily forgot about the baby. Quickly returning to the kitchen with Flora, they saw Trisha sitting in a rocking chair humming, rocking Violet to sleep. Taking the baby Elizabeth said, "You'll make a fine mother."

Being a man, Luke had his own cabin. After saying goodnight to her mother and Trisha, Luke and Elizabeth returned to the quarter. Before settling in for the night she asked, "What I was telling you about New Orleans, it won't make you do anything stupid, like run away would it?"

"No. Momma and Trisha; they be two pretty good reasons to stay."

Feeling a little better with his answer she said before going to bed, "I'll make you breakfast in the morning."

At day break she awoke to Luke getting dressed ready to chop wood for Trisha. He had taken over the job when John left, and for Elizabeth, it was like looking in a mirror. While he was out she made him breakfast, and when he returned, Elizabeth and Flora sat down with him to eat. After a hearty breakfast he left for the fields with the other field hands.

Elizabeth and Flora went back to the big house kitchen where Trisha was already making breakfast for Master Tom, Miss Sharon and Miss Anne. They were in the dining room when Elizabeth went in.

"Are there many changes since you lived here Elizabeth?" Miss Sharon asked.

"Other than Luke being grown, everything seems the same Miss Sharon."

Scanning them seated at the table she thought, *if what my momma said was true about your attitudes, it would make all the difference in the world. If it wasn't for seeing my mother and Luke, I would have just as well stayed in New Orleans.*

***

The following week David came as he promised. Tom was particularly anxious for his arrival because he was bringing the proceeds from his investments in the shipping business. Using some of Tom's money, David purchased the ships they used to transport cargo cutting out the middle man. Upon arrival he told Tom, "I had one of our ships converted for longer sea voyages to England. Most of the cotton is processed there and we carry back the finished bolts of cloth to the north where most of the manufacturing of clothing is done. Tom, if you could raise more cotton it's a better money maker even with the expense of a longer voyage."

Tom replied, "I have a chance to buy more land from the South Port Plantation. As long as I can get enough people to grow it, I'll be willing."

"Approximately how many more would you need? I can get them in New Orleans," David said.

"If I can open up three more fields, about 10 or 12 should do."

"Isn't it too late in the season to plant?" David asked.

"It's too late this year, but in a few weeks we could start clearing the fields to plant crops in the spring."

Tom left the room to tend the business of the plantation, and David sat finishing his breakfast. When he was alone, Elizabeth came in to say hello. Looking up he asked, "Well, Elizabeth, how are you enjoying your visit?"

"I'm glad to see my family, and Luke; he's so big I could hardly recognize him. It seems like he's thinking about marrying Trisha the cook."

"I'll mention it to Tom, but I don't know how much influence it would be with Miss Sharon."

Sharon had gained quite a bit of weight after the baby, obviously enjoying the cooking done by Flora and Trisha.

"Are you ready to return to New Orleans?" David asked.

"Yes, I think so," she replied.

With Trisha taking over the kitchen, Elizabeth was able to spend more time with her mother and brother and the two weeks went by quickly.

During the time David was there, Tom was able to show him the land he was going to purchase and all the improvements made at Cliveden since David's last visit.

"I'll have to leave in the morning. Let me know when you can use the extra field hands," David said.

The following morning after saying goodbye, they were about to get in the coach when Elizabeth noticed the way Flora was holding Violet. It appeared without actually saying it she was begging Elizabeth to stay.

As the coach pulled away, Elizabeth turned to look back. She saw her mother wiping the tears from her eyes with the corner of her apron just as she did the first time Elizabeth left. She felt bad about leaving, but realized as probably her mother, Elizabeth had her own family now.

Chapter 12
John

In two days they were in Biloxi. Elizabeth and the baby stayed a few nights at David's until the next ship came in. While Elizabeth was there news reached David that one of his ships hadn't reached port. It was two days overdue and he went to the dock to find out more from Jeremiah. He was told there hadn't been any storms since they left, and no one knew why the vessel hadn't made port. David, anxious to find out why, was able to get passage on another vessel heading for New Orleans, and quickly boarded the ship. The whole time at sea he slept very little wondering what could have possibly happened.

***

Docking in New Orleans, he was stunned to see the charred hull of his ship tied to the bollards of another dock. After disembarking, he ran to his own dock to find out what happened. There had obviously been a fire, and as he walked onto the dock he was approached by Charles.

"Charles, what happened?" David asked anxiously waiting his reply.

"A fire broke out during the night after the crew unloaded the cargo. John was the first one on board and tried to put out the blaze," suddenly Charles' exuberance to tell David turned to sorrow. Looking down as if the next few words were lodged in his voice-box fighting against being spoken, he said, "I'm sorry to say David; John was trapped by the flames below deck and died in the fire."

Stunned, David's first thought was, *how was he going to tell Elizabeth?* Booking passage on the next ship back to Biloxi, he wasn't looking forward to the task.

***

Upon arriving he told Jeremiah what had happened, and Jeremiah asked, "Master David, what we gonna do for somebody runnin' things in New Orleans? John was the best you had."

"You'll have to take his place temporarily until I can find a replacement. I thought about bringing Elizabeth's brother Luke from Cliveden. He would have to learn as John did, but I could eventually send him to New Orleans. It will also be a comfort to Elizabeth having Luke there."

Before getting in the coach, he told Arthur what happened. After seeing Arthur's shocked reaction, he wondered how bad it would be telling Elizabeth.

When he walked in the front door she confronted him immediately wanting to know what happened. In his absence, she found out he had gone to New Orleans to see why the ship hadn't come in. In almost a week that it took for him to return, for her, it seemed like an eternity. Taking Elizabeth by the hand into the study he poured her a brandy. She knew something terrible had happened, and was becoming increasingly impatient wanting to hear the bad news.

"Elizabeth, the reason I was gone so long, I had to go to New Orleans," pausing for a moment he continued, "I found out there had been a fire on board one of his ships when it was tied to the dock," hesitating again, "There's no easy way to tell you this, but trying to put out the blaze, John died in the fire."

She froze at his words for a moment then let out a blood curdling scream. "No! No! Not my John!" She screamed, her legs collapsing beneath her breaking the glass as she fell to the floor. He rang for Thelma who heard the scream, and was already opening the door with Anne close behind. Picking her up, he laid her on the sofa. Anne excitedly asked, "What happened? What's wrong?"

After telling them about John, they both looked at Elizabeth lying on the sofa wondering how she would ever cope. Getting smelling salts from the cabinet he waived it under her nose. As she came to, she said in a daze, "I had a bad feeling about going to Cliveden by myself, I'm partly to blame."

"That's not true," David quickly replied.

"It was providence child. It would have happened even if you didn't go," Thelma added.

"Is there anything I can do Elizabeth?" he asked.

Crying, she replied, "No David, I just want to be alone with my baby for awhile."

"Elizabeth, I was thinking about bringing Luke here to learn the same as John, then transferring him to New Orleans so you wouldn't be alone. How would that be?" he asked.

Not answering, he realized although he was speaking, she wasn't really hearing him still trying to comprehend her loss.

"Thelma, take care of her and the baby," David said before leaving the room.

Elizabeth looked up at David and said, "No David, Violet's the only family I have now. I just want to be alone with her."

With that, Anne, Thelma, and David left the room.

***

For the next few days Thelma took care of the baby while Elizabeth tried to gather enough strength to map out a future. She wondered, *would her and John been better off staying at Cliveden? There, everyone was like family. When someone died everyone else in the quarter made a difference.*

David knew what she was going through having to do the same with the loss of his wife and child. Avoiding conversation or questions about what she planned, he knew like himself, she would eventually get around to talking about it. The baby kept her busy and she thanked David several times for what he was doing for them.

"I mentioned it to you before, but I know you weren't hearing me. I'm thinking about bringing Luke here to learn how to run the dock just like John. After he learns how to do it, I'll send him on to New Orleans to run the dock there. At least you'll have a family member close by," David said.

"Luke and Trisha the cook planned on getting married. I wouldn't want to see them split up on account of me," she replied.

"I wasn't only thinking of your position, but my own as well. I need someone there and don't have anyone in mind I feel I could trust. There's going to be 10 more people added to the field hands at Cliveden, and within the week I'll be going there. If you feel strong enough to go I'll take you with me."

"Thank you, David. That might be a good idea."

***

A few days later he arranged for Jeremiah to bring the new field hands to Cliveden, and traveled with Elizabeth and the baby while Anne stayed home. When they reached Cliveden they were met by Sharon, wondering why Elizabeth returned. After David told her about the fire, he said, "I thought it would be better for Elizabeth to return and be with her mother for awhile."

Sharon replied looking at Elizabeth, "I'm so sorry for your loss. Your mother will be sorry too, but you being here will be a comfort to both of you."

When the door opened to the kitchen, Flora and Trisha were surprised to see Elizabeth standing in the doorway with the baby. Realizing something was terribly wrong Flora excitedly asked, "Why did you come back? What happened?"

Repeating the story over and over became burdensome for Elizabeth, and each time she had to repeat it her eyes would well up with tears.

"John died in a fire on the ship at the dock in New Orleans. David told me he was thinking about bringing Luke back with him to train for the same job. I'd like to stay here for awhile," looking up from Violet she continued, "I just want us to be around people I know."

A look of fright came over Trisha's face, and she asked, "Do you think Master David would let us marry up first, so's I could go with him?"

"I don't know but I'll ask. I can take over in the kitchen here with Momma," Elizabeth replied.

Luke, hearing about Elizabeth's return, went to the back door, knocked, then stepped in. Putting his arms around Elizabeth, he gave her a pat on the back, "I heard 'bout John, I'm sorry," pausing, "Least he knew what it be like to be free, something I dreamed of all my life."

Flora angrily replied shaking her finger, "I dun told you befo', don't you be lettin' Master Tom hear you speak on that. You almost got whipped for it last time... 'member!"

"Momma, I heard some slaves at the cotton market, they be talkin' 'bout people running away north," turning he asked, "Elizabeth, you know where 'dat be?"

Flora quickly snapped back, "They ain't never been an overseer since I been here and I hear Master Tom talkin' on it to Miss Sharon 'bout hirin' one. Don't you 'member what's happened to Harvey when he up and run away?"

"You mean Harvey from the quarter?" Elizabeth asked, looking up from attending Violet.

"Yeah, the same Harvey you growed up with," Flora replied.

"What happened?" Elizabeth asked with a concerned look.

"He ran away. After he was catched, he was whipped then got sold to Dumont, and Bein' sold to them, is like bein' whipped each and every day."

"When we lived in New Orleans, John sometimes came home and told me about the auctions at the dock. Some of them were sold to Dumont," continuing after handing Flora the baby, "John said he heard the first time you run away from Dumont it's a whippin'. The second time it's chains around your ankles and a whippin'. The third time, you just don't come back." Looking at Flora she asked, "Momma is that the reason you thought Master Tom changed?"

"No, he changed after Miss Sharon's baby was born. That's when she started drinkin' whiskey. When Master Tom cut her off she started eating and put on too much weight. That's when the arguments began. That's 'bout the time they both changed," Flora explained.

Elizabeth, looking at Luke, reminded him, "Remember what you promised about not doing anything stupid?"

"Yes, and I don't know what I do if I'm told to go back with Master David," he replied.

"We'll talk on that later. Bring my bag down to the quarter. I'll stay with you while I'm here, just to keep an eye on you," Elizabeth said.

That evening when Trisha was serving dinner, she heard Master David say, "Tom, the new people for the cotton fields will arrive tomorrow afternoon. Think about what I mentioned. With the extra hands you won't need Luke. He can go back with me and eventually be the replacement in New Orleans. He's someone we can trust."

While Trisha was bringing more food to the table she moved slower straining to hear as much of the conversation as possible. As she was leaving the room she couldn't hear the last few words; they were inaudible. Whatever was being said was about Luke and it concerned their future. She thought, *What Elizabeth told him about living in Biloxi or New Orleans, would it mean more to him being there than with her? If he gets there and enjoys the feeling of being more independent, will he still want us to have a life together?* All of a sudden these were questions she couldn't be sure she knew the answers to, and felt uneasy thinking about it.

After dinner the table was cleared and Trisha asked, "Miss Flora, could I go down to the quarter with you and speak with Luke?"

"If you wait a couple minutes we can go together," Flora replied.

After straightening the kitchen they walked out the back door and down the path toward the quarter. En route Trisha told Flora what

Master David said. Collecting her thoughts, Flora didn't answer for a few seconds; then stopped. Grasping Trisha by the arm she said, "Don't you go mentioning anything 'bout it to Luke... not tonight anyways."

As they continued walking to the cabin, the night air was cool and Flora pulled her shawl tighter around her neck. When they got to the cabin Luke had already lit a fire in the cook stove and Elizabeth already had a kettle of water on for tea. While she was rocking the baby to sleep the tea began to boil. Trisha took the baby, laying her in the crib while Elizabeth poured the tea. In spite of what Flora told her about being silent Trisha couldn't contain her fear any longer.

"Luke, I heard Master David talkin' 'bout taking you to Biloxi when he leaves out tomorrow."

"You don't say 'dat soon?" he replied.

"Yeah. Dat's what they was sure 'nough talkin' 'bout."

Flora looked at Trisha with contempt for violating her wishes but Luke replied putting Flora at ease, "I already dun' spoke to Master David. He told me he don't mind if I brings you after I learned what he wants me to know."

Feeling better about being included in his conversation with Master David, the burden of worry was lifted off Trisha's shoulders. They talked for about an hour until Flora said, "Trisha, we best be gettin' on up to the big house, it's gettin' late."

Flora kissed the baby then they left.

Next morning before Luke left for the field Master Tom told Solomon and Sam, "Ten new people are coming this afternoon. Solomon, I want you to stay in the quarter and wait till they arrive. After they get fed, take them on up to the field. I want everybody to help clear the trees and brush for the cotton I want planted in the spring. Both of you will be responsible that it gets done."

"Don't worry, Master Tom. We see's to it. Them extra hands, they surely will help," Solomon replied.

After his conversation with Master Tom, Solomon went into his cabin to ask his wife to make a pot of cornmeal so the men could eat when they arrive.

Getting there later than expected, Solomon took them to the barn. Looking over the group he said, "Ya'll be beddin' down here for the night just till we can make spaces for ya."

After putting their meager belongings in the barn Solomon commanded, "Follow me on up to my cabin. My missus dun made some cornmeal so's you can eat."

While they were eating Tom and David walked over to get a look at the men. Looking over the group Tom said, "I won't stand for anyone who takes to running away, and I won't give you a second chance. If you run you'll be sold to Dumont."

After he walked away, Solomon hitched up the flat wagon and loaded it with extra shovels and picks. Pulling up in front of his cabin so the new hands could get on, one of the men asked, "Solomon, what kind of master he be?"

Climbing up on the wagon seat he replied, "So far, they ain't never been an overseer on the place. Only two people tried running away 'dat I ever knew," pulling up his shirt to show them his back, he said, "And I be one of them!"

"Why ain't you get sold to 'dat place -Dumont?" another asked.

"That's where I thought I was suppose' to be sold when it weren't me at all. It was just somebody startin' trouble."

Another man said, "The plantation I come from had an overseer 'dat be hard on everybody. One day when he be whippin' up on someone in the barn, one of the other slaves dun' hit him with a board."

"What happened then?" another asked.

"He ain't never come out. They dun' hung him in there."

The wagon pulled away and when it got to the field, the men got off taking the tools with them. Solomon pointed out what had to be done, and Sam who was already there had them follow him. There were about two hours of daylight left and when the sun was almost down everyone began walking back to the quarter.

When they got there Master Tom asked, "Solomon, did the new men do their fair share of work?"

Solomon took off his dusty hat and slapped it against his thigh replying, "Well Master Tom, I can't rightly tell with just two hours of daylight. Best we wait till tomorrow night for 'dat answer."

"I'm counting on you and Sam. Now don't let me down," Tom said before taking his leave.

Later that evening Tom told Luke, "Get your things; you'll be going to Biloxi tomorrow with Master David."

Excited, Luke ran to the big house kitchen to tell Trisha.

"I'm gonna miss you and hopes you can bring me soon," she said giving him a kiss.

"Master David if it's all right with you I'd like to stay at Cliveden for a little longer," Elizabeth asked.

"It's fine with me if it's alright with Miss Sharon," he replied.

"I already asked and she said it was okay."

"That's fine Elizabeth. I think it will do you both good."

The next morning Tom saw them off, but Sharon stayed in her bedroom and didn't bother coming down until they were gone.

Chapter 13

Trouble in New Orleans

In two days they arrived at Biloxi. Like John and Elizabeth, Luke was surprised that everything Elizabeth told him was true. Looking around, it seemed so much better than he imagined. He rode up front of the coach with Arthur during the trip and when they arrived at the dock David asked Luke to climb down.

"Luke, I want to introduce you to Jeremiah. He's the head man here," David said.

"Jeremiah, this is Luke, Elizabeth's brother. He'll eventually take John's place in New Orleans. Teach him what he's supposed to know just like you taught John."

Jeremiah was closer in age to John when he came but by Luke being much younger, Jeremiah realized he may have a problem with the other dock hands. It would all depend on his attitude. For now they considered him another dumb field hand like John when he arrived, until he proved himself.

"Luke, Elizabeth wanted me to make sure you learn everything as quickly as possible so you could get to New Orleans with Trisha," David said.

"Yes Sir, Master David. I sure do my best," he replied.

Getting back in the coach, David left for home. Upon arrival Thelma greeted him, "Master David you have a few letters from New Orleans, one was delivered by special messenger."

The idea of a letter being delivered by special messenger always held a connotative tone preceding disaster. Wondering what it could be, he hurried into the study to open it. It was from Charles, his partner in New Orleans. It read that Charles suspected three dock hands stowed away on one of the ships bound for England. The fugitive slave law was still in effect here and slaves that were caught going north could be brought back to the state or territory where they came from. It was in itself, a deterrent from running away but sometimes challenged. Some were successfully settled in the north, but the majority were caught and returned, given back like a stolen piece of property. Not wanting to take a chance on being brought back, the three that stowed away decided to go to England where slavery had been abolished years before.

Abolitionist fervor in the north was high and people that were stirring it didn't realize it only made the noose of control tighter with slaves still wearing the yoke of bondage. There had been plenty that tried going north from different plantations, even around Cliveden, but were eventually brought back.

"Thelma, I'll be leaving for New Orleans on the next ship. It's due in day after tomorrow. Would you pack my bag? I'll need enough clothes to last a few days."

Looking down at David opening another letter she asked, "Master David was that special delivery letter important?"

"My partner in New Orleans wrote that three people from the dock crew were missing. He believes they stowed away on a ship bound for England."

Thelma, walking out of the room expressed her thoughts aloud, "I can't rightly understands them runnin' away from a place where they ain't bein' mistreated. I surely hopes no more take up to runnin'."

With a smile David said, "I'm going up to lay down for awhile. Wake me when dinner's ready."

In an hour Thelma went up and knocked lightly at his bedroom door. Opening it, she peeked in quietly saying, "Master David, dinner's ready."

"Thank you Thelma. I'll be down shortly."

After dressing he went to the dining room and sat down to dinner with Anne. Finishing, he got up and poured a brandy from the liquor cabinet and said, "Anne, I know you don't drink, but sometimes I hate to drink alone. Do you want one?"

Hesitating for a moment as if she needed a drink before asking a sensitive question, she replied, "Yes David. There's something I want to talk to you about. While I was at Cliveden I met the son of the owner of Five Oaks Plantation. His name is Beau...Beau Henry. He came to Cliveden on business a few times. On one of his visits he invited Tom, Sharon and me to a house party. While we were there he asked me for permission to speak to you about courting me."

Swirling the brandy in his glass David watched the contents as it revolved around. Realizing she was anxiously awaiting his answer he finally said, "The next time I get to Cliveden I'll send for him and he can ask."

Anne quickly replied, "I told him you probably couldn't tell when you would be back so he's going to send you a letter."

"Then I'll wait to read his letter. In the mean time, I have important business in New Orleans and have to go there the day after tomorrow."

Pleased he was at least agreeable, she left the room knowing by the time he returned the letter would probably be there.

∗∗∗

Two days later he boarded the ship Caroline to take him to New Orleans. The name of the captain was Captain Taylor. Taylor was in his mid 40's with salt and pepper black hair. Thin and about six feet tall, his British accent added to his authoritative demeanor. He ran cargo from Jamaica and Cuba to New Orleans and cities as far north as Boston and New York.

At dinner one evening Captain Taylor said, "David, far be it from me to tell you how to run your affairs. With the temptation of slaves running away to England where they can experience real freedom, I can only see your situation getting worse. Most of the dock owners in New Orleans are thinking since they had so many trying to leave, they're favoring a plan to free them and pay them a small salary. New Orleans is different from Biloxi."

"What do you mean by that?" David asked.

"It's a larger center of commerce and has a larger population of free Negros. It's been that way for a long time. If people that worked the dock were freed and paid a small salary, they would feel independent and have to pay for their own food and housing."

David looking up from his plate replied, "That sounds like a pretty good idea. I'll speak to Charles about it when we dock."

During the voyage he recognized one of the ship's crew who helped on Captain Jarvis' vessel the night of the storm. Remembering him from several sailings he asked, "Joseph, do you have any ideas on how to handle the runaways?"

"Master David, Captn's right. If you freed them and gives them a little money to work you could build some small houses close to the dock. They could rents them and with the little extra money they be makin', they probably won't be runnin' off," pausing for a moment he continued, "and you be gettin' back some of the money you be payin' them too."

Surprised he had a similar answer as Captain Taylor, David gave it serious thought. After reaching port he got together with Charles at a pub to discuss it.

"Charles, Captain Taylor said he thought it was a good idea to free the dock hands and suggested we give them a wage. I asked one of the crew, a darkie I knew by the name of Joseph what his thoughts were. He said the same and suggested we build housing and charge them rent. That way we'll be recapturing some of our money and won't have to be responsible for their keep. It sounded reasonable to me. What do you think?"

Thinking for a moment he replied, "That's a good plan. We already own a piece of land not far from the dock. We could make arrangements to have a few houses erected there. Some of the men that worked the dock could marry like Elizabeth and John and have a place to raise a family. I think it would also make for a better working environment too."

After toasting the idea, they went back to the dock to speak to Nehemiah, who had taken over as head dock foreman after John was killed.

"Nehemiah, have everyone gather around I have something to say," David said.

Climbing up on a crate Nehemiah called out to the dock hands, "Ya'll gather round, Master David has somethin' to tell us."

Looking at one another not knowing what to expect, they did as he asked. Nehemiah stepped down and David got up on the crate to address them, "I'm drawing up papers to make all of you free." Looking over the group he continued, "I'm making plans to pay you for working the dock and I'm having some houses built where you can live."

Silently they looked at one another. What they were hearing came as a shock. No more threats of getting sent to Dumont for running away, money for working on the dock, could this be true?

David continued, "Charles and I hope you'll stay and try the new system before deciding to run off. Other dock owners have already started doing it, and it seems to be working."

Nehemiah had enough courage to say, "Master David, that's why they stowed away. If this was dun befo' they might not have run off."

It was 1858 and most slave owners around cities had already freed their people. Outlying plantations still kept slaves to keep the plantations going, but with the amount of runaways, most plantation owners realized that time was rapidly coming to an end.

***

The two weeks David was there he saw to it his plans were put in motion and drafted paperwork giving the men their freedom. The effect was immediate. It seemed in doing so, gave them an added sense of responsibility to their job and they looked forward to getting paid. Before leaving for Biloxi, David enlisted a carpenter to build the houses on the ground he and Charles owned, not far from the dock.

"Charles, if you no longer need me I'd like to get back to Biloxi. I have other matters to attend to."

"I think I have everything under control David. I don't think I'll need you. If anything comes up I'll write."

Departing on the next ship, David returned home.

***

After arriving, Anne anxiously greeted him at the door excitedly saying, "There's a few letters on your desk. One of them is from Beau. Did you take care of the problems in New Orleans?"

Scanning the letters he looked up replying, "They've been solved for the present but I'm not sure for how long."

Following him to the study she stood patiently waiting for him to open Beau's letter. Realizing her impatience he slowly examined each one putting Beau's letter at the bottom of the stack. Trying to avoid eye contact to keep from laughing he pretended not to notice her impatience. The wait became too much to contain and she shouted, "Damn it, David! I've been waiting for eight days since that letter came for you to open it. Please! Don't keep me in suspense any longer."

Laughing he took it from the bottom. Opening it, it was penned eloquently and David realized immediately Beau must have been well educated. It read like a formal request to court Anne and after he finished reading, Anne anxiously asked, "What did he have to say?"

"Beau wants to come to Biloxi and make the request face to face rather than just send this cold letter. I'm impressed; especially with the last few lines. If his demeanor is as eloquent as his pen, I'll give my whole hearted approval."

Snatching the letter from his hand she clasped it to her breasts then spun around like a ballet dancer and with a heartfelt gesture hugged David.

Before she could leave the room he said, "Better than waiting for him to come here, let's make arrangements to go to Cliveden so I can meet this paragon of your admiration."

"Do you mean it? Do you really mean it David? ...We're really going to Cliveden?"

"Yes, get your things ready. We'll leave tomorrow."

Quickly leaving the room, she met Thelma in the hall. "Thelma! Thelma, we're going to Cliveden in the morning. Help me pack."

Thelma remarked, "You young girls needs to know sometin'. Even if yo' heart tells you to be excited... always act like you be doin' him the favor. Go on upstairs now. I'll help you packs for the trip."

David listening to what Thelma said, laughed to himself thinking, *How boring life would be in the house without her,* then sat down to open the rest of the letters.

Most were correspondence from friends. However, one of the letters was of some concern. It was from a friend who owned a plantation just outside of Hattiesburg, Mississippi. He mentioned a slave revolt where the overseer and owner of a plantation were killed and the slaves were quickly caught and publicly hung. It went on to explain it made for a bad experience and long time slaves that had always been loyal were being cast in the same lot as the ones making trouble. The letter further explained the townspeople would sometimes harass them when they ventured away from the plantation. His friend expressed concern of how Tom's plantation was doing and whether he or the other owners near him had any trouble.

Taking a paper and pen from the drawer, David wrote a reply about the trouble he had in New Orleans and what he did to try to remedy the problem. After adding a few words about Anne and her intended, he sealed it and gave it to Arthur to post.

In the morning David was awaken by Anne in the hallway outside his room. "Thelma, did you pack my pink chiffon dress? Did you remember to pack the peach colored gloves?" she said, going on and on in a flurry asking questions.

Thelma replied, "Lawd! Lawd, you in such a fuss to see this Master Beau! I 'spect you be pulling the horse and coach to Cliveden, all by yourself."

At breakfast, Anne only took a few bites of food anxious to get started. Thelma was coaching Anne on how to act when she sees Beau as David came down the stairs. He interrupted saying, "Thelma if any more special delivery letters come, have them sent to Cliveden. I'll be there for several weeks."

"Yes, sir, Master David; I'll be sure to do that."

Arthur brought the coach around front and loaded the luggage. Opening the door of the coach, David helped Anne in.

"Arthur, drive by the dock. I want to make sure everything's alright before we head out," David said.

When they arrived David spoke to Jeremiah, "I'll be at Cliveden for several weeks. If anything important happens, let Thelma know so she can forward the message."

"I will Master David. Don't you be worryin' none," Jeremiah replied.

Luke came over to the coach and asked, "Master David could you tell Miss Trisha I'm doin' fine and misses her?"

"Luke I'll do just that. Now pay attention to everything Jeremiah teaches you, and before long, you'll be able to tell her yourself."

With that said, David told Arthur to start out, "Drive by a few docks so I can speak with some of the other owners," he asked. Everyone David spoke to seemed to agree with what he was doing in New Orleans, and they decided to form a business council to discuss any future problems that may arise. At each stop, Anne sat impatiently waiting until he was through, and after the last stop she was happy they were finally on their way.

During the trip it started to rain and a cool rain in the winter can be uncomfortable. Anne didn't seem to mind the weather anticipating the prospect of a marriage at some point in the near future. A small thin girl due to her premature birth, she was ill most of her young life. David kept a heavy blanket in the coach and insisted she keep it wrapped around her for most of the trip.

***

When they arrived, they were met by Tom and Sharon. Anne and David were supposed to have been there several days ago, and without word, Tom wondered what was wrong. After going in the house, David and Tom went into the study so David could bring him up to date about what was taking place in Biloxi and New Orleans.

"Tom, I think I solved the problem with the runaways. It's going to require additional money at first and for a short time be less profitable. After the initial cost though, there will be less responsibility for having to feed and house the dock hands. With the rent they'll be paying, in a sense, we'll be getting most of our money back. The other dock owners agreed with me and began doing the same. We decided to form a group to discuss any future problems."

"That sounds like it might work David. Thanks for taking the initiative to get it done."

Changing the subject David asked, "Tom, about Beau Henry from Five Oaks. What's he like?"

"I've known the Henry family since I bought Cliveden. I've had several business transactions with his father Simon that were amicable. Beau's a graduate from a university in Charleston. He's a friend of Sharon's brother Franklin. They graduated at the same time. He seemed to be very sincere when he asked about Anne, but I told him you were the eldest in the family. He would have to speak with you."

"I received a well written letter from him. I'm anxious to meet him in person," David said.

Just then there was a gentle knock on the door. It slowly opened to Anne asking in a low tone, "Can I come in?"

"Come in, we were just discussing Beau. What do you think Tom? How should we respond to his request?" David asked.

"I think a formal house party would be in order. Sharon could make out a list of people she thinks should attend. Anne you'll find fancy writing paper in the top drawer of my desk."

Anxiously opening the drawer, she searched for stationary. Finding the one she liked she hurriedly left the room. They could hear her in the hall calling out, "Sharon! Sharon! David said we should have a formal house party for me and Beau. Would you help me write the invitations?"

"We'll start writing them after dinner," Sharon replied.

Just then Elizabeth came in the back door. Seeing Miss Anne they greeted each other with a hug and Anne told her the good news.

"That's fine Miss Anne. I hope you'll be very happy."

"How's Violet?" Anne asked.

"She has a cold. I didn't want to bring her outside, so she's with a friend at the quarter."

"It's no wonder with all this damp cold weather. I thought I was going to catch my death in that coach. I had to keep a blanket wrapped around me the whole trip from Biloxi," Anne said.

Dinner was about ready and Elizabeth helped set the table. Going into the dining room she saw David.

"Hello Master David. How's everyone at home?" she asked.

"Thelma keeps everyone on their toes," he replied.

Elizabeth smiled reminiscing, "I miss being in Thelma's company. She sure could make a bad day seem better."

David told her about the problems in New Orleans and how he missed John running things. Stopping for a moment listening to his words, she remembered it hadn't been that long ago since John was alive and how she missed the comfortable feeling she once had.

"I'll be here for several weeks. I'll enjoy speaking with you again," David said.

After the food was set in place everyone sat down to dinner. The conversation was light and Anne did most of the talking about her upcoming party. The invitations were written and sent out to the people Sharon thought should be invited. It included invitations to all the plantation owners within several miles of Cliveden. It was the beginning of December and Anne wanted it to be held just before Christmas, her favorite time of year.

Chapter 14
The Engagement

It was Saturday and although the sun was shining, there was a cool breeze in the air. When Beau arrived for the engagement party, Tom introduced David to him and his father and mother. Beau was 6' tall, 27 years old with brown hair, and had the physique of someone who hadn't done much physical work. His father Simon was around 5' 10" balding and on the portly side. Amy Henry was Beau's mother. She had graying hair and was slightly heavy. Around five feet two, she appeared to be a perfect match for Beau's father Simon. Saying a few words after the introduction, they went into the study. After David spoke with Beau he seemed to be every bit the person David imagined. When Beau asked formally about courting Anne, David gave his wholehearted approval.

After shaking hands, the men went into the study and Amy joined the women. Going into the study, Tom went to the cabinet and poured a brandy to toast the occasion. After the toast they returned to the other guests gathered in the hall awaiting the announcement. In a few minutes Anne came graciously sweeping down the stairs and about two steps from the bottom, she stopped where Beau joined her. Standing side by side Beau placed an engagement ring on her finger. Everyone clapped at the occasion and Anne announced their wedding would take place in the spring. After her announcement, she came down the stairs mingling with the guests proudly showing off her engagement ring.

After the announcement, most of the men retired to the study and resumed the conversation about the secessionist movement in South Carolina, and how it might affect them. David mentioned the trouble he had with the shipping business and what they did to remedy it. He knew things were different for plantation owners. Their livelihood came from the profits of mainly two crops, cotton, and tobacco, both requiring a large work force. Unlike shipping, a plantation's success was not only subject to prices, they were also subject to labor and favorable weather conditions. Large established plantations with little or no overhead were fine, but the smaller ones like Tom's which were newly established, couldn't weather a financial loss if it presented itself.

"Beau, have you heard from Franklin, Sharon's brother at Belmont?"

David asked.

"I heard from him several weeks ago. He told me they had some slaves run away, but the majority stayed. They never mistreated their people and there wasn't much need for them to leave."

Simon remarked with confidence, "I think the word being passed around about brutal overseers may have exacerbated the problem."

David candidly replied, "The attitudes are different even between people in New Orleans and Biloxi. I think the hostility for some reason is more of an attitude with people that don't even own slaves."

The main dining room had been cleared for the engagement party and the men in the study could hear the music.

"For now it's a lot to think about and the ladies are probably wondering where we are," Tom said.

"I think you're right Tom," David replied.

Opening the door they joined the women.

The sun shining in the afternoon made it worthy of a walk around the grounds and some of the guests took advantage of it admiring the flowers still alive in December.

At dusk, most of the guest's carriages were brought to the front and after being thanked by Tom and Sharon for coming, they departed.

Anne saw Beau and his parents to their carriage, and before it departed Beau said quietly, "Miss Anne I haven't left yet but I'm already anxious for our next meeting."

After kissing the back of her hand he got in the carriage and it pulled away.

Anne watched until the carriage passed the front gate and disappear into the darkness. After going inside, she did a few swirls in the hall imitating still being in Beau's arms thinking, *The next time I see him will be at Five Oaks in two weeks where we're invited to spend Christmas.*

David and Tom seeing how happy she was; went into the study for a nightcap. They talked about the funds being spent on their shipping business, and after discussing it for an hour, Tom yawned. After covering his mouth he said, "David it's been a long day. I'm going to retire for the evening."

"Goodnight Tom," he replied.

Elizabeth helping gather glasses used by the guests came into the study. Looking at David she remarked, "Miss Anne sure looked happy about where she's going to live after they get married."

"I guess so," he replied.

He didn't quite know for sure, but suspected Elizabeth had more to say. Not wanting further conversation he left the room.

***

A few days went by and Trisha asked, "Master David, how's Luke doing?"

"He's doing as well as John when he first arrived. At the rate he's learning you'll be with him in no time."

She smiled then David asked looking around the room, "Where's Flora?"

"Elizabeth's baby's been real sick. She got worse yesterday so Miss Flora went on down to the quarter to stay with the baby," Trisha replied.

The thought came immediately to David's mind, *"Maybe that's why Elizabeth wanted to talk the other night?"* Feeling bad that may have been the case, he hurriedly went out the back door and down to her cabin. After knocking he stepped in.

"Elizabeth has the doctor been here?" he asked.

Flora promptly answered for her, "No Master David. Master Tom never sent for one. Miss Sharon use to come down whenever anyone got the misery, but she don't do that anymore either."

"What changed all that?" he asked annoyingly.

"When her baby was about a year, Miss Sharon came down with a sickness after visiting someone in the quarter. She thought she might have passed it on to her baby too. Her baby got real sick. Almost died:"

Raising his voice David replied, "That shouldn't have anything to do with getting a doctor." Annoyed he rushed outside. "Arthur, saddle a horse for me please. I'll fetch the doctor."

Doctor Cook's home was a few miles away and after getting there David discovered he had just left on another visit. Before returning home, he left a message with the servant for Doctor Cook to come to Cliveden immediately upon his return.

On the ride back a cold rain began to fall. Getting to Elizabeth's cabin he went in.

"Elizabeth, I went for the doctor. He'll be here later. He's on another visit."

"Thank you Master David." Seeing he was drenched she said, "You best be getting to the house and get out of those wet clothes before you catch your death. Get in a hot tub and get something warm in you."

When he walked in through the kitchen, Trisha seeing he was soaked, put on several pots of water to boil.

"After they boil Master David I'll bring them up to your room."

"Thank you Trisha. I want to get out of these wet clothes."

After the water warmed she put it in the tub and gave him a glass of brandy. He drank it then slid into the warm water. It felt good to take the chill off and drinking the brandy warmed him through and through. In a half hour he was comfortable again. After drying he dressed and went downstairs.

"Where have you been?" Tom asked.

"I went to get the doctor for Elizabeth's baby. Why didn't someone help her?" he angrily asked.

"Sharon refuses to go there as long as she has a young child she might pass something on to. It happened once when she was a year old and we almost lost her," Tom replied.

"I know, Flora told me, but that's no reason for not summoning the doctor," he sternly replied.

"You're right David, but I didn't realize the baby was that sick. Elizabeth never said anything."

They were in the study for about an hour when the doctor arrived. Stepping from the study David said, "Doctor Cook, the child that's sick is down in the quarter. I'll take you there."

After examining Violet Dr. Cook said, "This baby has pneumonia; she's pretty sick. Why didn't anyone call on me sooner?" he chided looking at everyone. Without getting an answer he instructed Elizabeth on what to do, leaving medication to be rubbed on Violet's chest. "I'll stop by again the day after tomorrow," he said before leaving.

David thanked him for coming and paid him for his visit. Seeing that he couldn't be of any further assistance, David was ready to leave when Flora grabbed his hand. Holding it tightly she said, "You did so much for my family Master David, we could never repay you."

"You don't have to thank me. I'm just sorry it took so long to have the doctor come. You people are like family."

Smiling at his comment Elizabeth thanked him as well before he left.

Walking up the hill to the house, the rain stopped and the sun began to shine. Looking up at the clearing sky he thought, *It's a good omen, Violet will be fine.*

***

Christmas was a few days later and they were making plans to join Beau's family for the holiday. They were invited to stay a few days and although David didn't feel comfortable in unfamiliar surroundings, he went for Anne's sake.

They arrived at Five Oaks, a plantation built in the early 1700's that had been in the Henry family for almost 150 years. It was a large white very impressive home with a Grecian portico and round pillars almost as high as the main roof, similar to Cliveden, a design fashionable at the time they were built.

As they rode past the quarter David noticed there were more cabins than Cliveden. He didn't know how many people they had on the plantation currently, but realized in years past the amount of slaves had to number over 40.

Pulling up to the front steps they were greeted by Mr. and Mrs. Henry along with Beau and several of the guests that arrived earlier. Anne had been anxious since the engagement party to see Beau again, and being able to stay for several days, to her, was a real fantasy.

After the house servants settled their travel bags in their rooms everyone came down to the parlor. Beau and Anne were admiring the Christmas tree enjoying eggnog, when David and Tom entered the room.

"Beau do you intend on staying at Five Oaks after you're married?" David asked.

Obviously giving it prior consideration, he bluntly replied, "No. I'm concerned with the future of plantations. I thought about going north to a large city, maybe New York or Philadelphia and possibly getting into the banking field. When I was in college economics was my favorite subject. I know I could make a good living there without worrying about cotton prices, runaway slaves, or any of the other problems father's experiencing. I'll sure miss Five Oaks though," looking around he continued, "But I can see a time when most plantations like this will be gone."

Although in his mind Tom was agreeing with him, he didn't comment.

Anne taken aback by his answer said, "Beau, you can't be serious! This plantation is beautiful. It's been in your family for 150 years. Why on earth would you want to leave?"

Beau gave her a stern look of disapproval for making her opinion known in front of her brothers. Realizing she spoke out of turn embarrassing him, she quickly excused herself leaving the room.

Noticing the friction between them David said, "Your insight of the future in owning a plantation was interesting, but moving north to a big city? That would be a hard adjustment for Anne to make. Whenever she visited Cliveden she would always say this is the life she wanted to live and not in a city like Biloxi or New Orleans, or for that matter even Charleston."

Without replying it gave Beau something to think about and he planned on having a discussion about the subject with Anne before she left.

Tom and David were already impressed with the furniture and paintings inside, and Beau offered to show them the grounds so they went outside.

Some of the guests were relatives of the Henry's and one in particular was a beautiful young lady who was a second cousin to Beau. Her name was Brenda Atchison. She was 25 and David took an immediate liking to her with her beauty grace, and charm. She was about 5' 1', well-proportioned with long black hair curled at the ends. Her family was from New Orleans and they too came for the holiday. David tried to spend as much time talking with her as he could and Tom saw immediately David's interest in her.

Beau got a chance to speak to Anne privately about her not wanting to leave Five Oaks and explained some of the problems his father had in the past. He told her about the financial adjustments his father had to make by mortgaging the property several times and didn't want her to live with that same uncertainty. He also mentioned his concerns for the future of plantations if war comes, which at this point was almost a certainty. She never thought about it from that point of view, and was happy his concern was for her more than his own. They did set a date for their wedding in June and made their announcement the evening before

Anne left to go back to Cliveden.

In the morning when everyone was saying goodbye David told Brenda, "It was my great pleasure to have met such a charming woman as you. If I may be bold enough to ask. Could I call on you when I return to New Orleans?"

Politely reassuring him she would enjoy his visit she replied, "That will be fine. I'll look forward to our meeting."

After kissing the back of her hand he departed.

On the way back to Cliveden Anne thought, *Three days went by so quickly; it felt like I just arrived.* Thrilled with the fact she knew the exact date of the wedding she looked forward to spring.

When they got to Cliveden, David's first thought was to see how Violet was doing and went directly to Elizabeth's cabin. He found out the doctor had been there two more times and the baby seemed to be improving.

"I'll be leaving for Biloxi in the morning Elizabeth. I think it will be too dangerous to move the baby in her condition."

"I know it would David. I'd like to stay here in place of Trisha to help my mother."

"I'll have to speak to Sharon about it, but I'm sure it will be alright," he replied.

Getting back to the house he asked, "Sharon can Elizabeth stay here to help with the cooking? Trisha can go to Biloxi with me."

"I think that will be fine David."

Overhearing their conversation Trisha excitedly said as David returned to the kitchen, "Master David, I already heard you ask Miss Sharon. I be ready to go when you are!"

The next morning Elizabeth and Flora were in the kitchen when Trisha came in to say goodbye. After hugging them she thanked Elizabeth for allowing her to leave. Walking her to the door they waved as she boarded the coach for the journey back to Biloxi.

***

Arriving in the city, like John, Elizabeth and Luke, Trisha was just as impressed with what a city looked like.

"Arthur, go to the dock first so I can speak to Jeremiah. I want to make sure there hadn't been any problems since I left," David said.

When they got there David helped Trisha get out of the coach. When Luke saw her, he came to where they were.

"Luke, talk to Trisha. I want to speak with Jeremiah," David said.

"Yes Sir, Master David," he excitedly replied.

Meeting with Jeremiah David asked, "Do you think Luke knows enough to handle the dock in New Orleans?"

"I don't think he be ready just yet Master David but he be a fast learner just like John."

"How's the construction on the houses progressing?" David asked as he walked with Jeremiah in that direction. Unanswered he could see several houses that looked like they would be ready within the month and a few others framed out waiting for the roofs to be finished. Pleased with the progress he knew he made the right decision hiring the carpenter doing the work. Satisfied, he walked back to the dock.

"Trisha, you'll have to stay with me for a few days until the next ship for New Orleans comes in. You'll have to go to New Orleans by yourself and live in the house Elizabeth and John had until Luke's ready to join you."

Getting back in the coach they headed for home. When they arrived Thelma with her usual jolly self came out to greet them. David introduced Trisha and mentioned she would be staying for a few days before going on to New Orleans.

"Should she be put up in the room across the hall from you?" Thelma asked.

"No, a room downstairs will do just fine," David said before going into the study and closing the door.

Taking out pen and paper he began to write a note to Brenda wanting to give it to Trisha before she left. He began the note by saying how much he enjoyed her company and how the few days he spent with her gave him a privilege all men would envy. He also wrote he would like to call on her at her convenience the next time he's in New Orleans.

Leaning back in his chair with his hands clasped behind his head he thought, *How should I end this note? Would it be too bold ending it, 'Your most devoted, and patient admirer?'* After writing it he held it to his chin thinking with a devilish smile, *No, that wouldn't be too bold.* Satisfied with the ending, he sealed it then put it down. He was happy with the thought he may again have someone he was interested in. After dinner he retired for the night.

***

For the time he spent at Cliveden, his ledgers were far behind and he put most of the next few days bringing them up to date. The morning the ship was to arrive. David gave Trisha the note he had written telling her who she was to give it to upon her arrival in New Orleans. After saying goodbye, Arthur took her bags and put them in the carriage.

"Trisha: don't lose my letter now," David said.

"I won't Master David. I make sure the note gets delivered. Thank you for everythin' you be doin' for me and Luke."

When she got to the dock, Arthur helped her down from the carriage and Luke quickly came over to carry her bags aboard. Nervously looking around she said, "I'm afraid traveling by myself. Being out there on all 'dat water, I can't swim Luke."

"Don't you be thinkin' on nothin' but us bein' together in a little bit," he said. After kissing her he went back ashore.

The lines were untied from the bollards and the ship slowly slid away from its mooring. Trisha didn't know what to expect and asked the captain, "Sir, is they anything I can do to help?"

"If you feel up to it, you can help Ming. He's the cook in the galley," pointing in that direction.

After finding it she knocked at the door.

Ming seeing her happily said, "I know Missy Elizabeth, she cook good in galley when she was aboard she help me plenty. What your name?" he asked.

"My name's Trisha. I know Miss Elizabeth," she replied. Looking at the size of the room, she too said, "No wonder you're so small. I can hardly fit in this room."

An hour into the voyage, Trisha began to feel woozy and Ming gave her a few dry crackers which helped.

"Mister Ming, maybe if I help with the cookin' it might take away this bad feelin'."

"Maybe so," he replied.

Tying on an apron she began to help. As she expected, being busy took away the sea sick feeling. This was a whole new world that opened up for her and she helped in the galley as if she had been doing it for a long time.

Adam, who was aboard said, "I knew Elizabeth and John at Cliveden, but I never did see you there."

"I got there when Luke was 'bout 15. I come from Five Oaks Plantation. I was sold with a few others cause the Henry's, well, they be needin' some money. My daddy and mammy both passed when I was 12, and I was raised by my momma's friend until I was 15. That's when I was sent to Cliveden."

Adam was about 20 years her senior and when she went to put some dishes away he stood in her path.

"What you be goin' to New Orleans for?" he asked.

"I'm staying there for 'bout a month till Luke can come. We gonna be married."

Grabbing her around the waist he said, "A month's too far away to be waitin' on a man when they be one right here in front of you."

Picking up a knife from the butcher block she pointed it at his stomach saying, "Miss Cora lived in the quarter and was a friend to my mammy. After my mammy passed, I wents to live with them. Her husband started visitin' my bed regular from the time I was 13 till I left. I didn't have no choice then, but I do now, and ifn' you come closer, I gonna show you just what 'dat choice be."

Realizing she wasn't the type of woman that couldn't or wouldn't do what she said, he left.

***

Arriving in New Orleans Trisha quickly left the ship and found Master Charles giving him the letter. She said, "Master David say he be wantin' you to send this letter on to Miss Brenda.... Miss Brenda Atchison. He say 'He wants me to live in Elizabeth's house 'till Luke comes in 'bout a month. Miss Elizabeth she be stayin' at Cliveden."

Charles replied, "I'll have someone deliver it. I have some of the dock crew living in the house temporarily until their houses get finished, but you're welcome to stay in one of the rooms," pausing for a moment examining the manifest of the cargo being unloaded he looked up at her, "You could make a little money by cooking and washing their clothes if you want."

After pointing in the direction of the house, he went back to reading the manifest.

"Thank you, Master Charles," she replied, heading in the direction of the house.

Chapter 15
The Boarding House

After finding the house, Trisha opened the door then stepped back. From the doorway she realized it showed every sign of not having a woman present for a long time. There were dirty clothes piled in corners of all the rooms and beds that weren't made. The kitchen was a mess, and a stack of dirty dishes were patiently waiting in the sink for someone's attention. The windows were soot covered and could hardly admit sunlight even on this bright sunny afternoon. The floors had mud-caked footprints and probably hadn't been swept since Elizabeth left some months ago.

Going upstairs she took the smallest room that looked like it wasn't in use, put her belongings on the bed, then changed into an old dress. She began by sweeping her room then the rest of the rooms upstairs carrying the task into the hall and down the steps to the first floor. Piling the debris by the back door she looked down at all the dirt saying in a low tone, "Humph could plant a crop with it."

Realizing the kitchen would be her major problem she postponed it. After examining the empty cabinets she realized she would have to find a place that sold groceries. Knocking at a neighbor's door to inquire, she introduced herself.

"My name's Trisha. I be your new neighbor. I needs a place that sells groceries, could you tell me where one be?"

The neighbor pointed to the end of the row where she could purchase the much needed supplies. Before leaving, Trisha thanked the neighbor who replied, "If you needs anythin' else, just ask."

Before leaving the house she started the fire in the cook stove so it would be ready to use upon her return. After returning, she put on a pot of stew stirring it occasionally while straightening the rest of the kitchen.

Hearing the men coming in she ran to the living room. The first one hadn't taken more than two steps into the house when she yelled, "Don't you be bringin' yourself in my clean house without wipin' yo' feet!"

Although they were forewarned by Master Charles, they were surprised. Trisha continued instructively, "I don't know who slept in each room or what, but I don't wants clothes scattered all over my clean floor either."

After looking at each other, they could smell the pleasant odor of dinner and thought it best to obey replying, "Yes, Ma'am."

While they were eating she asked, "If you wants to pay me, I'll wash your clothes and cook your meals. I puts a basket on the back porch so's you can leave your dirty clothes in."

With the taste of a good hot dinner fresh in their mouths, after looking at one another they gave her a resounding, "Yes."

After they left the kitchen, she cleared the table washed the dishes and put them away. After a long day she went up to bed and as a safety precaution, braced a chair under the door handle.

Before dawn she was in the kitchen and had the cook stove already going. A pot of coffee was boiling and the aroma filtered throughout the house. As the men came into the kitchen they each placed $2 on the table for her services. Looking down at the money she felt odd having black folks paying other black folks for something she always did for nothing but thought, *When Luke get's here, we could have a few boarders until the houses being built are finished. I could cook and wash clothes for the men that weren't married and have a few dollars when he arrives.* She felt good about her future enterprise, and after the men left, she began cleaning the kitchen.

She went into the living room and looked around thinking, *I surely have to do somthin' 'bout these windows. The sun's shinin' bright and it still dark as midnight in here.* As she wiped the soot from each one, sunlight invaded the rooms revealing more work that had to be done. She thought, *Shoulda' left well enough alone.*

She hadn't had time to scrub the floors but as tired as she was, thinking about the money she could possibly earn, she dove into each room with renewed energy. It took the better part of the week to finally get the house the way she wanted, and each day the men came in there was always an improvement. With the changes, they became more conscious of the neatness in their surroundings which made her job easier.

Enjoying the little extras she did along with her cooking and baking skills, the $2 a week seemed well worth the price. She was glad to have a home of her own, and with the man she loved joining her in the near future, was something she could only dream of a year ago.

***

The month passed quickly cooking and washing clothes for the boarders, and she would be proud to have saved a few dollars to surprise Luke when he came.

While at the stove one afternoon she heard the front door open. Thinking it was the men returning early she turned around to see Luke standing in the living room. The shock of it made her drop a hot pan of fresh baked bread she had just taken from the oven. Running to him they threw their arms around one another showering each other with kisses.

"Master Charles said I don't have to go to the dock till mornin' so we could have some time together. I figure we gots 'bout two hours to spend fo' the men come home."

Wanting it to be intimate as possible, she took him up to her room. Although they weren't officially married they spent the two hours making love and returned to the kitchen just as the boarders were coming in.

As they were seating themselves at the table one of the men commented to Luke, "Miss Trisha, she dun' straightened up the whole house real good and the food be so good too. It goes down real easy like. You sure is lucky findin' a woman like 'dat. They ain't many round these days."

Another boarder commented looking up from his plate of food, "And dat's fo' sure 'nough the truth."

Trisha, embarrassed with the compliment replied, "You just ain't looked in the right places."

Luke remarked excitedly, "Master Charles wants me to take over as dock foreman. I'm not sure how ya'll like takin' orders from me?"

Looking up from the table the men looked at one another, then at Luke. One of the men replied, "We ain't got nothin' to say. Master Charles, he be the one what owns the dock. He be the boss."

One boarder named Joshua seemed to have an objection. In a disgruntled voice he said, "I don't know why Master Charles he don't make me headman? I dun' been here the longest. I knows everythin' they is to know 'bout the dock."

Surprised at his objection Luke replied, "I guess you have to ask Master Charles why he didn't," passing on the discussion going any further.

When dinner was finished the men went outside to smoke and enjoy the evening. Luke began helping Trisha with the dishes when she asked, "You thinks 'dat Joshua be trouble? He sure spoke up kinda quick."

Replying as he put his arms around her waist kissing the side of her neck, "Don't you be thinkin' on it. I just has to wait and see."

Lying in bed Trisha asked, "Luke, when you thinks we can be married? I surely would like 'dat."

"When I gets to the dock tomorrow I'll ask Master Charles if the captain of the ship will marry us. Will 'dat suit you?"

"Dat be mighty fine," she said as he put his arms around her. Comfortable embracing they fell asleep.

When Luke got to the dock in the morning he dove into the work helping rearrange cargo already on the dock. By his actions he made it known he was going to be a working foreman and like John, wanted to make a good impression. Working in Biloxi, he got to know most of the ship's captains but wasn't familiar with Captain Stewart commanding the ship coming in today.

After it moored and the gangway was put in place, the captain waved for Luke to come aboard. Thinking it would be a perfect time to ask Luke quickly went up the gangway to where the captain was standing.

The captain, a short, bald portly man in his mid 50's, told Luke, "I didn't know you were Elizabeth's brother. I had a special arrangement with John when he was alive," Captain Stewart said.

"What 'dat be Captn'?" Luke asked.

"Every once in awhile I bring in a few crates of goods that belong to me. I mark them special. John would make sure they were put aside for me to get later."

"What be in them Captn'?"

"Fine linens and liquor from France that isn't taxed," he replied.

Looking at the captain suspiciously, Luke never did anything like this before. "You don't thinks I gets into trouble do you, Captn'? I surely won't like to lose this here job. I just started today."

"No one need know about it except you me and Master Charles," Captain Stewart replied.

Luke looked surprised, and Captain Stewart reassured him by saying, "Yes, Charles knows about it too. We always gave John a few dollars for doing it and you'll get the same."

Going back to the dock Luke directed the marked crates as they came off the ship to a spot where they wouldn't be noticed. Captain Stewart watching from the ships rail gave Luke thumbs up where he placed them. It was Luke's first time doing it, and he was nervous when the port inspector came to look over the cargo. Captain Stewart came off the ship and walked over to the port inspector. After exchanging a few words they shook hands and the captain gave him an envelope. Luke, realizing it was probably money, felt better about not getting caught. After the port inspector walked away, Luke went over to the captain.

"What I'm suppos' to do now Captn'?"

"They'll be a wagon along sometime this afternoon to pick them up. Just make sure they handle them with care," Captain Stewart replied.

"I make sure of it captn'."

Feeling a little better being in the captain's confidence he wasn't afraid to ask, "Captn', excuse me for the askin'. I only just got here yesterday. I ain't had a chance to marry the woman I be with. She asked me last night if you could do it for us."

"I'd do just about anything for the brother-in-law of John. Bring her on over here. I'll do it now," Captain Stewart replied.

After seeing most of the cargo unloaded, Luke quickly went ashore and ran as fast as he could to the house. Getting there he threw open the door calling, "Trisha! Trisha! Captn' wants to marry us this afternoon."

Caught completely off guard she had on the flour covered apron from baking. Pulling her by the hand towards the door she exclaimed, "Wait a minute Luke! Wait a minute! I got's to change, I looks a sight."

Taking her by the hand he wasn't listening. With the long strides of his fast walk she was hard pressed to keep up. One of his steps equaled two of hers and she had to run most of the way to keep from falling. Trying hard to address her appearance as best she could with the free hand she kept saying, "You didn't even give me a chance to wash my face or puts on a clean dress," repeating it several times. He was hearing her words, but wasn't paying much attention. When they got to the dock most of the cargo was on the pier and Luke took her aboard.

"Here she is Captn', this here is Trisha!" he said proudly.

Stewart looked at her wearing the flour-covered apron, with traces of flour still on her nose and chin. He realized it wouldn't have been the way she would have presented herself having a little advance notice. Laughing to himself he also realized she was out of breath because Luke must have hurried her back to the ship as fast as he could.

"We have to have a witness," Captain Stewart said calling to his first mate to stand beside them. After the mate took his place Captain Stewart opened the book and read the passage for a marriage. When he was through he congratulated them. Going to his cabin he retrieved a bottle of French Champaign and handed it to Trisha. "Here's a wedding gift from me. Take this home."

Taking the bottle she replied, "Thank you Captn'." Happy she was finally married she walked proudly down the gangplank. A few of the dock crew knowing what took place began to clap. Embarrassed by her appearance she began to walk a little faster toward home.

Suddenly remembering she had bread dough in pans waiting for them to rise she began to run as fast as her legs could carry her. When she got to the kitchen it was just as she thought. The dough had risen over the pans onto the kitchen floor. Getting ready to clean up the mess she looked in the mirror and thought, *The sight of me on my wedding day. I must have made the captain and his first mate wonder what kind of woman Luke be marryin'? Well, it be done and official, and that's all that matters.*

Back at the ship, Captain Stewart said, "Luke, all the cargo's ashore. After they pick up the special marked crates you can go home. Spend the rest of the day with your wife."

Wanting to make something special for the occasion, Trisha began making Luke's favorite food, cornbread!

When the men came in they could smell it, and after washing, they sat down to dinner.

To Luke, the whole day was an experience. First helping Captain Stewart bring in the crates, something he was afraid to do, then getting married.

***

Several months went by and most of the boarders moved to other houses that were finished, but Trisha continued to do their laundry. One of the boarders that stayed made her feel uncomfortable. It was Joshua the only one who complained about not being chosen to be headman at the dock.

Lying in bed with Luke one night she said, "Luke, I just don't trust that Joshua. You should tell him to leave and go finds himself another place to live. Seems like he always be 'round tryin' to hear or see somethin' that ain't none of his business."

Thinking for a moment he realized Joshua seemed to be acting the same way recently at the dock, replying, "I think you be right, Trisha. I'm gonna tell him today."

When Luke got to the dock the following morning, Captain Jarvis' ship was being unloaded. When Captain Jarvis saw Luke, he called down to him, "Luke, come aboard. I want to see you in my cabin."

After boarding, Luke knocked on the door and removed his cap before stepping in. After Captain Jarvis closed the door he said, "I have three crates on this trip. I marked them with a red stripe. Put them in the same spot you put the last crates. Handing Luke an envelope he said, "Here's a little something for the last shipment."

"Thanks Captn', I be sure to put them in the same place."

After Luke stepped from the cabin he saw Joshua standing in the passageway outside the captain's door.

"What you be doin' here? You suppose to be on the dock," Luke demanded.

"We has a problem with one of the wenches. I wants to know where you wants us to put three crates. They has a different mark."

Luke realizing he must have been standing at the door listening, replied, "Get on back to the dock. I'll be there in a little bit, I gots to go down to the hold."

Luke said it wanting Joshua to think going to the hold was what the conversation with the captain was about. When he returned to the dock the marked crates were already ashore and put aside.

Later in the day Joshua approached Luke.

"I knows what you be doin'. I keeps quiet for some of 'dat money you be gettin'.""

Luke thought Joshua was bold by asking, but not wanting to lose all the money or expose the captain he agreed.

***

Several times during the month Trisha asked, "When you gonna tell Joshua to leave?" wondering why he was putting it off.

"They's no reason to put him out just yet. The extra money, well, it be commin' in handy too," he angrily replied.

He always let Trisha handle the money and recently she began to wonder why he wasn't bringing home as much. She sensed something was wrong at the dock and whatever it was, was contagious with the rest of the boarders.

When Joshua was around everyone seemed to be hushed not like it was the first few months they were there. Finally getting up enough courage she asked one of the boarders, "Is they be somethin' wrong at the dock. Ya'll seem to be actin' different from when I first come?"

One of the men realizing she understood something was wrong replied, "Miss Trisha, don't be tellin' nobody I told you so, but they ain't nothin' wrong here. It be Joshua. He be actin' like he be the boss now when we be workin'. He don't be doin' any work himself, and everybody on the dock don't know why Luke ain't say nothin' to him."

As she suspected, Joshua was the root of the problem, and was determined to say something again to Luke that evening.

When he got home she said, "I asked one of the mens, why everybody be so miserable when Joshua be 'round. They say, Joshua was actin' like he be the boss at the dock. Is you, or is he be the boss?" she demanded.

Luke snapped back, "Woman, 'dat ain't nobody's business but mine!"

It was his first harsh words to her and she felt bad but didn't question him any further that night.

The next morning when he got to the dock, Captain Jarvis' ship was docking once again. Luke standing on the dock observing, realized Trisha was right. Joshua had taken over giving the orders. When the special marked crates came off Joshua quickly told the dock hands, "Put these crates over younder," pointing to an inconspicuous spot. When Luke went over to examine the crates Joshua followed. Luke realized by being silent, he was losing control and quietly told Joshua, "You actin' like you be the boss. You not doin' any work and everybody be wonderin' why."

Standing next to the marked crates Joshua said as he patted one of them, "Yeah we both knows why. I thinks maybe I deserve even mo' of 'dat money for keepin' quiet."

Surprised at his boldness, Luke replied, "You be gettin' too much now. You ain't gettin' another penny." Pausing for a moment he turned to look at Joshua, "Maybe I just tell Captn' Jarvis and let him and his crew deal with you. I was thinkin' on it today anyway."

Pushing Joshua out of his way Luke headed in the direction of the gangway. Joshua fearing he would be exposed grabbed a bailing hook and swung it catching Luke on his left forearm. The sharp pain was excruciating but Luke was able to ward off a second blow with a punch to Joshua's jaw with his right hand.

The dock crew seeing what was going on gathered around to watch the fight, and the ship's crew stood by the rail cheering and yelling. Joshua was getting the best of Luke with Luke only having the use of one arm. They struggled rolling around on the dock choking and punching at one another, falling over small crates and tripping over ropes. Joshua kept swinging the bailing hook and Luke was able to avoid getting hit by ducking and dodging. Whenever he had an opportunity, he would get in a punch with his right hand.

Nearing the end of the pier Joshua swung the hook and Luke ducked. The bailing hook embedded deep in a bail of cotton and Joshua wasn't able to pull it free. Luke, taking advantage of him trying to free it began to pummel Joshua with his right hand. Joshua grabbed him around the waist and lost his balance sending them both headlong into the river. Joshua, not able to swim, grabbed hold of the ships rudder but with the strong tide going out soon lost his grip and began getting swept downstream, frantically yelling out, "Luke, help me, I can't swim!"

Luke, knowing how to swim, was barely managing to stay afloat himself. With only the use of one arm, he was rapidly tiring fighting the current. Looking back at Joshua thrashing at the surface trying to stay afloat he wondered how he could help.

Joshua went under briefly then quickly resurfaced still calling for Luke to help. Tiring rapidly, Luke kept fighting the swift current barely able to save himself. Two of the dock hands quickly grabbed ropes tossing it to each of them. Luke was able to grab one end with his good arm and held on, while they began to pull him back to safety. The other rope was tossed to Joshua bobbing up and down on the surface, but it was just out of reach. Throwing it again, it was still out of reach and they watched helplessly as Joshua frantically fought the current. After several attempts he lost his battle and went under.

Luke, holding onto the rope, was pulled to the ladder attached to the dock. After grabbing it with his right hand, one of the ship's crew climbed down and helped him up. He had a bad laceration on his forearm and was quickly bandaged by Elijah another dock hand.

Master Charles hardly came to the dock since Luke became dock foreman, but just happened to come that day to speak with Captain Jarvis. When he saw Luke bleeding he asked in a demanding voice, "Luke what happened?"

Luke remained silent but Elijah spoke, "Master Charles, Joshua, he never did like Luke bein' boss over him and for no good reason, he hit Luke with a bailin' hook."

"Where's Joshua?" Charles sternly asked.

"They both fell in the river. Luke was able to grab the rope we threw but Joshua couldn't and the river carried him on down. We tried to throw it to him again, but he still couldn't grab it and went under. I 'spect he drowned."

Looking at the damage to Luke's arm Charles said, "Elijah, use my carriage and take Luke to the doctor. Have him sew up that arm. When he's finished, make sure he gets home."

"Yes, Sir, Master Charles," he replied walking Luke off the dock. After helping him into the carriage they left for the doctor's office. After Luke was treated, Elijah took him home.

Trisha seeing him early in the day excitedly asked, "Elijah, what happened? What happened to Luke?"

After telling her she annoyingly said, "I told ya, Luke. I never did trust 'dat Joshua. He always did think your job was suppose' to be his. I knew he'd be nothin' but trouble. I just knew it!"

After helping Luke get his shirt off, he sat at the kitchen table while she made him something to eat. Stirring a pot of stew she looked over her shoulder, "I hates to speak on the dead Luke, but peoples like 'dat, they won't never be any good. They always be lookin' at what other folk's be havin'. I just ain't never trusted him."

After Luke finished eating he went upstairs to lie down. He wouldn't be able to go to the dock for awhile and asked Elijah to take his place.

***

In a few days Luke was able to go back. He tried valiantly to work with one arm, but couldn't. He wasn't kidding himself. With that wound, he'd never be the man he was physically.

Charles asked, "Luke, what was that fight about?"

"Well, Master Charles, Joshua always thought he should be the head dock man. He never did like me bein' over him."

"Was that all the fight was about, being foreman?"

Luke went silent for a few moments and Charles insisted, "Come on Luke -tell me what that was about."

Reluctant at first to speak, he finally gave in to his question. "Well, Master Charles, Joshua was outside captn' cabin one day and heard him talkin' to me 'bout the special marked crates. He said I have to give him half my money to keep quiet."

"Why didn't you come to me or one of the other captains? We would have taken care of it,"

"I don't rightly know. I was just scared I guess. I thought it be easier if I just give him some of mine."

"You go home and take it easy. Don't try to do too much," Charles said.

Luke came to the dock every day doing the best he could, but his contribution was minimal to what it once was.

***

In three weeks Captain Jarvis' ship came back to port. After waving Luke aboard he said, "I only have two crates marked this trip," pausing for a moment he asked, "Why were you fighting with Joshua?"

Luke repeated the same story he told Charles omitting the fact of having to pay Joshua.

After telling him, he returned to the dock directing where the crates should be placed.

That afternoon Charles came to the dock and boarded the ship.

Jarvis said, "It's a shame Luke got his arm tore up like that. Maybe we're partly to blame for making him in charge over Joshua."

Looking at Captain Jarvis Charles said, "Don't you know the real reason Luke was fighting with him?"

"He told me Joshua didn't like the idea he was passed over and didn't become head dock man," Captain Jarvis replied.

"That's all he said?" Charles asked.

"Yes, is there any other reason?"

"That's only part of it. Joshua overheard you talking about the marked crates one day and Joshua told Luke he had to give him half his money to keep quiet. The fight happened when he told Luke he wanted more money and Luke told him no. He threatened Luke with telling the authorities on us. That's what the fight was really about."

Completely surprised Jarvis replied, "Luke should have said something. I know how to handle someone like that. He would have been shanghaied to the west-coast. That arm looks pretty bad. Do you think he'll ever be able to get full use out of it?"

"I don't think so. I spoke to the doctor that sewed him up. He said there's a lot of ligament damage. If he can't handle the physical work that he's been doing, I'll give him other things to do. He won't have any problems hauling freight. I think we at least owe him something for his loyalty."

"I agree. Oh, I almost forgot. Here's a letter from David to Brenda, he asked if I could see it get's delivered."

"I'll give it to Luke, he can deliver it," Charles said.

Calling Luke to where they were standing Charles asked, "Luke, do you know where Miss Brenda Atchison lives?"

"Yes Sir."

"Take this letter to her. It's from David."

Brenda lived on a tree-lined street that had a few estates, but the one she lived in stood out from the rest. It was a beautiful white mansion with a meticulously manicured garden surrounded by a black wrought iron fence. When Luke knocked at the door the butler answered and Luke handed him the letter.

"Come in," the butler said.

Brenda being inquisitive about who was at the door came into the foyer. The butler handed her the letter and she recognized immediately who it was from. Smiling she anxiously opening it to read. Finishing she said, "Please, come to the library with me until I compose a reply."

With Luke following she asked, "Do you work on the dock?"

"Yes Ma'am; my names Luke. I came from Cliveden."

"I remember David talking about you. I thought you were head dock man in Biloxi?

"No, Ma'am, I was just learned there by Jeremiah."

"Oh, I see."

It only took a few minutes to write the reply then she handed it to him. Escorting him back to the front door she said, "David's coming to visit for a few days. He'll be here in two weeks."

Seeing his bandage she asked, "What on earth happened to your arm?"

Looking solemn he replied, "Miss Brenda, I hurt it working on the dock." Not wanting to continue the conversation he left.

Returning to the dock he handed the reply to Captain Jarvis and related to him David was coming for a visit.

Chapter 16
David's Visit

When David boarded the ship in Biloxi for New Orleans, he asked Captain Jarvis, "How's Luke working out as a dock foreman?"

"I guess you didn't hear about what happened?" he replied.

Looking at Captain Jarvis he anxiously asked, "No, what happened?"

After Jarvis related the story, David asked "What was the fight over?"

Although Captain Jarvis knew it was over money from his elicit business, he used an answer David would be able to recognize, and told him about Joshua wanting to be foreman.

"How bad is his injury?"

"I don't think he'll ever be able to get the full use of that arm. That's what Charles told me the doctor's diagnosis was."

David, having a special interest in Luke being Elizabeth's brother, wondered just how bad the injury was. He was carrying a message for Luke from Cliveden, a message telling him his mother had apoplexy, and was paralyzed on the left side of her face and suffered the loss of the use of her left arm. The letter said Elizabeth had taken over the kitchen and asked if Luke could come back for a visit.

***

During the trip David wondered how he could compensate Luke for being put in a bad situation that caused his injury. After docking he left the ship. Shaking hands with Charles he asked, "Where's Luke? I have a message for him from Cliveden."

"He's not here right now. I sent him to the supply house to get some canvas I ordered."

"Is he still able to work with his injury? Captain Jarvis told me it was pretty bad."

"He isn't able to do the physical work he used to, but since you seemed to have a special interest in him, I decided to let him supervise the loading and unloading instead of being a working foreman. I know he feels bad about it, so whenever I can, I send him on errands I think he can handle. You know David, he's a proud individual and I know it bothers him to feel like he's less than a man."

"I know Charles. Would you mind if I use your carriage while I'm here? Luke can be my driver?"

"I don't mind. Where do you plan on staying during your visit?"

"I thought I could impose on you and use a room at your house. That is if you don't mind."

"Certainly, I don't mind. I'll look forward to having your company."

Walking to the end of the dock together David could see the progress on the houses they were having built. A few more were finished since his last visit and a couple more were being worked on. He asked, "Charles is the new system of having the men pay for their board working?"

"Yes, in fact a few other dock owners are beginning to do the same. By the way do you know we have the busiest dock in New Orleans? We handle more cargo than anyone else."

"Yes," David replied, something he already knew with the profits he was receiving every month.

"Charles, I think I'm going to walk down to take a look at the houses. I want to stop and see Trisha. Tell Luke to pick me up there when he gets back."

"I'll do that. Will you be going directly to Brenda's?"

"I'd like to get freshened up and change clothes first," he replied.

"When you get to the house tell Adam my butler to set you up in the guest room."

"Thanks! I'll do that," David said before leaving.

Walking the row of houses admiring the progress, it reaffirmed he made the right decision with the carpenter he hired for the project, just as he did in Biloxi. When he got to Trisha's he knocked. Opening the door she stepped back surprised to see him.

"Come in Master David. Come in and sit down. I just now brewed me some tea. Would you likes some and a piece of this fresh bread I dun' baked?"

"I could smell the bread even before I stepped in the house. No thank you Trisha. Tea will be just fine."

Sitting at the kitchen table he looked down at the red and white checkered tablecloth and said, "I'm sorry for Luke having that trouble at the dock. I hear his arm is pretty bad."

Trisha, turning to look at him replied, "Yes Master David, it's pretty bad. 'Dat Joshua, I knowed he dun' spelled trouble from the first day he dun' came. I ain't never trusted him." She was about to continue when he suddenly cut her short.

"Trisha, I have something else to tell you," pausing for a moment looking up at her, "Flora has apoplexy. She's lost the use of her left arm and the muscles on the left side of her face."

Shocked to hear it, she realized Luke would take it much harder.

Staring down at his cup he continued, "If you and Luke want to return to Cliveden, I'll see you get passage back to Biloxi."

"Luke will want to go fo' sure but I don't thinks I can. I have a few boarders and do the wash for most of the men in the other houses."

"Yes I heard you've become quite a business woman."

With a smile and an uplifted voice she said, "Yes sir, I not only takes in laundry, I have a friend 'dat's husband goes out fishin' on the river. He brings me his catch and I gives him a few pennies. I cooks it up, and sells 'dat to the mens too."

"Sounds like it won't be long till you have your own restaurant."

Pausing for a moment she smiled again, "I surely wants to thank you for takin' a likin' to Luke the way you did. We owes everything we gots to you," pausing for a moment, she turned her back to pour the tea then said, "I guess Miss Elizabeth's bein' the cook now at Cliveden?"

"Yes, she has a young girl she's training just like Flora trained you."

In a half hour Luke came in and went directly to the kitchen. Trisha gave him a hug and David asked him to sit down.

"Luke, there's no easy way to put this, your mother has apoplexy. She's paralyzed on her left arm and part of her face. I told Trisha if you want to go back, I'll send you on the next ship."

"I already knowed, Master David, Master Charles dun' told me. When you leaves for Biloxi, I'd sho' like to go back with you."

"Will the both of you be going?" David asked glancing at Trisha.

"I don't know. Me and Trisha has to talk it over," Luke replied.

As he stood up to leave David said, "I'll be here for almost a week. Let me know what you decide. Thank you for the tea Trisha," turning to Luke he asked, "Would you drive me to Charles' house?"

"Yes Sir."

Arriving David said, "I'm going to freshen up before I go to Miss Brenda's. Come back for me in about an hour."

Still feeling sullen about the news of Flora, Luke quietly replied, "Yes Sir, Master David." Turning the carriage around, he headed for home.

Upon his return, David was ready to go. On the way to Brenda's Luke said, "Master David, I went back to the house and talked it over with Trisha 'bout goin' back. We thinks I should go by myself."

"Maybe that's the right decision, seems like she's too busy," pausing for a moment he asked, "What happened between you and Joshua at the dock? Was the fight worth the use of your arm?"

"No sir, but I ain't have no choice. Joshua was the one 'dat started it when he dun' sunk 'dat bailin' hook in my arm for no good reason."

"I understand. It's still a shame it had to happen."

Arriving, David was greeted at the front door by George the butler, and escorted into the parlor. When Brenda entered the room David said, "Your home is quite impressive, Miss Brenda."

"Will you excuse me David? I want to tell Papa you're here."

"Certainly."

After she left the room he looked around admiring the paintings that adorned the walls. One large life size portrait in particular captured his attention and he stood staring, transfixed at its beauty. When Brenda's father entered the room he said, "Good evening," extending his hand to shake David's, "I'm Edward Atchison, Brenda's father. Would you care for a brandy?"

"Yes I would, Mr. Atchison," he replied.

"Please don't call me Mister Atchison. Edward would be fine."

After pouring the brandy they sat down.

Edward, a man in his late 50's, was very distinguished looking for his age. Slightly on the heavy side he was tall with gray hair.

"I don't know if my daughter told you but the Henry family who are friends with your brother, are related to me by marriage. Beau's mother and I are cousins. I understand your sister Anne and my nephew Beau are to be married in the spring."

"Yes, I met Beau at Christmas. He seems as anxious as my sister for spring to arrive."

"When I entered the room I noticed you staring at that portrait," he said pointing to the one David seemed to be transfixed on.

"Why, yes. It's a beautiful painting of Miss Brenda. It looks as though she could step down from it and join our conversation."

Edward smiled, "Thank you for the compliment, but that's not Brenda. It was my wife, Charlotte, Brenda's mother. She passed away when Brenda was 12. I had a nanny raise Brenda after her mother died. I was absent about six months of the year spending a lot of time at my sugar plantation in Cuba."

Surprised at the likeness David replied, "Well the painting captures the image of a beautiful woman that bore a child in her image."

Edward smiled again replying, "Thank you so much for the compliment."

In a few minutes the maid came into the room announcing dinner. David wondered why Brenda was absent for the conversation in the parlor, but understood as she entered the dining room. She came in with a vibrancy he hadn't seen since his wife died. She wore a blue chiffon dress with an elegantly designed necklace made of silver, with blue sapphires and earrings to match. Her long black hair was accented with a black onyx hair comb, and an ornately designed mother of pearl inlay. Mesmerized by her beauty as she approached the table, he rose, then pulled out her chair so she could seat herself, then gently pushed it back.

The conversation during dinner shifted towards the secessionist movement and how it might affect the shipping business in New Orleans.

"What do you think of the war talk, David?" Edward asked.

"I think if some of the western territories were to secede the North would probably try to cut off any port that could supply the South with war materials, and in fact, may cut off shipping all together. They would definitely try to curtail the south's finances from trade with foreign countries.

Brenda replied, "I hope South Carolina stops with all this secession talk. They don't realize their shipping business would be jeopardized too. Charleston and the rest of the Carolina coast are almost as busy as we are."

David was surprised she had input not like most southern belles who were pampered and catered to. Edward noticing his reaction, was amused saying, "David don't look so surprised. I taught my daughter to think and express her opinion just like her mother when she was alive. My wife was instrumental with starting the sugar plantation, I valued her opinion so much she took care of the correspondence and book-keeping in my absence."

"Edward, that's interesting." Looking at Brenda, David could see she was aglow with Edward's compliment.

Turning to Edward David said, "My wife did the same when she was alive."

"David, my friends in the shipping business tell me you worked out an unusual arrangement with your people working the dock? I'd like to hear about it."

"Edward, with all the runaways, my partner and I decided to free our people. Most of them are already free to go as they please within the confines of the city as long as they return to work anyway. The days of keeping them contained at the dock are all but at an end. With outside influences they're heading north or as three people that worked for me did, stowed away on a ship bound for England seeking freedom. We decided to pay them a wage and alleviate the problem of feeding and housing them. We've even built housing for them to live in and they pay rent."

Looking down seemingly concentrating on what David said Edward slowly looked up asking, "Well, how has the policy worked out?"

"So far the policy seems to be working. It gives them more of a feeling of independence and that in itself creates a better work environment."

"That's an interesting point of view. You've obviously given it a lot of thought."

After a little more discussion about David's policy with his people, Edward came to the same conclusion his friends had. Times were changing and a worker more self-sufficient worked better. Informed by friends that were in the shipping business, Edward already knew David's docks here and in Biloxi were some of the busiest. He realized without question David's ability to support Brenda in the lifestyle she's become accustomed to, wasn't a concern.

After retiring to the living room Edward approached the painting of his wife once again. Looking up at it he said, "Yes, she was truly beautiful," turning to look at David he asked, "You mentioned at dinner how your wife helped with your book-keeping. If it's not too painful when did she pass?"

"She died over 10 years ago in child birth two years after we were married. The baby died too."

"I'm so very sorry to hear that; how tragic. It must have been heart rendering. I know how it affected me when my wife passed. I spent six months out of the year in Cuba but fortunately I was here when she died. In spite of her untimely death, I still had Brenda," looking at Brenda he continued, "She gave me the courage to carry on. Losing your wife and child at the same time, that's tragic, truly tragic," pausing again remembering Brenda's mother.

David asked, "Edward, may I have the permission, and privilege of courting Miss Brenda?"

The question seemed to snap Edward out of reminiscing, and turning to look at David he replied. "You ask as though I'll have an objection. Is it because of the distance between your ages? If it is, I realize there's 13 years between you. I feel someone that's older and wiser would be more attentive and a better match for my Brenda. She's more mature than her age and if that's what she wants, then yes, you have my approval."

They both stood up and David shook Edward's hand, "Thank you Sir. I'll be looking forward to seeing you again during the week."

"That won't be possible David. I sail for Cuba tomorrow, but I'll look forward to seeing you again in the near future. If you'll excuse me I have to retire for the night. My ship sails early tomorrow morning."

Before leaving the room he glanced up at the portrait once again. Brenda hurriedly got up embracing her father kissing him gently on the cheek. He paused kissing her on the forehead saying, "Good night my darling," then left the room.

"Would you like to retire to the parlor and talk for awhile David?" Brenda asked.

"Miss Brenda, I would like that."

After going in she poured him another brandy.

"I think father was impressed with the way you handled yourself, just like a true southern gentleman. How long will you be in New Orleans?"

"I have a few meetings with my business partner and a few other errands before I go back. I'll probably be here most of the week."

"Then I hope we get to see each other again before you go."

"I certainly hope so Miss Brenda."

"Well then, you wouldn't mind another invitation to dinner?" she asked.

"I would like that very much," he replied.

"If it doesn't interfere too much with your schedule, how about the day after tomorrow?" she asked.

"That would be fine!"

They small talked about likes and dislikes until they were surprised when the mantle clock was chiming 10. So taken by each other's company the time seemed to fly by. He rose from his chair and Brenda walked with him to the front door. Before making his exit he turned. In anticipation for him to kiss the back of her hand she raised her arm. Instead, he took her hand and pulled her close, passionately kissing her on the lips.

Gently pulling back she smiled saying, "Sir, do you always take such liberties with the ladies?"

"No, but one with the grace and charm as lovely as you Miss Brenda, makes one abandon himself. I hope you weren't offended."

Without answering she smiled as he made his exit. After closing the door she thought, *I'm happy some of that grace and charm he displayed all evening was only masking part of his true self, passionate!*

Returning to Charles' he went straight to his room. Having business to discuss with Charles he wanted to do it early in the morning. Thinking about Brenda, he retired to bed.

After waking, he went downstairs straight to the dining room where Charles was already eating breakfast.

"Good morning David, how was your evening?" he asked.

"Entertaining, very entertaining. Mr. Atchison's point of view is interesting. I think he gave me an idea without realizing it. Did you know he has interests in Cuba?"

"I heard about it, but I don't know much more than that."

The servant interrupted asking, "What would you like for breakfast Master David?"

"The same as Charles, bacon, eggs and some coffee please."

Giving David his undivided attention Charles asked, "What kind of idea did he give you?"

Pausing for a moment from stirring his coffee David said, "Why don't we try to start a shipping business in Cuba?"

Looking concerned Charles replied, "I don't know David. I think I just want to concentrate on business here. I don't want to take on too much."

"It was just a thought, but if the South does secede we'll still be in business."

"What did he say about our policy to pay and house the dock workers?"

"He didn't say. He more or less confirmed the other dock owners were in agreement with what I'm doing in Biloxi. Everyone would benefit if they joined a coalition to deal with any problems that may arise. Charles, if you don't need me, I'd like to go to the dock this morning to see Brenda's father off. He's leaving for his plantation."

"You can ride with me. I'm going to the dock," he replied.

Going outside they found Luke waiting to drive them. On the way to the dock Charles quietly talked about what they could do for Luke. After voicing his opinion David said, "I'm fine with whatever you want to do. I think we owe him that much. I do want him to go back with me when I leave though. His mother developed apoplexy and he wants to visit her."

When they got to the waterfront, Luke let Charles out and proceeded to the pier where the ship was moored that would take Edward to Cuba. David was a little late and saw Brenda standing on the dock waving as the ship was moving away from its mooring. When he approached, Brenda was surprised. Standing next to her they looked at each other then waved at Edward until the ship was down the river and out of sight.

"Thank you David for being so considerate," she said as she wiped a tear from her eyes. "It seems like since he's getting older, every time I see him off, I think it may be the last time I'll see him."

"Don't think that way. Just anticipate the joy of him returning. Brenda, would you like to have dinner this evening at a restaurant in town?"

"I would love to David. What time should I be ready?"

"I'll pick you up at 6 o'clock."

Escorting her back to her carriage, he held her hand as she got in. As it pulled away, he could see her turn to look at him until the carriage rounded the corner out of sight.

He saw the people he had to see during the day and by late afternoon had completed all his appointments. Going back to Charles' he got ready for his dinner engagement and at 6 o'clock sharp was at Benda's door. After knocking he was admitted by the butler.

Standing in the hall he marveled as Brenda came down the stairs. She was wearing a peach colored dress and a white finely knit shawl around her bare shoulders. With what she was wearing and the contrast of her long black hair, tonight, she would make everyone man or woman look with envy.

The open carriage ride with the clear sky made the ride seem that much more enchanting. As they passed through the French Quarter, people would turn and watch in envy. A few people taking advantage of such a gorgeous evening were sitting on their ornately trimmed balconies of wrought iron overlooking the street. As they passed below Brenda could hear a woman comment to her friends on the balcony, "Look at this! Now this is the height of southern gentility."

The French Quarter seemed different than the one Brenda knew. She only saw it during the day with the hustle and bustle of fish mongers and other people selling their wares.

Luke pulled up in front of Antwonett's, an elegant restaurant built 12 years before the Battle of New Orleans. After going inside, all conversation seemed to cease as David removed the shawl from her shoulders handing it to the maitre d'. After ushering them to a table in the middle of the room, another maitre d' helped Brenda seat herself then lit the candle on the table.

The establishment was elegantly adorned with polished panels of dark teakwood and smoked-glass mirror inlays. The tables were covered with white linen, and the fine china as well as the silverware sparkled from the light being cast by four exquisitely designed chandeliers. There were 15 tables in the restaurant, and about half were occupied. The menu was Cajun Creole, Brenda's favorite food.

"David, I'm looking forward to Cousin Beau's wedding with Anne in several months and I'm looking forward to seeing you there too."

"I hope I don't have to wait that long. I'm afraid you may have a change of heart toward me," he replied with a smile.

Leaning toward him she quietly said, "I don't think you have to worry about that. I think the way we parted last night was the real you behind all that southern gentility."

Without returning her comment, he smiled again.

After dinner the night was so perfect they decided to take a stroll through the streets of the French Quarter. After taking in the sites they wound up at a coffee house for a light repast. Café Durmontee' was once owned by the pirate Jean Lafitte, and after having their drink they walked back to the carriage.

The ride home was bringing to an end an evening Brenda wished could go on forever. The carriage pulled up in front of her house and David escorted her up the steps to the front door. After stepping inside he embraced her then kissed her on the lips. The kiss she gave him in return was not like the evening before when she was taken by surprise. It was to let him know he meant more than just a dinner engagement.

Returning to Charles', over a night cap they discussed more of their business. Charles asked the big question that most dock owners were concerned with in their own minds these days, but hesitant to openly talk about.

"David what are we going to do if war comes?"

"I don't really know. But it will surely curtail our foreign trade and maybe even domestic trade as well. It all depends on what they do here in New Orleans."

"David you mentioned this morning about investing somewhere else. It might be a good idea for you to cut back on buying anything right now and just focus on what we already have. Brenda's father has his sugar plantation and it's going to affect him just as much as it does us."

"Not really Charles. Unlike us, he can still transport his sugar north. If a blockade does come it won't affect him at all."

"I agree. If there is war they'll definitely blockade New Orleans. The British did the same thing in the war of 1812. I guess the North already realizes that."

"Charles we'll have to wait until morning to continue this discussion. It's been a long day. I'm getting tired."

After climbing the stairs David was somehow rejuvenated with the few words they exchanged. After undressing he got into bed. Lying there staring at the ceiling he wondered whether it wouldn't be better if his brother Tom sold Cliveden. If he can't get his crops to market, the plantation couldn't make it financially and he'd lose everything in the long run too. He realized the South didn't have a navy to protect its ports if war did come. The only way it would pay to stay in business is if the South was allowed to separate, something Abraham Lincoln wouldn't consider if he got elected. With all the questions circulating in his mind he decided to lay them aside; focusing instead on the next time he'd be able to see Brenda. He thought, *I leave for Biloxi the day after tomorrow. I'd like another chance to see her before I go.*

It seemed like he just closed his eyes and after opening them again it was morning. Going downstairs he picked up the conversation with Charles where they left off the previous evening.

"David I'm here in New Orleans. It's a much larger hub of commerce than Biloxi. I hear more news than you from not only southern states, but northern states, and foreign countries as well. With all the heightened secessionist fervor in South Carolina and now other states joining in, I think you're right. War is pretty much inevitable probably before the end of next year."

"Charles I realize that. I was thinking last night about telling Tom to sell Cliveden while he still has a chance to get out. Like it or not we're in the same boat. If we can't ship or receive goods we don't make any money. If Tom can't get paid for his crops, he can't make money. All of us have the potential to go bankrupt. When I get back to Biloxi I think I'll write Tom a letter for Luke to carry back to Cliveden."

"Good idea. I don't know where all this will lead. I had hoped the hot heads would reconsider the mistake they're making and how it's going to affect so many businesses, including theirs."

"Charles, if it's alright with you I'd like to visit Brenda. It's my last day here."

"That's fine with me. Maybe you should tell Luke to be ready to go back to Cliveden," Charles said.

After dropping Charles off David proceeded to Brenda's. Before getting out of the carriage he turned to tell Luke, "You better spend the rest of the day with Trisha. We'll be leaving in the morning. I'll find my own way back."

"Yes Sir, Master David. She helped me pack last night. I was hopin' we could spend my last day here together."

David went up the stairs and was led into the parlor where Brenda was waiting. As he entered the room she put down her needle work and rose from her chair. "David, thank you for such a beautiful evening, I never felt so regal. It was like a fairy tale."

Remembering how Brenda's father spoke about her mother's input in their business he thought he would confide in her about the conversation he had with Charles. Asking her opinion on the subject she paused for a few moments then said, "David, my father's in a uniquely different position. His business is more flexible because he has many places to deliver his sugar. It's a commodity most people use, whether it's here or abroad. However, Tom's or Beau's father's plantation is fixed with only two types of crops, cotton and tobacco. They depend on shipping. Sorry to say if you can't get the product out because of a blockade, everything comes to a halt."

David realized he not only wanted her for her beauty but for the obvious intelligence she just displayed replied, "Thank you for being so perceptive. Now what would you like to do today?" he asked.

"I think I'd rather stay here this morning and if possible go out for lunch."

Over the course of the day they talked about a possible merger between Brenda's father and David. The day went by quickly and before David realized it was time to leave. Brenda saw him to the door and after kissing, he departed.

In the morning when he arrived at the dock, Luke was already there saying goodbye to Trisha. To David's surprise Brenda came to see him off, just as she did her father. It made him feel good the relationship meant that much to her, and as the ship pulled away from the dock she waved.

Chapter 17

Flora

The trip was uneventful, and three days later they were tying up to port in Biloxi. Jeremiah already hearing about Luke's injury asked, "Luke what you be doin' in Biloxi?"

"I'm on my way to Cliveden. My momma dun' has the weakness."

"I sorry to be hearin' 'dat. When you be leavin'?" Jeremiah asked.

"Soon as I can get somebody to carry me on out there," he replied.

"I surely hopes she's not too bad off. I see you when you gets back," Jeremiah said.

That afternoon David secured a ride for Luke on a freight wagon going to Cliveden. The whole time traveling Luke wondered how bad Flora was. In Biloxi, Thelma never got any letters that she was any worse and that was encouraging.

When he arrived at Cliveden, Elizabeth came out to greet him. Looking at her eyes welling up with tears Luke realized his worse fear was probably correct. He asked solemnly, "How's momma?"

Embracing Luke she broke down sobbing, "Luke, she's gone. She passed three days ago. I was hoping you could get here before."

Master Tom and Miss Sharon were there and both conveyed their sorrow. "Luke, your mother was a good woman," Master Tom said.

"Thank you Master Tom," he replied.

With his head lowered, Luke put his arm around Elizabeth and they slowly walked back to the kitchen. When they walked in Elizabeth said, "Luke, this is Mary. She's going to be in the kitchen taking momma's place. Mary, this is my brother Luke, he's been the dock foreman in New Orleans. He's married to a girl from here named Trisha. She used to help Miss Flora just like you're helping me."

Mary turned to Luke wondering if her words would have a positive effect on him saying, "I'm sorry Miss Flora died but she won't want to be liven' like that, all crippled up with somebody havin' to feed her."

Elizabeth added, "Yeah, Luke, she was pretty bad in the end. She wouldn't have wanted it that way."

Solemnly Luke replied, "I didn't know she was 'dat bad off. I guess it be for the best."

"Are you still in the same cabin Elizabeth?" he asked.

"Yes, there's a neighbor taking care of Violet while I'm up here."

"I think I'll just wander on down and put my bags in there."

"Miss Elizabeth, why don't you walk on down with Luke, I be fine here by myself."

Elizabeth smiled at Mary, then her and Luke walked out the backdoor.

Getting to the cabin Elizabeth asked, "How's Trisha? Is everything in New Orleans alright?"

"Everything's fine. Master David, he sure 'nough gave us a good start."

"Yes, he's been a blessing to this family that's for sure," she replied.

Stacking some kindling in the cook stove he started a fire. Looking up at Elizabeth he said, "We live in the house you and John lived in. Trisha dun' took in some boarders. She cooks and washes they clothes and they pays her money."

With a chuckle Elizabeth said, "Luke, did you ever think we would see the day when black folks would be payin' other black folks?"

"No, I surely didn't. Is Master Tom and his missus treatin' you good?"

"Yes, but the only problem we have is the poor white folk pickin' at us when we go off to the store or when the men go to the cotton market," pausing to stir a pot of stew she made earlier she continued, "They beat William pretty bad."

Shaking his head and looking down at the floor he asked, "Why everything be changin'? It surely don't seem like the place it used to be."

Looking at him she replied, "I don't know," pausing for a moment, "You just be careful! Don't you go pokin' your nose where you're gonna get it in trouble."

After dinner she poured some tea and they talked about when they were young, the secure feeling they always had when Daniel was alive and the people they once knew who added to that sense of security. After talking for awhile, Luke decided to go out back to the cemetery where Flora was buried to pay his respects. Looking down at the freshly disturbed earth he thought, *If I had only been a few days earlier.* Looking at his father's marker, it was tilted and he straightened it. Noticing other markers were tilted he straightened them too and after doing it, he decided to take a walk trying to relieve his sorrow.

Before long he found himself walking the same path he and James used to take to the swamp. He remembered the day they heard the shot and watched the slave catchers tie George over the horses back taking him back to Dumont. He remembered how they were so afraid that day; they hid in the tall grass until almost dark before running home. The sound of the field hands singing as the harvest was being done, was all coming back.

Before he realized he was standing next to the hollow log he and James used to sit on when they were fishing. Staring at the mirror like surface of the water a ripple disturbed its tranquility. Someone behind him tossed a pebble over his head into the swamp. He'd been so deep in thought he never heard the group of men behind him.

"What are you doin' here boy?" one of the men asked.

Quickly turning he replied, "Nothin' Sir. I be stayin' at Cliveden, at Master Tom Stewarts."

"You sure you ain't one of them runaway's what's been causin' all the trouble round here?"

"No Sir. I just came back to burry my momma. She was the cook here at Cliveden."

"How come I ain't never seen you round these parts befo'?" another man asked after spitting a hefty mouthful of tobacco juice.

"I dun' been gone out of here quite a spell. I be workin' for Master Tom's brother, Master David Stewart, in New Orleans. He dun' freed me and my missus."

"You got papers to prove that boy?" another man asked.

"No Sir, but we can go on up to the big house. Master Tom will tell you I ain't lyin!"

"You're one of those uppidy niggers what's been freed. Some of the kinds we just don't like round here. Suppos'en we just kinda stretch your neck a little and take some of that sass outa you?"

The other men standing there, laughed.

Luke realizing it was futile getting anywhere talking to them knew his only chance was to bolt into the swamp. Pushing the one closest who had been vocal, he made a dash for the water. One of the men fired a shot and began to run after him, when the man who was pushed got to his feet and said, "Don't chase him. Let the alligators and snakes get him."

Wading fearfully through the swamp Luke found a piece of dry land next to an old cedar stump to hide behind. With almost a full moon he waited until it was overcast and darker before attempting to move. He could see men in the distance carrying torches looking for any signs of his exit along the edge of the swamp and thought, *they'll never suspect me coming out at the same point I ran in. When the clouds cover the moon again, I'll take a chance.* Wiping the sweat from his face he strained to see if there was anyone around. Assuring himself there wasn't, wide-eyed, he slowly waded back to shore. There seemed to be more men than when he first saw them and realized they were probably two groups that came together. Afraid to make a run for Cliveden he thought, *if I could hide long enough they may just give up the search.*

Stumbling around in the dark he found a log to hide behind. When the clouds parted the moon-lit-night revealed he was hiding behind the same log he and James would sit on when they came here to fish. He would have never imagined it would be his temporary refuge from the mob that was chasing him. Hearing the hounds and men coming closer he wondered whether it would have been better staying in the swamp. They were close enough for him to hear one say, "We'll find him. He can't stay in the swamp forever."

Another man asked, "What we gonna do with him when we catches him?"

"Well, he's got two choices," another man said.

"What kind of choices?" the inquiring one asked.

Laughing he replied, "He can choose which end of the rope goes round his neck," then they all laughed.

One of the men said, "Hey! Quick, come over here. I think we got somethin'."

The lead hound picked up Luke's scent and he was unleashed heading in Luke's direction. Before Luke had a chance to run back in the swamp, one of the hounds had him firmly by the trouser leg. Trying to pull away a second hound clamped his jaws down hard on Luke's thigh. The excruciating pain shot up through his body as the dog began shaking his head trying to render a piece of Luke's flesh.

Desperate to loosen their hold, he kept punching at the dogs with his right arm. A third hound grasped him by the wrist limiting him the ability to use it, and as hard as he tired he soon realized fighting off the dogs was futile. Trying to protect his face and neck a forth dog joined in, jumping up biting him on his side. He knew he was trapped and the dogs kept attacking biting at his legs and ankles.

When the men got to him one of them hit him on the head with a club knocking him to the ground. Getting to his feet, he was dazed and in great pain bleeding from his good arm, both calves and his side. He realized the dogs had done a fair amount of damage to him, and wondered what was going to happen.

The men with their incoherent speech began pushing him back and forth dragging him along the ground, and stopped at the base of a hundred year old swamp-oak. With its thick branches extending they resembled outstretched arms. Two men climbed up on the first branch wide enough to comfortably walk on and threw a rope down to lift Luke up.

After they had him standing on the first branch one of the men threw the rope over a branch just above fastening it to a limb. There was still a lot of talking and cussing going on and a strange feeling came over Luke, something he never experienced. He realized it was near the end, but somehow the feeling he had made him insensitive to what was about to take place.

He wasn't paying much attention to the men. Instead, he looked up at the clouds racing by the face of an almost full moon and it reminded him of the night Solomon was whipped for running away from Cliveden. He remembered the Spanish moss stirring that night and it was doing the same now. He could feel the dampness of the swamp-mist on the branch under his bare feet. No longer felling the pain of the bite wounds to his arms and legs, he prepared himself for the inevitable.

After one of the men put the rope around his neck Luke could smell it must have been stored in a shed that had kerosene, the odor permeated the rope. He thought about the question his friend James asked the day James was bitten by the snake. 'Luke, what you think it be like dyin'?' It all seemed so long ago, and the irony of where he was going to experience it was their favorite spot. One of the men grabbed him by the collar forcing his head around to look at him, "I guess by now you wished you ain't pushed me, huh boy?" he said.

Instead of replying Luke gave him a blank stare. Smiling, the man gave Luke a shove causing him to lose his balance. He could feel the rope tighten for a brief moment then nothing. It was like he had never been born.

When he didn't show up at the cabin after dark Elizabeth began to worry and went to the big house to tell Master Tom.

"Are you sure he just didn't stay with someone else at the quarter?" Tom asked.

"No Sir. He told me he'd be right back after he went to Momma's grave."

"Get Sam, Solomon and some of the other men together. Tell Solomon to bring torches and we'll see if we can find him," Tom instructed.

In a panic she ran to Solomon's cabin and frantically knocked at the door.

"Solomon, Luke didn't come home. He's missing. Master Tom wants you to get Sam and some of the others. He said you should bring torches, he wants all of you to go look for him."

"Tell Master Tom we be up right away," Solomon replied as he put on his shoes.

In a short time about 15 men gathered together at the front steps of the big house. After lighting the torches Tom said, "I want you to break up in three groups. I want one group to look in the tobacco fields and the woods near there. Sam, you take a few and search the meadow. Solomon, you take your group and search along the edge of the swamp. I'll be with you. Does everyone know where you're assigned?"

After acknowledging him they left. They searched their assigned area, and in two hours after returning unsuccessful, they decided to go out again at daybreak.

As dawn broke they were out front of the quarter again and Master Tom gave them the same areas to search. Not going with any of the groups he returned to the house.

Within two hours Sam's group came back with Luke's body. Elizabeth seeing them ran out of her cabin screaming, looking in horror at what she anticipated. After they laid Luke's lifeless body on an outside table, Elizabeth, who was being restrained by two of the women broke loose and ran to him, cupping his face and kissing it. The rope marks were visible around his neck and she wondered what kind of animal could take the life of someone so innocent. Luke was dead and there was nothing anyone could do to bring him back. A few of the women from the quarter walked Elizabeth back to her cabin consoling her. Master

Tom, looking at Luke's lifeless body shook his head in disbelief saying, "They need to hang the men who did this. Sam, Solomon, make a coffin, we'll bury him alongside Miss Flora and Daniel."

Later that evening everyone came by Elizabeth's cabin to pay their respects. Still in a state of severe morning with the loss of her brother, she began slowly humming the spiritual Daniel liked, *Wade in the Water*. Soon the rest of the mourners joined in. Master Tom and Miss Sharon came down to pay their respects and as they were leaving Tom told Elizabeth, "I know now isn't the time, but I'd like to speak to you after the funeral."

Seeing his concern for her, through saddened eyes she made a gesture confirming his statement.

The next morning with a bright blue sky they buried Luke. He would be at rest with the people he loved dearly.

***

After a few days Tom went to Elizabeth's cabin to speak with her. He asked, "Do you think you'd like to go back to New Orleans and be with Trisha for awhile? She's going to need someone."

"Yes, Master Tom, I think that would be best. She's is goin' to need help. It would be good if I could be there."

"That's settled then. You can leave tomorrow if that's ok. I have some paper work for David you can carry along."

"Thanks, Master Tom, me and my daughter will be ready in the morning."

Looking down the row of houses in the quarter he said, "We'll sure miss you around the place. Your family has been like our own kin," then went back to the house.

The next morning when the coach pulled up at the front steps Elizabeth said goodbye and got in. As the coach was going down the dusty road heading for the front gate she turned to look back. As if she was seeing a mirage she clearly remembered her mother wiping the tears from her eyes the day she left and realized she was seeing Cliveden probably for the last time. Although she was part of the property of Master Tom and Miss Sharon she did have a life here that held some pleasant memories.

***

When she arrived at David's home in Biloxi she was met by Thelma and Sarah.

Thelma quickly asked, "Where's Luke?

"Luke's dead," Elizabeth sadly replied.

"Dead! What happened to him?" Thelma asked.

"He was too late to see Momma before she died and was feeling pretty bad about it. He went for a walk that evenin' and never came back. When the men went out searching for him the next day they found him hanging from a tree. There must have been 12 or more people that done it. They said there were a lot of foot prints on the ground."

"Hung him for what?" Thelma angrily asked.

"We don't know. Where's Master David? I want to tell him."

Thelma replied, "Arthur took him to a meeting with the other dock owners. They talkin' bout what to do about all this war talk. Folks just a hangin' and shootin' at each other. Umph, Umph, Umph! What this world be a commin' to? I just don't understands it! What they be doin' to each other next?" pausing from her triad for a moment she said, "Here Elizabeth let me take Violet."

When Thelma ran her finger over the sleeping child's chin Violet smiled. Carrying Violet up the front steps Thelma asked, "How long will you be stayin'?"

"I don't know. I'd like to get the first ship to New Orleans. Trisha has to be told about Luke."

Thelma raised her eyes remarking, "And that ain't gonna' be easy. You sho' gonna' have a time doin' that!"

Sarah added, "Ain't that the sho' enough truth. Elizabeth would you like something to eat? Master David should be along any time now."

"I think I'll wait till he gets here," she replied.

Within the hour David arrived. Surprised to see Elizabeth he realized something was wrong and asked, "What on earth are you doing here? Come into the study."

As she told him about what happened to Luke, he sat there trying hard to absorb her words. Getting up from his chair he walked around the desk to embrace her. Without saying it she knew he was sharing her sorrow, something she clearly understood.

"You've experienced so much tragedy in such a short time. How can I help you?" he asked.

"I'd like to get back to New Orleans to tell Trisha. I think I should be with her for awhile. She sure gonna need me."

"I'll see you get passage on the next ship. It leaves day after tomorrow."

Thelma entering the room said, "Master David, dinner's ready."

"Thank you Thelma. Did you set a place for Elizabeth?"

"Yes Sir. I thought you would have her join you and Miss Anne."

"Where is Anne?" he asked.

"She went to her friend's to talk about her wedding plans. You knows her, she get's so caught up with her intended she forget's her own stomach."

They smiled as Thelma left the room.

As they sat looking at each other David asked, "How's everything else at Cliveden?"

"Oh! I almost forgot. Master Tom gave me some papers to give you. I'll get them."

"No, sit down and finish your dinner, they'll wait," pausing for a moment he looked up from his plate, "I wish you wouldn't keep saying Master Tom or Master David when you're speaking to me."

"Ok, I'll try to remember," she said.

"Did they find out who killed Luke?"

"No, I don't think they really trying. It seems like the poor white folk are mad with all the runaways stealing everything trying to figure a way north," she said.

"I know, I don't think that's all the reason. I think it has to do with the people up north pushing for freeing the slaves. That's what the meeting this afternoon was about."

"Well, you did free everyone already," she said.

"I know, but the plantation owners need slavery to survive."

"What's going to happen to Cliveden?" she asked.

"I don't know. I warned Tom what was coming and to prepare for hard times with a blockade, something that I'm sure will happen. When I go back next month for Anne's wedding I'll speak with him again."

They were talking about different things they had done and how their lives took different paths when Anne came in the room.

"Elizabeth. Thelma just told me about Luke and your Momma. I'm so sorry."

"Thank you Miss Anne. Here, I'll let you talk to David while I look in on Violet."

"I just saw her. She's just the sweetest thing," Anne said.

After she left the room Anne asked, "David, when will we be leaving for Cliveden?"

"I thought we would leave in about two weeks. I want to go with Elizabeth back to New Orleans. I want to tell the dock owners there about the meeting this afternoon."

"What did you decide to do?" she asked.

"The war seems to be going well for the South right now but it's just starting. I don't hold much for our success. The news travels so damn slow. I don't think it will be long before our ports are blockaded."

"What will that mean?" she asked as she sat down.

"That will mean everything will stop as far as getting anything in or out of port. Even if we win on the battlefield, we still don't have a navy and that will make a difference for us. Everything will come to a standstill."

"Maybe Beau was right about leaving Five Oaks," Anne said.

"I certainly wouldn't dismiss what he said. It's going to get pretty bad for plantation owners. I tried to tell Tom but he just sent me a reply and wants to keep Cliveden going as long as he can. Maybe I can convince him when we get back for your wedding."

***

The day the ship was to leave Elizabeth said goodbye to Thelma and Sarah thanking them for everything they had done over the years, and somehow hoped she would see them again. Sarah held Violet until Elizabeth got in the coach then handed her to Elizabeth.

"You take care of this sweet little thing," Thelma said kissing the baby on the forehead.

Elizabeth replied, "I will. She's my whole life now."

Then the coach pulled away.

Arriving at the dock, it seemed like everyone already knew about Luke from the people driving the tobacco wagons coming from Cliveden. Seeing Elizabeth they all paid their respects, and she boarded the ship.

***

The three days at sea went quickly and when she arrived in New Orleans all the dock hands wondered where Luke was. After Elizabeth told them they too were stunned. Charles was at the dock to greet David and David told him what happened to Luke.

"Charles, arrange a meeting with the other dock owners this evening at your house. I'll let them know what the dock owners in Biloxi have to say. I'm going with Elizabeth to see Trisha."

"Ok David, I'll let them know. That's really a shame about what happened to Luke, ignorant damn people. He was a good person," Charles said in a disgusted tone.

Elizabeth and David walked to Trisha's house and knocked at the door. Answering it, Trisha stood back immediately sensing something wrong.

"Where's Luke?" she said beginning to tremble, "I know it must be bad, dear god in heaven, please don't tell me he's dead."

"Trisha sit down, we do have some bad news... Luke is dead," Elizabeth said.

"No! He just can't be dead. He just can't be," she began crying hysterically then screamed. "Master David, tell me it ain't so. Please! Tell me it ain't so."

"I'm sorry Trisha but there's no way to tell you without it being painful."

Trisha regaining some composure solemnly asked, "How did it happen?"

Elizabeth replied holding Trisha's hand, "Luke missed Momma's funeral. We already buried her three days before he came. He was feeling pretty bad and wandered down by the swamp. There must have been some men looking for somebody stealing from them and thought Luke was the one."

Looking at Elizabeth Trisha asked, "How'd they kill him?"

"That isn't important to know?" David quickly replied.

"Yes, I want to know if he suffered any," Trisha pleaded.

Elizabeth interrupted, looking at David she realized Trisha wanted desperately to know and said, "They lynched him down by the swamp."

Trisha screamed, "Oh no! I knew I should have gone with him. I just knew it."

"Trisha, I went through the same thing when John died. I hated myself for not having him go with me. It's providence that's all."

"What happened to his body?" Trisha asked.

"Sam and Solomon brought his body back and we buried him out back of the quarter with Momma and Daddy."

"Trisha, I thought Elizabeth could help you get over this crisis by staying with you. It would be good for you to be in each other's company for awhile."

Sobbing Trisha replied, "Thank you Master David."

"No Trisha, it's just David."

After saying how sorry he was again, Elizabeth walked him to the front door. Looking back at Trisha then at David, she said, "Thanks David, I think she'll be fine in a few days."

"Let me know if you need anything. I'll be here for the week," he replied.

Returning to the dock to speak with Charles he asked about the meeting.

"I already asked several owners, they'll be there at seven if that's alright with you David?"

"Seven will be fine. Now, can I impose on your hospitality and stay with you again?"

"You don't have to ask. I take it you'll want to stop and see Miss Brenda before the meeting too?"

"I'd like to, this whole thing with Luke really took its toll on my nerves. I need some comfort with her conversation to help settle them."

"Take my carriage. I'll get a ride home with one of the other dock owners."

Arriving at Charles', David quickly washed and changed clothes then hurried to Brenda's. When he arrived she was surprised to see him.

"Brenda, I had to speak to you. Your conversation is something I need desperately."

"What on earth are you talking about? You seem so solemn. Come in and tell me what's wrong?"

After telling her about Luke and having to tell Trisha the bad news, she understood leading him into the parlor. After confiding his thoughts with her, it seemed to help. After an hour he returned to Charles'.

Chapter 18
The Plan

In the morning he returned to Brenda's. Knowing Edward returned from Cuba he asked, "Brenda is your father at home?"

"Not right now. I expect him shortly for dinner. You'll stay of course?"

"I'd like to but I have a meeting already set with some of the dock owners at Charles'. I have to let them know what's being done about what those damn hotheads in South Carolina started. Oh, forgive me dear for swearing."

"That's okay. I've heard Papa say worse since the fighting's begun. What do you think is going to happen?"

"For now it will remain the same until the blockade happens. After that no one really knows."

At that moment Edward entered the room. "Hello David, and what brings you here?" with a slight laugh he smiled then continued, "Wouldn't be my Brenda, would it?"

"Papa you're such a big tease."

"Yes Sir, and a meeting we had in Biloxi about a potential blockade. Unfortunately I can't stay very long."

"At least come into the parlor for a brandy, it won't hold you back that long," Edward continued mumbling in a low voice, "Damn South Carolinians, starting a war they won't be able to win. Not thinking about the rest of the South."

Entering the parlor he turned to David asking, "What do the dock owners have to say in Biloxi?"

"Some decided to hold out as long as they could; hoping for the best. Some of the others were talking about getting smaller ships that could sneak past the blockade."

Edward asked, "Where would they carry their cargo? Smaller ships couldn't hold as much and wouldn't make the long voyage to England profitable."

Edward, noticing Brenda sitting silently asked, "Brenda, you seem to be thinking about something. What is it?"

David glancing at her waited patiently for her reply.

"They wouldn't have to make a long voyage if they took it to Jamaica.

They're a British colony and the North wouldn't be able to stop them," Brenda said.

Surprised at her input David replied, "That's a good idea. I never thought of that."

"I told you David I taught my daughter how to think," Edward said looking at her with a smile.

David replied, "I'm glad I heard her. At the meeting tonight I'll bring it up with the other dock owners." Swirling the brandy in his glass David looked at Edward then asked, "Edward, could you possibly look into a port in Jamaica where we could ship our goods?" pausing, "I wouldn't want you to jeopardize your own business affairs."

"David, I don't think that will be a problem. Tell that to the other dock owners at the meeting tonight."

"Yes sir, I certainly will and thank you Miss Brenda for your wisdom."

They talked about the upcoming wedding of Anne and Beau and how the three of them looked forward to meeting again at Five Oaks.

Edward said, "I think Beau might be right about getting out of the plantation business before things really get bad."

"I understand he's the only child of the Henry's?" David asked.

"Yes. From what I hear they had to mortgage the place several years ago to get out of a financial burden."

"Yes I know. When we were there at Christmas I heard Beau tell that to Anne. Beau said he's considering going north and possibly working in the financial sector, possibly New York," David said.

Not realizing the time had slipped by so quickly David got up from the sofa. Before excusing himself he said, "Edward, I'll see you again at the wedding."

"Papa, I'm going to walk David to the door."

"That's fine dear. You go right ahead."

Brenda and David entered the vestibule and she closed the door behind them. After giving him a kiss she asked, "I'll see you again before you have to leave won't I?"

"I'll call on you again day after tomorrow," he replied.

After he left Brenda watched until his carriage pulled away.

Arriving at Charles' there were already three carriages there. It seemed everyone arrived early wanting to know what was being said in Biloxi. After entering the living room Charles introduced David to people he wasn't familiar with. David told them what was discussed about getting smaller ships to run the blockade adding, "While I was at Mr. Atchison's tonight, his daughter, Miss Brenda, gave me an idea. She suggested we secure a port in Jamaica. They're a British colony and our cargo can be transferred to larger vessels then transported to Europe."

"Who's going to set things up in Jamaica?" one person asked.

"Mr. Atchison said he would do it. He knows other sugar plantation owners and said he would use whatever influence he has," David replied.

Looking at each other they nodded in approval. Talking quietly to one another the inquiring one said, "Gentlemen that seems like the best idea. Here's a toast to the South and the success of our new policy."

Rising to their feet, they all replied, "Here! Here!" lifting their glasses before drinking. After the toast there was some light talk about how bad they thought it would be if the North tried to occupy New Orleans and David expressed his opinion, "I think we'll eventually be shut down and won't be able to move anything... a terrible prospect," he added.

As the guests walked to the front door they were discussing between themselves what each other's thoughts were.

"Good night, Charles, David, we'll be seeing you again soon," a few of them expressed walking out the door. After they left, Charles and David continued the discussion. "Charles, what will we do if we have to shut down?"

"I've been thinking about that for the last few months. I can't say right now what I'll do. I'm hoping for the best but expecting the worst," Charles replied.

The following morning David went unannounced to Brenda's wanting to tell Edward about the meeting. Going in Brenda heard his voice and came out to the hall.

"Is your father at home? I'd like to tell him about the meeting last night."

"Why, yes. I think he's in the back garden reading the newspaper. I'll take you to him."

As David stepped out the back door Edward rose from his chair.

"Good morning David, how was your meeting?"

"Fine, Sir. I wanted to tell you, all the other dock owners wanted to thank Miss Brenda themselves for her idea," both of them looked at

Brenda then smiled. David continued, "They also wanted me to let you know whatever it costs to set up in Jamaica financially, you can depend on them."

"Thank you David. Tell them I appreciate their confidence but I hope we don't need it," showing David the front page of the newspaper he said, "The Yankees just suffered another defeat. I was reading about it this morning."

"Do you think it will end soon?" David asked.

"I really don't know. I certainly hope they'll call a truce and let the South leave the union in peace. I'd hate to see this nation at war with each other very long. Are you going back to Biloxi and tell them what I'm going to do?"

"I was thinking about going back tomorrow," David replied.

"Well then, let me allow you two young people to spend some time together. It's such a beautiful morning. I think I'll take a walk."

"Thank you Papa," Brenda said kissing him lightly on the cheek.

Turning to David after her father left the room, Brenda said disappointedly, "I was hoping you would stay a few more days."

"I would Miss Brenda but the other dock owners are anxious to know what's happening here in New Orleans."

"You could come by for dinner again this evening. I'm sure Papa wouldn't mind," she replied hoping he would accept the offer.

"Thank you for the invitation."

After a few hours of conversation he said goodbye. As he was about to leave Edward entered the parlor and said, "You're welcome to dinner tonight, David."

"Thank you sir, Miss Brenda already extended the invitation."

Edward laughed.

Returning for dinner that evening, they enjoyed pleasant conversation until 8 o'clock, when David departed.

The following morning he was on a ship bound for Biloxi, a ship commanded by Captain Jarvis. At dinner Captain Jarvis was saddened to hear about the loss of Luke.

"Captain Jarvis, have you seen any significant naval activity by the Yankee fleet in our area?"

"Yes David, I spoke to a captain I know that sails out of Charleston. He was boarded twice for inspection to see if he was carrying war material."

Looking across the table at Captain Jarvis David said, "I think it's only going to get worse. They'll eventually strangle the South by closing all southern ports. This war is just beginning and although the south won the first few battles decisively, I think if it's a long fight the South will ultimately lose."

"I agree... What do you intend to do?" Captain Jarvis asked.

"I already have a proposal from Brenda's father."

"Who's Brenda?" Captain Jarvis asked.

"She's the daughter of Edward Atchison. Do you know him?"

Captain Jarvis appeared to be searching his mind. Finally remembering he replied, "Why yes, he owns one of the biggest sugar plantations in Cuba. I have a friend who captains a ship that carries his sugarcane to Philadelphia for processing. What's he going to do?"

"He's going to secure a port for us in Jamaica where we can ship our goods. From there larger British ships can transport it to Europe unmolested. The North wouldn't dare interfere with them," David said.

"That's a good idea. Now, how are we supposed to get through a blockade?" Captain Jarvis asked.

"I was thinking about getting smaller ships that would stand a better chance of not being detected. They're much faster and although they won't carry as much cargo the trip is much shorter than making the trip across the Atlantic. All we have to do is register our larger vessels in Jamaica under the British, and use it as their home port," David replied.

"That would probably work. When are we going to test this theory?" Captain Jarvis asked with a little skepticism in his voice.

"I'd like to do it after Brenda's father secures a port."

"You speak about this Miss Brenda as if you may have intentions?"

Running his finger around the rim of his wine glass David looked at him smiling, "I do. I'm going to ask for her hand in marriage when I attend my sister Anne's wedding next month. Her father is related to my sister's intended through marriage. His mother is Mr. Atchison's cousin on his mother's side. In fact this whole idea about getting our goods to another port was Brenda's idea."

"Sounds like a woman that uses her brain as well as her beauty. I recall a woman in a carriage waiting for Edward coming in at another dock. She had black hair and was very attractive as I recall. Is that her?"

"Yes, I think it must have been," David replied.

"Good luck with your proposal," Captain Jarvis said, as he raised his wine glass to toast David's success.

***

Arriving in Biloxi David went to several piers where he knew the owners and asked them to attend a meeting at his home later that evening, wanting to inform them about the plans discussed in New Orleans.

Arriving home he was greeted by Thelma excitedly saying, "Master David, you needs to speak to Miss Anne; she needs to settle down. She's just a runnin' round like a chicken with its head cut off. I dun' told her, she's gonna' make herself sick."

"Okay, Thelma, I'll speak with her."

At that point Anne lightheartedly came sweeping down the stairs moving her arms like a ballerina. Seeing David she excitedly asked, "When are we leaving for Cliveden?"

Thelma looked back over her shoulder before leaving the room, "See what I dun' told ya, she needs to settle down."

"The wedding's not for two more weeks. If you want to go sooner I'll send you tomorrow. It'll give Thelma some peace and quiet."

"Do you mean it David? Can I sure enough go?"

"Yes, I'll have Arthur take you."

Running into the hall, she excitedly said, "Thelma! Thelma! You have to help me pack. David said I can leave tomorrow."

"Don't you be botherin' me now. I wants to set the table for dinner. We'll do it after you eat."

Coming into the hall David said, "Thelma, I have some business people coming around 7 o'clock. Tell Sarah I'd like to have some light refreshments for them," then returned to the library.

"Yes Sir. I'll tell her."

At 7 o'clock when the business associates arrived, David escorted them to the living room where he laid out the plans discussed in New Orleans. Without exception they approved. One of the men asked, "David, if we can use a private port why not take it a step further?"

"What do you mean?" he asked.

"Why don't we try a rendezvous at sea and transfer the cargo?"

David replied, "I already asked that question to one of the ship's captains. He said it would be too risky and we run the chance a Yankee war ship confiscating both ships. Even if they returned the British ship it would scare the other British ship owners from taking that chance."

Thinking for a moment, the person asking the question replied, "I guess you're right, we'll have to try it your way."

The meeting ended and David escorted them to the front door. Closing it he could hear them talking to one another about the success of the plan as they walked down the front steps. Confident with their agreement he returned to the study wanting to compose a letter to Brenda to let her know about the approval of her plan. He also wanted to convey some private thoughts about seeing her in two weeks at the wedding. After finishing he sat staring at the painting of his wife wondering how he would feel being married again.

Thelma came into the room and asked, "Master David, how did things go in New Orleans with Trisha?"

Looking up he replied, "As hard as can be expected but with Elizabeth and Violet there for her, I'm sure she'll be fine."

Looking at the letter in David's hand she asked, "Do you wants me to post your letter in the mornin'?"

"No, I want to make sure it goes out with Captain Jarvis' ship tomorrow. I'll have Arthur deliver it."

With a smile noticing it was written on fancy stationary and not his normal business paper Thelma said, "Is that letter to the lady Miss Anne talked about?"

"Yes, Thelma. You're very observant."

Thelma sheepishly asked, "I takes it, you might want to marry her?"

"I'm going to ask for her hand when I return to Cliveden for Anne's wedding."

"That's fine, that's just fine. Will you be needin' me the rest of the evening?"

Smiling he replied, "No, I won't need anything, you get some rest," pausing for a moment he added, "You'll need your strength to deal with Anne in the morning."

Leaving the room she replied in a low voice, "And that ain't no lie... I surely will."

Chapter 19
Anne's Wedding

In the morning Anne was scurrying around the house making sure she had everything in order for her trip. She would be gone from the house and didn't know whether she would ever return. Finally getting all her clothes and personal items she wanted to take with her, she said goodbye to the house servants. Before going out the front door she embraced Thelma giving her a kiss on the cheek.

"I don't know what I'll do without you Thelma. You've been practically like my mammy all these years."

With a tearful eye Thelma gave her a hug, "I'm gonna miss you, Miss Anne, but we sees each other once in awhile when you comes to visit."

"I don't know. Beau plans to go to New York. He doesn't want to live at his father's plantation."

Surprised Thelma asked, "Why would he wanna do that? All those people living on top of each other; just don't seem natural."

"Maybe I can still talk him out of it," Anne said.

As Anne was leaving, Thelma walked with her down the front steps, hurling instructions at her on how to act around Beau. After Anne got in the coach Thelma stood next to it holding her hand while they waited for David. Coming out of the house David handed Arthur a letter instructing him to go by the dock first and deliver it to the captain of the outgoing ship.

As the coach pulled away Thelma threw Anne a kiss. Waving goodbye she said aloud, "Bye, Miss Anne. You be sure you keeps yourself warm now... Bye!"

Thelma and Sarah watched until the coach was out of site. They both solemnly returned to a house that just a few minutes ago abounded with Anne talking and scurrying around making sure she had everything for her trip. Although she sometimes created a fuss, the house seemed abnormally empty without her.

"Thelma, now you can relax," David said.

Turning to look at David she threw her apron in front of her face and started crying. "Master David she's been my little lamb all her life just like she was my own."

David looking over a paper he was reading said, "Don't fret! I'll take you to Cliveden with me for the wedding."

"Yes Sir, Master David. I surely would like that," she quickly replied.

Smiling he said, "See, you feel better already, don't you?"

***

Two weeks went by quickly and the day he was to depart for Cliveden Thelma was packed and ready to go. Looking around Anne's room she gathered a few things for the trip that Anne forgot to pack and after putting them in the coach they left.

***

Two days later they arrived at Cliveden. The first thought Thelma had when she saw the place was when she was a young girl at the plantation she was born.

When the coach pulled up to the front steps, Tom, Sharon, and Anne, came out of the house to greet them. Anne, seeing Thelma, quickly rushed to her throwing her arms around Thelma's neck.

"Thelma, I was praying David would bring you. I'm just so glad."

"Where's this Master Beau you had yourself so upset over?" Thelma asked.

"You'll meet him tonight. He's coming to dinner."

"Miss Sharon, is there a place I can stay at the quarter?" Thelma asked.

"No, Thelma, you'll stay here in the house right next to Miss Anne's room," she replied.

Anne, happy with Sharon's decision, quickly picked up Thelma's bags saying, "Here, Thelma, I'll help you with your things. I want to show you my wedding dress and all the clothes I bought when I was staying here," going on and on as if she hadn't seen Thelma in years her exuberant voice fading as they entered the house.

David said with a chuckle, "I wonder how long it will be before Thelma misses the peace and quiet in Biloxi?"

Everyone laughed as they went inside.

After Anne showed Thelma the room she'd be staying in she excitedly pulled Thelma by the hand across the hall to show her the wedding dress.

"Look Thelma this is my wedding dress. Isn't it beautiful?"

"That surely is," pausing for a moment, "You sure this Master Beau's worth it?"

"He's more than worth it. You'll see for yourself tonight."

After helping Thelma unpack they spent the rest of the afternoon talking about the wedding.

Around 5 o'clock Beau and his parents arrived. After Tom greeted them at the front door they went into the parlor to await the announcement for dinner. Anne, taking Beau by the hand led him into the hallway.

"Thelma this is Beau," Anne proudly proclaiming.

Looking Beau up and down as if she was examining a thoroughbred at an auction Thelma said, "Hello, Master Beau. You sure looks like the somethin' Miss Anne's been braggin' 'bout for the last year. You treat her real nice, you hear?" Thelma commanded.

Blushing, Anne smiled looking at Beau. "Why Thelma, that's so embarrassing. Certainly he's going to treat me nice."

Beau added, "Yes, Thelma, Miss Anne told me all about you. I'm sure she won't be disappointed."

With a nod of approval at his statement Thelma turned toward the kitchen. Halfway down the hall she turned to look at Beau again judging his sincerity. Assuring herself he was sincere she continued to the kitchen to help put out dinner.

In a few minutes, the dinner bell was rung and they filed into the dining room taking seats. After everyone was seated David tapped the side of his glass with a spoon getting everyone's attention then stood up. Raising his glass he looked at Anne and Beau.

"I'd like to propose a toast to the bride and groom. May they always be as happy as they are tonight."

Everyone rose from their chair toasting his speech then sat back down.

"Thank you David," Beau said, "On a less pleasant note. I received a letter from my friend Franklin in Hattiesburg, Mississippi. He wrote that more slaves are running away to the North and it wouldn't be long before they'll have to pay them to stay or go out of business. It seems like the only way to stop it, is do something drastic like what happened to Luke. It's only a matter of time before it happens here."

"I refuse to succumb to brutality Beau. This isn't the time or place to discuss this matter," Mr. Henry said.

Tom adding, "Your father's right Beau. I think we can forego this conversation for now. It can wait 'till after dinner in my study."

"I think that's a good idea," Mr. Henry said before continuing, "David, Brenda's supposed to arrive tomorrow morning with her father. I guess you'll want to spend some time at Five Oaks while she's there?"

"If possible Mr. Henry... That is, if you feel you have the room."

"Please call me Simon. When I get home I'll see that you have a place ready."

After dinner the women went into the parlor and the men retired to the study. After Tom closed the door the conversation Beau began at dinner resumed immediately.

"Beau, I wish you wouldn't talk like that in front of your mother, it upsets her."

"I'm sorry father I apologize, but it's the truth. Where will Five Oaks be if we have to pay the help?"

Simon sternly replied, "We never mistreated our people. I don't see any call to be alarmed about it now. David, I heard from Edward. You had the same problem in Biloxi. How did you handle it?"

Not wanting to take sides with either Beau or his father David replied, "We wound up giving them their freedom and pay them a wage. That has more of an advantage in our type of business; it's all manual labor without a crop failure downside," after a brief pause he added, "We built small houses they live in and they pay rent. It serves two purposes. We've relieved ourselves from the financial burden of feeding, clothing and housing them. They seem to be much happier and work much better realizing there's a pay waiting at the end of the week. I don't know what effect the war is going to have on the shipment of cotton and tobacco, but if the North cuts our lifeline with commerce, you'll whither on the vine."

After a moment of silence absorbing David's last few words Tom said, "According to the newspaper our boys are giving them damn Yankees a good licking."

David, listening to Tom's optimism replied, "Tom it's only the beginning. We don't have the materials to fight a sustained war. If they don't call a truce soon, it's inevitable, the North will eventually win. In Biloxi and New Orleans we're already making contingency plans for an eventual blockade of our ports. Brenda's father is looking into securing a port in Jamaica so we can at least attempt running the blockade in smaller sloops. They can't carry as much cargo but they're fast and the trip is a lot shorter. From there we can have our larger ships transport the cargo to Europe. Monetarily wise, we'll only lose our transportation cost. In essence we'll be doing the same thing we did before we bought the ships, when we had to pay the shipping cost."

"I never thought of that David. That's a good idea."

Pausing for a moment with a smile David said, "Well it wasn't exactly my idea, it was Miss Brenda's. I'll be able to find out how successful Edward was securing us a port when he and Miss Brenda arrive tomorrow."

"Beau told me he's thinking about abandoning Five Oaks for a job in the banking industry up north," Simon said.

"Father, I wish you wouldn't keep saying the word abandon. It makes me sound like a deserter. I'm sorry that I'm an only child. If I wasn't we wouldn't be having this conversation. I could just leave it to a brother or sister to take care of. I have to think about the future for Anne and myself. It'll be a big change and adjustment for both of us I'm sure, but I won't have to face the financial hardships with failed crops and runaway slaves."

Tom, giving those words serious thought for a few moments suddenly remarked, "I think we've been absent from the ladies too long."

Looking at the clock on the mantle Simon replied, "It is getting late, it's a five-mile trip back to Five Oaks. We had better be heading back home Beau."

The ladies had been busy chatting the whole time, and when the men exited the study they joined them. It was getting late and the ladies were anxious to leave.

Anne was the first one up the following morning and it didn't take long before she had everyone else awake.

"Thelma, where did I put Momma's broach? I want to wear it on my wedding dress."

"You go on and get dressed. I'll find it," Thelma said continuing in a lower tone, "I don't know why we all has to travel all the way to Five Oaks for the weddin'. Why couldn't you just have it right here?"

Anne looked at her explaining, "Well, you see it's this way. Tom only had this plantation for a few years but Five Oaks has been in the Henry Family for over 150 years. The first Henry wedding was under an oak tree there. Everyone since then has been married under that same tree.

On such a beautiful day it will be just lovely."

Searching for the broach Thelma whispered, "I don't spect' that old oak tree would miss just one weddin," pausing for a moment, "Supposin' it would rain? they'd have to do it in the house anyway. What some folks does just don't make no sense. Here, I found your broach. So's you don't lose it again I'm pinning it on right now."

Looking around the room to make sure she had everything Anne replied, "Thank you, Thelma. I think I have everything ready."

Looking around the room before closing the door Thelma replied, "I think so."

Going downstairs everyone was in the hall ready to go. Seeing Anne, David remarked, "Why aren't you in your wedding gown?"

"I don't want to get it dirty from the road dust before I get married," she replied.

"I never thought of that," David said.

Thelma, shaking her head added, "Mens! All you got's to do is slicker down they hair and put on they pants to be ready. Takes us women a long time," everyone laughed.

The coaches pulled up and everyone climbed in. It was a beautiful late spring morning and the trip through the country was ideal. As they pulled up at Five Oaks, David could see Brenda standing on the veranda talking to Mrs. Henry. Exiting the carriage he went straight to where she was standing.

"Hello Mrs. Henry, Brenda. It's a beautiful day for a wedding," he said.

"Yes it is. If you'll excuse me I have to receive the other guests arriving," Mrs. Henry replied.

After she walked away David asked, "Brenda, where's Edward?"

"He's talking to Uncle Simon in the study. I think it's about your thoughts and fears about this war."

"Did he go back to Cuba after I left New Orleans?"

"Yes, I think he has a port you can use."

"That's good. If you'll excuse me Miss Brenda I'd like to get the particulars."

Smiling she replied, "You just got here and you want to abandon me so soon?"

"No, Miss Brenda, as a matter of fact I was going to ask you later today after Anne's wedding, if you'll marry me?"

Blushing she replied, "You take me back with your question. You completely catch me off guard."

"Well, now that you know... Would you?"

"Yes, I want to very much and I think Papa will be very proud."

"After he's through talking to Simon I'll ask his permission," he said before hurrying away.

An hour after they arrived, Anne in her wedding dress came down the stairs. Thelma, teary eyed, was behind her holding up the long wedding train from her head piece. David and Tom were staring at their little sister on her wedding day and couldn't have been prouder.

Beau, obviously nervous, fumbled for the right words to express his gratitude to both David and Tom. Accompanied by his best man they went outside to the shade of the oak tree for the ceremony just as his father, grandfather, and great grandfather before.

Anne, being accompanied on either side by her brothers, was escorted to where the minister, groom and best man were waiting.

After the ceremony they kissed and the festivities began. The food was a traditional pig roast with all the trimmings. As everyone was getting their food David asked, "Brenda, shall I get you a plate?"

"Yes, David, that's very thoughtful of you."

As David looked around at the guests in the yard he asked, "Brenda, I haven't seen your father. Where is he?"

Looking around at the other guests she didn't see him and replied, "I guess the long trip tired him out. He must have gone in to lie down."

"I'll get your food. Then I want to see whether he got us that port in Jamaica."

When he returned with Brenda's plate Edward had already joined her.

"Hello, David, I'm sorry I missed the ceremony. I was just so tired I needed a cat nap."

"That's quite alright. I know what a long trip can be like. Were you able to secure us a port?"

"Yes, I'll tell you all about it over a julep."

After retrieving the drinks David returned to continue the conversation.

"When I went back to Cuba I met a sea captain who ports in Jamaica regularly. He has a dock of his own and a few ships that will carry your goods to England if you'll carry some of his contraband back to New Orleans," Edward said.

"What's the contraband?" David surprisingly asked.

"I don't know but that's a question I would certainly ask before exchanging any monies."

"Where and when do I get to meet this captain?" David asked.

"I can arrange a meeting the next time he comes to New Orleans. It might be a little tricky since you spend most of your time in Biloxi."

"That's alright. If it comes down to it I'll spend a few days in New Orleans when he's expected. Our paths should cross eventually. Is there any other option?" David asked.

"Since Britain's not certain who's going to come out of this war a winner I personally think they'll choose to remain neutral and come out later to congratulate the winner, whoever that may be. I know you were looking for something more positive but that's the best I could do on short notice."

"Thank you, Edward, that's more than I expected. There's something else I'd like to ask it concerns Miss Brenda."

Edward smiled in anticipation of David's question said, "Go on."

"I'd like to ask your permission to marry Miss Brenda."

Patting the back of David's hand Edward replied, "If my Brenda wants to marry you, that's fine with me."

"Thank you, sir, may I excuse myself and tell her the good news?"

"Certainly David, you go right ahead."

Wandering through the crowd of guests he found Brenda in conversation with Anne and two of her bridesmaids.

"Brenda may I speak to you alone?" he asked.

"Yes, what is it?"

Taking her by the arm he quickly moved her away from the others. "I asked your father if we could marry and he gave his permission."

"Oh! That's wonderful. Where is he?" she excitedly said as she looked around, "I want to thank him."

Pointing in the direction of where he spoke to Edward David replied, "I left him over there talking to Beau and Simon."

"Let's go over and thank him together," she suggested.

As they approached the table where he was seated, he stood up as if he was expecting them then slumped over. Brenda screamed, "Papa!" racing to him.

He was pale and sweating but wasn't unconscious. Brenda frantically called out, "Dr. Cook! Dr. Cook! Come quick, it's Papa."

Dr. Cook, who was attending the wedding, got his physicians bag from his carriage. "Carry him inside, I'll examine him there," he said as a few men helped bring Edward to the house.

Brenda, David, and most of the wedding party followed. Edward was awake and after being examined asked if Brenda, David and him could be alone. After everyone left the room Edward said, "From the first day I met you David, I was hoping you would ask for my Brenda. Now I know she'll be in good hands."

"Papa you still have to give me away. I don't have anyone else."

"Brenda, I'm old and lived a full life. If it wasn't for you I would have just as soon died when your mother passed. It was you that gave me the strength to go on," reminiscing, he continued, "I got a lot of amusement from you with only a few months a year we could be together. Do you remember how you would make me sit down at your pretend tea parties and serve me tea with your play set? You always made sure I used my napkin. You were such a fun child. You made my life worth living."

Tearfully she replied, "Yes, Papa, I remember."

David opened the door asking Dr. Cook to join them. "Doctor, will he be alright?" Brenda asked.

"I gave him a sedative to help him sleep. With a few days rest he'll be fine. I think the trip from Cuba and the two day journey here from Biloxi just tired him out. He's running a slight fever but I don't think it's anything to be concerned with. I'll check in on him again tomorrow."

"Thank you Doctor," Brenda said as he left the room.

Returning to their guests Beau asked, "How's Uncle Edward?"

David replied, "The doctor gave him something to make him sleep. He looks like he's resting comfortably now," pausing for a moment, "We didn't tell you the good news. Edward gave his permission for Brenda and me to be married."

"That's wonderful cousin Brenda," Beau said embracing her. "David we're happy for you. Have you set a date yet?" Beau asked.

"We haven't discussed it but I'd like it to be in the fall if that's ok with you my dear?"

"I'd love a fall wedding," she replied.

Looking at Brenda David said, "Then it's agreed. October will be the month."

"Beau, how long are you and Anne going to be at Five Oaks?" David asked.

"I think we'll be here for the rest of the month then go on our honeymoon to Niagra Falls. I was going to stop in New York City on the way back and speak to someone that was my classmate in college. He's taken a position in one of the major banking firms there and said he thinks he could get me in. After what just happened to Uncle Edward, it has me taking stock in myself."

"What do you mean by that?" Brenda asked.

"Seeing him ill made me feel like an ungrateful wretch leaving mother and father here alone at Five Oaks. Just like father said, like I'm abandoning them."

"Don't be silly. You two have your own life to live. Just like our parents when they married," Brenda quickly replied.

Anne, not wanting to get involved in a long discussion said, "Beau, let's not forget our other guests."

Prolonging the discussion David asked, "Beau, with the war going on how do you propose to get north without difficulty?"

"I thought if Anne and I could get on a ship that could run the blockade we could escape to Cuba or Jamaica. We could then reenter the country on another ship from the Caribbean, a British ship perhaps."

"That's a good thought. I guess you were going to ask your Uncle Edward to help?" David asked.

"Yes, I was."

By dusk people started to make their way to their carriages to leave, and as they did, Beau and Anne bided them farewell thanking them for the gifts. It was time for Tom and Sharon to go too and they said goodbye. Before getting in the coach Tom asked, "How long will you be staying here David?"

"I think I'll stay until I can see Brenda and her father safely back to New Orleans. Would that be alright with you?"

"Certainly, do you want Thelma to stay with us?"

"No Tom, I think she'll be fine here."

"Well, goodnight David, Beau, Anne, Brenda."

"You too Tom, I'll let you know what happens," David said as the coach pulled away.

Brenda and David returned to the house where Simon was sitting on the front porch. "I'm just enjoying the night air David won't you join me?" he asked.

"Thank you Sir. I think I will."

"David I hear congratulations are in order?"

"Yes. Edward gave Brenda and me permission to marry."

"That's fine. Have you set a date?"

"Yes Sir. We were thinking about an October wedding."

"Mighty nice time of year, that's when Mrs. Henry and I were married," Simon pointing across the yard, "Right under that same oak tree where Anne and Beau were married."

"It's a shame there's no one else to carry on the tradition. I understand Beau's your only child," David inquired.

"No, we had another after Beau. It was a little girl. She died shortly after being born. The doctor told my wife she could never have another. It was hard for Mrs. Henry but I told her at least we were gifted with one. Some people aren't that lucky."

"That's true, my wife and baby both died in child birth two years after we were married."

"If it's not too painful David how long ago was that?"

"Over 12 years ago."

"Well, it's time you thought about an heir for your property. I wish you and Brenda all the best. It's been a long day. I think I'll retire," Simon said as he rose from his chair.

"Good night Simon. I think I'll do the same," David replied as he too rose from his chair.

Before breakfast David looked in on Edward asking, "How are you feeling today?"

"Fine, David, I embarrassed myself getting everyone upset at my condition. I should have rested a little more before mixing with company."

"I think if everyone knew all the running around you've been doing helping me they would understand. From New Orleans, to Cuba, to

Jamaica, then back again, not to mention a two day trip here, that much traveling would exhaust anyone."

"David, I know you have questions about the arrangement for the dock in Jamaica but the only thing I can suggest is a trip there with me and talk to the people personally."

"I think I'd like to do that after you're well enough to travel."

"I'll be up and around in a few days. The doctor's coming this afternoon."

"I want to thank you again for giving Brenda and me permission to marry. We're considering an October wedding. Most of the shipping should be about completed and it's a beautiful time of year."

"That's fine. That's when Brenda's mother and I were married too."

"Is there anything I can get for you?" David asked.

At that moment Brenda came into the room, "Good morning Papa, you gave me such a fright yesterday. Can I get you anything?" she quietly asked.

"David just asked. No thank you dear. Now, you two run along."

Leaving the room they joined Mr. and Mrs. Henry, along with Anne and Beau in the dining room.

"Brenda, how's your father?" Anne asked.

"He's looking better after a good night's rest. I think he should stay a few days before traveling, don't you David?"

Mrs. Henry replied, "I think you're right! That cousin of mine is awful hard headed."

Simon quickly added, "You're right dear... and remember, that's your side of the family," everyone laughed.

"What are your plans today Beau?" David asked.

"Anne and I are doing some packing. After thinking about what you said last night, I think if I wait too long the blockade will only get tighter. Maybe we should leave with you when Uncle Edward's ready to travel."

"I think that may be wise," David replied.

Beau's mother became teary eyed and said, "With this war going on it will probably be near impossible to get letters through directly. If mail could be sent to Cuba then to New Orleans we would be able to at least hear from you Beau," wiping away a tear with the end of her napkin.

"Mother, don't fret. I'll find a way," Beau replied trying to lift her spirits.

After breakfast Simon went to check on the cotton fields that were planted in late March and Anne and Beau went upstairs to continue to pack with the help of Mrs. Henry.

David asked, "Brenda, would you like to take a stroll in the garden?"

"Yes, I would," she replied.

As they were walking through the garden Brenda asked, "David, what if the North does cut off shipping? That is a real possibility you know."

"I've been thinking about that. I wanted your opinion on me getting out of the shipping business altogether?" David replied.

Thinking for a moment she said, "That's up to you. If the war goes on for a long time we'll be bankrupt anyway. There's no better time to sell than right now. What would you want to do with the proceeds?"

"I was thinking about getting a plantation in either Cuba or another place where we could raise tobacco or other crops, possibly sugar. You were right when you said we could transport it anywhere. It's something everyone wants. The money will still be invested in something and with the profit we make we can come back and reinvest after the war. I already spoke to your father this morning about going back to Cuba and Jamaica when he goes back."

"I think that's your decision. It seems like they'll be a few passengers, Father, Anne, Beau, you and I," she said.

After returning to the house, there was a knock at the door. It was Doctor Cook coming to look in on Edward.

"Is he still in his room Brenda?" Doctor Cook asked.

"Yes, he is. I'll see if he's awake."

Taking her by the arm he said, "That's okay, I'll take a look myself."

In a half hour he returned to the parlor.

"How is he doctor, will he be able to travel soon?" Brenda asked.

"I think with two more days rest he'll be fine. When he gets back to New Orleans have him look in on his own doctor. I've written him a note. You can deliver it," handing it to her.

"Thank you, I will," she replied.

After he left Brenda opened the note. It was written in Latin, something she couldn't understand.

"I wonder why he wrote it in Latin?" she asked.

"I think all physicians do that. I wouldn't worry," David replied.

***

With a couple days rest as the doctor predicted, Edward was looking and feeling much better. He was ready to travel and when David's coach pulled up in front, Brenda, Edward, David, Beau and Anne said goodbye to Mr. and Mrs. Henry.

Teary eyed, Mrs. Henry hugged Beau and Anne. Simon wished them luck wherever they decided to live and Edward said goodbye to his cousin thanking them for their hospitality. Edward realizing his cousin felt bad about saying goodbye tried to cheer her up by saying, "If all goes well by October when Brenda and David are to be married, maybe we could have the wedding here?"

"That's a wonderful idea Cousin Edward," Mrs. Henry replied, "Let's pray we'll all be together by then."

As the coach was leaving, Beau turned to look at his mother and father standing on the front porch waving. He thought of the many wonderful years he had growing up here and felt the same way now as he did when he left for college. Five Oaks was his birth place and seeing it for the last time, he wondered if he was making the right decision.

Chapter 20
Running the Blockade

Arriving in Biloxi David asked Jeremiah when the next ship was bound for New Orleans. Realizing Mr. Atchison was at risk without seeing his doctor, he didn't want to take a chance on him having a relapse in Biloxi.

"Master David they dun' boarded one of our ships and took some things off."

"Who boarded our ship and what did they take?" David alarmingly asked.

"Them Yankee's, they gots' they ships out there just a waitin' for us."

"They didn't take the ship did they?"

"No sir, but they's some 'dat say they be doin' 'dat befo' too long."

"Has Captain Jarvis been in?" David asked.

"He's supposed to come in day after tomorrow," Jeremiah replied.

"Thanks Jeremiah. Has anything else happened?"

"I almost forgot. Steven the boy you kilt in the duel, his daddy died last week, 'dats 'bout all."

"I'll be leaving for New Orleans with Miss Brenda and her father. Miss Anne and her husband will be going too. Make sure there's room for their baggage."

"Yes Sir!"

Returning home he told everyone when they'd be leaving and went into the study. Edward followed asking, "David, you seem troubled. What is it?"

"I was told the Yankees boarded one of our ships and took some cargo off but I don't know exactly what."

"You mean they actually boarded the ship?"

"Yes, that's what Jeremiah said. Now you realize why I'm so concerned about this war. I'll get a better idea of what happened when I speak with Captain Jarvis."

"Will we be able to get to New Orleans at all?" Edward asked.

"I have faith in Captain Jarvis' ability to outmaneuver the Yankee fleet. I think they may have been lucky stopping one ship but I don't think their primary concern right now is with the Gulf ports. I think their main focus will be on the Atlantic ports and anything that might be coming in from Europe."

"I think you might be right. They're probably stretched pretty thin right now."

"If you'll excuse me Edward, I'd like to get a letter off to Tom about what's happening."

"Certainly," Edward replied.

At that moment there was a knock at the door. Slowly opening it Brenda peeked in. "May I come in or is this just man talk?" she asked.

Walking to the door Edward said, "Come along dear, David's writing a letter to Tom about one of his ships the Yankees boarded at sea. I think we should leave him alone for awhile."

"Father, David was right. I think we should take his advice."

"I know dear. Now, let's not disturb him. Let him finish his letter."

Looking up David said, "I'll be with you presently; this won't take long."

Thelma stepped in, "Dinner's ready Master David."

"Thank you Thelma. I'll be there in a minute," waving for her to leave.

After finishing the letter he went to dinner. There was much discussion about current events of the war and its implication with business. Beau said, "The South's continuing to win major battles, maybe it will be in our favor."

David replied, "No Beau, Tom said the same thing. I told him the longer the war goes on the more advantage the North will have. They'll just be able to out produce us with war materials."

"Why don't we change the subject for awhile?" Anne suggested.

"That's an excellent idea," Brenda replied.

Thelma asked, "Excuse me for askin' Master David but will you be coming back here?"

"At some point yes, but I'm not sure when. Keep running the house as you have in my absence."

"Yes Sir, I surely will do that."

After dinner they left for the dock. When they arrived David helped the women from the carriage. Hurrying up the gangway to speak with the captain he said, "Jeremiah, show Miss Anne and Beau to their cabin and bring their luggage aboard."

Going to the captain's cabin he knocked before entering, "Captain Jarvis, I hear you had a little trouble, what happened?" David asked as he stepped inside.

"I tried to ignore their warning but they fired a shot across the bow. I had no alternative but to stop."

"I understand but what did they remove?"

He wasn't about to tell him it was contraband so he passed it off as checking for war goods and wanting tobacco for themselves.

"Do you think we'll have any trouble getting through to New Orleans?" David asked.

"I don't think so. I'll hug the coast line as best I can. The travel will be slower but it's safer."

"What do you mean by being safer?"

"I think they'll be several miles further into the Gulf. That way they'll be able to sail much faster covering more area. I spoke to a few captains in England the last trip. They tell me the Yankees confiscated two ships on the Atlantic Coast sneaking war supplies to the South."

"We're not carrying war supplies. Why would they bother us?"

"Right now they have no way of knowing until they board us. I think eventually they'll try to strangle the South's ability to even finance the war by confiscating all the ships and cargo. It also increases the size of their navy at the South's expense."

"Do you think you could run the blockade after we port in New Orleans?"

"I think so if we run it at night with no light showing. Where are we heading?"

"Cuba. To Mr. Atchison's sugar plantation. First I want him to consult his doctor in New Orleans. He had an episode at Five Oaks. That's why we're a week late."

"Suppose he can't go?" Captain Jarvis asked.

"Then I'll have to go myself. But we must have an alternative for a port outside the United States. Can we leave tonight?"

"I see no reason why we can't. They're almost finished loading. We can leave on the evening tide."

"That's fine. I'll tell the others," David replied.

At dusk the ship slipped its mooring, slowly entering the Gulf heading for New Orleans. Traveling close enough to land they could see faint traces of light from houses along the shoreline. The going was slow but at a point where Captain Jarvis felt he could safely navigate further into the Gulf he did. They ran all night in complete darkness and dawn broke to a beautiful clear sky. Extra lookouts were posted and if they could stay clear of northern ships for another day they could slip into New Orleans the following night. Without seeing another vessel during the day, dusk was a welcomed site.

Brenda said, "David, I think all this is having a bad affect on father. He's looking poorly again, the way he did at Five Oaks."

"I think he'll be fine dear. We'll be docking tonight or tomorrow morning. We'll get him to his doctor as soon as possible."

Suddenly a lookout shouted, "Captain! Light two points off the port bow!"

Captain Jarvis looked through his telescope then shouted, "Make sure no lights are showing!" he said aloud. In a quieter tone he said, "Everyone will have to function in the dark for several hours. Hopefully he hasn't seen us."

With a watchful eye they saw the light fade over the horizon and out of sight. Not really knowing who the other ship could be, Captain Jarvis didn't want to take that chance. In the dark with his remarkable seamanship they entered the Mississippi and within several hours they slipped into port.

Charles, greeting them, offered his carriage. Beau and Anne remained aboard while Brenda and David took Edward home. While Brenda was seeing to his comfort, David went for the doctor. It was late and there were no lights on at his residence but he knocked. The butler answered and David explained the situation. The doctor overhearing what was said came to the door. After David repeated it the doctor he replied, "Let me put on my jacket and get my bag. I'll ride there with you."

Arriving, they went directly to Edward's bedroom. Entering the room the doctor said, "Edward, what's all this about fainting at a wedding?"

"Yes, I embarrassed myself," he replied.

"Well, let's just take a look at you."

Removing his stethoscope from his bag he listened carefully to Edward's heart.

"Doctor, I have a note for you from Doctor Cook. He was the doctor who attended to him at Five Oaks. He told me to give it to you," Brenda said.

"Thank you Brenda. Why don't you go downstairs? I'll be down directly. I want to give him a sedative so he can sleep."

As they left the room she turned again to look at her father then slowly closed the door. They were in the parlor when the doctor came in.

Brenda nervously asked, "Doctor, how is he?"

"His heart sounds pretty weak. He shouldn't have made that trip."

"What did the note from Doctor Cook say?"

"It basically read what I'm telling you. He needs plenty of bed rest. I'll be by in the morning."

David said, "Thank you, doctor. I'll see you're driven home. Would you mind if I accompany you?"

"No, that will be fine," he replied.

On the way David asked, "Do you think he'll be able to make a trip to Cuba?"

Turning to look at David he said, "To be quite frank; he'll never see his sugar plantation again."

David surprisingly asked, "It's that bad?"

"Yes. Edward told me you and Miss Brenda plan to get married?"

"Yes, we intend to get married in October."

Pausing for a moment the doctor said, "If I were you, I'd try to have it within the next two months, anything after that I couldn't guarantee."

Arriving at the doctor's residence he got out of the carriage. Turning to David he said, "I'll see you in the morning. I wouldn't tell Miss Brenda what we discussed right away. Give her a little time."

"Thank you, doctor. I will."

Heading home he tried to think of an excuse to have the wedding sooner, *I could make it sound like I'm pressed for liquidating my affairs, and would rather have the wedding over before getting tangled up with business. That sounds like a better plan. I'll ask if we can do it after I get back from Cuba.*

At breakfast the following morning Brenda asked, "Are you still leaving tonight with Captain Jarvis?"

"Yes Brenda, I'd like to. Will you be alright with your father?"

"Yes, we'll manage. I'll see you when you return."

Brenda instructed the maid to have David's baggage sent to the ship for his voyage. The rest of the day was spent enjoying each other's company and occasionally looked in on Edward. At one point David looked in on him and thought he was asleep. Closing the door Edward asked, "David, is that you?"

"Yes Edward, what can I do for you?"

"Come in, sit by my side. The doctor isn't fooling me. I know how I feel. I'd like you and Brenda to move the wedding date to right after you return from Cuba. I'd like to be alive to see it."

David replied, "Not that I think you won't be but I think it would be better to have it sooner so it doesn't interfere with all the business I have to take care of."

Edward smiled realizing David understood the situation. It wasn't for business matters he wanted to make it sooner; it was Edwards' impending death.

"David I'll be gone soon enough. I wish you would consider taking over the plantation in Cuba. At least I'll know you and Brenda will be safe until the war is over."

"Thank you Edward. I'll think it over."

"Another thing I'd like to say. There's a man name Frank in Havana I want you to look up. If you run into a problem he may be able to help."

"Just Frank?" David asked.

"Yes, just Frank, he won't be hard to find."

Puzzled, David left the room.

That evening David said goodbye to Brenda then left for the ship. When he arrived Beau asked, "Where's Uncle Edward and Brenda?"

"They won't be going with us. Edward's pretty weak. Brenda's staying here to take care of him."

Captain Jarvis came out of his cabin and said, "We're ready to sail."

The ship glided out on the river and headed downstream for the Gulf.

The following morning with fair wind and sunny skies they were on their way to Cuba.

David was standing at the ship's rail looking out at the ocean when he was joined by Beau. David asked, "Beau, what's your next move? Are you still thinking about going north?"

"Anne and I discussed it last night. We decided we might try looking into Cuba as an investment."

"Do you mean starting a plantation there?" David asked.

"No, we don't have the money for that. Maybe we could find a small established business in Santiago or Havana maybe a hotel," Beau replied.

"Hotel! That sounds like a lot of work."

"Not really, we'll get help the same way you get laborers for your dock, pay them. What about you? Are you still seeking a dock to ship cotton and tobacco from? What if they close all the ports in the South, what will you do?" Beau asked.

"I've given that some thought too and may just close the dock in New Orleans and wait the war out. For now that seems like the best option. Brenda's father won't make it very much longer she'll have to take over his sugar business. Edward's concerned with our safety. He told me it would be better if we stayed on at his plantation until the war is over."

Anne, joining them heard David's statement and asked, "Do you think Edward will pass soon?"

"The doctor told me he wouldn't last more than two months."

"Does Brenda know?" Anne asked.

"No. I didn't tell her. What the doctor told me was in strict confidence. He also advised me to make our plans for a wedding sooner. I think Brenda's father knows he's going to die soon too and was pretty adamant we have it upon my return."

"Then he knows he's dying?" Beau asked.

"I'm sure he does. He as much as told me that's his reason for the request."

Holding onto Beau's arm Anne replied, "That's sure going to be some wedding gift, saying I do then having your father pass away. We probably won't be there so our best wishes to you and Brenda. We'll celebrate sometime later," Beau said.

***

Within several days, the ship entered the Caribbean and Anne commented constantly about the clear blue water. After docking she asked, "David, is the weather here always this hot and humid? It's terribly uncomfortable."

"I don't know sister. I've never been here. I have to find this Mr. Frank that Edward wanted me to meet."

"How will you know who he is?" Beau asked.

"Captain Jarvis knows his way around this port. Maybe he can help me find him."

After securing the ship they went ashore. Captain Jarvis spoke to the dock foreman, "Do you know where a Mr. Frank lives?" he asked.

Pointing in the direction of a small shack just off the pier the dock-hand replied, "There!"

"Isn't that a shack for storing ropes and tools?" Jarvis asked.

"Yes sir. That's where he lives."

Looking at him with some skepticism they asked someone else. When they too confirmed he lived there they looked at each other in amazement wondering why a person with supposedly that many connections would be living in a shack.

When they knocked at the door it was unlocked and swung open. They marveled at a dirty disheveled man who was in desperate need of a shave, lying face down fully dressed on a cot. A dog lying next to him raised its head to look then put it back down realizing they were no immediate threat. They seemed to be a perfect match. Frank appeared to be in his early forties, stocky with black hair.

As they stood in the open doorway scanning the room the inside was exactly what it appeared to be from the outside... a shed. The only light being admitted to the room was from a small dirty four-pane window partially covered by a dirty curtain. A closer look revealed it wasn't a worn curtain but a discarded towel suspended by two nails. Ropes and pulleys were hanging from wooden pegs and various parts for ships were leaning against the walls.

Knocking again harder seemed to make him angry for the disturbance but he rolled over and sat up. Scratching his head and smacking his lips together, it was obvious his mouth was dry from a rough night of drinking. Looking around the room trying to get his bearings he growled "Uhhh! What can I do for ya?"

"I was told by Edward Atchison you were someone that could acquire me a port."

At the mention of Edwards name his tone changed, "Oh! Edward sent you. That's different!" still grumbling and smacking his lips together he asked, "How is Edward?"

"Not so well. The doctor told me he wouldn't last another two months. I doubt very much you'll ever see him again," David replied.

Kicking an empty rum bottle across the floor to clear a path for himself, he still appeared to be trying to get his bearings, "That's a shame. I really like Edward. We did a lot of business."

David thought, *How could Edward consort with someone as disorganized as this?*

Frank waved his hand to gesture as if he was reading David's mind, "You don't have to say anything. I know what you're thinking. How can Edward deal with someone like me, right?"

David's face grew red. He looked at Captain Jarvis realizing Frank did in fact read his thoughts. Sitting on the edge of his cot he fumbled around trying to put on his socks occasionally glancing up at them. David intentionally hesitated to begin the conversation until he was sure he had Frank's full attention. Again, Frank was able to read David's thoughts.

"Go ahead. Go ahead. I'm listening," Frank said.

"With this war I'm afraid of my docks being shut down in Biloxi and New Orleans. I was thinking about running the blockade at night in small vessels, transferring the cargo to bigger ships then transporting it to England."

Frank waited a few moments then replied, "Well, it'll be easier to ship from Jamaica and you won't have the interference with the American Navy at all. They spend a lot of time here. This Spanish governor is pretty friendly with American politicians."

"That's what Edward said. That's why I'm here," David replied.

Frank grunted then scratched his head. Looking around for his other sock he asked, "Are we talking legal, or illegal goods?"

David smiled, "I primarily ship cotton and tobacco. On occasion I ship manufactured goods but not often."

Scratching his head again looking for his shoe Frank continued, "Well if you want my opinion, why don't you mix it up, a little legal with a little illegal, it's better profit?" he said, giving Captain Jarvis a wink.

David could see Captain Jarvis was red faced and appeared to be uneasy but didn't know the reason. Captain Jarvis didn't realize Frank knew his secret about bringing in contraband goods from France.

"As soon as I have my coffee we'll work on your problem. Care for a cup?" he asked.

"No thanks," they replied.

Getting up from his cot he bent down and scratched the dogs head, "Rough night last night, right Queenie?"

When the coffee was brewed he poured half a cup filling the rest with rum. A couple gulps later it was finished.

"Ok, let's see what we can do."

Leaving the shack they proceeded to a tavern a few blocks away. Entering, a woman from the bar came up to Frank throwing her arms around him speaking Spanish. He pushed her away saying, "Not now!" then scanned the tavern as if he was looking for someone.

"Ah! There he is. I thought I'd find him still here. Come on."

They went to a table where a man was seated with his head resting on his folded arms. He too looked as though he had a bad night drinking and David assumed he might have been Frank's drinking partner. Frank shook him then looked at us.

"I guess you figured it out. We're drinking buddies?" Frank said.

Shaking him again Frank said, "John, wake up! These guys were sent by Edward. They need your help."

Raising his head he looked as bad if not worse than Frank. Unshaven, he wore shorts and a T-Shirt. The Tee shirt was spotted with stains of various colors and didn't quite extend to his shorts challenged by his imposing belly. Finally fully awake Frank said, "John, this fella's someone Edward Atchison sent. He's looking for a place in Jamaica where he can run cargo to England without being bothered by the Navy. Can you help him?"

Scratching his head John replied, "If it's someone Edward sent I sure can. How's Edward doing?"

"From what he said it sounds like Edward's dying."

"Is this just a business deal or are you related to Edward?" John asked.

"Both. Well, I'm not related yet, but I'm going to marry Edward's daughter, Brenda."

"When's that?" John asked.

"Probably when I get back to New Orleans, it's what Edward wants."

Looking on the table John saw a glass with some whiskey that hadn't been consumed. Picking it up, he sniffed its contents then took a healthy swallow. He asked, "Is what you're shipping legal or illegal?"

Again, David looked at Captain Jarvis wondering more than ever what the connection was between them and Edward.

David replied, "It's strictly legal. I have to have a port to move my cotton and tobacco shipments to England."

John replied, "My usual fee is 10% but since you'll be Edward's son-in-law I'll only charge 5%. How's that for a bargain?"

"Better than I thought," David replied.

Pointing at Captain Jarvis John asked, "Who's this?"

"He's Captain Jarvis, one of the captains running the blockade. When can we start doing business?"

Disregarding David's question, John wiped his eyes and looked at Captain Jarvis, "Oh yeah. Edward told me about you."

Turning back to David's question John replied, "We can start right now. I'll take some money up front."

Opening a map of Jamaica Captain Jarvis brought ashore, he spread it on the table. John stood up and pointed to a spot on the map, "Lookey here Captain. Are you familiar with this cove?" John said, pointing to a spot south of Kingston.

"Yes, I know where that is but there's no port there," Captain Jarvis replied.

"There is if you're in my line of work. That's where you'll pick up a British captain that will take over from there," John tactfully said.

Looking at John then at Frank Captain Jarvis asked, "You mean we have to transfer the cargo on the water and not at a dock?"

Looking up from the map John replied, "That's right. The governor there is as crooked as a hog's tail. He's recently started taking money from the U.S. to hold all American goods being shipped out of Jamaica. When can we expect the first shipment?"

Captain Jarvis replied "I'd like to get underway tonight. I should be back again within two weeks."

"That's settled then," John said shaking hands with David, "Let's have a pint to make it official?"

David replied, "No thanks" turning to Captain Jarvis he said, "Captain

I think we better be getting back."

"Suit yourself. I'll see you in two weeks," John replied, as he picked up the bottle of rum and poured some in a glass.

Heading back to the ship David said, "Before we leave, I want to go to Edward's plantation and get my sister and her husband situated. I'd like to look it over. I'll see you back here later."

"Okay David. Make it around sunset; that's about high tide."

At sunset he returned as the last of the cargo was being put on board. Walking up the gangway he asked, "Am I on time?"

"You're fine. We're just about to get underway."

The last of the crew came aboard and the ship moved slowly away from the dock.

Captain Jarvis asked, "Did you get your sister and her husband situated?"

"Yes, the plantation is very impressive."

"I was about to have dinner. Care to join me?" Captain Jarvis asked.

"Sounds good, I have a couple questions I'd like to ask."

Looking at him suspiciously Captain Jarvis replied, "What about?"

"About the business with my future father-in-law, Frank and John mentioned. Was he involved with illegal contraband coming into New Orleans?"

Captain Jarvis' face became red with embarrassment saying, "Suppose we talk about it at dinner? I won't be long. I just want to clear the reef so the second officer can take over."

"I'm looking forward to the conversation," David replied.

Within the hour Captain Jarvis reentered his cabin where the table had already been set.

"Sorry you had to wait, but getting past that reef is kind of tricky. The first officer's relatively new. I didn't know whether he was able to navigate around it. Now, what did you want to ask?"

"Being quite frank, was Edward involved with contraband goods?"

Embarrassed by David's question he replied, "It depends on what you mean by contraband. If you want to ask about untaxed goods that's a different story."

"What do you mean? What's the difference?" David replied.

"We're all involved in bringing in fine linens and liquor from France or anywhere else we can get it."

"Edward too?" David asked.

"Yes! Edward too. In fact, he was the one that started it years ago along with Frank and John."

"Is it all done through Jamaica?" David asked.

"Yes, that's the place where he told you we were transferring your cargo."

"Isn't it a little risky?"

"Not really. The ships that make the run to Europe always bring back a full cargo."

"Who finances it?"

"We do. We buy the goods and finance the return trip. Do you want to take over Edward's part? It's pretty lucrative."

"I'll have to think about it. I have too many irons in the fire right now but it sounds promising."

"I wouldn't go embarrassing Edward with what you learned if I were you. By what you told me about the doctor's prognosis he probably won't be around very long anyway."

"I won't embarrass him but it's funny. I would have never guessed he would be involved in anything like this."

"Why not? John Hancock did the same thing back in his day."

Both chuckling they toasted the occasion. The rest of the conversation through dinner was about Edward's plantation and the potential of David and Brenda settling there if the war got worse.

"Do you think we'll have any problem with the blockade?" David asked.

"I don't think so. I guess we'll know for sure when the time comes."

***

David walked about the ship for the next few days giving some serious thought as to whether he should sell his docks and relocate all together. Within three days they were in the area where Captain Jarvis suspected the naval ships were patrolling. He said, "I think we'll just have to lay off for awhile and try going in under the cover of darkness."

As the sun was setting under full sail he resumed his race towards shore. With lookouts peering into the darkness for the slightest sign of light they never saw another ship and were soon in sight of land. Captain Jarvis took over and as dawn was breaking, they entered the mouth of the Mississippi heading for the dock. David tried to get a few hours sleep but with the anticipation of getting back to Brenda and her father, he wasn't successful. After the ship was secure he quickly headed to Brenda's.

Chapter 21
Brenda and David's Wedding

David knocked at Brenda's door and was admitted by the butler. "Hello Master David, I didn't think Miss Brenda was expecting you back so soon."

"I know. I think I'll surprise her. How's Mr. Atchison?"

With a tearful eye he replied, "The doctor was here the other day and told Miss Brenda his heart seems to be gettin' weaker. I don't know what all else he said, but Miss Brenda just cried and cried the rest of the day."

"Where is she now?" David asked.

"I think she's in his room. Shall I tell her you're here?"

Just then she appeared at the top of the stairs and ran down to David's outstretched arms.

"David I missed you so much. I don't know what to do. Father seems to be getting worse. I think we should have the wedding as soon as possible. What do you think?"

"I think you're right. I should write to Tom and the Henry's. There won't be time to have the gala affair you deserve but I think we're trading that for Edward's desire to be here when we marry."

"I know David. I don't mind. Father's my first priority."

With his arm around her waist they both ascended the stairs. Brenda opened the door slightly to Edward's room and peeked in.

"I'm not asleep my dear. Come in."

Opening the door a little farther Edward could see David standing behind her.

"Come in David. When did you get back?"

"I just arrived this morning and came here straightaway."

"Brenda, if you'll excuse us this is man talk. Pull up a chair David and tell me about your arrangements. Did you meet Frank? He's some kind of character isn't he?"

Pulling up a chair David replied, "I guess you could say he's a character. He sure looks like someone that wouldn't have a lot of influence."

"Don't let appearances fool you, he knows a lot of people... important people, and more importantly he's very trustworthy."

"I also met a friend of Frank's when I went with him to a tavern with

Captain Jarvis. His name's John."

Laughing Edward started to cough. Clearing his throat again he replied, "Oh -so you met John too?" chuckling lightly again and coughing once more he said, "They make quite a pair don't they?"

"Yes and they both wanted me to tell you how sorry they were you're ill."

"I'm not ill David, I'm dying. I'll probably never see either one of them again but you remember to thank them for me."

"I'll be sure to do that Edward. Did Brenda mention to you we're going to move the wedding date up?"

"She said something about it but never gave me a date, probably because she wasn't sure of your return."

"Well, we're thinking about two weeks from now if that's alright with you?"

"That's fine. Tell her to be sure she writes to my cousin at Five Oaks. They'll want to attend."

"She's down stairs writing the invitations now."

"Good! Then she's busy and we won't be bothered. I don't know whether Frank or John told you but I'm involved with bringing in untaxed goods from Europe. Frank's been my point man for quite a few years."

Lying to him, trying to avoid any unnecessary embarrassment David replied, "They never mentioned it but you giving me Frank's name and him asking whether I was going to ship something legal or illegal told me a lot."

"David, that's another thing I like about you. You live in the real world. Most people don't see the opportunity that surrounds them." Getting closer to David as if there was someone else in the room not privy to what he was about to say Edward continued, "Now here's what I suggest. After you and Brenda get married, I would seriously think about shutting down the dock in Biloxi. I think that will be one of the first places that will be affected by the blockade. Here in New Orleans there's a larger governing body with a lot more influence both North and South."

David asked, "Wouldn't it matter if the North is in control?"

"Not a bit. All wars are fought over economics of one sort or another. They're people in the North who are heavily invested here. They're not going to want to lose money no matter how the war ends. I'm leaving the sugar plantation in Cuba to you and Brenda. After the wedding, you get your personal business straight in Biloxi and go to Cuba until the war is over. I know Brenda will be safe there and the business will keep the cash flowing for both of you. Sugar can be transported anywhere in the world, even to the north."

Firmly grasping David's hand, in a gesture that let him know he had confidence in him, Edward continued, "It's too late now, but if I had a son, I would have wanted him to be like you. Now go down and talk to Brenda. She's had a rough time emotionally since you left."

"Thanks for the advice Edward. It's sound advice and I hope my brother Tom can be convinced to do the same."

Before he left the room Edward asked, "How did my nephew Beau and Anne like Cuba?"

A slight laugh from David he replied, "Anne asked if it was always that hot but she liked the tropical flowers. Beau was thinking about not going north at all and maybe just looking for a hotel in Havana or Santiago."

"A Hotel!" Edward laughed then coughed, "I wouldn't say anything to Simon about that just yet, or he'll be in bed right alongside me."

Laughing at the remark Edward coughed again then tried getting to his feet.

"Are you strong enough to get out of bed?" David asked.

"The doctor said no but I'm not dead yet. I will be if I take his advice and just lay here. Hand me my robe, will you please."

Handing Edward his robe David said, "Edward, let me help you downstairs."

After going down Edward sat in the parlor talking to David about his life together with Brenda's mother. David realized Edward wanted him to know how important she was helping him make sound decisions, and within the hour Brenda came into the room. Mockingly she said to her father, "Is all the man-talk over with? Can I be invited to sit down and join your conversation?"

"Certainly my dear. Did you send an invitation to Five Oaks?"

"Yes father. I also sent one to Myrna."

"Myrna! Why on earth would you send an invitation to a dressmaker?"

"She was mother's friend and she's going to make my gown."

Disappointed Edward replied, "I was hoping you would wear your mother's wedding dress. She packed it away neatly after we were married. I'm sure with a little alteration you'll look just as beautiful as she did the day we were married."

Not wanting to disappoint she said, "I'll get it out first thing tomorrow morning and take it to her."

"Thank you dear for giving a dying man his last wish."

"Don't be silly Papa. You'll be here for a long time."

"One more thing I ask of you two."

"Anything you want Edward," David said.

"If you have a son and name him after me, don't give him the same middle name."

"Why father, what's wrong with your name?" Brenda curiously asked.

"I never told you but my name's the same as my father. All my young life, I was called junior, and hated it."

David replied, "We'll be sure to do that. But like Miss Brenda said you'll be around for years."

Brenda gave the invitations to the butler to post and they went in to dinner.

"What was so secretive you two had to be alone to talk about?" she asked.

Looking up from his plate Edward replied, "Remember dear, curiosity killed the cat. David's mapping out a future for you and I know he's doing the right thing."

"Well then, I won't ask any more questions."

After dinner Edward retired to his bedroom while Brenda and David went into the parlor.

"Brenda, I think you should have made a note on the invitations, the urgency to have the wedding sooner."

"I did David. I do hope most of the people will come."

David said, "Tom and Sharon will probably be here by the end of the week. It's a shame that Anne and Beau won't be here. The timing just wasn't right."

"I know. Everything seems to be moving so fast since their wedding."

"As long as your father will be here I don't mind. Now, where would you like to have a honeymoon?"

"I was thinking about going to father's plantation in Cuba but I don't want to go until we see how he progresses, if that's alright with you."

"That's fine. It will give me some time to straighten my affairs here in New Orleans. I spoke to my partner Charles. We discussed a deal with the partnership that increases his percentage of the business while I become more or less a silent partner. It's like an insurance policy so we can still have a hand in it after the war. That way we'll still have a port where we can bring in our sugar. What do you think?"

"I spoke to father last night and he wished we would go to his... or rather, our plantation until the war is over."

"Yes he mentioned it to me several times too. We'll talk about it more after the wedding."

"You know David, I'm glad you include me in your opinion. I want to do what's right for our future family."

"When I told you my wife helped with my decisions before she died that wasn't just idle talk. Surface beauty eventually fades with age. Your intellect is an inner beauty that continues, and that's something I admire in you."

They continued to talk about the wedding and the refreshments they should serve until the chiming of the clock struck ten.

"It's getting late my dear. You have a full day tomorrow preparing for the wedding," he said as they walked together to the front door.

After a goodnight kiss Brenda said, "Goodnight David. I'll see you in the morning."

Arriving at Charles', everyone had already retired for the night and David decided to do the same. He found falling asleep difficult and was awake most of the night wondering if he was making the right decision about his business.

The following morning he slept in and was late for breakfast. After some discussion with Charles about their agreement they left the house.

Charles asked, "Should we drop you off at Brenda's, David?"

"Yes, if you wouldn't mind I'd like to see how Edward's doing."

Arriving at Brenda's David got out and said, "Charles, I'll have Edward's coachman drop me off at the dock after I check in on Brenda."

"Fine, David. I'll see you then."

After speaking with Brenda they both looked in on Edward. He seemed to be resting peacefully and they decided not to disturb him. Coming downstairs Edward's coachman asked, "Master David, will you be needin' the carriage today?"

"Miss Brenda's going to the dress maker this morning. You can drop me off at the dock on your way," David replied.

"Yes, Sir, she already mentioned it."

Entering the room Brenda put the back of her hand to her forehead. Seemingly confused on what she was going to do first she said, "David, I have so much to do today. I hardly know where to begin."

"You can begin by dropping me off at the dock if you wouldn't mind," he replied.

"No dear, it's on the way to the dressmaker."

"Brenda, was this dressmaker Myrna something more than a friend to your mother?"

Leaning toward David she quietly replied, "Don't tell anyone but Myrna's a quadroon. She doesn't look like it but she's one quarter Negro. My mother went there frequently. I think Myrna's grandmother may have been fathered by my mother's grandfather, my great-grandfather. She's actually mother's relative."

"Your secret's safe with me. I was just wondering like your father why she was invited."

"All these elegant dresses I have, she made them. She treats me special and I think that's the reason."

"I understand. When will you be ready to go?"

"After I finish my breakfast and look in on Papa again we'll leave."

Surprisingly Edward entered the room.

"Father, you looked as though you were sleeping soundly. Did we wake you?"

"No I was just lying there. I heard you close the door on your way out. You shouldn't be concerning yourself with me so much; you're pretty busy. I see you've got your mother's wedding dress on the sofa."

"Yes Papa. I'm taking it to Myrna's shop today."

"That's fine, that's fine. Good morning, David, and what are your plans for today?"

"I'm going with my partner Charles to a lawyer to draw up the contract about our change in the partnership."

"Well, I guess I'll see you both later," Edward said.

Within a few minutes Brenda and David left for town.

After dropping David off at the dock Brenda continued to the dress-shop. She entered the shop and Myrna said, "Hello Brenda, what brings you here today?"

"I've moved up my wedding date to have it while Papa's still alive."

Putting a dress on a hanger Myrna quickly asked, "Has something happened?"

"Yes, while we were at Five Oaks he passed out. The doctor says his heart's very weak."

"I'm very sorry to hear that. Is there anything I can do?"

"Yes, I have mother's wedding dress. Papa wanted me to wear it for the wedding. Can you look it over and make any alterations it may need?"

"Certainly, let me see it."

Gently taking the dress from the box Myrna looked it over. "You know Brenda your mother was a very special person to me. I remember making this dress for her."

"Mother must have cared for it a lot; she had it packed away so neatly," Brenda paused, "I sent you an invitation to the wedding. You should be getting it tomorrow or the next day."

"I'll be glad to go. My gift will be making this dress as new as when your mother wore it."

"Thank you so much Myrna."

"Who's the groom? Do I know him?"

"He's actually from Biloxi but he's part owner of a dock here in New Orleans. His name's David Stuart."

Continuing to examine the dress Myrna looked up, "I don't think I know him. Where will you live after the wedding, here in New Orleans or Biloxi?"

"We haven't figured that out yet but we have plenty of options."

"Your parent's home is one of the most beautiful in New Orleans. I would have loved to have lived in it."

After examining the dress she said, "It shouldn't take more than two days to have this dress ready. Would you want to pick it up or should I send it?"

"If you wouldn't mind, I'd like to pick it up. I'll be able to match it with a few accessories."

"Okay. Then come by day after tomorrow."

"I will and thank you."

As Brenda was opening the door to leave the shop Myrna said, "Be sure to tell your Papa I said hello."

"I will."

After the dress-shop Brenda went to a local florist to have floral arrangements made. When she was through she asked her driver to go by the dock to see if David was ready to go home. She waved as he came off the pier. Walking to the carriage with Charles David asked, "Charles, will you need me tomorrow?"

"Not here David, I assume you'll be at Brenda's this afternoon?"

"Probably."

"I'll pick you up there about 1 o'clock; then we can go to the lawyer's office to sign the papers."

"That will be fine."

After getting in the carriage David asked, "Well my dear, did you get everything done you had to do?"

"Yes Myrna said she'll have the dress ready in two days. I also ordered the floral arrangements."

"My, my, you have been busy."

"What did Charles say about you being a silent partner?"

"He liked the idea. I think he's going to hang on as long as he can financially for however long that may be. I heard some news today about a few more Yankee victories. I hope our boys won't get beat too bad before they call a truce."

"Oh David, Wouldn't that be wonderful!"

"Yes, it would, but that depends on Jefferson Davis."

"Let's change the subject. I don't want to spoil a nice day with politics."

"You're right dear."

Pulling up in front of the house the doctor's carriage was there. Before they came to a complete stop Brenda leaped from the coach and ran up the front steps. Going in the door the doctor was just leaving.

"What happened doctor. Is Papa alright?" she frantically asked.

"Yes Brenda but he's got to get it through his head he needs bed rest. You'll have to make him listen... I can't. I gave him another sedative and got him to go to bed. I'll be back in the morning."

"Thank you doctor," David said.

***

The next few days went by quickly with Brenda making her wedding arrangements and David taking care of the legal paperwork with Charles. During that time they both periodically looked in on Edward seeing to his comfort.

By Friday morning Tom and Sharon arrived from Cliveden along with the Henrys from Five Oaks.

"Hello Tom. I signed the paperwork the other day with my partner. We're now officially silent partners. I wish you would reconsider your position at Cliveden," David urged.

"Well David we'll be here for the week. We have plenty of time to talk about it. How's Edward feeling?"

"The doctor says he should get plenty of bed rest but he keeps getting up. Does he remind you of someone?"

"Yes, father before he passed away," Tom replied.

"That's right Tom. It's a shame Anne and Beau couldn't be here but I'm glad at least you, Sharon, and the Henrys are."

"When's the ceremony?" Tom asked.

"We're thinking about Sunday."

"Will everything be ready by then?" Sharon asked.

"Yes, Brenda's been working feverishly on the arrangements. We thought in light of Edward's condition something small would be better."

"Whatever Sharon can do to help I'm sure she wouldn't mind," Tom said.

Simon came into the room, "Hello David! How did Anne and Beau like sailing to Cuba? They must be well on their way to New York by now?"

David replied, "I don't know if it's my secret to tell but they're thinking about staying in Cuba."

Simon looking a little confused asked, "You mean, starting a plantation of some sort?"

"No they were thinking about getting a hotel or shop in Santiago or Havana."

A bewildering look came over Simon's face indicating to David not to say anymore and changed the subject. "I was just telling Tom here about selling my half of the dock and becoming a silent partner financially. I wish Tom would give up Cliveden. I hate saying it but with more Yankee victories I think most plantations are going to fail."

"Do you think the blockade is going to affect us to that degree?" Simon asked.

"I know it will. I was on the trip to Cuba and during the day the captain had to post extra watches to look for any sails. Whenever one of the lookouts reported seeing one the captain changed course. At night we traveled in complete darkness trying to avoid the few ships they have guarding the Gulf ports. It'll only get worse with more ships they'll eventually bring here.How will you get our cargo to market?"

"That's the chance we're taking. They boarded one of our ships already and took a few crates they said were contraband. The longer this war drags on the worst it will be. I'm going to sell my interest in Biloxi after the wedding, and may just wind up in Cuba on Edward's sugar plantation to sit out the war as he suggested."

"David, your analysis of the future of the South isn't very encouraging to say the least. I hope you're wrong," Simon remarked.

Simon, looking concerned with what David said, broke his concentration by asking, "Shall we see how Edward's doing? He might be awake."

"I'll check. Better yet. Why don't we all go up? I'll peek in and ask if he wants visitors," David said.

Opening the door slightly David saw him awake. Tapping lightly at the open door he asked, "Can I come in? I have a few visitors who want to say hello."

"Certainly, who's with you?" Edward asked.

When David opened the door all the way, Edward could see his guests.

"Come in... come in. I'm sorry you have to visit me in my room but that doctor worries more than I do about my health."

"We just wanted to say hello," Simon replied.

"I'll be able to socialize a little more on Sunday. Thanks for coming on short notice."

After a few words of encouragement to Edward, they left. Going downstairs Tom said, "He looks pretty weak David."

"I know Tom. Now you know why we moved the date up so soon."

Mrs. Henry coming up the steps asked, "How's Cousin Edward?"

"We just walked out. He's awake but I wouldn't stay too long," Simon instructed.

"I won't, I just want to say hello."

After tapping lightly on the door she went in. "Hello, Edward. They went downstairs so I thought I'd drop in and say hello too. What's all this about you not wanting to stay in bed?" she chided.

"Ah! Doctors, they're not happy unless they can give people orders," Edward annoyingly replied.

"Well, it's good advice. I don't want to bother you too long. I'm going back downstairs."

Before leaving the room she said, "You listen to the doctor, he knows what's best."

With a wave of his hand Edward replied before she closed the door, "You women are just as bad."

**

On Sunday, about 20 people gathered in the parlor where the ceremony was to take place. The room was beautifully adorned with floral arrangements and glasses filled with champagne were being served. Edward was helped downstairs and seated by the make shift alter. When Brenda came into the room she was wearing her mother's wedding dress. The portrait of her mother hanging on the wall was her exact likeness and everyone present gasped at the similarity. It was as though her mother stepped down from the painting. Edward looked up at the painting then at Brenda saying, "My dear, you look even more beautiful than your mother on our wedding day."

The ceremony began and within a half hour it was over.

Edward said, "David, I want to thank you and Brenda for changing your plans to let me share in this very special day. I know you two will have a wonderful life together. I have something to add to that. Don't waste a moment of it."

"We won't Edward," David replied.

Myrna came over to congratulate Brenda and David and say hello to Edward. Before she could speak Edward said, "Myrna, you did a masterful job with Brenda's dress. I'm deeply indebted to you."

"Edward, seeing Brenda today was like looking into a mirror going back almost 30 years. Like her mother she made a beautiful bride," Myrna said.

Everyone was enjoying themselves when the doctor who was present came over and said, "Edward, I think you've had enough company. I think you should retire for the rest of the day."

"I just want to stay down here with the guests for another hour," he replied.

"Ok, I warned you. I have to leave, I'll be back tomorrow," turning toward Brenda he said, "Here Brenda, make sure he takes these pills before he goes to bed. Don't let him stay down here for more than another hour."

"I won't doctor and thank you for coming to my wedding."

"I was glad to have come. Now don't forget, no more than one hour. Good luck to both of you." After kissing Brenda lightly on the cheek, he shook David's hand then left.

Within the hour, Tom, Simon, and David, helped Edward up the stairs and put him in bed. Brenda, following them into the room said, "Papa, the doctor wants you to take these pills before you go to sleep."

"Okay, but first, I'd like to see you and David alone."

Everyone else filed out of the room and David closed the door behind them.

"What you two have done today made my entire life worth living. There are some papers in a wall safe behind your mother's painting. It's my last will and testament leaving everything to you two. The only thing missing is a sum of money I'd like to leave Myrna. For some reason and I don't know exactly why, she was always a favorite of your mother. What she did for me today with your wedding dress brought back a lot of fine memories."

"Yes, Papa, we'll do as you ask."

"Good. Now stand together for a moment. I'd like to get another look at you."

Doing as he asked they couldn't help but think it may be the last time he sees them.

"Good night Papa," she said kissing his forehead.

"Good night Edward -and thank you," David added.

Brenda turning down the light could see him smile. "Good night," he replied.

Going downstairs they rejoined the rest of the company and by 7 o'clock most of the guests were gone. As the last of them were leaving Tom asked David to step into the parlor.

"David, I know this isn't the right moment but before I leave for Cliveden I'd like to talk to you about my interest in the Biloxi dock."

"Fine, Tom. We'll discuss it tomorrow."

After Tom, Sharon and the Henry's went to bed, David and Brenda slowly ascended the stairs. Before entering Brenda's room which would be their bridal suite they looked in on Edward once more. He was sleeping, but Brenda said in a whisper before closing the door, "Goodnight Papa."

Retiring to their room they were undressing in front of each other for the first time. Brenda said, "David, I'm so worried about Papa. I think our first night together might not be what you expect."

"My dear, we have our whole lives to make up for whatever you think we'll be missing. If you're not yourself I'll understand."

Moving closer she embraced him for being understanding. After a little effort on Brenda's part, the wedding was consummated.

By the time Brenda awoke David had already gone downstairs. He was seated at the breakfast table talking to Tom when she entered the room.

"Good morning dear. I was just talking to Tom about his interest in the Biloxi dock. He's agreed to sell his share too."

"That's good. It will be one less problem for you. Are you still going to keep Cliveden?" she asked.

"I haven't given that a lot of thought but what David's been warning me of, if you'll excuse the expression... scares the hell out of me."

"Tom, it wasn't to scare you it's what I'm afraid will happen. I see no other alternative. I looked at the newspaper this morning. The South lost a few more battles. The North has all but sealed off any outside help with the blockade of the Chesapeake and our ports in Savanna and Charleston."

Tom replied, "Then after you sell your part in Biloxi, you won't have any business attachment in the United States."

"That's right. We'll only have our house in Biloxi and Brenda's house here."

At that moment the butler entered the room announcing the doctor's arrival. Entering the dining room he said, "Good morning!"

"Would you care for some coffee doctor?" David asked.

"No thank you. I have a rather busy schedule today. If you'll excuse me I'll just go up and check on Edward."

With David and Brenda following they went into the room. Edwards arm was extended off the bed and David realizing something was wrong, quickly turned Brenda away from the room. Her fears of the night before had come true. Her father was gone and she began to weep. David put his arm around her escorting her downstairs. She tried to turn and go back to his room but David blocked her path saying, "There's nothing more we can do Brenda. He's with your mother now."

Sharon got up from the table and escorted Brenda to the parlor, comforting her.

"Is there anything I can do to help David?" Tom asked.

"No, it seems as though he passed away quietly in his sleep."

"If you need help with any funeral arrangements let me know. I think Sharon and I should stay at least until the funeral is over."

"Thanks Tom, Sharon will be a big relief for Brenda."

***

Within the next two days funeral arrangements were made. Even with the light gentle rain the day of the funeral, it seemed like the line for his viewing was endless. Edward had quite a few friends and business associates in New Orleans and the funeral parlor was packed with floral arrangements. After viewing Edward in the casket Myrna gave Brenda a hug.

"You know dear, your father paid me the most beautiful compliment at your wedding. He thanked me for the alterations and told me I brought back a lot of great memories for him."

Wiping away tears Brenda replied, "Thank you Myrna. Mother thought so much of you as a friend."

After the viewing the undertaker closed the casket and six pallbearers carried it to an awaiting hearse. The light rain turned to a mist as it pulled away and the procession that followed was long. The family gravesite was an aboveground vault, within a walled cemetery. The crowd of mourners gathered to hear the last words, were sheltered under what seemed to be a sea of black umbrellas.

After everyone left the gravesite David escorted Brenda back to their awaiting coach comforting her, then went home.

***

Within two days, Tom, Sharon and the Henrys made their departure. After waving goodbye Brenda and David went back inside. It was actually the first time they were alone since the wedding and it felt awkward.

"What would you like to do today Brenda?" he asked.

"I would like to go into the French Quarter for lunch, but first I'd like to get a letter off to Anne and Beau, telling them what's happened in the last week."

"Okay dear, I'd like to go to the dock and see if we can get passage to Cuba. I'll post your letter."

"When are we going?" she asked.

"I'd like to go within the next two weeks. When I sell the dock in Biloxi, I'm demanding payment in gold. I don't want it to be accessible to either the North or South so I'm carrying it to a bank in Cuba or maybe Jamaica."

"This whole war is getting you very nervous isn't it?" she asked.

"Yes, I'm afraid it is."

"Then go and make your plans," she said.

After giving her a kiss on the forehead he left.

Getting to the dock Charles greeted him. "You've had a busy week haven't you David?"

"Yes, I have, first the wedding, then Edward dying. I'm glad we made our agreement before all this started."

"How's Brenda taking it?"

"Right now she's still in a state, but giving it a little time I think she'll be fine."

"That's good, that's good. What brings you here today?" Charles asked.

"I want to get passage within the next two weeks for Cuba. I have some business to take care of for Brenda concerning her father's plantation."

"Captain Jarvis is due in the end of the week if that's soon enough. He's coming from France," Charles said.

"Is he making a run to Biloxi first?" David inquired.

"No, he's coming straight here. Why?"

"I have to book passage for Biloxi too. I'm selling Tom's interest in the dock as well as mine. He made his decision a few days ago."

"There's a ship coming in today if you want to leave tomorrow evening?"

"Who's the captain?" David asked.

"Captain Bailey. Have you ever sailed with him?"

"I seem to remember I have. When's he leaving?" David asked.

"Well, he won't be leaving until day after tomorrow. Do you want me to make sure you have a cabin?"

"Yes, please do."

"Oh by the way, Elizabeth and Trisha stopped by the dock last night. They wanted to pay their respects to you and Brenda."

"Are they still running the boarding house?"

"Yes, and from what some of the dock hands say they're doing pretty well too. They also opened up a small seafood restaurant a few blocks away."

"I think I'll walk down and pay them a visit," David said.

Leaving the dock he headed for the house he had given John and Elizabeth. The chain of events that happened with eventually Luke and Trisha owning it, now Elizabeth and Trisha seemed like fate. Peering in the window he saw someone walking about and knocked at the door. After Trisha opened it she was surprised and stepped back.

"Master David! I'm so glad to see you. Elizabeth and me, we wanted to pay our respects to you and Miss Brenda but we weren't sure we'd be welcomed."

"Don't be silly. You two are some of our dearest friends. Where's Elizabeth?"

"She be right back. She went to gets the fish for the restaurant."

"I hear you've become real business women."

"Yes Sir, come on in the kitchen while I fix'es you some tea. How's Miss Anne? We heard she's married now too."

Just then the front door opened and a little girl came running into the kitchen.

"Aunt Trisha! Aunt Trisha! Mommy gave me a penny to buy this candy," she excitedly said.

Seeing David she suddenly stopped talking, and hid behind Trisha's apron. David stood up as Elizabeth entered the room.

"Hello Elizabeth, Violet is getting big."

"Thank you David. We owe everything we have to you."

"I was just telling Trisha, I heard you're two successful business women.

I understand you even have a seafood house. Does it have a name?"

"Yes, we call it the E & T Catfish House."

"That's grand. Brenda and I will have to try it sometime."

As Trisha poured the tea Elizabeth told him about the two old men that catch fish out on the river and her cooking it for the restaurant. David filled them in on all the news and after tea, pardoned himself to leave. Walking him to the door Elizabeth said, "Goodbye, David. Tell Miss Brenda we're sorry to hear about her father passing."

"I will," as he tipped his hat and said, "Goodbye to you too little one. Maybe the next time I come you won't be afraid of me."

Still not sure of the visitor she hid behind Elizabeth's apron.

Elizabeth said, "Violet, don't you be afraid of Master David. Come around here and say goodbye."

Bashfully looking out from behind Elizabeth in an almost inaudible voice she said, "Goodbye!"

Elizabeth, stepping out on the porch with David asked, "Master Charles told me you sold him your half of the dock. Are you and Miss Brenda leaving?"

"I'm selling the dock in Biloxi and transferring the proceeds to Cuba. Miss Brenda's father has a sugar plantation there and left it to us. We're not sure whether we want to live here or there. It hasn't been decided."

"What about the house in Biloxi? If you sell, what will happen to Thelma, Arthur and Sarah? Where will they go, what will they do?" she asked.

"I'll give them the option of coming with us, or maybe just bring them here to New Orleans for the time being," pausing for a moment he asked, "You didn't think I would leave them stranded did you?"

"No David, I'm sorry. I was just concerned."

"That's one of the things about you that made me care for you, thinking about everyone else."

"Thank you but that seems like a whole lifetime ago," she replied.

"Yes but people that have consideration for other people always have that quality. Like a leopard, they don't change their spots."

After taking his leave Elizabeth watched as he walked down the street and turned the corner out of sight. When she returned to the kitchen Trisha said, "He's so thoughtful 'bout us, it was sure nice seein' him again."

Elizabeth, listening to her words paused to reflect on the pleasant times they spent together. Smiling, she said, "Yes indeed. He's very thoughtful."

Arriving home he said, "I'm sorry dear for being late. It's too late for lunch. Why don't we make it an early dinner?" pausing, "I'm going up to lie down for awhile."

"When do you want me to wake you?" she asked.

"Why don't you just come up and lie down with me? Then we can wake up together."

"I'll be right there," she replied.

He slowly climbed the stairs and Brenda as soon as she could anxiously followed. Stretching out across the bed they held each other close and Brenda asked, "David is there something wrong? Don't I make you happy?"

"It's not you dear. I just have so much on my mind, with all the business, the wedding, and the funeral all coming together. It's been overwhelming."

"Relax, everything will work out," she said.

Within a few minutes holding each other, they drifted off to sleep.

When they awoke the sun was going down, and they realized how much they must have been exhausted. Two hours had passed.

"Let's get dressed and go to dinner. Where would you like to go?" he asked.

Without hesitating Brenda replied, "Antwonette's, the restaurant you took me to the first time we went out to dinner."

"Then, Antwonette's it is my lady."

Unlike the first time she went there she was now getting undressed and dressed in his company. The romance was still there and she wondered if it would always be. They finished getting ready and he escorted her to the carriage, holding her hand as she stepped in. The ride was just as she remembered and the city lights were just as enchanting as they were then.

Entering the restaurant, coincidentally, they were seated at the same table they had on their first visit.

"As I remember dear, you're favorite food is Cajun Creole. I'm not very familiar with it so I'll let you order."

After dinner, they had a light repast at Dumonte's then returned home.

Brenda asked, "Could I go with you to Biloxi tomorrow or would I just interrupt your business there?"

"I would like your company and the input you may have. It's always a good idea to have another opinion and I trust your judgment."

"I'll run up and pack a few things, so I'll be ready in the morning."

David watched as she went up the stairs and then went into the study to prepare some paperwork he needed for the trip.

The next day, they enjoyed each other's company and that evening headed for the dock to depart.

"Good evening, Charles. When will the ship be leaving?" David asked.

"In about an hour, I'll have your luggage sent to your cabin."

Escorting them aboard, he introduced them to Captain Bailey. "This is David my partner and his wife, Brenda. They were married last week," Charles said.

"Welcome aboard," Captain Bailey said as he stood up to greet them.

"I'm glad to meet you, Captain," shaking his hand. "Looks like fair weather; I hope it holds for the trip," he said.

"I think we'll be fine. Congratulations on your wedding. If you need anything ashore you should get it. We're about to leave."

Brenda excitedly looked around at all the activity. She was witnessing something she hadn't seen since she was a teenager, the last voyage she took with her father to his plantation. She recalled to memory the handsome second officer, a young man she fell instantly infatuated with as only a young girl in her teens could.

"Brenda, let's get to our cabin and not be in the way until the ship leaves port."

"Okay David, it's just so exciting."

They went to their cabin and in a short time, could hear the first mate commanding orders to untie the ship. As it slowly glided out on the river they emerged once again from their cabin.

"It's hard to imagine us giving up this life style," she said.

"That's only because we haven't had a chance to experience another lifestyle," he replied.

"I guess you're right. I shouldn't condemn what I don't know. We'll just have to wait and see."

Chapter 22
Beginning a New Life

At dinner David asked, "Have you had any trouble with the blockade Captain Bailey?"

"No. Not so far. There aren't that many ships patrolling the Gulf. I suspect there will be before too long. They'll eventually bring their ships in closer and cut off Biloxi and New Orleans from being used for war materials."

"How are the shipping ports on the Atlantic doing?" David asked.

"They shut down the ports on the Chesapeake. They did the same in Norfolk, Virginia; Wilmington, North Carolina and Charleston. The only way the confederacy can get war supplies in is on desolate sections of beaches wherever they can find them. There are civilians looking out for spots that aren't controlled by the Yankees. They signal the ships when it's safe to land. Are you going to Biloxi on business?" Captain Bailey asked.

"Yes, I'm liquidating all my interest in the dock and plan on selling the home I lived in."

"Charles told me you already sold him most of your share and you're only a silent partner as an investor. That doesn't sound like you have a lot of faith in the South winning the war," Captain Bailey said.

"You're right. It was a stupid thing to begin with. Those hot heads in South Carolina don't realize the manufacturing ability of the North and the longer the war goes on the harder it will be for a Southern victory. Before it's over they'll be a lot of economic hardships for people and businesses I'm afraid, including theirs."

"I think you're right. What do you intend to do?" Captain Bailey asked.

"Through my wife's father we inherited a sugar plantation in Cuba. We might just stay there and wait out the war."

"Mrs. Stewart, is your maiden name Atchison by any chance?" Captain Bailey asked.

Looking up Brenda replied, "Why yes. Why do you ask?"

"I knew your father quite well. I'm sorry to hear Edward passed. When did it happen?"

Looking solemnly down at the table she replied, "He died last week, the day after we were married."

David, hoping the captain wouldn't mention Edward's hidden past of smuggling quickly changed the subject.

After dinner, David and Brenda took a walk around the deck. The sky was clear and the stars were like a canopy that stretched endlessly across the sky. The ship traveling without a light being visible made the stars appear even brighter. Looking down at the water, they saw phosphorous churned up, riding the top of each wave as it spread out from the bow cutting through the dark water.

When the ship docked in Biloxi, David heard a familiar voice.

"Hello, Master David."

"Why, hello Jeremiah. I heard you were here breaking someone else in to be foreman."

"Yes Sir. He's not a quick learner like John and Luke but he be gettin' there."

"That's fine. This is my wife Brenda. We were married last week."

Tipping his hat to acknowledge her Jeremiah said, "Nice meetin' you Ma'am."

"Think you can get us a ride home?" David asked.

"Yes sir, I get one. Your house people will surely be glad to see you again."

David asked, "How's Thelma and Arthur doing?"

"Since you dun' left they ain't much call for them to come here."

"Well I guess we'll just surprise them," David said.

Brenda, extending her hand to the captain, said "Goodbye Captain Bailey. Thanks for the pleasant trip."

"You're welcome Ma'am. Goodbye David, I guess our paths will cross again."

"I'm sure they will," David replied as he and Brenda walked off the dock to the awaiting carriage Jeremiah procured.

"Brenda, it'll be good seeing Thelma and the rest of the servants again. I sort of miss Thelma keeping everyone on their toes."

With a slight laugh Brenda asked, "Have you made a decision on what their future will be when you sell?"

"I've been thinking about giving them the option of staying here or coming with us. What do you think?"

"I think we should wait and see how they react after you tell them."

As they pulled up in front of the house Thelma was sweeping the front porch and looked up. "Master David! I'm so glad to see you. We thought you weren't never commin' back. Hello, Miss Brenda, I'm glad to see you again too. Master David, shall I takes her bags upstairs?"

"Yes you can put them in my room."

Thelma paused... raising her eyebrows she said, "You say... puts them in your room?"

"Yes, if you please. We were married last week."

With a wide smile she replied, "Sure thing Master David! Come on honey!"

"Where's Arthur?" David asked.

"I think he's 'round back at the carriage house."

"Good. I'll only be a minute dear. I want to tell him I need him to drive me this afternoon."

After speaking to Arthur, David returned to the house.

"Hello Sarah. I sure missed your cooking," David said.

Smiling, she replied, "Your wife's sure enough beautiful Master David. I'll make somethin' special for dinner."

"Thank you Sarah. I'll look forward to it."

As David was leaving the room he turned and said, "Brenda, I have to visit a friend. He's always had an interest in this house. I want to see if he still wants to purchase it. I'll see you when I return."

"Okay David. Good luck," she said, quickly rushing across the room to kiss him before he left.

"Are you ready Arthur?" David asked.

"Yes Sir."

"Do you remember where Franz my fencing master lives?"

"Yes Sir. I ain't never gonna forget that day. We was all worried you were gonna die." Pausing for a moment Arthur asked, "How's Trisha and Elizabeth likin' New Orleans?"

"They like it fine. They run a boarding house and have a restaurant."

"Restaurant! What are they servin'?" Arthur asked.

"Seafood," David replied.

"I know they be good cooks but a restaurant, now if that don't beat all."

"They've been pretty successful so far," pausing he said, "Tell me something Arthur. If I sold the place would you rather stay here and work for someone else or go with me?"

Making sure he heard David correctly he replied, "That depends on whether the new owner treats me good. Is that why we going there?"

"Yes it is. You see I sold most of my interest in New Orleans and I'm selling my share of the dock here in Biloxi. After I sell the house I'll be leaving for good."

"You mean you're gonna live in Miss Brenda's house in New Orleans?"

"No. Not for long. We're thinking about going to the plantation Brenda's father left us in Cuba."

After a few minutes of silence Arthur replied, "That's a powerful amount to be thinking on right now. Have you asked Thelma or Sarah?"

"No, you're the first one I mentioned it to. I was going to sit down with everyone tonight and discuss it."

After reaching their destination, David could see Franz standing on the front porch. He got out of the carriage and went up the front stairs to shake his hand. "David, it's been a long time since we last met. The circumstances that day weren't exactly pleasant. What brings you here today? Not another duel I hope?!"

"No. Not this time. Tell me Franz, you always admired my home. Are you still interested in it?"

"This comes as a surprise. Are you leaving?" Franz asked.

"Yes. I was married last week in New Orleans. My father-in-law left us a sugar plantation in Cuba. We're going to settle there until the war is over."

"I don't blame you. When the list of war dead gets posted every week I always find names of former students on it. As I see their names, I can remember their faces, some as young as 16. They haven't even had a chance to live. What a waste of young lives."

"I know. It sounds unpatriotic but that's one of the reasons I'm leaving. It's all a waste." David said.

"How long will you be here?" Franz asked.

"Only long enough to get my affairs in order. I take it you're still interested then?"

"Yes, I am. Can we meet tomorrow to discuss the property?" Franz asked.

"If you can come by tomorrow morning I'll be able to show you the house and we can discuss a price," David replied.

"Will 10 o'clock be alright?" Franz asked.

"That will be fine."

After exchanging a few more words David departed.

On the way home Arthur said, "He seems like a nice enough master. I remember how he was after the duel. Do you think he'd let us be as free as you have?"

"I don't think you have to worry about that," David replied.

Thinking about it for a few moments Arthur said, "I don't know about the others but if it's okay with you I'd like to stay."

"That's your decision Arthur."

After arriving home, David went inside and Arthur followed after putting away the horse and carriage. Within a few minutes Thelma announced, "Dinner's ready Miss Brenda, Master David."

After the dinner was placed on the table Brenda told Thelma, "Get Sarah and Arthur and sit down with us."

Thelma at times was invited to sit down especially when David was sitting alone, but never with Arthur and Sarah. Looking at each other suspiciously Thelma asked, "Is they somethin' wrong Master David?"

"No, we have something to ask you. Please get a plate and sit down," he said. Looking at each other they did as he asked.

After they were seated David said, "We're selling the house. We want to know whether you want to stay here with the new owner if he needs you or go to Cuba with me and Miss Brenda."

"Cuba!" Thelma quickly replied.

"Yes Cuba. My father-in-law left us his sugar plantation. With this war we don't know what's going to happen here. They'll be plenty of room for you and the work won't be as hard. They'll be more servants."

Listening intently Thelma's eyes began to well up with tears hearing the cutting words about a place she's been for so many years being sold.

Arthur said, "The new owner will be Master Franz. He's the fencing teacher that helped bring Master David home the day of the duel. He seems pretty nice."

Noticing the look of shock on their faces David quickly added, "You don't have to make your decision right now. He's coming in the morning to discuss the terms for the house."

The rest of the dinner was quiet, as though someone had thrown a bleak shadow over what was to be an enjoyable dinner. After several minutes Brenda broke the silence, "Sarah, this meal is delicious. How did you ever get chicken to taste so good?"

Looking up from her plate Sarah smiled at her compliment replying, "Miss Brenda, over 20 years of cookin'."

"Well if the new owner has his own cook I'd love to have you come with us. Our cook in New Orleans was getting old and went to live with her daughter."

It seemed to break the icy silence once more and Brenda continued, "It isn't so much the house but the people that occupy it that count."

Thelma, with a smile on her face asked, "I wonder what's that Cuba's gonna look like... are they natives Master David?"

You could always rely on Thelma to somehow make a bad day seem better and David replied, "No they're normal people. Cuba has gorgeous flowers all year round and the temperature is always pleasant. The people are very friendly and our plantation is beautiful."

After thinking for a few moments Thelma asked, "I have one question Master David."

"What's that?"

"Do we have to be crossin' a lot of water to get there? I can't swim."

With a chuckle he replied, "Don't worry about that. They have lifeboats."

Looking back at her food Thelma mumbled quietly, "Sure is a good name... lifeboats. I sure hopes they means it."

The following morning as David looked out the front door, he saw Franz surveying the outside of the house. He was there on time and David stepped out on the porch to acknowledge his presence.

"Good morning David."

"Good morning Franz. Come in and have a cup of coffee."

David led him into the study where he opened a portfolio with all the papers concerning the property laying them on the table.

"Here's the deed to the house and all the documents that show how it's been transferred, from my grandfather to my father and then to Anne, Tom and myself. I think everything's in order."

As soon as Franz examined the folder he understood immediately

David was well organized and it wouldn't be a problem transferring the property.

"Would you like to take a tour of the house?" David asked.

"Yes, after we have our coffee. Do you have the power of attorney to sign for Anne and Tom?" Franz asked.

"Yes, we discussed it a few months ago. I have those documents here too," opening an envelope to show him.

"It seems you have everything in order." Looking at the signature on the bottom of the paper Franz said, "I see we have the same lawyer so the transfer shouldn't be a problem."

Entering the dining room they sat at the table while Thelma poured the coffee. A few minutes later Brenda entered the room and they both rose from their chairs.

"Franz, this is my wife Brenda."

"Good morning Brenda. Congratulations on your marriage."

"Thank you. Did you come to an agreement on the house? It's such a gorgeous place. I'm sure your wife will just love it."

After David and Franz looked at each other, Franz replied, "My wife passed away two years ago but if she were still alive... I'm sure she would."

"I'm so sorry. I hope I didn't stir sorrowful memories," Brenda said.

"That's okay Miss Brenda. You had no way of knowing."

Getting up from the table David said, "If you'll excuse us my dear I was just about to show Franz the house. Franz, would you like to begin upstairs?"

"That's fine David."

On the second floor they saw Thelma who acknowledged them.

"Good morning Master David. Hello, Master Franz."

"You remember me?" Franz asked.

"Yes sir! I ain't never gonna forget that day. Do you have a house maid coming with you?"

"Why yes I do."

Thelma looked at David as though she was waiting for him to comment. A few moments later David asked, "Franz, how many house servants do you have? Thelma here and Sarah my cook wanted to know if they'll be needed."

"I've had my servants since my father was alive. They're getting quite old and if you're asking whether your people will be kept on that's strictly up to you. They're welcome to stay if they want."

"Do you have a coachman?" David asked.

"That's something I don't have. I remember your driver. I was hoping he would stay on," Franz replied.

Thelma entering their conversation said, "I'm pretty sure he would but you have to ask him. I don't know if Sarah the cook be stayin' either. I thinks I be goin' to Cuba with Master David and Miss Brenda."

Franz replied, "Well, as I told David. My cook's getting old and I need a replacement. I'd like to keep Sarah if she wants to stay." Pausing for a moment, he continued, "You don't have to make a commitment right now. It will take a few days for the property transfer. David, I think I've seen enough of the house. Let's go down stairs to discuss price."

After retiring to the parlor they came to an agreement.

"Now that that's settled, David, when do you want to go to the lawyer's office?"

"We can do it tomorrow if that's alright with you," he replied.

Walking Franz to the front door Franz asked, "If you could pick me up in the morning around 10 o'clock, I'll make sure I'm ready. I'll have to go to the bank this afternoon and get a draft for the sale price."

"Then I'll see you in the morning Franz."

David watched as he walked down the front steps and turned to survey the outside of the house once more before closing the door.

Brenda came into the hall and asked, "Did you agree on the sale price?"

"Yes dear, we're going to make the transfer tomorrow morning. I suggest we spend the rest of the day with Thelma helping us pack whatever we're going to take with us. There are some old trunks in the carriage house. I'll ask Arthur to get them."

The rest of the day was spent sorting through clothing that wasn't wanted, clothes left by Anne, and things that no longer fit or were out of fashion. Some of the personal items Anne and Tom inadvertently left were packed neatly for transport to the dock. As David looked at some of the items his mind drifted back to things reminding him of when Violet and Elizabeth lived there. The perfume bottles in particular reminded him of the night Elizabeth splashed too much on herself and was embarrassed. The broach he bought for Violet for helping him get out of his depression after losing his wife did as well. Yes he thought, *There were plenty of good memories within these walls.* They worked diligently long into the evening getting everything packed.

Brenda looked up and said, "David, I think we've done a lot today. I'm exhausted. Can we continue tomorrow?"

"I'm sorry dear. I didn't realize the time went by so quickly."

They carried the clothing they no longer wanted to the library so Arthur could take them to the poorhouse in the morning.

After getting washed they got ready for bed. This would be the first night they were able to spend together without a lot on David's mind and Brenda wanted to take full advantage of it.

Everyone was busy the following day and after David returned home from the lawyer's office they resumed packing.

"Arthur, there's quite a bit of old clothing we left in the library last night. Take them to the poorhouse."

"Yes Sir."

"Don't take too long. I want you to help me pack the books in the library."

"How soon would we have to be out of here David?" Brenda asked.

"I'm sure Franz isn't in a rush. He probably has as much packing as we do," he replied.

Stopping for lunch David asked, "Thelma, have you or Sarah made up your mind yet?"

"Yes Master David. We both be goin'."

"That's fine. We hoped you would."

After lunch they continued packing and didn't finish until early evening.

"For the life of me Brenda, how do people gather so much without noticing?" David remarked.

"David, if you think this is a lot, we haven't even started with our house in New Orleans."

Thinking about what she said for a few moments he replied, "Well then, maybe we should just keep that house in case we wanted to come back. This way we wouldn't have to pack everything."

Looking at him with a wide smile she replied, "Do you mean it? Do you really mean it? We won't sell it?"

"I didn't think you wanted to part with the memories," her loving husband replied.

Smiling she threw her arms around his neck, "I was hoping you would say that!"

***

By the end of the week everything that was going to New Orleans was sent to the dock. Some things that were needed in Cuba were packed and labeled also. They wouldn't have to leave the ship until its final destination.

Thelma and Sarah, excited to know they would still be together, were packed and ready to depart. As they were walking out the door Thelma looked back with a tear in her eye.

Brenda asked, "Thelma, what's wrong?"

"Well, Miss Brenda, I feels like this house been part of me. I raised Miss Anne here and seen so much of the family growin' up. It's like leavin' some of my heart here."

"Well, look at it this way. You'll be able to take care of Miss Anne again. Didn't you know her and Beau are going to live in Cuba?"

"No, Ma'am, I surely didn't," with a rejuvenating smile she said, "That makes some kind of difference. We ready now, ain't we Sarah?"

"We certainly are. I wonder how they cooks down there in that Cuba place?" Sarah said.

David remarked smiling, "You'll just have to teach them Sarah. Okay Arthur we're in. We can go now."

It seemed strange going down the street for the last time realizing they would never return. On the way to the dock David posted a letter to Tom telling him about the sale of the house and that they were leaving for New Orleans.

Chapter 23
Renewing Old Friendships

After arriving at the dock, Arthur helped the ladies from the carriage. After hugging Thelma and Sarah he bid them farewell. Taking off his hat he said, "Master David, I want to thank you for takin' me off that plantation years ago and making me your coachman. I ain't never gonna forget you." Taken with emotion teary eyed, he embraced David.

"Thank you Arthur for serving me so well. I'll miss you too."

As Thelma and Sarah were ready to board they marveled at all the activity of the ship being loaded.

"Hello, Miss Thelma. You 'member me?"

"You be Jeremiah," Thelma replied.

"Dat's righ. I seen you at Master David's a few times. Let me takes yo' bags to yo' cabins." Motioning with his head, "This a way please!" he said.

Following him up the gangway to where they would sleep Thelma remarked, "All this noise. I sure hopes they not this noisy when people be tryin' to sleep."

Jeremiah laughed, "No Miss Thelma, dat's just when we loads the ship. It get's quieter later on. You gonna live in Cuba with Master David and Miss Brenda?" he asked.

"Yes. They dun' sold the house in Biloxi. I didn't want to stay. The new owner asked if we wants to and he seemed like he be good to work for but bein' in that house with different owners, I don't know, it just won't seem right.... He let Arthur stay on though."

Opening the door to their cabin Sarah looked in remarking, "Kind of small ain't it?"

"It's the biggest we gots unless you wants to sleep with the crew, and dat's kinda crowded." Laughing he continued, "I be willin' to share my bunk with you though."

Sarah replied, "You old rooster. I dun' past that stage. I ain't no young girl you can be coaxing easy like. Besides, you be an old man!"

He replied laughing, "Miss Sarah, Just cause they be frost on the roof don't mean they ain't no fire in the cook stove," then laughed again.

Surveying the cabin again she said, "I recon it'll do. Who does the cookin' for the mens that runs the ship?" Sarah asked.

"Let me puts yo' bags up and I takes you to him," Jeremiah replied.

After putting the bags in the cabin he led them to the galley.

"Hello Ming. These ladies wants to see who does the cookin' and where you be doin' it."

Ming asked, "Did you ladies know Missy Trisha, Missy Elizabeth?"

They looked at each other then at Ming replying, "Yes, how do you know them?"

"When they come to New Orleans she helped me in galley plenty. She very good cook... very good! She make some nice dishes for men. Everyone talk about leaving Ming behind." Pausing for a moment Ming asked, "You ladies cooks?"

"No. I mean, I ain't, but she is," Thelma replied.

Sarah remarked, "You needin' some help? I be glad to help you. Where the kitchen be?"

"I do right here."

Looking at the small room she replied, "No wonder you so small! I couldn't hardly fit in that kitchen let alone cook in it."

Laughing he replied, "That's what Missy Trisha say. You get use to after while."

Giving Sarah an apron, she began helping.

Thelma said, "You two don't needs me. I'm goin' back to see if Miss Brenda or Master David be needin' anything." Looking over the side rail she continued, "I'm still not sure 'bout all that water and these here lifeboats. They don't look none too big." Surveying them again as she walked by she thought, *sure is a good name for 'em though, lifeboats.*

Captain Jarvis oversaw the crew setting sail and the vessel moved slowly out into the Gulf.

"Hello David, did you get all your affairs in order?" Captain Jarvis asked.

"Yes, everything here is finished. I have no more financial ties. I'd like to have the key to my cabin if there is one."

"There aren't any keys but you can lock whatever you have in the safe in my cabin."

"That'll be fine. By any chance is there a bottle of French wine there?"

"Maybe there is. Let's go see," Captain Jarvis replied.

David went to his cabin and retrieved the box of gold coins from the sale of the house and dock. Bringing them to the captain's cabin he opened the box. Captain Jarvis looking at the contents said, "Now I know why you wanted a key for your room."

"Yes, I was able to transact the sale of the house and the dock in gold. I never thought I could but confederate money isn't all that secure."

"I know, if the South loses it won't be worth the paper it's printed on," Captain Jarvis replied.

After securing it in the safe Captain Jarvis poured two glasses of wine.

He said, "That's a mighty peculiar smell coming from the galley. It' doesn't smell like Ming's cooking."

"It's probably Sarah my cook from Biloxi. She's going to Cuba with us."

"Well, it will be a treat for the next few days having her aboard."

Raising their glasses, they toasted the journey as the ship headed out to sea.

"Here's to a safe voyage. How long will you be in New Orleans?" Captain Jarvis asked.

"Enough time to secure the house. We hope to be traveling to Cuba with you when you leave."

***

Within the next two days, one of the conversations at dinner Captain Jarvis suggested, "Why not hold onto the house in New Orleans? It would be a place to come back to after the war ends, no matter which way it turns out. It will also give Tom and his Missus. a starting point when they follow. Thelma and Sarah could stay and keep the place occupied." Pausing for a moment, he continued, "That is... in case they didn't want to continue any further."

"We've already made up our minds. Brenda wants to keep it." David replied.

After reaching port they were met by Charles.

"Did you get your affairs in Biloxi straight David?" he asked.

"Yes. I was able to sell the house to a fencing master I knew. We were able to transfer the property in less than a week. I think we've pretty much decided to keep the house here. We'd like to sail with Captain Jarvis tomorrow if we can. Why don't you stop for dinner tonight and I'll tell you about my plan," David said.

Looking at Sarah he asked, "What time shall I tell him dinner will be served?"

"Seven o'clock Master David, same as usual."

"Then 7 o'clock it is," Charles replied.

Walking off the dock, Thelma excitedly asked, "Master David, ain't that Elizabeth?" pointing to a woman walking down the street.

"Why yes, it looks like her. Driver, pull up," he said.

Thelma quickly exited the carriage, "Elizabeth! It's me... Thelma."

Surprised to see her they embraced. "What are you doing in New Orleans?" Elizabeth excitedly asked.

"Master David sold everything in Biloxi and we gonna stay here in New Orleans or in Cuba."

"That's fine. I live down the street," she said, pointing in the direction of the house. "I live there with my daughter and Trisha."

"We be sure to stop first chance we gets," Thelma replied.

"Elizabeth, this is my wife Brenda," David said.

"Pleased to meet you Miss Brenda -congratulations!"

"How's Trisha and Violet?" David asked.

"She's doing fine. Between the boarding house and the seafood house it keeps us pretty busy. She still ain't over losing Luke. I can hear her crying sometimes at night, but she'll be alright."

"Yes, that was a blow to all of us. We'll see you again I'm sure. Right now we're pressed for time," David said.

With an acknowledgement to the driver they continued home.

As they pulled into the street Thelma and Sarah were in awe at the big homes with manicured gardens, some finer than Biloxi.

"Miss Brenda this sure is a fine house. I thinks I'm gonna like it here," Thelma said.

Going in they were met by the butler, "Hello Miss Brenda, Master David. How was your trip?"

"Fine, George. This is Thelma; she's going to be in charge of the house. This is Sarah, she's the new cook. Show them around the house will you please while I freshen up."

"Certainly, if you ladies will follow me," George said.

He began by showing them the upstairs then a brief tour of the downstairs. The house was much larger than David's in Biloxi but Thelma knew she would have it organized to her liking in no time. Sarah settled into getting familiar with things in the kitchen then began dinner.

"Sure is some house Sarah, I'm glad we stayin'. I wasn't looking forward to that trip to Cuba. I was prayin' the whole time getin' here," Thelma said.

"Me too," Sarah replied.

"After Master David and Miss Brenda leaves, we has to pay Elizabeth and Trisha a visit," Thelma said.

"Yes, I think George could find a way to get us there. He seems like a nice person," Sarah replied.

Sarah opened and closed a few kitchen cabinet doors and drawers trying to find the right utensils for cooking. Frustrated, she leaned back on the butcher block and said, "I have to straighten this whole kitchen just so I knows where everything's at."

"I'll give you a hand after they leaves tomorrow. I have some straightening out to do myself. I wonder who worked here befo'?" Thelma asked.

"I heard Miss Brenda say they went to the sugar plantation thinkin' Miss Brenda was gonna sell this house. I'm sure glad Miss Brenda changed her mind and decided not to sell."

At that moment, George entered the room and asked, "Thelma would you like me to help set the table for dinner?"

Sarah and Thelma looked at each other then looked at him. Never having the offer, with a light chuckle, Thelma replied, "Yes, you can."

At 6 o'clock Charles arrived. He had a small box in his hand and David led him into the library.

"What's in the box?" David asked.

"It's your share," Charles replied.

"My share! My share of what?" David asked.

"Well it was actually Edward's share," Charles said as he opened the box revealing a hefty amount of gold coins.

"What's this for?" David asked.

"It's from the last two shipments of liquors and other things we brought in."

Looking at the coins David replied, "I didn't know this business was so lucrative."

"It's more than profitable. If your brother decides to join us financially, we could get much bigger," Charles said.

"How were you able to run the blockade so easily? From what Captain Jarvis said they're bringing in more ships to make it more difficult."

"We have an arrangement with several captains that are part of the blockade. They turn a blind eye as long as it isn't war supplies."

Surprised at his statement David asked, "How do you arrange payment?"

"Through Frank, the guy Captain Jarvis introduced you to," Charles confessed.

Rubbing his chin David replied, "Now I understand why it was so successful. No one would suspect a slovenly character like Frank to be a ring leader of something so sophisticated."

"That's right, it would seem as though it was a perfect disguise.... wouldn't it? The truth of the matter is, that's the real Frank. That's the way he's always lived. You would have never guessed it, but it was him, John, and Edward who really started this thing. Do you think your brother Tom would be interested?"

"I can only ask. Tom's a little cautious when it comes to risking a dollar."

Just then Thelma knocked lightly at the door. Opening it halfway she said, "Master David, dinner's ready."

Through dinner David was weighing what Charles told him, wondering why he never said anything about smuggling before now. Like Captain Jarvis, it was a question he wanted to ask and after dinner they retired to the study.

"Charles, how long has this been going on?" David asked.

Slowly looking up from his glass of brandy Charles confessed, "For about eight years. We started before the war avoiding tariffs by only paying the port inspector. However since the war began, everything's become harder. We have to pay off a lot more people. Making the right connections has to be more clandestine."

As David patted the top of the cash box Charles gave him he replied, "I'm almost positive Tom would want to be part of it."

After an hour of light conversation David walked Charles to the front door.

"Goodnight Charles. I'll see you in the morning."

"Goodnight: and thank you for an enjoyable evening David."

After he left, David went into the study to compose a letter to Tom describing in detail how much profit was involved with only a small risk. He pointed out once more in the letter something he spoke to Tom about twice before. Being a plantation owner Tom was facing at best, an uncertain future. He also explained to him the house in New Orleans was still available if he had a change of heart. At the bottom of the letter he wrote he was going to the sugar plantation the following day and any correspondence should be sent to his partner Charles to forward. After sealing it he laid it on the hall table then retired to bed.

The house was buzzing with activity in the morning with Brenda and David preparing to leave.

Thelma announced, "Your breakfast is ready in the dining room Miss Brenda."

"Thank you Thelma. Could you tell David? I believe he's in the study?"

"Yes Ma'am," she replied.

Just then David entered the room asking, "Tell David what?"

"Only that breakfast is ready Master David," Thelma said.

"Oh, okay Thelma. There's a letter I'd like George to post this morning, it's on the table in the hall. If any letters come for me after we leave, have them taken to the dock. Charles will know how to forward them."

"Okay Master David. I see to it," she replied.

After they finished eating Brenda sat there toying with a napkin holder. She seemed to have something on her mind and David asked, "Brenda, you seem to be deep in thought about something. What is it dear?"

Looking up at him she said, "David, I'd like to take a last look around the house before we leave."

"You're not getting homesick already are you?"

"No it just seems strange leaving the house I called home for so many years."

Replying sympathetically, "We'll be able to return one day I'm sure. Don't be too long. I don't want to be late getting aboard."

"I won't David. I promise."

Wandering through the rooms she remembered small things that happened throughout her life and somehow doing it was fulfilling. When George finished loading the baggage Brenda and David said goodbye to everyone then left.

After boarding the ship, within the hour they were leaving port.

"Captain, last night Charles told me all the details of the operation. I'm a little surprised I wasn't filled in on it sooner. Did someone think I wasn't trustworthy?" David asked.

"I don't think it was that. I think between all your other investments in Biloxi they thought you wouldn't want to get involved," the captain replied.

"Tell me something Captain, was my dock and Edward's dock, the only ones involved?"

"No the boy you killed in the duel Steven Watson, his father was part of it too. Why do you ask?"

"I'm thinking with so many people involved there could possibly be a leak that could spell disaster," David said.

"So far it's been very profitable. We have a policy of a need to know only basis."

"That's a little more reassuring. When you unloaded at my dock, who's the one that kept the cargo separated?" David asked.

Hesitating at first to answer he realized by the look on David's face he couldn't avoid telling him.

"It was John first, then after him it was Luke. That's one of the reasons he had his arm injured. The man he was fighting with, after finding out what we were doing, threatened to tell if Luke didn't give him most of his share."

"I see. Is that why you and Charles felt it was necessary to compensate him?"

"In a way yes, but he was a good foreman too. I never had to worry about cargo shifting in transport. He knew his job. He did it well."

"Thanks for clearing up a few things in my mind," David said.

After excusing himself David went to see how Brenda was taking the trip.

"Hello dear. Are you comfortable with the cabin?"

"Yes David. Let's go out on deck and watch the sun go down."

"I'll be ready in a moment. I just want to get a cigar."

They went out on deck and watched as a beautiful orange sun faded away over the horizon.

"Maybe we should go inside? This night air with an ocean breeze can be quite chilly," he said lovingly putting his arms around her shoulders.

"I'd really like to stay out for awhile. I want to stay on deck to see the stars come out. Will they keep all the lights off on the ship?"

"I'm sure they will, but if you're intending on staying out I'll bring your shawl."

"Thank you David."

Within a half hour daylight was completely gone and the stars were crystal clear. Brenda looked over the ship's rail and could see the reflection of the full moon on the black water below. In the distance they could make out a light from another vessel, but with the captain quickly altering course. It too was soon out of sight.

When morning broke the ship was under full sail heading southeast in perfect weather. The water was a deep blue and Brenda could see a few porpoises racing alongside the ship occasionally racing to cross in front of the bow as it cut through the water. Captain Jarvis, taking a bearing on the ships compass looked up, "Good morning Miss Brenda. You're up early this morning."

"Yes the motion of the ship is like a cradle. I slept sound as a baby."

"Where's David this morning?" he asked.

"He wanted to get a few more minutes sleep; he'll be along directly."

"If you're hungry I'll tell Ming to prepare breakfast," he said.

"That will be fine." Turning around she said, "Why, here's David now."

"Did I hear someone mention breakfast?" David asked.

"Yes Dear. Captain Jarvis was about to tell the cook to prepare it."

"Good. I'm hungry enough to eat a horse!"

They went into the dining room and just as they were taking seats, they heard the watch in the crow's nest yell, "Captain! Ship two points off the starboard bow."

Captain Jarvis leapt from his chair with David quickly following. Getting out on deck, Captain Jarvis yelled to the lookout, "Can you make it out?"

After a few moments the watch yelled down, "Looks like a navy war ship Captain. Looks like she spotted us... yes sir, she's heading in our direction."

Captain Jarvis looked through his telescope at the oncoming ship.

"Will it be trouble Captain?" David nervously asked.

"I won't know that David until they get closer. Most navy ships look alike. If you mean is he one of our contacts I don't know that either. We'll have to wait and see."

Within the hour the ship was at hand giving a signal for them to halt. Captain Jarvis looked again through his scope and said with relief, "David, he's one of ours."

The watch in the crows-nest called down, "Captain, they have a longboat overboard. There's a boarding party coming."

"I thought they would be more aggressive trying to stop ships heading in," David asked.

"Not really. They know the cotton and tobacco trade brings back money to help finance the South," Captain Jarvis replied.

"Do we pay both ways?" David asked.

"Yes. That's the only way we can operate without having our ships confiscated."

Within 15 minutes the longboat was fastened to the side and a naval captain with another officer came aboard.

"Hello Captain Jarvis. What's the cargo?" the captain with the boarding party asked.

"A few passengers and some cotton, not much at all. These people are a few of my passengers, David Stewart and his wife Brenda."

"Good morning Ma'am, Sir," Tipping his hat to Brenda he identified himself, "I'm Captain Samuel's from the U.S.S. Liberty. I have to inspect the cargo with Captain Jarvis. Will you excuse us?"

"Captain Samuels, would you mind if David comes along?" Captain Jarvis asked.

Listening suspiciously at the request, Captain Samuels reluctantly replied, "No I don't mind. Shall we proceed to your cabin and have a look at the manifest first?"

After entering the cabin Jarvis closed the door and retrieved a small bag of coins from his desk.

Captain Samuels looked at David and hesitated. Before taking the coins he asked, "Captain Jarvis who is this gentleman?"

Realizing Captain Samuel's suspicion, Captain Jarvis replied, "That's okay Captain Samuels. David's half owner of the dock in New Orleans and has a plantation in Cuba. That's where we're en route to."

Once reassured, Captain Samuels took the bag extending his hand to David in friendship.

"Glad to make your acquaintance David. Will you be making the trip often?" Captain Samuels asked.

"No, my wife and I just inherited her father's sugar plantation. We're on our way there now."

Captain Jarvis poured three glasses of brandy and after finishing, Captain Jarvis took Captain Samuels below to examine the cargo. Returning to the deck 15 minutes later, Captain Jarvis asked, "There's some word that they'll be confiscating ships. Is that true Captain Samuels?"

"It depends on the flag it's flying naturally, but we haven't been given those orders as of yet."

"Thank you Captain Samuels. Until next time, safe sailing," Captain Jarvis said before the boarding party returned to their longboat.

After they were clear of the ship's side Captain Jarvis gave the command, "Resume sail," and they were underway once more.

"I see what you mean captain but I don't like the words, 'Haven't been given the orders yet.' Is there another way we could know the patrol areas ahead of time?"

"When we get to Cuba we'll talk to Frank. He knows a lot of captains from other countries. Maybe we could arrange for payment through one of them. I'll look in on him at the first opportunity."

The rest of the voyage went without incident and the ship docked in Havana several days later.

***

Arriving, they were met at the pier by Anne and Beau. When Brenda and David came down the gangway they promptly congratulated them on their marriage, and expressed their disappointment for not being there for the wedding or Edward's funeral.

"How are my father and mother taking us leaving the country?" Beau asked.

"As well as can be expected Beau. I told them about your plan to stay here and possibly purchasing a hotel. Although your father disapproved, your mother may have had the same feeling but didn't express it. She did say it seemed like a lot of work."

"Anne and I like it here so much we intend to stay and follow through with our plans. I'm not sure whether we have enough money, but we have an opportunity to buy a hotel right here in Havana. It's an established business and fully staffed. They said they'll remain if we purchase it," Beau excitedly said.

"Well Beau I don't think you'll have a problem. Your father gave me a tidy sum to give you and I have Anne's proceeds from the sale of the house in Biloxi."

"Thank you David. That relieves my mind about having to ask you for a loan to finance our adventure."

Laughing they continued to the plantation. As they pulled up in front, they were greeted by a house servant who escorted them inside. The main house was elaborately furnished and Brenda commented on things she remembered from the time she was very young.

With deepest sentiment as she ran her hand over the back of an ornately carved rocking chair and said, "This was my mother's. Father brought it from New Orleans after mother died."

"We're sorry to hear about Edward's passing Brenda. It must have been very traumatic," Anne said.

David replied, "He expected it and wanted to be alive for the wedding. I'm glad we moved it up; he passed away satisfied."

"Brenda it must have been hard to sell the house in New Orleans. It's such a beautiful place. It probably has so many memories for you too," Anne said.

"We didn't sell it. We're keeping it as a foothold and a place to go back to if necessary. Thelma was glad not to have to make the trip too. Sarah and Thelma are going to occupy it so it won't stand empty. It will also be a place for Tom and Sharon to go after they come to their senses and sell Cliveden," David said.

Anne replied excitedly, "Thelma, in New Orleans? I was so worried about what was going to happen to her."

"Now sister you wouldn't think for one minute I'd give up having Thelma in our family. She's always been a part of it."

"How long will you be here David?" Beau asked.

"I have to learn how a sugar plantation is run and get to know the people who are running it. I also have to see a few people that may have input on how to get through this blockade."

"Would you need my help?"Beau asked.

"I don't think so. I know a man here that has a few connections for this sort of thing."

After the house servant poured them a cool drink they went out on the veranda to discuss the hotel Beau wanted to buy. A light rain began to fall accompanied by a breeze and with the palms and tropical flowers; it was a perfect picture of what a Caribbean Island looked like. An iguana made his presence known by scampering along the top of the veranda railing then leapt onto a tropical bush before disappearing, blending in with the surrounding fauna. Shaking at the site of it Anne quickly re-marked, "That's one of the things I won't get used to. They have them at the hotel to keep the bug situation under control." Pausing for a moment she continued, "No one seems to mind them though."

"When are you going to take over the business Beau?" David asked.

"Now that we have the necessary funds we could have the paperwork drawn up this week. I think Anne would like to have a few days with you and Brenda in her company. She hasn't been able to make many friends here. The plantation doesn't have any close neighbors as she had in Biloxi. That's another reason she wants the hotel; they'll be more people around that can speak English."

"Well for the present let's just enjoy each other's company," Brenda suggested.

The rain began coming down a little harder and with a slight wind blowing it on the veranda they retreated to the house.

"It's the rainy season and after the rain, which is practically every day, it gets a little muggy," Brenda said.

"Beau, walk down to the field with me. I'd like a word with the foreman. I want to know what kind of person he is," David said.

"He's no different than any other overseer," Beau replied.

David looked at him for a moment. Not understanding in which context to take his statement he said, "I hope you don't mean that the way it sounded. I don't think Edward would hire anyone who would mistreat his people; he just didn't seem like the type."

Beau replied, "I guess I used the wrong phrase. Anne and I met him several times since we've been here. He seems like he's not a hard person as long as the work gets done. His name is Andrew."

"Then let's go and meet him," David said.

Walking down to the sugarcane field they saw him at a distance directing the laborers. After noticing them he approached and introduced himself.

"Hello Beau. This is David I presume?"

"I am," David replied.

"I'm Andrew, the overseer here."

David looked at him on his horse and by his appearance alone he looked commanding. He had both shirt sleeves rolled up over bulging forearm muscles, and leaned down extending his hand to shake David's.

"Where's Edward?" he asked.

"Edward passed away several weeks ago. I'll be taking over the plantation. I'm married to Edward's daughter Brenda."

Shocked at the news Andrew said, "I haven't seen Miss Brenda since she was about 17. How did she take Edward dying? I know they were very close." Pausing for a moment he added, "The last time Edward was here I thought he seemed awful tired."

"Yes, she's quite upset. It was a shock to all of us. How long have you been in Edward's employ?" David asked.

"About 15 years. Yes let me think -it's been about that long."

"I'm sure Edward had a good judgment of character. I'll have to learn the ropes about running things so I'll be relying on you," David said.

"Will you be staying here full time or will you be living in New Orleans and only spend half the year like Edward?" Andrew asked.

"That will depend on how the war goes. For now we'll be here most of the time."

"Well, any questions you have I'll be glad to answer."

"I don't think Edward would hire anyone that mistreats workers. Do you mistreat them?"

"Not really. There is some grumbling about some owners but it hasn't affected us so far. We have a pretty good group. They know as long as the work gets done I'm satisfied."

"That's a good answer Andrew. It's what I wanted to hear."

"Please David, call me Andy."

"I'll do that. Are the mosquitos always this bad?" David asked as him and Beau swatted at them landing on their arms and waving them from flying around their face during the entire conversation.

"No this happens to be an unusually wet season. I better get back to work," Andrew said before riding away.

As Beau and David walked down the path through the sugarcane fields back to the house, they moved a little faster trying to avoid more mosquito bites. Several steps further down the path they were forced to run trying to avoid them. Breaking out on the other side of the cane-field was much better.

"Well are you satisfied with Andrew?" Beau asked.

"He seems to know what he's doing. I'll have to rely on him," David replied.

They were greeted by Brenda when they reached the house.

"Brenda, Andrew said he was sorry to hear about Edward. He told me you were a devil of a child when you were young. Is that true?" He jokingly asked.

"He wouldn't say that. You're teasing me." Pausing for a moment she continued, "I have to confess though... I thought he was the most handsome man sitting on his horse. Like a knight in shining armor."

David laughed then they went inside.

At dinner David asked, "Beau, will you be going to town tomorrow?"

"I'd like to. I'd like to get started on the paperwork for the hotel."

"I'll join you. In fact maybe we could all enjoy the day and go into town," David said.

"That sounds good David. Maybe we could even stay for a few days," Brenda coaxed.

"Maybe. We'll see." he replied, without a commitment one way or the other.

Chapter 24

Hotel Havana

The sun was warm on their faces as the carriage made its way to town. Passing the docks they noted the hustle and bustle of cargo being loaded and unloaded, made Biloxi seem small by comparison. The ships flew flags from many nations but they all had one thing in common, the moving of commerce.

David commented, "Looking at this reminds me of what that stupid war between the North and South is doing to America, stifling trade."

Brenda replied, "Let's not get involved in politics David. We're supposed to be enjoying the day."

"You're right dear. I apologize."

The carriage pulled up in front of the hotel and the white sign with green letters boldly read, *HOTEL HAVANA*.

"This is it! This is where our home's going to be!" Beau said.

"Why it's gorgeous! It looks so tropical in design!" Brenda replied.

A member of the hotel staff came down the stairs. Opening the carriage door he said, "Good morning, Mr. and Mrs. Henry."

"Compton, this is my brother-in-law David and his wife Brenda. They'll be spending the day with us in town. Could you make sure lunch is provided for four please?"

"Yes sir."

When they entered the lobby they noticed a young boy pulling a cord attached to a large embroidered tapestry in a frame suspended from the ceiling. As he pulled the cord the tapestry gently swung back and forth creating a breeze that was welcomed on such a hot day.

"Well what do you think of it David?" Beau asked.

Looking around he replied, "Impressive, very impressive. Does the current owner live here?"

As David asked that question, a man approached. He appeared to be in his late 50's, thin, and about 5'7" with a full head of snow white hair. Dressed in a white tropical suit he looked like the image of a person who would own this kind of establishment.

"Good morning Beau. Is this your brother-in-law?" he asked.

"Yes it is. This is David Stewart and his wife Brenda."

"Hello I'm glad to make your acquaintance," he said extending his hand to shake David's, "My name's Garfield, Garfield Simmons."

Brenda thought, *even the name fits!* then remarked, "Your hotel is very impressive. It's just what one might imagine reading a book without actually seeing it in person."

"Thank you madam I'm glad you approve," proudly replying with a smile.

Beau looked at David who seemed to approve of their decision to buy the place. "Garfield, I've brought the funds to initiate the sale. I'm going to the lawyer's office. Would you care to come along?"

"I'll be with you in just a minute," he replied.

As David turned around he noticed Frank coming in the front door just as disheveled as the first time they met. His dog Queenie at his side was about to follow when Frank said, "Stay Qeenie!" mumbling quietly but still audible, "I look bad enough."

"Hello David I saw you passing the dock. What brings you to Havana?" Frank asked.

Beau asked quietly, "David do you know him?"

"Yes, believe it or not he wields a lot of power and has friends in high places."

Brenda replied with a strange look sizing Frank up and down, "I hope he combs his hair and changes clothes before he goes to see them."

In a hushed tone David replied, "Brenda my dear, believe it or not he doesn't have to change clothes they seek him out."

David said, "Frank, I'll be living in Cuba most of the time. I was going to try and see you today."

"I'll be at my shack on the dock most of the morning. You know where it is."

"Would you mind if I stop this morning while my brother-in-law Beau is at the attorney with Garfield? Beau's buying this hotel."

Turning to Beau extending his hand Frank said, "Congratulations. This is a popular place. I know Garfield was looking to sell it. Who are the pretty young ladies?"

"I'm sorry Frank. This is my wife Brenda and my sister Anne, Beau's wife."

"Good morning ladies," Frank said tipping the old navy cap he wore.

Brenda and Anne nodded, acknowledging his gesture.

At that moment Garfield came out of his office, "Hello Frank. May I have a few private words with you?" he asked.

"Sure!" Frank replied.

Going to a secluded corner they had a few undistinguishable words. Brenda quietly remarked, "David I guess you were right. Even the owner of the hotel requested a private conference."

David softly laughed thinking to himself, *If you only knew what an instrumental player he was with your father, I'd have to run for the smelling salts.*

After Frank and Garfield were finished talking they shook hands. Coming to join them Frank remarked, "Beau, are you ready to become a hotel owner?"

"Yes. This is the day I've been waiting for," he excitedly replied.

"Well good luck. I'll be seeing you again I'm sure. Ladies it's been a pleasure meeting you," Frank said before exiting the hotel.

Going out the door where his dog Queenie was patiently waiting, she got up wagged her tail then meandered down the steps with him.

As David, Brenda, Anne, and Beau walked out of the hotel, David excused himself from them, and hurried down the street to catch up with Frank.

"Frank, I might just as well walk back to your shack with you."

"That's fine. What's on your mind?" he asked.

"We were boarded en route here and the captain of the naval vessel mentioned about possibly getting orders to confiscate ships coming from the southern states. I was wondering whether there could be something done to prevent it?"

"I heard that. I've been asked by several other ship owners to see if there's a way around it," he said.

"Then I'm not the only one concerned."

"No, but the problem here is political not a military decision. I'm working on an angle where it can be worked out with some politicians in Washington. They're the ones that create policy for the military. The main issue with them is they don't want a scandal attached to their name. If a ship tries to get through carrying weapons to help the southern war effort that would be political suicide.

"I see. Then I take it that it's not completed yet?"

"No not yet. It's just about how much it will cost and how to arrange the payments. I'm working through a bank here that does business with England and the United States. We're in the process of setting up an account for the politicians involved."

"I guess it will be a tidy sum?" David asked.

"Yes it probably will. Politicians don't come cheap."

"That takes a huge burden off my mind. Is there anything I can do to help?"

"Yes as a matter of fact you can. Beau's buying the hotel that the people involved will be staying at. Ask him to make sure they're accommodated as Garfield has."

"Is that what your private conversation was about?"

"Partly," he said not wanting to divulge any more information than necessary. He continued, "Make sure Beau and Anne know."

"I will!" laughing lightly, David continued, "I don't want you to feel offended but by your appearance, but my Brenda was surprised that you were so influential."

Looking down at himself he replied, "Well, when they see me they see money and that's what really counts." They both laughed heartily.

After talking about all the possibilities of avoiding detection and what's to be expected from the politicians, David thanked Frank repeating his offer, "If you need me let me know. I'll be here for several months. Now I best get back to the ladies. I've been here for about an hour."

"Taking them shopping?" Frank asked.

"Yes, they're anxious to see the sites."

As David walked back to the hotel he couldn't help laughing to himself about what Brenda had to say about Frank combing his hair and changing clothes before meeting important people. If she only knew what his living quarters looked like she'd probably faint.

Approaching the hotel he met Beau and Garfield coming back from the lawyer's office. "Did you get the paperwork for the transfer finished?" he asked.

"Yes, with Garfield's influence we were able to get through it rather quickly. Anne and I are now the proud new owners of *Hotel Havana*."

"Garfield what do you intend to do now that you've sold the hotel?"

David asked.

"I was thinking about some travel abroad that I should have done two years ago before my wife's passing. She asked me many times to do it but by the time I was ready she became ill and we never had the chance. While I'm away I'll give more thought as to where I'll live."

Surprised at his statement David asked, "Wouldn't you want to live here?"

"No I'm originally from Philadelphia and will probably go back nearer to the city. I've made quite a few friends since I've owned the hotel. Some are from Philadelphia and New York. A small apartment will do me just fine."

David turned to Beau saying, "Beau it seems you came to Cuba at exactly the right time. I wish you and Anne all the luck with it."

"Yes it seems so David. I hope to be just as successful as Garfield."

"I'm sure you will. I'm sure you will," Garfield replied.

As they entered the hotel they saw Anne and Brenda patiently waiting to have lunch before taking in the sites of Havana.

"Where have you been all this time? We're hungry," Anne asked.

Beau replied, "How fast do you think we could have completed the transaction? By any standard it was rather quick. We're now the proud owners of the hotel."

Jumping up from the table she put her arms around him, "Oh Beau... it's perfect. I can't wait to move in."

He replied jokingly, "Let's see what kind of lunch this establishment offers maybe we'll have to complain to the new owners."

Compton, the hotel valet, smiled then escorted them to a table in the dining room. The furnishings were white wicker with white tablecloths, and red hibiscus flowers adorned small green glass vases in the center of each table. With the open sashes the deep green tropical fauna outside was a perfect backdrop. While they were being seated Beau asked, "Compton, how long have you been with the hotel staff?"

"I've been here since I was 17, about 30 years now sir. I came just after Mr. Garfield bought it."

"Since you must know everything there is to know about running the hotel, I'm making you the assistant owner."

"Thank you kindly Mr. Henry."

"Don't call me Mr. Henry Compton, Beau will be sufficient."

"Yes Sir."

"Compton, another question if you don't mind. During your time here have there been many important people stay?"

"Yes Sir, quite a few. We've had a few very important people stay here recently. They were politicians from Washington. They were here several times since the war began."

When he said it, David smiled with interest knowing what Frank told him was the truth and thought, *they were probably the people being paid off who had bank accounts set up for them by Frank.*

After finishing lunch over pleasant conversation, Beau said, "Now let's see what Havana has to offer for entertainment."

Leaving the hotel they went on their adventure to explore the city.

The women were amazed at all the different shops selling everything imaginable. Being a duty-free-port goods from all the countries were available for purchase without import taxation.

Anne remarked, "Gracious me Brenda, the first time I saw these shops I swear I thought I just died and went to heaven." Taking a silken scarf from a table she draped it over her shoulders quietly saying, "We'll have to explore this when the men aren't around."

"Yes, I think so!" Brenda quietly replied.

"David this is even busier and has more shops than New Orleans."

"I know dear and I also know you'll be spending more time here with Anne. I can see it now, closets bulging with new dresses."

They laughed as they continued exploring the market area.

Anne asked, "Beau can we have dinner here? This seems to be a very attractive restaurant. Don't you think so Brenda?"

"Yes it looks like a perfect ending to a perfect day," she replied.

Going inside, they enjoyed a nice diner of Cuban cooking, part Creole and part Caribbean: spicy, just as Brenda likes it.

"Why don't you stay the night in our hotel and go back to the plantation in the morning?" Beau asked.

Brenda, looking at David for his approval replied, "That sounds like a good idea."

"Then it's settled. We'll put you up in one of the best rooms," Anne said.

After dinner they walked back to the hotel. Anne took Brenda to a room with a beautiful view of the harbor and handed her the key. "I hope you enjoy the room, it's the best we have," Anne said.

Coming into the room, David overheard Anne's comment. Looking around he remarked, "I guess this room might just do for a couple that own one of the finest plantations on the island."

Anne smiled then gave David a light kiss on the cheek. "Thanks David for giving Beau the money. Sleep well!" she said before closing the door after exiting.

"Would you like a drink Brenda and sit out on the terrace for awhile?"

"Yes just let me slip into something a little more comfortable."

Sitting on the edge of the bed he looked down at the floor and sheepishly asked, "Brenda do you really think Andrew is the most handsome man sitting on his horse with his sleeves rolled up?"

Stopping for a moment to look at him she replied, "Why David! Is that what's praying on your mind? I was wondering why you were unusually quiet all day. No, don't be jealous of something I thought when I was 16 or 17. You needn't worry."

"Okay dear, for a moment you just made me feel like a jealous little school boy."

"Don't be David. I'm flattered."

They sat out until late discussing plans for the future, and wondered whether Tom and Sharon would have the good sense to join them. In about an hour they retired for the evening.

After breakfast the following morning they departed for the plantation. Approaching, they saw smoke and smelled the strong odor of something burning coming from the cane fields. Arriving they were met at the front door by Eva the Cuban house maid. Extremely excited she clamored, "Senor, three of the workers in the cane fields, they come down with the yellow fever."

The terrified look on her face was an indication of how much of an epidemic it could be.

Yellow fever is a highly contagious disease and could sweep through a community with devastating results, both mortally and economically. David's first thought was to get Brenda back on a ship as soon as possible, out of harm's way.

"My dear I think you should pack a bag and make arrangements to go back to New Orleans on the first available ship."

"David let's just wait a few days until we see how bad it really is. Have you ever lived through an epidemic before Eva?" Brenda asked.

"Se', when I was very small but I don't remember too much. Two of the house servants already left the low ground. They go higher into the mountain to get away from the mosquito's. They don't want to be near the swamp," Pausing for a moment she said, "I don't think they come back."

"Well we'll just have to fend for ourselves, won't we?" Brenda replied.

Looking at the smoke rising from the cane fields, Eva nervously replied reluctantly, "Se' Senora."

"I still think you should leave until this thing passes," David said.

"David how would it look if I left and the servants stayed? It would be as if I ran out on them."

After thinking for a moment David said, "Well, maybe we can arrange for you to relocate to higher elevations too? Eva do you know a place where it might be a little safer?"

Excitedly replying, "Se', Senor. My family lives in the mountains and you would be much welcomed there."

"I was only speaking for Miss Brenda, I'm staying here," he replied.

"Se', we can leave tomorrow," Eva said looking out at the thickening smoke.

"Thank you Eva."

Hurrying off the front porch David said, "I'm going down to see Andrew about the fever. I'll be back this afternoon."

"Be careful David," Brenda said.

"Wait, Senor!" Eva said heading for the kitchen.

Returning in a few minutes with a bottle of olive oil she said, "Rub this on your face and arms. It will protect you from mosquito bites."

"Thank you Eva," he said applying a generous amount to his face, neck and arms. Rather than walk through the swampy area he and Beau went through, he saddled a horse to make his way faster. Getting past the wet area he could see part of the cane field closest to the swamp still smoldering. Looking down he could see a light sheen of oil that had been spread on the stagnant water trying to check the mosquito infestation.

"Andrew how bad is it?" he asked.

"When the first worker became ill I thought it may have been just swamp fever. Not often, but it sometimes happens. Usually within a few days the fever breaks and they recuperate. After the first case two more workers came down with it within 12 hours. The fever never broke on the first person and he died. That's when I sent for the doctor. He immediately quarantined their living quarters and told me two neighboring plantations have a few cases also. That's why we're burning off the fields."

"Do you think it will get much worse?"

"I asked that question to Doctor Drake. He said it's hard to tell. It depends on how long this rainy season keeps up. It's the worst I've ever seen."

"Would draining some of that swamp help?" David asked.

"Probably, but yellow fever is highly contagious, that's the problem."

"I was asking Brenda to consider going back to New Orleans but she may just go to a higher elevation with Eva. I believe Eva's relatives live up there."

"That might be a good idea," Andrew replied.

"Well Andrew, if you need me I'll be back at the house."

"Okay David."

The next morning Brenda and Eva were ready to leave.

"Goodbye dear. I'll see you soon," David said.

After embracing, Brenda kissed him and said, "I love you, try to keep in touch."

Eva looking on was becoming impatient with the parting gestures. Nervously looking around tapping her foot she said, "We should be going now Senora."

"Okay Eva. I'm ready." After getting in the carriage they departed.

It seemed strange with the house empty but David busied himself getting into Edward's ledgers from the last few years. The plantation was quite successful and he was going to try his best to insure it would continue to do so. Noting there were profits that couldn't be accounted for, he sat back in his chair with his hands folded behind his head, he thought, *I wonder whether they were the proceeds of the untaxed goods going into New Orleans. It made perfect sense putting all his illegal gains into the banks here, rather than New Orleans where they could be scrutinized.* David chuckled to himself, *and I thought Edward was beyond reproach.*

There was a knock at the door and when he looked up he noticed it was already 2 o'clock. Answering the door, a messenger handed him a note. It was from Anne and he was shocked to read Beau was down with possibly yellow fever and the doctor quarantined the hotel. He told the messenger, "Wait just a moment. I have a reply you can take back."

He wrote that Brenda had already left for high ground and three people here had yellow fever. Not wanting to upset her further he didn't mention the one who died but added he would join her in two days. After handing the note to the messenger he closed the door. Thinking he must see Brenda before going back to Havana he went first to the cane fields to speak with Andrew.

"Andrew, I just got a message from my sister Anne. Beau is down with the fever and the doctor quarantined the hotel. I'll have to see Brenda before I leave for Havana. I don't want you to think I'm abandoning you."

"I'll be fine here David. Good luck."

Going back to the house he packed a few clothes for the trip. He wanted to tell Brenda the news, and if possible, spend the day before going to Havana.

Being there before the carriage driver knew the village where Eva lived. It was a small village on one of the highest points of the island. The trade winds there were constant which reduced the threat of mosquito infestation. He knew if contaminated people didn't come there Brenda would be fine. As the carriage approached the village they stopped a young boy walking alongside the road. David asked, "Which house belongs to Eva's parents?"

The boy shrugged his shoulders not able to understand English. The driver asked in Spanish and the boy pointed to a cluster of about 15 wooden structures with thatched roofs on both sides of the road, elevated four feet off the ground. Chickens roamed at will and there were a few pigs in penned areas. It looked like one would expect of people living in poverty. After inquiring to several people the coachman pointed to a cottage almost at the end of the row.

"That's where Senorita Eva lives Senor."

As the coach came to a halt at Eva's parent's home, curious neighbors exited their cottages. Not receiving many visitors, some of the people just stood in their doorway looking to see who it was. Brenda, seeing the carriage came to the door.

"David, is something wrong? The look on your face is distressing."

"Yes Brenda. I received a note from Anne yesterday afternoon. Beau has yellow fever and the doctor quarantined the hotel."

"No! He seemed fine the other day. Of course you'll want to go. Shall I go with you?"

"No I think you'll be better off here." Looking at the surroundings he continued, "If it isn't too inconvenient?"

"No David, in fact, I'm enjoying Eva and her parents. Her brother and his wife live across the road. They're teaching me how to cook Creole style with a flare of Caribbean."

"Eva, do you think you could spare another boarder for tonight? "I promise I won't be a burden. I'll be leaving first thing in the morning," David asked.

"Se' Senor."

Even with extreme poverty the people had good hearts willing to share what little they had without question. Around 5 o'clock, they sat down to dinner of black beans and rice. After they finished, Brenda and David settled in for the night.

In the morning, David boarded the carriage and as he was leaving, Brenda held on to his arm and said, "Tell Anne I was sorry to hear about Beau. I'll join her as soon as possible."

"Okay my dear. I'll be sure to tell her."

On the way back down the hillside smoke was now visible on much of the low lands from several plantations. The feint smell of charred sugarcane kept getting stronger until they passed the last plantation.

Reaching the city David went directly to the hotel. As he walked up the steps he saw placards fastened to several porch posts warning of the yellow fever inside. When he walked in, Anne sobbingly greeted him with a hug.

"How's Beau?" he asked.

"He's not doing well at all. His temperature is still well over a 100 degrees and he's been delirious since yesterday. If his fever doesn't break soon the doctor doesn't hold out much hope for recovery."

"Well we can hope for the best," David replied.

"Where's Brenda?" Anne asked.

"She went to the mountain with the housekeeper Eva. Eva was afraid to stay at the plantation and several other house staff left too. There's no one there for the exception of Andrew and the field hands. I wanted Brenda to go back to New Orleans until this thing passed but she won't go."

Anne said teary eyed, "David, if anything happens to Beau I'll never forgive myself."

Looking around he embraced her replying, "It wouldn't be your fault. This is what Beau wanted."

Just then the doctor walked in, "Who are you? Didn't you read the signs out front?!" he adamantly demanded.

"Doctor this is my brother David. He's married to Brenda Atchison."

"I'm sorry. I didn't know," the doctor replied.

"Anne, is Beau the same as he was last night?" the doctor asked.

"Yes doctor I'm afraid he is."

"If you'll excuse me David, I'll see how he's doing."

"Doctor I'd like to join you."

"Maybe that's not just a good idea right now. Why don't you stay down here with Anne?"

Reading into his statement David knew it was far graver than the doctor made it out to be.

"Let me go to him doctor," Anne anxiously said.

"No Anne. Stay here with your brother."

Throwing herself into David's arms, she cried out, "Oh David! I'm so worried."

"I'm here now. Beau's young and strong. He'll pull through."

Within a half-hour the doctor came down the stairs.

"How is he?" David asked.

"I won't kid you Anne, his condition is worse. I feel he won't make it through the night."

Breaking down sobbing she threw herself down on a couch in the lobby saying aloud, "We should have never left Five Oaks! We should have never left Five Oaks!"

As David was escorting the doctor to the front door, the doctor quietly asked, "Where's Five Oaks? Is that where they lived?"

"Yes doctor. It's a plantation his father owns about 50 miles from Biloxi."

"What will she do with this fine hotel they just purchased?" the doctor asked.

"I don't know. I guess we'll have to figure that out when the time comes. Will you be coming back again?"

"I don't think it will be necessary. There are other sick people. We're just overburdened with this epidemic. It began so sudden. Let me know when he passes."

"I will. Could you leave me a sedative in case Anne needs one?"

"Certainly," reaching in his bag, he took out a small bottle and handed it to him.

"Thank you Doctor," David said as the doctor left.

David went behind the bar to pour a brandy for Anne and himself, handing it to her he said, "Here Anne you need this."

"David, the whole world seems to have just tumbled down in the last few days."

"I'll stay here with you for awhile. Brenda is safe where she's at and Andrew is doing all he can at the plantation."

"How do you think he got sick?" Anne asked.

"That's hard to say. It could have been through a mosquito bite or coming in contact with someone who had it. Andrew said the mosquitoes have been horrible this year since the rainy season began. I remember walking back from meeting Andrew the first day I was here. Beau and I were actually running back to the house to keep from getting bit."

In an hour they went up to look in on Beau. Anne kept putting damp cloths on his forehead trying to break the fever but he was still delirious. Putting her hand to his forehead she said, "David he's burning up with fever."

"There's no use in you staying here. You've been up for two nights keeping watch. No sense wearing yourself down and becoming sick yourself. Here's something the doctor left for you. It will help you sleep. Go and lie down."

With David keeping watch, Beau passed away peacefully in a comatose state. David didn't wake Anne thinking sleep was the best thing for her, and with the help of two hotel staff members, they took the body to an undertaker close by. The undertaker was mentioned in Edward's ledger in the event Edward passed away while he was here. Upon returning they saw Anne in the lobby. Without seeing Beau in his room she knew he died. Seeing David she wept saying, "David, I should have stayed with him at the end."

"No, you did the right thing. He never regained consciousness. I'll write the letters to Beau's parents, Tom, and Sharon. If you're okay, I'll use the office to write them."

"Thanks David," looking down at herself she added, "I'm just an awful mess. I hardly know where to begin."

"Leave everything to me. You'll be fine," he said, then went to the office and took out writing paper and envelopes.

Never having to write this type of letter he paused for a few moments wondering how he would word it. Carefully choosing the right words he began to write,

"Dear Mr. and Mrs. Henry," he wrote, pausing to gather his thoughts again he dipped the pen into the ink bottle. *"I'm writing this letter to inform you that Beau has passed away after contracting yellow fever."* Pausing again worrying about Brenda's safety he continued, *"Anne was at his side right to the end disregarding her own health to insure Beau was properly attended to. He was happy these last several weeks and looked forward to being the proprietor of a hotel anyone would be proud to own."*

"At this time Brenda has gone to a higher elevation to get relief from the lower wetter areas where this terrible disease spawned. I'll be bringing her back to the hotel to stay with Anne until we can get their affairs straight. There's no question that you or my brother Tom, would have wanted to be here for the funeral, but time and distance make that impossible.

"Rather than have him buried at the sugar plantation where there's no guarantee we will own in the future. I think it best we have a small service and chose a burial site at a nearby cemetery. Hopefully you'll be satisfied with the arrangements."

"I know you'll be coming at some point and I'd be more than glad to see to your comfort. If you happen to see Tom, tell him Anne's weathering the death as well as can be expected. But seeing her and Beau in each other's company the last few weeks tells me the road ahead for Anne is going to be hard. In closing you have my deepest sympathy, David Stewart."

Having finished the letters, he took them out front to post. When he returned to the lobby, he took Anne into the kitchen and brewed a cup of coffee. They sat down and David told her what was in the letters he posted.

"I'm happy you're here. At least there's someone from the family," Anne said.

"I'm sure if there was a way Tom and Beau's parents could be here, they would. You didn't sleep very long. Why don't you try to get some more rest?" David said.

"I think I will David."

As he watched her slowly walk up the stairs to her apartment on the top floor, it looked as though she was carrying the weight of the world on her frail shoulders. He called out, "Anne, I'll be here when you wake. I want to get a message off to Brenda."

Looking over the banister she replied, "Fine David. I'll see you when I wake."

After composing the note he had one of the hotel staff deliver it. He thought, *Brenda will probably get the note today and start down tomorrow.* The note read for her to stop at the plantation and tell Andrew Beau died, and sometime after the funeral he would return to the plantation.

Chapter 25

Beau's Funeral

Anne bore the heavy burden of losing the man she loved as well as could be expected and although David was there, she was happy to see Brenda arrive.

"I'm so sorry for you. Will you be okay?" Brenda asked.

"Yes Brenda I'm fine. David's here, but having you is a big help. Women somehow seem more sensitive than men. They understand each other."

Brenda asked, "David, what arrangements have you made?"

"It's going to be a small private funeral. The undertaker that's going to do it is someone Edward wanted to do his in the event he passed away while he was here."

Brenda looked at David as though what he said was something that never passed her mind until now, "David, a horrible thought just crossed my mind."

"What's that dear?"

"I never gave that a thought, Papa use to spend about six months every year here. If he had died while he was here I would have never had a chance to see him."

"Well, we're fortunate it turned out the way it did. Did you tell Andrew I'll be here for a few days?"

"Yes, and he said he sends his deepest sympathy to you Anne."

Anne smiled, "That was thoughtful of him."

***

Within two days the funeral was held with Anne, Brenda, and David present. When they got to the gravesite there was a man they didn't recognize. At first glance it was hard to tell it was Frank. He was clean shaven and had a tie and suit jacket on. The giveaway was his dog Queenie lying at his side.

After the service he approached them and said, "Anne, I was sorry to hear about Beau. I know it must be hard since the both of you had such high expectations with buying The Havana."

"Yes it is. Thank you for being so thoughtful by coming to pay your respects."

"If there's anything I can do to help, let me know," Frank said.

Anne, while holding onto Brenda's arm, nodded in approval of his offer.

"David I take it you'll be at the hotel for a few days?" Frank asked.

"Yes Frank, I'll probably be here for a few weeks. Is there something you wish to discuss?"

"Yes, and if you could stop by my place later I'll let you know what's happening with our discussion the last time we met."

"Now that Brenda's here I could be there tomorrow if that's okay with you?"

"That's fine. I'll see you then," Frank said.

"If you'll excuse us Frank I'd like to get Anne home."

"Certainly, again Anne I'm sorry."

With Anne sobbing, David and Brenda walked her back to the carriage. Arriving at the hotel she broke down completely and Brenda quickly took her to her room.

"Brenda I'll be in the office if you need me," David said.

"We'll be fine," she replied.

The next day David went to see Frank. Entering his shack Frank said, "David there's several legislators coming. I don't know exactly when but keep an eye out for them. Don't say too much until we can all meet together. Like all politicians, they have a way of being intimidating."

"I won't Frank. Thanks for the warning."

***

Several weeks went by and the quarantine placards were taken down. The epidemic had subsided and things were beginning to return to normal. David had taken over running the hotel and with the help of long-time employees like Compton it was as though he had been the proprietor for years.

One afternoon several guests accompanied by their wives arrived.

"Can I help you?" David asked.

"Yes, we'd like two adjoining rooms if at all possible."

"We have the space for you but the dining area will be closed for awhile. You'll have to dine elsewhere. We're in the process of hiring new kitchen help."

"That's fine. We can manage," one of the guests replied.

Turning the book in their direction David asked, "Would you please fill out the registry?"

After they signed he turned the book back around and could see their addresses.

"I see you're from New York," David said.

"Yes, we're here with our wives on vacation. I'm Senator Harold Thompson," he said pointing to his right he added, "This is Congressman James Lewis."

Senator Thompson was about six feet tall and on the portly side. He appeared to be in his late 50's and had the demeanor of a politician. As he spoke he had his hands on his hips as though he was about to address a crowd of potential voters. Congressman Lewis on the other hand was around 5 foot 10, with straight black hair. He was on the thin side and appeared to be in his early forties. He seemed reserved with his opinion and before he spoke, he looked at Senator Thompson seemingly for approval.

David rang the bell for the porter and instructed Compton to bring their bags to the 2nd floor.

"Compton, please take these people to rooms 8 and 9."

"Yes Sir," turning to the guests he said, "Would you follow me please?"

As Compton was taking them to their rooms they could hear Anne crying as they passed her apartment.

"Is there something wrong here Compton?" Senator Thompson's wife asked.

"Yes Sir. That's the wife of the owner of the hotel. Her husband died several weeks ago. Sometimes she gets overwhelmed and has to go to her room until she regains her composure. Her brother's the person that checked you in."

"We don't want to be a burden. Will it be alright if we stay?"

"Yes, there's enough staff here to accommodate and there's supposed to be a cook and waiter at the end of the week. We have several other guests. They dine elsewhere."

"That's a relief, it's such a beautiful hotel," one of the wives commented.

Compton replied, "It's the finest in Havana. May I ask your names?"

"I'm Senator Harold Thompson and he's Congressman James Lewis. We're from New York State. Do you know where that is?"

"Not exactly but I know it's up north somewhere and gets pretty cold. That's all I want to know."

They laughed.

"How long will you be staying in Havana Sir?" Compton asked.

"We're supposed to meet with a man that owns a sugar plantation nearby. His name is David Stewart. Would you by chance happen to know him?"

"Yes Sir. He's the man that just checked you in. It's his sister's husband who died. He's helping out for awhile. Shall I tell him you're here to see him?"

Congressman Lewis handing Compton a dollar replied, "No that's okay. We'll introduce ourselves later. You can leave the luggage here."

"Thank you Sir. If I can be of any further assistance please let me know."

After entering their separate rooms they went out on the adjoining balcony, leaving their wives to unpack.

"That's convenient James. We won't have to travel any further. We'll let him know we want to speak with him later and just enjoy the day with our wives."

When Compton returned to the lobby David asked "Did you get them situated in their rooms?"

"Yes Sir."

"Did they mention why they were here?"

"They said they were supposed to have a meeting with you. I told them you were the one who checked them in and asked if they wanted me to tell you. They said 'No,' they wanted to speak with you later."

"Which one seemed to be the spokesman," David asked.

"The heavy set one, Senator Thompson," he replied.

David's assessment of the two was accurate. Senator Thompson would be the one Frank would have to deal with.

"Thank you Compton."

A short time later, David looked up and saw Senator Thompson coming down the stairs. Approaching the desk while eyeing the lobby, he lit his cigar saying, "You have a beautiful hotel. I'm sure we'll enjoy our stay."

"Well, it belongs to my sister and her husband who died recently."

"Yes Compton told us. I'm very sorry to hear that. I'm told your name is David Stewart?"

"Yes it is. Why?"

"We have a mutual friend," he said, pausing for a moment to butt cigar ashes into a tray, "His name is Frank."

Pretending to look surprised David thought, *Frank was more widely known, than David ever imagined.* Senator Thompson continued, "There's something we have to discuss before we leave but we want to enjoy the rest of the day with our wives."

"That will be fine. I'm sure we can find time to talk about what our mutual interests are. Havana has some interesting places and shops the ladies will enjoy visiting."

"I'm sure they will," Senator Thompson replied with a chuckle.

In a few minutes Congressman Lewis came downstairs with the two wives and approached the desk.

"David this is Congressman James Lewis," Senator Thompson said.

Extending his hand David said, "Glad to meet you Congressman. I'll be looking forward to our meeting."

"Likewise David. Well ladies, are we ready to go on our adventure?"

"Yes, and we hope there's a lot of clothing shops," Mrs. Thompson added.

"There's more than enough!" David replied with a smile.

After they left the hotel, David rang for Compton. Approaching the desk David said, "I have to go out for awhile. Would you ask Brenda if she could watch the desk until I return?"

"Yes Sir. We'll manage."

Quickly leaving the hotel, David went to the pier and knocked at Frank's door. There was no answer but as he turned to walk away Frank was coming in his direction. "Hello David. Did you meet your guests?"

"Yes, they're out with their wives doing the town. I just wanted to know what input you have before I meet with them."

Jokingly Frank said, "The input is within your pocket. Come in and we'll have a drink."

Opening the door they stepped inside. David, looking around for a place to sit cleared some papers from a chair then sat down. Frank was searching a cabinet for a clean glass and after finding two, he looked inside. Taking a towel from a drawer he wiped them clean before pouring two Brandy's. Realizing David saw him wiping the glasses clean he said, "I'll have to have one of the girls from the tavern come in and straighten up this mess one of these days."

David smiled thinking, *Frank meeting with a senator and congressman is taking second place to a tavern girl straightening his shack,* He chuckled to himself and asked, "Frank, how do we proceed with the meeting?"

"If they ask you any questions before the meeting try to postpone giving them an answer. If they persist, the first question to ask is what kind of arrangement can be made in regards to getting through the blockade. The second question should be, if confiscation of ships is enforced and one of yours is taken, how can we go about getting it released? The third question and the most important, is how much will it cost and how the money will be exchanged?"

"Will you be at the meeting?" David asked.

"Yes, and so will John, our contact in Jamaica."

"I remember him from the meeting with Captain Jarvis," David said.

"Yes, he's the one that could clear it with the British as long as there's a profit for him. But again you have to remember, the most important thing is politicians won't jeopardize their position at home."

"It seems like a lot of hands have to be taken care of," David said.

"Yes, so we'll have to make up for it by increasing the illegal goods. The congressman and senator will have to realize that. When is this meeting going to take place? I want to make sure John's here," Frank asked.

"Should I try arranging it for later this week, possibly Friday?" David replied.

"That's good. It'll give me time to get John. They aren't likely to want to leave until after the meeting," he said chuckling, "As the saying goes. It's money in the bank."

David finished his drink and with a smile remarked, "I hope my pockets are deep enough for these politicians."

"We'll see. We really don't have an alternative. The war doesn't seem like it will end any time soon. I heard there was a second big battle in Manassas with heavy losses for the South. The North thought the South would have stopped fighting but they escaped and regrouped."

"Yes, I heard that. I told my brother to sell his plantation outside Biloxi and come down here. I hope he takes heed."

As Frank opened the door for David he asked, "How's Anne holding up?"

"She'll be fine. Brenda's going to stay for about a month. By that time my brother and his wife should be here and so will Beau's parents. I sent letters when Beau died. They'll be staying at the hotel so Anne won't be alone."

"That's good. Tell her again how sorry I am."

"I will, and thanks for the advice."

Returning to the hotel he saw Brenda behind the counter looking at the guest registration book. She asked, "David who are these people that checked in earlier?"

"They're politicians from New York. They've taken their wives out for the day."

"Did you have your meeting with Frank?" she asked.

"Yes how did you know?"

"I suspected it has something to do with avoiding the blockade with our shipping. Are these people here to help?"

"Your father said you were a thinker. He sure brought you up properly. Yes it's about our shipping business and how we can avoid the blockade. I have to arrange a meeting with them and Frank at the end of the week." Smiling he continued, "Now don't say anything to them about your suspicions."

"I won't dear." Laughing she added, "A meeting with Frank of all people!"

"Yes, his influence is nothing short of remarkable."

Later that afternoon Senator Thompson and Congressman Lewis returned to the hotel with their wives. David met them in the lobby and escorted them to the dining room. After pouring them a brandy, he informed them the meeting was scheduled for Friday at 9 p.m.

"I have to return to my plantation to attend some business. I'll be back on Friday. How did you enjoy your day?"

Congressman Lewis replied, "We had a wonderful time and with all the bags our wives are carrying you can tell they had a great day exploring the shops too."

"Yes, this is a woman's dream come true when it comes to shopping. If I don't see you before I leave in the morning enjoy your few days until my return."

Senator Thompson replied as he raised his glass with approval, "Thank you David, until then."

In the morning, as David was packing his bag to leave he asked, "Brenda will you be alright here with Anne?"

"Yes, with Compton knowing how to run the hotel we'll do just fine. Did you make the arrangement for your meeting?"

"Yes we're going to have it on Friday evening. Frank sent for John in Jamaica and by Friday he should be here."

When they got to the lobby Compton took David's clothing bag and brought it out front to his awaiting carriage.

"Compton, I know with your help, Brenda and Anne won't have anything to worry about."

"No Sir we'll be fine. It may be better for Miss Anne to be busy. It'll take her mind off Mr. Beau."

"You're probably right. Well, goodbye."

After the carriage pulled away, Brenda and Compton returned to the lobby just as Anne was coming down the stairs.

"Did I miss David?" she asked.

"Yes he just left. We'll be on our own for the next few days. How are you feeling?"

"I think I'll try and get another cook to help in the kitchen. With all the guests we'll have to have more help. I don't want the service to be less than excellent."

"Where will you look?" Brenda asked.

"I have my eye on one at a local restaurant. She's not very happy working there and she turns out a tremendous Creole menu."

***

As David was approaching the plantation area he could still smell the charred remnants of the cane fields. He knew the loss of revenue would be devastating and would have to carry the burden financially. He realized the money he had from the sale of the house and dock in Biloxi would probably have to be used for the safe passage of contraband to New Orleans. That too would depend on what the senator and congressman wanted along with who they have to influence in the navy. He realized financially he would be cutting it close.

"Hello Andrew. It looks pretty bad."

"David, there won't be much of a harvest this year but the problem with the mosquitos is all but eliminated. Firing the cane fields and spreading oil on the low lying marsh helped considerably. With the end of the rainy season I think we pretty much licked it."

"Has there been anyone else down with the fever?" David asked.

"No, we had three die during the height of the crisis and several that recovered. One of the worker's wives attended the sick which helped a lot."

"That news is encouraging. Maybe Eva will return soon. Is there anyone you would recommend to take her place until she does?"

"There's one of the field hand's wives. She'll probably do it. Will you be staying at the plantation for good?"

"No, I'll be here for a few days though. I have to return to Havana on Friday for a meeting. Why don't you join me for dinner?"

"I'll do that. There's something else I want to discuss with you," Andrew said.

"It sounds important. We'll talk about it at dinner," David replied.

Andrew rode back to where the work was being done in the field and David's carriage continued to the house. Pulling up to the front door, Eva came out to greet him.

"Senor, where's Miss Brenda?" she asked.

"She's staying with my sister in Havana helping her with the hotel. My brother and his wife will be coming to Havana within the next few days to stay with her for awhile. I didn't know you returned."

"I just come back this morning," she replied.

"Andrew didn't know you were back. He was going to ask one of the field hand's wives to cook until you returned. You better tell him. Oh! Andrew's coming for dinner tonight so set out a place for him."

"Se' Senor."

David went into the study and opened the safe. Counting out fifty five thousand dollars from the sales in Biloxi, and half his share from the dock sale in New Orleans, he wondered, *will this be enough money to cover expenses? When Tom gets here, he'll have money and probably want to invest in the contraband trade too.*

After examining Edward's ledgers closer, he read where a few of the cane fields were destroyed by an accidental fire over 20 years ago. The ledger revealed Edward had to borrow money against his home in New Orleans to recover the loss. Reading it was an inspiration for another option he hadn't thought of.

Although Edward's fields weren't completely destroyed being a recent purchaser, Edward must have already been holding a mortgage. He thought, *I wonder if that's when he began the illicit trade. If Edward was able to do it, I'll be able to weather this financial loss too.*

He was distracted from the ledgers by a knock at the door. Looking up he said, "Come in Andrew. How's the work progressing?"

"It's coming along pretty well. We'll be able to plant again very soon."

"That's good to hear. I was just going over some of Edward's ledgers. I read he sustained a heavy loss not long after he bought this place."

"Yes I know, he told me about it. He thought he would go bankrupt until his wife's father helped financially." Not knowing whether David knew about the illicit trade he avoided embarrassing Edward's secret by not exposing what he knew. Instead he diverted the conversation by saying, "We still have the two fields that weren't affected so it should help."

Before Andrew could continue, David said, "If it wasn't for your knowledge I'd be at a total loss."

At that moment Eva entered the room announcing, "Dinner's ready Senor's."

Going into the dining room, they sat down. David asked, "Andrew, what did you want to speak to me about?"

Taking a chance he may have been wrong about David not knowing about the illicit trade he replied, "David, I have some money put aside. I'd like to invest in the New Orleans trade you're taking over. When Edward was alive he always let me invest a few dollars that gave me a return on my investment."

"I wasn't aware of your knowledge about that. Edward must have been very fond of you."

Happy he took the chance to ask, Andrew said, "He was. I was the one who introduced him to Frank." Pausing for a moment, Andrew looked down at his plate, "Frank's my older brother."

Looking in astonishment, David wanted to know more about their relationship and asked,"How is it you're not in Havana helping him?"

"Well we're actually half brothers. His father died and our mother remarried. Frank never approved and I think he never quite accepted the fact me and my younger brother never came from the same father."

"It must be hard not to be accepted by your brother," David said.

"Enough talk about my family history. Would you consider me investing?"

"Yes, I'd be glad to let you in, but there's a small complication I must warn you about."

"What's that?"

"With the war between the states it's getting more difficult to get cargos through. There are a few politicians at the hotel Frank and I must have a meeting with. We'll learn more about how we can get around the blockade and how much it will cost. It's untried at this point and I wouldn't want to deceive you as to its success. We're taking a chance."

"I understand. I'm willing to try."

Excusing himself from the table, Andrew went outside. When he returned, he had a saddle bag and withdrew a small sack emptying it on the table, fifteen thousand dollars in gold.

"Here David you can invest this."

"I'll do my best Andrew."

"I know you will."

***

Four days went by quickly and David was once again on the road back to Havana. Passing the cane fields he could see Andrew on his horse directing the workers thinking, *how lucky I am to have him.*

When the carriage pulled up in front of the hotel Brenda came out to greet him.

"David I've missed you so much." Throwing her arms around his neck, "I've been dying to find out how everything is at the plantation?"

"Everything's fine. Andrew has everything under control. How's Anne?"

"We've been so busy during the day she doesn't have time to be sad. But I can hear her crying when she's in her bedroom at night."

"Well that's to be expected. As time passes I'm sure she'll be fine. How are our politician guests?"

"They're out again shopping."

David chuckled. "Is there anything else I should know?"

"There was a Yankee war ship that anchored offshore, and two of the officers came here to speak with Senator Thompson."

"Do you know what it was about?"

"I didn't hear the conversation but I think after the meeting they're going back home on that ship."

"Did you by chance see Frank?"

"He came in yesterday and spoke with Senator Thompson and Congressman Lewis. I think it was about the meeting this evening but I'm not sure."

"That's fine dear."

Seeing Anne approaching, he gave her an embrace and said, "Hello my little sister. How are you doing?" Putting his arms around her he continued, "Brenda tells me you've been quite busy."

"Yes, there's a lot to keeping the hotel going. Compton has been a lifesaver. He was able to get another cook so the dining room is fully staffed. You'll be able to taste the food for yourself tonight at dinner."

"I'll look forward to it," he replied with a smile.

Brenda asked, "Was there a lot of crop loss?"

"Andrew said it wasn't as bad as it could have been. Three workers and one of the children died, and a few were sick, but they're getting better."

"Is there anyone cooking at the house?" Brenda asked.

"I forgot to tell you. Eva's back and she asked me to say hello." Continuing he said, "If you don't mind I think I'll go up and lie down for awhile dear. I didn't sleep well last night."

"Ok David. I'll wake you in time for dinner."

Chapter 26

The Meeting

Around 5 o'clock, Brenda gently knocked at the bedroom door. Opening it slightly, she quietly whispered "David it's 5 o'clock. You should get ready for dinner."

Waking from a sound sleep he replied, "Hello my dear. I think I had the deepest sleep since Beau died."

Brenda sat on the edge of the bed then kissed him lightly on the forehead. "You looked so exhausted when you arrived. I'm glad you were able to rest. I don't want you to become ill trying to keep everything together."

"I'll be fine. Why don't you go downstairs? I'll be with you presently."

Walking to the door, she looked back to make sure he was sitting up then closed the door behind her.

As he entered the dining room he acknowledged the Senator, Congressman, and their wives seated at a different table. He asked with a smile, "Have you ladies had your fill of being away from home?"

Senator Thompson's wife replied, "I could just stay here forever. Unlike New York, the weather here is always warm and the flowers are gorgeous."

The Senator added with a chuckle, "And you can shop to your heart's content." Turning to David he asked, "How was your trip?"

"It was fine. My overseer at the plantation is in control."

Senator Thompson's wife alarmingly replied with a frown, "Do you mean to tell us you keep slaves?"

"No. I guess I used a poor choice of words. The people we have, have a long history with the plantation. We pay them."

"That's refreshing to know. I thought most sugar plantations in Cuba keep slave labor," she said.

"Some do, but they're mainly large commercial plantations controlled by investment groups. Slavery is an outdated institution. I've freed the people I had in New Orleans and Biloxi several years ago. I was involved in the shipping business there."

Looking surprised at his statement she replied, "Then if it would have ended eventually, why did South Carolina secede?"

"Most southerners didn't agree with South Carolina's decision but were forced into defending their individual states rights. If you'll kindly excuse me, I haven't dined with my wife for most of the week. Senator, Congressman, we're having a meeting here at 9 o'clock, I'll see you then."

"Yes, that's correct," Congressman Lewis replied.

Retreating to the table where Brenda and Anne were seated, he sat down. Through dinner David casually spoke to Anne about what her future plans might be.

"I think I'll stay here and keep the hotel. With the experienced help it's something I'll be able to direct and it will give me a constant income."

"If you feel you can handle it I think it's a wise decision," David replied.

Halfway through the meal David remarked, "You were right dear, this cooking is straight from the quarter in New Orleans. Now I know why you hired her. It's your passion for Creole."

Brenda smiled, "I knew you'd like it. You can thank Compton. He knew she was looking for a job in a hotel instead of cooking for a restaurant."

After dinner the women retired to the lobby with the Congressman and Senator's wives talking about their shopping experiences, while David entertained the Senator and Congressman.

"Frank and John will be here at 9 o'clock. Then we can get on with the meeting." Looking toward the door David said, "Here they are now."

Coming into the dining room, they moved a few tables together in one corner for privacy. At ten of nine two men came in and sat down at the table.

"Who are these gentlemen?" David asked.

Senator Thompson replied, "They're naval officers who'll be controlling vessels used for the blockade of New Orleans."

Congressman Lewis added, "We're very close to their commander in New Orleans, Admiral Stark."

"Oh, I didn't know. They're dressed in civilian clothes."

Frank replied looking up from the table, "Well it doesn't pay to advertise."

After introductions all around John said, "Now let's get down to business."

David asked bluntly, "How can we go about avoiding contact with the war ships in the Gulf?"

Before he got a reply, Senator Thompson said, "We must be strictly assured the contraband you're bringing in isn't war material."

Seemingly in deep thought while focusing on the glass he was holding Frank replied, "No, it's strictly luxury goods mainly from France. It comes to Cuba and Jamaica by way of David's ships then transferred to smaller sloops that are fast enough to get by the blockade undetected." Looking down at his glass again concentrating on the discussion Frank said, "Now that that's settled gentlemen let's proceed. Congressman Lewis, what if one of David's ships gets confiscated by someone that's not in the loop. How will we get it back?"

"The captains of the vessels where you'll be passing are handpicked. They know where to patrol at the time you're supposed to be passing to avoid contact," Senator Thompson replied.

"How will they know when we're leaving port to make a run?" David asked.

Frank, evaluating the conversation to ensure nothing was left to chance, looked at him replying, "John will get the word to them from Jamaica through British ships. I'll be the man here in Havana." Pausing for a moment he said, "Now gentlemen let's get down to cost. How much can we do this deal for?"

Senator Thompson quickly responded, "Frank, you're rather blunt and to the point."

"Well it's business, so let's conduct it like business," he replied.

"I think you're right. We'll settle for four thousand dollars per ship," Senator Thompson said.

"Will that include taking care of the captains here?" David asked.

"That will take care of everyone on our end," Senator Thompson replied.

"How will payments be made?" David inquired.

Frank looked up interrupting, "Through me."

"Then it's settled," Senator Thompson said.

As they stood up to leave, David motioned for Frank to step aside for a moment. He asked quietly showing him the several thousand dollars in gold Andrew gave him, "Should I pay them now?"

"Let's wait until we get ready to ship some goods. Never pay before you have to," Frank replied.

"Okay Frank you're in charge."

The meeting ended amicably and they toasted their agreement with a glass of French imported cognac.

Senator Thompson asked, "When will your first ship sail David?"

"Within two weeks. Will you have time to set up your contact in Washington?"

"Yes, I think so. We're leaving tomorrow on one of the naval vessels in the harbor."

Adjourning for the evening, David escorted John and Frank to the front door.

David asked, "Do you think they'll keep their part of the bargain Frank?"

"That's why I told you not to give them any money. We'll see how honest their bargain is. Don't forget, they're going against their own government's policy. That isn't exactly what you would call a trustworthy person. Let's wait until he proves he can be trusted."

Laughingly John added, "Yeah, honest. Like all politicians."

After they were outside, Frank said, "Goodnight David. Come on Queenie let's go home."

Queenie, slowly got up and stretched, shook to wake herself, then meandered down the steps. David couldn't help but think as Frank and Queenie faded into the dark street, *how one unassuming man could influence so many people.*

Daybreak at the hotel was always accompanied by the odor of coffee and food being prepared in the kitchen.

"I'm hungry Brenda. Let's go down to the dining room."

Smiling devilishly she replied, "You go David. I want to catch a few more minutes sleep. Our love making last night just tired me out."

"I'll be in the dining room dear. Captain Jarvis' ship is coming in today. I'm hoping Tom and Sharon are aboard. Hopefully the Henrys will be with them."

Getting to the dining room he asked a waiter, "Coffee please... when you get a chance."

Picking up a newspaper he sat at a table. "Good morning Anne. I just mentioned to Brenda I think Tom, Sharon and the Henrys will be coming in this morning on Captain Jarvis' vessel. Is there anything I can help you with before they arrive? Are their rooms ready?"

"Yes. Compton had the maids make up two front rooms with the view of the harbor. Everything else is already taken care of."

"Well if you don't need me, after breakfast I think I'll go down to the dock and wait for the ship."

The waiter brought the coffee to the table and poured each of them a cup. Looking solemn at David's mentioning the Henrys arrival, Anne wasn't looking forward to having to go through all the pain again. Beau was their only child and knowing it would be hard on them, she feared a relapse of her own emotion.

"How did your meeting turn out?" she asked.

Looking over the top of the newspaper he replied, "About as well as can be expected. We'll see."

"Will you be alright with Beau's parents here?" he asked.

"Yes I'll be fine. It will be good to have Sharon here."

Taking a final swallow of his coffee, he laid the newspaper down. "Then if you don't need me I'll leave," he said.

Walking out of the room he passed another couple who were registered guests.

"Good morning," he said, "It looks like it's going to be a beautiful day."

"Yes it seems like it," they replied.

Arriving at the dock, he met Senator Thompson and Congressman Lewis with their wives. They were getting ready to embark in a small craft that would take them to a war ship at anchor several hundred yards out in the bay.

"Good morning David," Congressman Lewis said with a chuckle, "Are you making sure we're leaving?"

"No. My brother and his wife are arriving today along with Anne's in-laws."

Congressman Lewis' wife spoke, trying to apologize for the congressman's thoughtless remark, "We were so sorry to hear of her loss. It must be hard losing a husband so soon after marriage. Luckily they don't have children."

David agreed and bid them farewell as they went down the stairs getting into the small boat. "I hope your voyage is a safe one," he said, waving goodbye as the small craft slid gently away from the dock with six uniformed sailors pulling at the oars.

When he turned around Frank was standing behind him.

"Good morning Frank. The congressman wanted to know if I was making sure they were really leaving."

"Funny how they're suspicious of us. They're the ones we're paying for doing something illegal," Frank replied with a smile.

"Well I hope they keep their promise. To answer your question, I'm really here to meet my brother and his wife. They're coming in with Beau's parents."

"I think that's Jarvis' boat coming around the point. Why don't you come into my shack and wait until it docks? I put on a pot of coffee and with a little eye opener in it it's just what I need, especially after last night," Frank obligingly said.

"Was the meeting that strenuous?" David asked.

"No. It was the trip to the tavern with John afterward," Frank replied as he ran his fingers through his uncombed hair still trying to wake up. "It was a rough night for us wasn't it Queenie?" he said as he bent down to scratch the dogs head. Continuing he said, "Come on David the coffee will be like tar if we don't get back."

They strode the length of the dock entering Frank's shack. The place was still a disaster as it was the first day David had seen it, and Frank noticing David's expression said, "I know, I know, don't remind me. The last time you were here I said I was going to get someone in to straighten things out. I think I found someone at the tavern last night. I just don't remember her name or what she looked like."

With a chuckle David replied, "If a woman shows up with a mop and a broom in her hand you'll know."

Frank smiled then found two cups and poured the coffee. "Care for a chaser in yours?"

Covering his cup with his hand David said, "Not this early... Thanks."

"Well, you don't mind if I indulge, I need it!" Frank said, pouring a generous amount of rum in his cup.

After some conversation about the plantation and the meeting with the politicians the night before, they went back to the dock. After the gangway was put in place the passengers began to disembark.

"Tom!" David shouted as he waved, Tom waved back in acknowl-edgement. When Sharon became visible standing behind him with their 4-year-old daughter, she waved. David saw the Henrys coming down right behind them, scanning the dock as if they were entering a strange land. After greeting each other, David introduced Frank.

"Sharon, Tom, this is Frank. He operates the dock here. Frank, this is Mr. and Mrs. Henry - Beau's parents. And this precious little thing is my niece Roselyn." Picking her up he asked, "Don't you have a big hug for your Uncle David?"

"Yes Uncle David!" she turned around pointing, "That's a big boat -it brought us here."

"I know darling," he said then put her down.

Mrs. Henry replied wiping away tears, "Beau so wanted to have a little girl he could spoil. He'll never get that chance now!"

David put his arm around her shoulder consoling her.

Simon moved closer to her saying, "I better take her David."

"I'm happy to make your acquaintance Frank. Pardon me for being emotional," Mrs. Henry said.

"That's quite alright. It's understandable."

Sharon put her arms around her to comfort her too. Something she had to do often during the trip.

"How was your voyage?" David asked.

"I'll tell you all about it later. Why don't we get to the hotel? I'm sure the women want to rest," Tom said.

"Good idea Tom," David replied escorting them to an awaiting carriage.

"Frank, I'll be back this afternoon with Tom. We can fill him in on what's taking place."

"Fine, you know where to find me," he replied as he and Queenie walked away.

David turned, instructing the carriage driver to proceed to the hotel. When they pulled up, the Henrys, Tom and Sharon, looked in approval at the beauty of the building.

"Look Tom, what a gorgeous hotel. I can't wait to see the inside," Sharon said.

Walking up the front steps, they turned to survey the view and Mr.

Henry added, "Yes it does look stately."

Stepping into the lobby Anne rushed forward first embracing the Henrys, then Sharon. Picking up Roselyn she said, "How's my little precious angel?"

"I'm fine Auntie Anne. You have a big house!"

"I'm so glad to see you," she said embracing Mrs. Henry. "Why don't we go into the dining room, and have some tea. Compton, would you and the porter take their luggage upstairs, they have the two front rooms."

"Yes, Ma'am we'll see to it."

Mrs. Henry walked into the room with her arm around Anne asking, "How are you holding up my dear? You know, my Beau loved you so very much." With those words it became too difficult to hold back their sadness. Embracing each other they both broke down crying.

Mr. Henry speaking to his wife asked, "Are you sure you don't want to go directly to your room dear?"

"No. I want to spend some time with Anne here in the dining room."

David said, "Mrs. Henry, writing that letter to inform you about Beau passing was one of the hardest things I ever had to do. I'm sure the words must have been deeply distressing as you read them. Tomorrow I'll escort you to the cemetery where he was laid to rest."

"David we're so happy you were able to be here to make the arrangements. I don't know how to thank you enough," Simon remarked.

"I was glad to be of service Simon. It was also much easier on Anne."

They sat down to lunch over much conversation about Beau, the hotel, and the yellow fever epidemic. News of the war and slave situation at Cliveden seemed secondary.

"Tom. Did you make arrangements to sell Cliveden?" David asked.

"I've been making inquires to the surrounding plantations but so far I haven't heard anything. Simon's facing the same problem. We haven't had any runaways as of yet, but in time I know they'll want their own land and freedom too. I think you've made the right decision to sell the dock and house in Biloxi."

"I could see it coming Tom. Are you here to stay?"

"I'm going to leave Sharon and our daughter here while I return to finish business, that is, if Anne doesn't mind."

"No Tom. I'm more than happy they'll stay," Anne replied.

"How about you Simon, will both of you return to Five Oaks?"

"I'll have to return for sure, but it's up to Mrs. Henry if she wants to go back."

"Can we postpone the conversation of leaving? We haven't been here half a day," Mrs. Henry replied.

"I guess you're right. I apologize," Tom said.

Through lunch, there was much conversation about Beau and how he was looking forward to their new life being the owners of the hotel. During the conversation about him, periodically Mrs. Henry would wipe a tear from her eyes.

"Will you keep the hotel Anne?" she asked.

"Yes. With the help that's been here for so long like Compton I don't think I'll have any problem. I have full confidence in him helping me."

"Thank you Ma'am," Compton said as he stood quietly aside.

After lunch David and Tom retired to the front porch to talk about Cliveden and David's new venture with the politicians.

"We just had a meeting last night with them Tom. They just left."

"As we were rounding the point, I saw a navy warship leaving. Were they aboard that ship?" Tom asked.

"Yes. There were two people at the meeting last night that were introduced as an admiral and a naval captain. They're supposed to be part of the plan."

"Will this be your business from now on?" Tom asked.

"No, only part of it. I realize the majority of profits will be from that during the war. After it ends I'll primarily be involved with the sugar plantation. This is only a temporary financial investment. Since I'm still part owner of the dock in New Orleans I'll be able to travel back and forth to oversee both."

"I have to give you credit David. You seem to have given your financial options a lot more thought than I have. I was sticking to a way of life that I refused to see was coming to an end."

"I'm afraid the war is going to change life for a lot of people Tom. It's not too late to change."

"That's why I'm here. Who was that man you introduced us to at the dock when we arrived?"

"Believe it or not he's one of the most influential people here in Cuba, and his friend John yields as much influence in Jamaica. Through them we'll be able to keep our contraband cargo getting through the blockade."

Tom laughed, "By the looks of him he sure has the ability to go unnoticed."

"Tom, there's some business I have to take care of at the sugar plantation. Would you like to go with me or stay here with Anne?"

"I think Anne will be fine with the Henrys and Sharon. I'd like to go. When are you leaving?"

"I thought I'd leave in the morning. We could be there by noon."

"Yes. I'd like to see it," Tom replied.

The next afternoon, as they approached the plantation Tom noticed all the charred fields.

"Is this the result of some sort of accident?" he asked.

"No Tom. It was mosquito control. The only way to control the epidemic was to burn the sugarcane, drain the swamp area and spread oil on the marsh to smother the mosquito larvae."

A short while later the plantation came in view. "There it is Tom."

"How many acres are here?" he asked.

"About 600 total. I don't know how many acres in sugarcane." Pointing he said, "There's Andrew; he would know. He runs the place."

David waved as he got closer to the house.

"How long has he been the overseer?" Tom asked.

"I think he told me 15 years. He seems to know his business."

Pulling up in front of the house, they were met at the front door by Hector, a house servant.

"Hello Hector. This is my brother Tom."

"Buenos notches senor!" Hector said.

David asked, "Hector, is Eva still here?"

"Se', Senor. How long will you be staying?" Hector asked.

"We'll be here for two days. Tell her there will be an extra person for dinner, and let Andrew know I want him to join us."

After Hector walked away, David took Tom on a tour of the house proudly showing him the elaborate furnishings. There were Persian rugs on the floors, and hall cabinets with inlaid mother of pearl from the Orient, a lifetime of collections by Edward.

"The whole thing is very impressive David. I wish you luck."

A short time later, Andrew came in, "Andrew this is my brother Tom. He's going to be a partner in the plantation."

Tom reached out shaking Andrew's hand.

"How long will you be here David?" Andrew asked.

"We'll be here for two days and then we're returning to Havana. It will be some time until I can get back. I want to be on the first ship that gets by the blockade just to see how it goes."

"That's smart. It sounds like you don't have a lot of trust in the people you're dealing with," Andrew said.

"Not completely. I just want to be sure. Your half-brother thinks it's a wise idea too. We don't know who we can really trust without testing them."

Tom remarked, "There was a major battle at a town called Gettysburg in Pennsylvania. The Yankees are pushing farther south."

"I know Tom; I read it last week. News travels slow but comes almost weekly from foreign ships coming in from northern ports."

"I'll go back to Cliveden with you when you leave and see if there's any interest in anyone buying the place," Tom said.

Andrew, looking concerned Tom was going to live here asked, "Will you be getting your own plantation?"

"I'll have to see how much I can get for the sale of Cliveden."

"There's a plantation not far from here. I know it's going up for sale. Maybe you could buy it," Andrew said.

"That will have to wait until I get back next month," Tom replied.

Chapter 27
Testing the Water

The next two days were spent getting familiar with the place, and Andrew pointed out many things that weren't much different from owning Cliveden.

Getting back to Havana, David's mind was constantly focused on the trip to New Orleans.

"Tom I want to see Frank before we go."

"Do you want me to go with you?"

"If you want," David replied.

Arriving at the dock, Frank was talking to Captain Jarvis. He had just made a run to Jamaica to pick up some contraband cargo and was about to put on more before sailing in the morning.

"Frank, if we should get stopped by a war ship that isn't part of the plan, how much should I bring to satisfy the captain?" David asked.

"Captain Jarvis will handle it if you're boarded. I don't think the Senator and Congressman had enough time to initiate their influence so we're still operating on the arrangement before their visit. Are you returning to New Orleans so soon?"

"Yes. I'm going back with Tom and taking care of some business of my own."

"Then I'll see you gentleman in the morning," Frank said.

Returning to the hotel, Sharon and Brenda greeted them in the lobby and went into the dining room for dinner where the Henrys were already seated.

"David, did you get everything done at your plantation?" Simon asked.

"Yes, Tom and I are going back to New Orleans in the morning. Do you want to come with us?"

Looking at Tom, Simon asked, "Are you going to sell Cliveden?"

"Yes, I am. Even if I have to take less I'm going to join David here in the sugar business. Andrew said there's another plantation near David's for sale. Depending on what I can get from selling Cliveden, I may just look into buying it."

Looking at Mrs. Henry to seek her approval Simon replied, "I think I might join you then."

"Simon I'm staying here until you return. It's been such a short stay," Mrs. Henry said.

"Whatever you care to do dear. I think I'd rather have you stay here with Anne for awhile anyway."

The following morning they said goodbye to their wives then headed for the ship. When they arrived, the cargo had just finished being loaded and they went aboard. Within the hour the ship's crew unfurled the canvas at the first mate's commands and it smoothly slid away from the pier.

***

Several days later, they were in the area of the blockade waters. Toward evening, Captain Jarvis warned, "After dusk the ship will be in a state of total darkness. Don't open your cabin doors without first extinguishing the lanterns. The slightest light even from a match can be seen for miles. We have to try avoiding ships that might be in or near the course I'm taking. Frank didn't think Senator Thompson wouldn't have had time to implement our agreement so this trip relies on getting through without detection."

David remarked, "I already forewarned them Captain."

In light of what Captain Jarvis said everyone decided to retire early for the evening.

As daylight was breaking David was awoken by hearing the lookout yell down to the quarter deck, "Captain ship abeam."

Captain Jarvis turned to see a ship trailing them but only the sails were visible over the horizon.

"Can you make out what kind of ship it is?" Captain Jarvis yelled.

"It doesn't seem to be the sails of a naval ship," he said leaning forward straining to see, as though a few inches would make a difference, he yelled down, "I can't tell sir."

"Keep your eye on its movement while I alter course. Keep a sharp eye to see if it alters its course too. Helmsman steer 10 degrees to starboard."

"Aye Captain." Everyone on deck watched patiently as the ship altered course. Within 20 minutes the lookout yelled down, "Captain it's no longer visible but there's another sail on the horizon."

"Where away?" Captain Jarvis exclaimed loudly.

"Ten points off the port bow."

"Can you identify it?"

"Yes Sir it's a navy war ship."

"Does it look like it's coming in our direction?"

"Yes Sir, I can see a signal. She's asking us to identify ourselves," he said. Pausing, the lookout yelled down, "Captain, I just saw a puff of smoke, I think they just fired a shot."

Within seconds a cannon ball ripped through the top sail causing a hole, and the canvas began to tear causing it to sag dramatically from loss of air and the ship quickly slowed.

"Captain she just let loose with two more shots." As the war ship came closer David asked, "What's your plan of action?"

Captain Jarvis replied, "There's a fog bank about three miles dead-ahead. If we can make it we'll lose her."

Just then another shot sent up a splash of water close to the port bow short of its mark. Another shot could be heard as it went over the ship landing in the water over its intended target.

"Keep a sharp lookout to see how much distance she closes," Captain Jarvis yelled to the lookout.

"Aye, Aye Sir."

With every stitch of canvas unfurled they headed for cover. Everyone was tense with the race to the fog bank and all eyes were on the pursuer closing fast. As the fog enveloped the ship, Captain Jarvis altered his position immediately. Instead of remaining on his current course he altered it running parallel just inside the front of the fog bank, hoping it was something the captain of the war ship wouldn't suspect. Within an hour the tense moment with watchful eyes seemed to have passed. Retiring to the captain's quarters for breakfast Tom asked, "Do you think we lost them?"

"I believe so. I never suspected they'd fire on us so soon after seeing us," Captain Jarvis said.

"Captain, when will we sight land?" Tom asked.

"Without anymore navigational disruptions we should be at the mouth of the Mississippi by daybreak tomorrow. It looks like we're heading into a storm and that does two things. First, it will cut down on visibility for any blockade ships which is in our favor. Second, it also means if the storm is worse than I expect we'll have to slow down which will increase our chances of being detected. I had originally planned on getting to New Orleans by dusk this evening but it doesn't look like that'll be the case. This is like a game of cat and mouse."

"How's that?" Simon asked.

"Well, at this point if we're not stopped we don't have to pay. If we do get stopped we run the risk of getting the ship confiscated if it isn't one of the captains we're paying off."

"I see. It is like a game of cat and mouse," Simon replied.

It was beginning to rain and with the wind increasing the fog disappeared. The waves were significantly higher and the movement of the ship was testimony of Captain Jarvis' prediction.

Tom and Simon looked a little seasick retiring to their cabins but the rough water didn't seem to affect David. The thought of being stopped by a naval ship may have been the reason. During the day, with the rain pelting the vessel, David spent most of it inside his cabin.

Late afternoon, there was a knock at his door. When he opened it, Ming the cook asked, "You be coming to dinner with Captain Jarvis?" he asked.

"I'll be there shortly. Did you ask Tom and Simon if they'll be there?"

"Yes, but Ming no think so... they still seasick."

David laughed, "Tell Captain Jarvis I'll join him after I finish this ledger."

On the way to the galley, David knocked at Tom's cabin door. From inside he could hear him say, "Don't even ask if I'm coming to dinner."

David opened the door slightly and asked, "Would you want me to bring something back like a thick greasy pork chop?"

"No thanks. Make fun of a dying man," Pausing before continuing he said, "I don't think you need to ask Simon either."

Closing the door and laughing, David headed for dinner. The rain was coming down a little harder but the wind died down considerably. As David entered the captain's cabin, Captain Jarvis rose from his chair, acknowledging his entry.

"I guess we'll be dining alone David," Captain Jarvis asked.

"Yes I believe so. I asked Tom if he wanted me to bring him back anything but he passed on the offer."

Captain Jarvis laughed.

"Captain, did the storm change our plans or will we still arrive just before daybreak?"

"I don't like trying to port in the dark especially in the fog. We'll anchor in the river until dawn. You never mentioned what you're going to do here. Are you coming back to help Tom?"

"That too but I want to check on Brenda's house and have a word with Charles at the dock. I want to know if he's had any problems with the port inspectors."

"None that I heard of," Captain Jarvis replied, "But it seems like there's a lot more hands we have to pay to stay in business."

David replied, "I guess we don't have a choice. Some profit is better than no profit. With the arrangement with Senator Thompson, we'll be able to bring in more goods."

Over small talk about the war they finished dinner and David returned to his cabin. After two more hours of ledger work he closed it for the night and retired to bed. After what seemed to be a few hours of being asleep he awoke to voices. "Let go the anchor."

When he pulled back the curtain in front of the port hole, he could see lights ashore faintly through the fog. They safely made the anchorage at the mouth of the river without detection and as dawn broke a few hours later they pulled up anchor and headed for the dock seventy miles upstream. Tom and Simon came out on deck a few hours later just as the ship pulled into its mooring.

Simon exclaimed, "Thank god we made it!"

David replied, "Thanks to that storm yesterday we were able to get by undetected."

Chapter 28
Selling Cliveden

Coming down the gangway, they were met by Charles. "Welcome back. How was your voyage?" he asked.

David replied, "There was only one incident with a naval warship but Captain Jarvis was able to navigate away from it. They fired on the ship within minutes after they signaled us to halt, something Captain Jarvis never expected."

"I've heard that from the other dock owners that are involved. The boy you killed in the duel, after his father died, his uncle took over his business. We've been friends for a long time. He said one of his ships was hit by naval gunfire and several crew members were injured."

Turning to Captain Jarvis David asked, "I wonder if it was the same ship that fired on us?"

"It could have been. Whatever ship that was it sounds like the captain's pretty aggressive."

At that moment Captain Jarvis waved for Jeremiah to join them.

"Hello Jeremiah good to see you again. How are you?" David asked.

"Thank you Master David. I'm doin' right fine." Looking at Captain Jarvis he continued, "Captn', where you wants me to put the crates for the port inspector's visit?"

"Same place but there are a few more than we usually bring. I want them mixed in with the other goods. We'll have to bring in more so it's going to be a little tricky trying to hide them. Has there been any change with the port inspectors?" Captain Jarvis asked.

"No, they hasn't. I takes care of these myself."

"Charles, may we borrow your carriage to get to the house?" David asked.

"Certainly David, how long will you be here?"

"I'll probably go to Cliveden with Tom in the morning to help him settle his affairs then return. I think Mr. Henry will return to Five Oaks and do the same. I don't know how long that will take. Why don't you come over for dinner? I'll fill you in on what's happening. I know you're anxious to hear."

On the way off the pier David asked Jeremiah, "How are Elizabeth and Trisha getting along?"

"They be doin' right fine. They seafood house and they boardin' house keeps them pretty busy."

"Glad to hear it." After boarding the carriage, they headed for home.

Upon arrival they were met by Arthur, David's former driver who was staying with Thelma and Sarah.

"Arthur what happened? I thought you were staying on in Biloxi with Franz?" he asked.

"Master Franz died last month. I didn't care for the new owner so I came here. Thelma told me to be the driver until you came back. She said you didn't have one and I thought you might be needin' me again?"

"That's good Arthur. I'm glad you're here."

Pulling up to the house Arthur said, "Master David, go on in, I'll unload the baggage,"

"Thank you, Arthur."

Entering the house David called out, "Thelma!"

Coming from the kitchen she exclaimed, "Why it's Master David. Where's Miss Brenda?"

"She stayed in Havana with Miss Anne. Did you know Beau died?"

Shocked at his words she looked solemnly down at the floor shaking her head. "No I didn't. My po' baby! She must be heartbroken."

"Yes. She took it pretty hard. I'm sure you would have been a great comfort to her. Could you ask Sarah to make lunch for us? We'll be here for dinner also and Charles will be joining us. Four places will be fine."

"Yes Master David. I'll let her know."

"Has there been any letters for me since I've been gone that weren't forwarded?"

"No sir. I carries all the mail over to the dock when they come. Master Charles, he sends them on the next ship. How long will you be home?"

"We'll be leaving for Cliveden in the morning. I suspect we'll be back in about a week or two. I'm going to freshen up before lunch. Tom, Simon, if you want to do the same Thelma will see to it the water pitchers in your rooms get filled."

"Thank you David," they replied.

At 6 o'clock Charles came in. David brought him into the parlor where he and Tom had been discussing the sale of Cliveden.

"Charles. What's the latest news on the war?" David asked.

"What we discussed about a year ago with controlling the Mississippi, it looks like they'll close it down sooner than later. We don't have any real defense against a Yankee invasion of New Orleans, so I guess most, if not all shipping, will cease."

"Is it that desperate?"

"Yes it is. We were doing well until a few months ago. That's when the rumor spread that we were going to be invaded by the Union Army."

"We have two forts guarding the mouth of the Mississippi: Fort Jackson and Fort St. Phillip. Won't they be enough to keep the Yankee navy out?" David asked.

"I don't think so. The war is only a little more than two years old, and we've already felt the economic effect. Before the South declared war there were thirty three different shipping lines here. We're now down to about twenty. Most have either suspended their shipping business as you did, or went out of business. We've gone from five hundred 500 million a year in trade to about half that with no bottom line in site."

Looking down at the floor Tom said, "They're pretty grim statistics. I think you just reinforced my opinion to sell Cliveden, that is, if I can. Simon will you be selling Five Oaks?"

"I think I'd rather sell. Beau's gone now so there's no reason to keep it. Since I have no other children I might just as well give the proceeds to Anne."

David shook his head saying, "It would have been good if Louisiana would have been able to separate from the secessionist movement when they tried. The inner parishes didn't realize the value of the river on their economies. All the cotton and tobacco they grow has to be transported by ship either from Biloxi or New Orleans. Without shipping they go bankrupt."

"We've hashed that out a hundred times. I'm sure they're aware of it by now. I'm getting out just in time," Tom said.

David stood up, "Here's to a successful trip to Cliveden and Five Oaks," he declared, raising his glass. Simon and Tom did the same warily toasting his statement.

In the morning after breakfast Arthur pulled the carriage around and they departed. Having to travel over land instead of traveling by ship to Biloxi, they were at Cliveden the following week. Going in the house, Tom's servant told them excitedly, "Master Tom! Master Tom! They was some peoples who came when you was gone."

"Who were they?" Tom asked.

"They were people from town wonderin' why you and Miss Sharon weren't here. I 'spect they thought we kilt you and took over the place."

"That's ridiculous! Why would they think that?"

"I guess with all the slaves runnin' away, and all the troubles they dun' been havin' with them stealin' they just don't trust us."

"It seems like things just keep getting worse since they hung poor Luke!" Tom said.

"Yes Sir, they surely have. Poor Solomon, he went to town by his self last week for supplies. They dun' ganged up on him pretty good they did. Like to beat him half to death. Beat him so bad he hardly made it back. He say if it wasn't for 'dat overseer from the Fairfield Plantation they would have hanged him."

"Is he ok now?" Tom annoyingly asked.

"Yes sir. His Missus been takin' care of him but nobody else wants to go to town and get beat up. We just figured we'd wait 'till you got back."

"Has Sam been able to get by on what we had?"

"Yes sir. He just keeps everbody doin' what they supposed to be doin' till you come."

"David, I'm going down to talk to Solomon. I'll be back."

"I might just as well go down with you. Arthur, take Simon to Five Oaks. I'm staying here."

"Yes sir, but with all the trouble shouldn't I have a note sayin' I have permission to be traveling alone since I have to come back by myself?"

"Simon will give you one. Come on Tom. Let's go talk to Solomon."

Going down the path toward Solomon's cabin, they passed other slaves acknowledging them. Looking at their forlorn faces, they appeared to be confused. Their normally regimented life was in question, and the uncertainty of their future in doubt.

"Good afternoon Master Tom. We sure is glad to see you," one of them said.

"Thank you!" Turning to David Tom asked, "What am I going to do with these people? They've been loyal to me for years. I don't know how to tell them they're no longer welcome to stay, and I don't want to leave them here to fend for themselves."

"Well, maybe it won't have to come to that. If we ask who wants to leave let them go, they wouldn't work out anyway. We'll ask the ones that want to stay if they want to be share croppers for whoever buys the place," David said.

"That might work. We'll just have to find someone in town that's willing to buy it and live here to oversee things."

"Do you have anyone in mind?" David asked.

"Yes, in fact I do. The man that owns the cotton-dock, his son Bruce asked about buying the place last year. I could ask him."

"Was he serious about buying it, or was he just asking?" David asked.

"At the time yes, but I don't know if things have changed since then. I'll ride into town tomorrow and ask."

Knocking at Solomon's cabin door, his wife Ester answered letting them in.

"Hello, Master Tom. Solomon be in his room. I get him."

"Thank you Ester."

Hearing them Solomon was already on his way out. Shocked at his appearance Tom remarked, "My god! Solomon, if the beating happened almost a week ago it must have been severe. The marks and swelling around your eyes look as though it happened yesterday. You must have taken a hell of a beating."

"Yes Sir, Master Tom. They dun' ganged up on me pretty good. I be fine though in a little bit."

"You just take it easy for now. Who did it?" Tom asked.

"I rather not say Master Tom. I tried not to start nothin'. I told them you had to travel to New Orleans for a funeral for Master Henry's son Beau. I told them they wasn't anyone else to oversee the place while you was gone," he said pausing, "I be thinkin', they must think, we done killed you and the Missus. They say we must have hid your bodies. When they come out here everybody dun told them the same thing. After they looks around a bit they just throwed me on out the wagon and left."

Ester added "We was all afraid they were gonna set fire to the quarter."

Tom being distressed at the situation said, "Don't fear Ester, I'm going to town tomorrow and see if I can get things straightened out. Sam will take over while you're recuperating Solomon. You take it easy for the next few days."

"Yes Sir, Master Tom. I surely will do 'dat."

Returning to the house they were surprised to see Arthur coming back. The horses were at a gallop and without Simon in the coach David knew it spelled trouble. They stood on the porch as Arthur brought the horses to an abrupt stop.

"Master Tom! Master Tom!"

"What is it Arthur?"

"On the way to Five Oaks, Master Henry he done passed out. I done took him straight away to Doctor Cook's house."

"Did the doctor say anything?" Tom asked coming down off the porch.

"Yes, Sir, he wants you to come as soon as you can."

"David, I'm going right away. Do you want to come?"

"Yes. It sounds kind of urgent."

Getting in the carriage Arthur sped off to Doctor Cook's with the horses at a full gallop.

Arriving, Doctor Cook met them at the front door. Tom asked in an excited voice, "What is it Doctor Cook, is he alright?"

"He's had a heart attack. He's resting right now. He was saying something about his son Beau but I couldn't quite understand him."

David replied, "Doctor. Beau died last month."

"Died? What from?" Doctor Cook asked.

"Yellow fever," David replied.

"Yellow fever? How on earth did he contact yellow fever in New York City?"

"He never went to New York. He and Anne were in Havana, Cuba, and bought a hotel there. There was an epidemic and he died."

"Well I guess that leaves his wife and Anne as the only heirs."

"Is it that bad doctor?" Tom asked.

"When you saw him earlier, was he complaining about chest pain?" Doctor Cook asked.

"He thought he had a little indigestion but said it might have been from the rough sea voyage we went through. He heaved a lot," David said.

"He was probably having a heart attack then and didn't realize it. Is Mrs. Henry at Five Oaks?"

"No, she stayed in Havana. Simon was coming back to sell the place or close it down, the same decision Tom here made."

"No wonder he had a heart attack. Beau was his only child. Losing him along with selling Five Oaks must have been too much of a strain."

"Just then the doctor's wife came into the hall and said, "He's calling for you."

They went quickly to his room and as they entered Simon said, "Tom, I'm so glad you're here. I want you to bring my lawyer, Harold Collins. He's the same lawyer you have. I want you to become legal trustee of Five Oaks. I'll need to draw up the paperwork before I die; there's no one else."

"I don't think it's that drastic Simon but I'll do as you ask."

Leaving the room, Doctor Cook remarked, "I wouldn't wait until tomorrow Tom. Get him now!"

Getting back in the carriage, Tom and David headed for town. Arriving at Harold Collin's office they explained what happened.

"Tom, I'll head out right away. Why don't you return to Doctor Cook's? I'll be there shortly."

Within the hour they were gathered around Simon's bed as Harold came into the room.

"Simon, what would you like me to do?" Harold asked.

"Harold, I want to make Tom my legal trustee to my property. Whatever he decides to do with it I know it will be best for Mrs. Henry and Anne."

The paperwork was written out in the dining room and with Doctor Cook's signature as a witness the document became legal.

Tom said, "Simon, we'll proceed to Five Oaks. We'll look the place over and see what we can do. Then we have to head back to Cliveden to see what we're going to do there. Bruce White who owns the cotton dock expressed his interest in buying the place several times. I want to see if he's still interested."

"Well, see what you can get for Five Oaks too."

"I'll do my best Simon."

Before leaving the room Simon said, "I do have one request though. When I die I'd like to be buried in the family plot there."

"As you wish Simon," Tom said before leaving.

Looking around after they arrived at Five Oaks, they noticed the place was already showing signs of neglect. The shrubs were beginning to grow out of shape and a fence was broken down. Much like Cliveden, there were a few people sitting around that hadn't taken to the road looking forlorn at their future. Seeing David and Tom riding up to the house the butler stepped out on the porch. Recognizing them he asked, "Master Tom, where's Master Henry and Mrs. Henry?"

"William, Mr. Henry's at Doctor Cook's. He's had a heart attack. Doctor Cook said he doesn't think he'll recover. Mrs. Henry stayed in Cuba. I don't think she'll come back either. Mr. Henry wants me to try and sell the place. How many people stayed on?"

"They's only a few field hands, me, one house maid, and the cook. If you sells the place what's we gonna' do? I don't know nothin' 'cept bein' the butler."

"I'll figure that out later. Has there been any trouble with the locals?"

"No Sir." Pausing he said, "They did come 'round one day, but one of them that knowed Master Henry, knowed he was going to see Beau. After he say that to the others they dun' left us be."

"William, keep doing what you're doing. I'll go down and speak with the field hands," Tom said.

"Sure thing Master Tom!" he replied, retreating to the house shaking his head unsure of his future, an uneasy feeling he never experienced.

They walked down to the quarter to speak with the few people that were there and as they approached, the top field hand, Homer, came forward to speak with them.

"Master Tom, where's Master Henry?" he asked.

"He's at Doctor Cook's. He had a heart attack and will probably die within the next few days. I spoke to William and told him to keep doing what he's doing just as if Master Henry were here. How many field hands stayed on?"

"Only 'bout six of us dat' have family. Everybody else dun run off. What we suppose' to do now?" he asked.

"Don't do any more field work; that's not necessary. Just see to what's already planted. Is there enough garden to feed everyone?"

"Yes Sir. We make it do."

"That's good. I'm going back to Cliveden. If you need me for anything come and get me. I'll write a few passes in case you're stopped on the way."

"Thank you Master Tom. I looks after things."

"Tom, why don't we head back to town first and see if Bruce White still wants Cliveden?"

"Okay David." Then they headed for town.

Mr. White was standing on the cotton dock counting burlap bags used for packing cotton when they arrived.

Tom said, "Good afternoon Randall. Is your son Bruce here?"

"He's inside the store tending to a customer. Go on in."

"Hello Bruce. Tom said, "Can I have a word with you?"

"Sure Tom. Wait until I finish with this customer. Will that be all Mr. Stone?"

"Yes Bruce," Mr. Stone replied before leaving the store.

"Now Tom, what can I do for you?" Bruce asked.

"I was wondering if you still had an interest in buying Cliveden. I know you mentioned it in the past."

"Are you selling?"

"Yes. I'm going with David to Cuba. He has a sugar plantation there."

Bruce, thinking for a moment said, "Buying it depends on the price. With all the runaways I know plantations are harder to run these days... How much were you asking?"

"I haven't exactly set a price but it can be worked out I'm sure. Would your father object if you bought it? It's rather a large undertaking for someone your age. If you don't mind me asking how old are you?"

"I just turned twenty three last month. I have some money put aside and I'm confident if my father would cosign a loan, I'll be able to do it."

"If you have the time, why not come out to Cliveden tomorrow? We can work out a price," Tom said.

"Then I'll see you tomorrow afternoon," Bruce replied.

Walking off the porch Tom said, "Goodbye Randall."

Randall, eyeing them suspiciously wondered what the conversation with Bruce was about. After they pulled away he jumped down from the shipping dock and went into the store.

"Bruce. What was that conversation about?"

Looking up from some merchandise he was counting he replied, "He asked me if I was still interested in buying Cliveden."

"Are you serious?"

"Yes, I am father. I think most plantation owners are over a barrel with all the runaways. They're forced to sell or board up and leave. I might just be able to get it cheap."

"When are you supposed to look the place over?" his father asked.

"Tomorrow afternoon."

Well, so you don't get taken advantage of I'll go out with you."

Later that afternoon, Doctor Cook walked in the store. "Randall, I ordered some alcohol and other medical supplies. Did your supply wagon bring my package from Biloxi?"

Checking the manifest of supplies he replied, "Dr. Cook, according to this sheet they weren't in this order. Seems like you've run out of just about everything; you must have been busy?"

"Since I'm the only doctor I've been seeing quite a few patients," he said eyeing a piece of fabric he could possibly use for bandages. "I was interrupted this morning with an unexpected case. Simon Henry had a bad heart attack and he's at my home."

Randall looking at him with a thought in mind replied, "I guess Mrs. Henry will have to run the place until he gets well."

"No, from what Tom Stewart told me, she's in Cuba. Their son Beau died last month during a yellow fever outbreak."

"Do you think she'll be coming back?" Randall asked.

"I wouldn't think so. I don't think Simon will last more than a few days. He turned it over legally to Tom Stewart."

"What do you think Tom's going to do with it?" Bruce asked.

"I don't know. He was mentioning selling Five Oaks, but with Tom's plantation to get rid of too I wish them luck. I was told all but about 10 people remain to work the place and that's hardly enough. That's the trouble with these plantations. Unless they find another way to find the labor to run them they'll all disappear," he said. As he walked towards the door he looked back adding, "Just like the dinosaur."

Just before he stepped out Randall asked, "So what you're telling me, they have two places to sell?"

"Yes, and as I said, it isn't going to be easy."

After he left Randall said to his son, "Did you hear that. Maybe we can get two places for the price of one?"

"How would we be able to work both plantations father?"

"We could always try to work a deal where we tell them if they work the fields as share croppers they can have part of the profit. If we charge them for the land until it's theirs they never get it paid off. If the sheriff tells them they can be arrested for not paying the bill they'd be too afraid to run off."

"But I always wanted to own a place for myself," Bruce complained.

Slapping him across the face Randall replied, "Don't be stupid! Just listen to your father."

The next afternoon they rode out to Cliveden.

"Hello Tom, David. I spoke to Doctor Cook after you left yesterday afternoon. He said you were trying to sell both, Cliveden, and Five Oaks... is that true?"

"Yes it is. Simon asked me to be legal representative in selling his place."

"Well, let's start here," Randall said as he looked around adjusting himself in his saddle. "How much were you asking for the place?"

"Before we get into price, I want to know what you intend to do with the people here? Some of them have been here for years."

Looking at his son he replied, "We haven't figured that out yet so how much were you asking for the place?" Randall anxiously repeated.

"There's over six hundred acres here: the house, the barns, stable, and the fifteen houses in the quarter. I was thinking fifty thousand dollars would be reasonable."

Randall adjusting himself in his saddle again pushed his hat back. "Well, let's see now that's a heap of money now days... how much for both places?"

"I'll tell you what. I'll let you have both for eighty five thousand dollars in gold," Tom said.

Randall and his son looked at each other. Randall replied after smirking at Tom, "I'll give you eighty thousand for both, how's that?"

Tom replied, realizing he was at Randall's mercy, "I think we can work out a deal, as long as it's in gold. I'll get Harold Collins to draw up the papers."

As they rode away David said, "Tom! He's just stole this place."

"I know, but what am I going to do, eighty thousand dollars in gold is a bargain. I don't think I could have done any better."

Looking over the property David asked, "What are you going to do with the people? Solomon, Ester, Sam and the rest... they deserve to be taken care of. You said, 'They've been here before you bought Cliveden.' I wouldn't trust Randall to do the right thing by them. We could offer them passage to New Orleans, Cuba, or even Jamaica. For that matter they could even work the cane fields at my sugar plantation or we could find other places for them where they wouldn't be mistreated."

"I think you're right David. I don't trust Randall either."

After gathering everyone from the quarter and the house servants in front of the house, Tom said, "I know you're concerned with what's going to happen with you, so we'd like to make a few suggestions. The property will be sold to Randall White and his son Bruce. They're buying both Cliveden and Five Oaks. We don't know what they intend to do or how you'll be treated, but it's a sure thing you won't do as well as when Miss Sharon and I owned it. If you would like to try your chances in New Orleans or going north, that's up to you. Cuba is where we're relocating to. We have a sugar plantation there, and I intend to start growing tobacco. You're familiar with doing that and you'll be more than welcome to come."

"Master Tom, what that Cuba be like? Where it be?" Solomon asked.

"It's an island in the Caribbean. There are tobacco and sugarcane plantations there. Some of you house servants may find work in New Orleans if you don't choose to leave the country. Wherever you choose we'll make sure you'll be transported. We'll be here for the next few days. Try and decide what's best for you."

They began walking back to the quarter mumbling to each other where their chances would be better. Suddenly, Solomon abruptly turned and walked back, "Master Tom, I thinks me and my missus, we like to try goin' to 'dat place you call Cuba. I thinks some of the others might wanna' go too."

"That's fine Solomon. I was hoping you would." Walking away satisfied, Solomon put his arm around Ester heading back to the quarter with the others.

Going in the house David said, "Tom, we have to do the same thing tomorrow at Five Oaks. I don't know how many would want to go."

"Well if they didn't want to stay they would still be better off in New Orleans than here," Tom replied.

"I think you're right, I guess we'll know tomorrow after we ask."

The next morning on the way to Five Oaks, they decided to stop at Doctor Cook's to check on Simon. Pulling up to the house Doctor Cook was coming off the front porch.

"Doctor Cook, how's Simon?"

"He died in his sleep last night. Could you arrange to have someone come by and pick him up? I remember him saying he wanted to be buried at Five Oaks."

"We're on our way there now. We'll have someone come back for him. Whatever burial service we arrange will have to be short. Randall White and his son are buying Five Oaks and Cliveden. The papers will probably be signed day after tomorrow."

"Well, while you're there have them open a grave for him. I'll notify the minister. I have to pass by the church to visit a patient. Maybe he can come for the service."

"Thank you Doctor. We'll see to it."

When they reached Five Oaks they were met by William the butler.

"Master Tom! How's Master Henry this morning?"

"Master Henry died last night. Would you get everyone together later, we want to speak to you."

Stepping off the front step, William summoned a young boy from the quarter passing by, "Go on down to the quarter and tell whoever' be there, they have to come up to the big house tonight. Master Henry died, and Master Tom wants to speak with us."

"Everybody, Mr. William?"

"Yes! Everybody. Now mind what I say, go on now, hurry up!"

Around 7 o'clock all the field hands with their families gathered at the front steps. Whispering amongst themselves they weren't sure of what was going to be said. When Tom and David stepped out on the porch the gathering went silent.

"Who's the head field hand here?" Tom asked.

One of the men stepped forward, "That be me, Master Tom. I be Homer."

"I remember you Homer, when I came to borrow the oxen years ago. First I want to tell you, Master Henry died last night," a few murmurs came from the group then became silent again as he continued, "His last request was to be buried at his beloved Five Oaks in the family burial plot. Will someone see that a site gets opened? Doctor Cook went by the minister's house to ask if he would come by tomorrow to say a few words. I've sold Five Oaks and I sold Cliveden too. Randall White and his son Bruce are buying both places. I told the people that are at Cliveden they're free to go if they want. We don't know what kind of owners they'll be, so you're taking the chance if you stay. If not, we would see to your transportation if you want to go to New Orleans. I think you'll have a better chance there with your new freedom. We made the same suggestion to the people at Cliveden. The second suggestion I have, if you want to go to Cuba, you can work at our plantation there. We already have sugarcane fields and we want to start growing tobacco. You can make up your mind overnight. We'll be here until after the funeral tomorrow."

Homer asked, "If you please Master Tom, who all be goin' from Cliveden?"

"Do you know Solomon or Sam?" Tom asked.

"Yes Sir. We knows them from the cotton dock. We dun' heard Solomon was beat up pretty good when he went to town. 'Dat be true?"

"That's right. That's why we're giving you the option of going to New Orleans. I think you'll find the people are friendlier than here or Biloxi. Like I said, make up your mind and let us know tomorrow."

Staying overnight at Five Oaks they went inside. David asked, "Tom, what are we going to do with all these furnishings? There are several pieces here that look like family heirlooms."

"I don't really know David. Do you think we should have mentioned it in the sale?"

"It's a little late now. Let's walk through and see what we should bring for Mrs. Henry. I don't know how many field hands are going or how many wagons they have for travel, but I guess we'll find all that out tomorrow."

Walking through the house was like going through an expensive museum, family treasures obviously dating back over several generations. One piece stood out in the main hall which looked to be oriental. It was made of black mahogany with inlaid mother of pearl birds and flowers, almost identical to the one at David's sugar plantation.

"This looks to be the oldest piece here. I'm sure Mrs. Henry would want to keep it," David said as he ran his hand over the piece.

"I think you're right David. We'll definitely have to take it."

As they toured each room David remembered spending the Christmas holiday where he first laid eyes on Brenda. It seemed as though a whole lifestyle was slowly disappearing. A lifestyle that had taken years to build was being torn down by war. He thought, *It's lucky there's only one surviving family member. The family's that at one time could pass down a way of life to other generations would soon be gone.*

The South was losing the war and they realized confederate money would be worthless. Either gold or property, were the only things that would maintain any value. Realizing the limited options he had, Tom knew he was doing the right thing by selling. After the funeral tomorrow, the only thing that will be left behind would be the memory of Simon Henry... and the generations before him that were resting in the ground.

"Tom I was thinking. If there aren't enough wagons here maybe we could buy a few? With gold in our hand I don't think it will be a problem."

"We'll work on that tomorrow. I'm going to walk down to see if they're opening up a gravesite," Tom said.

"Wait, I'll go with you."

When they got there they saw Homer and another man just finishing the grave.

"Is this good enough Master Tom? We be buryin' Master Henry where his Momma and Daddy are buried."

"Yes Homer. I don't think he'd mind at all. Yes, that's fine."

"Homer, is there a coffin for Master Henry?"

"Yes Sir. He always thought it was a good idea to have one handy."

"That's fine. How many wagons does Master Henry have?

"We has the carriage, the coach, and three flat wagons."

"How many of you will want to go?" Tom asked.

"Since Solomon was beat up, I thinks just 'bout everybody –'bout twelve of us. After we get away from here, maybe some strikes out on they own, but I'z sure they stays at least 'till we get's to New Orleans," Pausing, Homer looked at the ground, "Um! Um! Um, Master Tom, this whole thing's 'bout scarin' me to death."

"I wouldn't worry. I think you'll be fine when you get to where we're going. Are you going to Doctor Cook's tomorrow to pick up Master Henry?" Tom asked.

"Yes Sir. Me and Poe here. We be leavin' bright and early."

"That's fine. I'll see you in the morning. Oh! By the way! Don't mention to anyone that you'll be leaving Five Oaks. We don't want that word to get around."

"No Sir. If'n you say so. But I still not sure 'bout 'dat place Cuba," He said turning to look at his helper, "You Poe?"

"No, sure 'nough," Poe replied.

At daybreak they watched as the flat wagon passed with Homer and Poe leaving to pick up Simon's body.

"Well, Tom. Why don't we get a few people to gather the things we're going to take with us and put them here in the hall? This way after the funeral we can load up and leave."

"That sounds good."

Several hours passed with still no sign of Homer or Poe. "David, I'm beginning to get worried about them. They should have been back an hour ago. I'm going to saddle a horse and ride out to see what's keeping them."

"Wait a minute. I'll go with you," David replied.

About halfway, they saw the wagon off to the side of the road with no one around it. Approaching David heard a moaning sound coming from a patch of high weeds. Riding up to it, they saw Homer. It was obvious he had been badly beaten.

"Homer what happened?" Tom disturbingly asked climbing down from his horse.

"Master Tom. We was stopped but didn't have no pass. I dun' tried to tell em' we was goin' to Doctor Cook's to pick up Master Henry's body but they didn't believe us. They hit me on the head and knocked me out. I don't know what happened to Poe."

David still mounted, followed a trail where the high weeds were pushed down. Getting to the wood-line he saw Poe hanging from a tree and yelled out, "Tom! Poe's over here. He's dead. The bastards hung him!"

Running over to where David was he exclaimed, "Damn ignorant bastards... just because I forgot to write him a pass. I'll hitch my horse to the back of the wagon. We might just as well keep going to Doctor Cook's."

"Okay, but let's not leave Poe hanging there."

Cutting him down, they laid him by the road. "We can pick him up on the way back," Tom said.

Getting to Doctor Cook's they had him treat Homer. After he finished they put Simon's body in the flat wagon, then headed back to Five Oaks, picking up Poe's body on the way. When they arrived the Minister was already standing at the gravesite.

"We're sorry we're late. We had an incident on the road getting to Doctor Cook's."

Homer's wife Sally seeing him bandaged ran to the wagon, "Oh sweet Jesus! What happened to Homer?" she frantically asked.

"Some men stopped them on the road. Because they were without a pass they beat them up," Tom said.

"Where's Poe? She asked, "He be with him."

"They killed Poe. He's in the back of the wagon too. Does he have a Missus?"

"No Sir. She died two years ago, they ain't have no children."

"Well we'll have to have another coffin made and bury him too. Where's the cemetery for the quarter?"

Two other field hands stepped forward to get Poe's body and one of them said as he pointed, "It's over yonder Master Tom. We opens another grave and sees to buildin' Poe's coffin."

Stepping down from the wagon the field hands carried Simon's body to the gravesite and laid him in the coffin. After sealing it they lowered it in the grave. The few people still left at the quarter gathered around the gravesite. After the minister recited a passage from the bible they appeared to be solemn. Although they were owned by Master Henry, there was some measure of remorse. He wasn't a hard Master to serve.

Poe being hung only created an added fear in them if they stayed which gave them all the more reason to leave.

"Master Tom, what you want us to be doin' now?" Homer asked.

"Hitch up the flat wagons and load them with your belongings. Don't take any furniture. We won't have room for that and the people from Cliveden too. We're only bringing a few things that we think Mrs. Henry would want; the rest will stay here. After they finish with Poe's coffin we'll burry him then leave."

Everyone hurriedly left the gravesite to do as he asked. Two young people ran to the barn to hitch the horses to the carriage and mules to the flat wagons. With everyone running about doing what Tom said, it resembled organized chaos. The sad event with Master Henry and Poe dying, was giving way to a new hope of a life far different from Five Oaks, a life they weren't sure of but looked forward to with apprehension.

Several hours later Poe's coffin was finished and everyone gathered around the gravesite near the quarter. Poe was laid in it and it was lowered into the hole.

"Master Tom," Homer said, "Could you be sayin' a few words? We ain't never had a burial here at Five Oaks without somebody sayin' somthin'. Master Henry he always did it. I have this here bible. It belonged to Mrs. Henry. I packed it just in case she wants it."

"That was very thoughtful of you Homer. Let me have it," Tom said.

After reciting the Lord's Prayer they closed the grave. Loading into the wagons they headed for Cliveden.

As they were heading for the front gate Tom looked back at the place. Without anyone walking about it seemed desolate. He remembered his wife Sharon saying the day she arrived at Cliveden, 'The people are what make a plantation a home' and more than ever he realized she was right.

Several hours later they arrived at Cliveden. Solomon, his wife Ester, and Sam came out to meet them.

"Solomon, see that these people are put up for the night in the empty cabins. They're going with us tomorrow after we sign the papers for the sale."

"Will you be takin' anything from the big house?" Solomon asked.

"Not much. We won't have the room. Tomorrow before we leave to sign the papers I'd like to have everything packed and ready to go."

"Master Tom, we be ready," Solomon replied.

"Tom, with these three flat wagons, and the two from Five Oaks along with the carriage, it should look like some caravan."

"That's exactly what I was thinking David, but it's the only thing we can do," he replied.

The next morning at 10 o'clock they rode into town.

"Good morning Randall. Are you and Bruce ready to sign papers?"

"Yes. We'll be ready in about 30 minutes. I have to get my son and of course the money."

"We'll head on over to Harold's office. We'll see you there," Tom replied.

After walking into Harold's office they sat down.

"Good morning, Tom, David. Where's Randall?" Harold asked.

"We just saw him, he'll be along soon," Tom replied.

"Tom, I never asked, but what are you going to do with the furnishings at Five Oaks?" Harold asked.

"David and I talked about that yesterday. We really don't know what to do."

Harold, tapping on the desk with his letter-opener said, "If you wouldn't mind. I'd like to buy it. How much do you think it's worth?"

"Whatever you want to give me for it will be fine. I have to say, I did take a few things I thought Mrs. Henry would like. They might be family heirlooms but there's still quite a bit left."

"Would you consider selling it for... let's say, two thousand dollars in gold?"

"Harold, that's fair. I know you'll be happy with it."

"I'm sure I will. I remember all the fine pieces of furniture on my few visits. I'm going to take it with me when I leave."

Surprised Tom asked, "Where are you going?"

"I've decided to take my wife and two children to New Orleans. We're leaving next week. In fact this is probably the last legal transaction I'll be doing here."

Just then there was a knock at the door. "Come in Randall, Bruce. Here are the papers ready for your signatures," Harold said.

Randall laid a bag on the desk heavy with gold coins asking with a smile, "Should I count this out?"

"I don't think it's necessary. Sign here," Harold replied.

After signing the deed Harold said, "Tom, you sign here as the lawful trustee." After Tom affixed his signature Harold said, "Now that's settled."

"Tom, when do you think I can take control of Cliveden?" Randall asked.

"Will the day after tomorrow be alright? I just want to load a few things that belong to Sharon's mother I'm sure she would want. The rest of the furnishings are yours."

"Why thank you Tom. That's quite generous."

After Randall and his son left the office, Harold opened a small safe taking out a stack of gold coins. After counting out two thousand dollars in gold, he closed the safe and said, "Tom, you did the right thing selling. Getting gold for it was a plus."

They stood up and shook hands, "Good luck wherever you go Harold," Tom said.

"You too," he replied.

Getting back to Cliveden everyone seemed anxious to get started. Tom and David took one last tour of the house making sure they didn't miss anything. When David looked in the kitchen he saw the door partially open to the small room Elizabeth once occupied. He remembered the fear she displayed that night lying in bed beside him and his restraint to take her against her will. It all came back. All he was thinking about at the time.... was an insatiable urge to possess her whether she agreed or not. The circumstances that happened after that and the eventual affair made him realize he made the right decision. Looking around the small room again he closed the door and met Tom in the hallway.

"Are we ready?" he asked.

"I think so," Tom replied.

Walking outside Tom looked around for the last time then mounted his horse.

"Solomon, let's go," he said.

Solomon quickly responded, "Giddy up old mule. We got's a long way to go. Dat' place Master David dun' talked about.... Dat' place called Cuba!"

Chapter 29

The Road to Safety

With a late start and slow travel, they stopped the second night in an area they were unfamiliar with. Although David and Tom traveled this area many times before, they always stopped at an inn about five miles farther.

"Solomon, you and Sam might as well pull the wagons side by side and rig up a canvas shelter like last night. Build a fire so the women can cook up something for your dinner. David and I are going up ahead. There's an inn where we can stay for the night."

"Yes Sir Master Tom."

Sitting around the campfire wondering what their new life would be like, they talked until several hours after dark trying to imagine it. Solomon was awoken during the night by the sound of men talking. Looking out from under the canvas he saw four men looking over the wagons.

"Where did you niggers come from?" one of them vehemently shouted. "Where'd you get all this stuff?"

"Sir, some of us came from Cliveden and some came from Five Oaks. They be plantations 'bout 30 miles from here."

"Where's your travel passes?" one of the mounted men asked.

"We ain't got none Sir. We be travelin' with Master Tom and Master David. They be on up ahead, stayin' at an inn on up the road a piece. Master Tom say he knows the man what owns it."

One of the mounted men looking over Solomon and the group said to the others with him, "There ain't too many good ones, mostly women and kids. They don't have too many men."

Sam stepped forward saying, "One of us can go on up to the inn and ask Master Tom to come down. He tells you we belongs to him."

One of the riders said, "He looks like he'll bring a good price. Why don't we just take the men?"

"Please Sir! Just let me go on down and fetch Master Tom. We all family here, please don't be seperatin' us."

"All you men line up here," the one who seemed to be the leader of the mounted group said.

Ester came forward, "Please don't take my Solomon!" grabbing the leg of the leader.

Lifting his foot from the stirrup he put it to her chest pushing her to the ground, "Get away from me wench, we're in charge here," he said.

Solomon seeing it became enraged. Sam, noticing Solomon was angered and about to do something grabbed his arm holding him back. He said quietly, "Solomon, we ain't got no choice. We might just as well go on with them. If'n' we don't, we just might all be killed."

The people in the caravan trembled in fear, wide-eyed wondering what was going to happen. Solomon asked, "Sam, what Master Tom gonna say when he gets here in the mornin' and we ain't here?"

Sam replied shrugging his shoulders, "They just gots to tell him we was took."

Ester ran to the mounted man begging as she did before grabbing his leg pleading, "Please don't take my Solomon!"

Taking out his revolver, he shot her in the head. Falling to the ground Solomon bent down holding her lifeless body.

"Come on you men get on that flat wagon or you'll all wind up the same way!" Pointing at Sam he said, "You there nigger, hook up that team of horses."

Sam grabbing Solomon said, "Come on, you can't helps her now. She's dead. De' means business."

Out of the group eight men were told to get on the flat wagon. With Sam driving they started down the road.

Buzzing with activity not knowing what to do, Sam's son Noah, a ten year-old, jumped on the back of one of the wagon horses.

His mother shouted, "Where you be goin'? Don't you be chasin' after them."

Riding in the direction of the inn he yelled back, "I gonna' find Master Tom and Master David, and tells dem what happened."

"You be careful!" she yelled as he sped away at a gallop.

Arriving at the inn he quickly dismounted and banged franticly at the door. "Master Tom! Master Tom!" he shouted looking up at the windows on the second floor. There was no answer and he hammered again with his small fist on the thick wooden door. A light came on and a window on the second floor swung open.

"Who's down there?" someone called down.

"Excuse me Sir. Is Master Tom or Master David Stewart up there? I needs to speak with dem in a hurry."

"Just a minute!" the man yelled down with irritation.

In a few minutes the front door swung open. "Come in," the proprietor said. Tom was coming down the steps with David and asked, "Noah. What is it? What's happened?"

Excitedly speaking he replied, "Some mens, they came and shot Mister Solomon's wife Ester. She be dead."

"Where's Solomon?" Tom replied.

"They done took him, my daddy too, and the rest of the men's. They dun' took dem' away on one of the flat wagons."

"Who's left back at camp?" Tom asked annoyingly as he tucked in his shirt.

"Just my momma, and some other ladies from Five Oaks... us kids and the peoples from Cliveden. I'm da' oldest."

The inn keeper remarked, "It must be them damn Sullivan Boys. They've been grabbing every darkie they find, selling them to any plantation that will buy them. Since so many slaves are running away they get a pretty good price for them too."

"Our wagons are at a clearing a few miles from here. Where do these Sullivan's live?" Tom asked.

The proprietor replied, "They have a small place not far. I'll draw you a map. It's back up in the woods. I wouldn't try tackling them by yourself, they're a pretty nasty bunch."

After drawing the map Tom asked as he stuck the map in his pocket. "Is there a sheriff here about?"

"There's one about a half mile back in the direction you're going. Sheriff Ward Jackson is his name. You won't have any problem with him helping. He hates them bastards."

After thanking the inn keeper for his help, David turned and said, "Noah go to the stable and bring our horses around."

Still excited at the event, wide eyed he quickly replied, "Yes Sir!"

On the way back to the encampment they stopped at the sheriff's home. Tom said, "David, you might as well go with Noah and find out how things are. I'll be along with the sheriff in a little while."

Getting back to camp, David was immediately surrounded by the remaining women and children, clamoring about what happened.

"Where's Master Tom?" one of the women asked.

"He stopped at the sheriff's. They should be along in a little while. Pack up the wagons. When the sheriff gets here he can tell us what to do. Noah, you'll be in charge."

Within a short time Tom and the sheriff rode into camp.

Tom said, "Sheriff, this is my brother David. We're taking these people to New Orleans to work for us there. Is there someplace they'll be safe while we're getting back the men?"

"Yes. There's a field right next to my house. They can wait there."

"Noah, do you remember where we left Tom at the sheriff's?" David asked.

"Yes Sir Master David," he replied.

"I'm appointing you the leader. Take everybody there. Think you can handle that?"

"Yes Sir, Master David. I knows where it be."

"Sheriff, are we going after them alone?" Tom asked.

"No, not a scurvy bunch like that. We'll have to pick up a few deputies on the way. There are quite a few people in these parts that hate them even more than me."

"Sheriff I noticed the wagon tracks lead off in that direction," David said, looking at the dirt road.

"Call me Ward. That's my first name. Yes. The wagon tracks are going in the direction where they wouldn't have to stay on the open road. That way they wouldn't be seen. First, let's get a few more deputies. Then we can concentrate on taking care of the Sullivan's."

Riding off following the wagon tracks they periodically stopped at a few farm houses where the sheriff deputized several more people. One house in particular a man came to the door "Hello Ward. What's the trouble?" he asked.

"Roger it's them damn Sullivan boys. This here is Tom and David Stewart. They were taking some darkies from a plantation they owned to New Orleans. Those damn Sullivan's jumped their camp, shot and killed one of the women then kidnapped all the men. Think you can help?"

Wiping the sleep from his eyes he replied, "Wait here." Returning to the house he said, "Boy's, wake up! Sheriff's here! He needs some help.

Ward, give us a chance to get some clothes on and get our guns. We'll be ready in a few minutes."

"Thanks, Roger," Ward replied.

"He's a pretty big guy. Sounds like he's as anxious to settle a score same as everyone else we picked up," David said.

"That's right David and his four sons are just as big. They would love to see the Sullivan's gone."

In a little while the boys strode out on the front porch. And yes! They were bigger than their father. "Good morning sheriff!" one said rubbing the sleep from his eyes, "Where they headed?"

"By the looks of the wagon tracks I think they're probably heading to that abandoned barn just through the swamp from their house. I figured we could surround the place on the woods side and leave the swamp area open for them to escape. Once we get Tom's people back we can concentrate on getting them out of the swamp. They won't stay in there too long."

"Sounds good, Ward. If we're in danger do we shoot to kill?" one of Rogers sons asked.

"You're deputies. You make that decision, I'm sure Judge Thomas won't object," he said. They all laughed as they rode away.

Daylight was breaking when they got to a clearing on a hill overlooking the barn.

"Roger, take your boys and spread out on the edge of the woods. Tom, David, Hank, and his son Jed here, will cover the high ground to the edge of the swamp."

"Sheriff, I don't see the wagon," David said.

"It must be in the barn. We'll find out when we get closer," he replied.

With everyone in place the sheriff snuck up to the barn. Peeking through a space between the boards, he could see the wagon and a few slaves standing near it with chains around their wrists and ankles. Quietly creeping around the back of the barn he gently untied their four horses. Realizing he was in luck.... all four brothers were still inside he gently swatted the horses on the rear and they ran away. Returning to the front of the barn he knocked at the door with the butt end of his rifle, "Hey you in there… Sullivan's… Come out with your hands up!"

A shot rang out from inside and a chunk of wood splintered from the bullet close to Ward's head. Looking through the space between the boards, he saw the back door of the barn swing open, and the four brothers ran for the swamp. Roger and his four sons were closing in from the edge of the woods and several more shots rang out. Ward waved for Tom, David, Hank and Jed, to come to the barn. Running around to the rear of the barn they could see two of the brothers running into the swamp. Another was lying face down at the edge of the swamp, and another was crawling in that direction.

Entering the barn, Tom and David found Solomon and Sam along with six other men chained to the wagon.

"Praise god you dun' found us Master Tom. They's gettin' ready to sell us," Solomon said.

"I know Solomon. I'm so sorry Ester was killed. We should have stayed with you."

"Master Tom, they just be evil mens. Wern't nothin' we could do."

"Tom, we'll have to break these wrist restraints with this hammer and anvil. Break Solomon loose first. He can free the rest."

After breaking Solomon free Tom handed him the hammer and chisel, "Here Solomon free the rest. I want to see what's going on outside."

Periodically hearing shots, wide eyed Solomon said, "You be careful Master Tom."

Going outside they saw one of the Sullivan's in handcuffs and the other lying on the ground dead. Ward and the rest of the posse were gathered around them questioning the wounded Sullivan.

"Sheriff, do you need us any further? We'd like to get these men back and continue our journey," David asked.

"No, we have everything under control. They'll come out of the swamp eventually. We'll just wait them out."

"Thanks sheriff. And thanks to the rest of you men," David said.

Solomon hitched up the team to the wagon and they got aboard. He asked, "Master David, where everybody else be?"

"They're camped in a field next to the sheriff's home about a half hour away. After we get back we'll continue to Biloxi."

After returning to the women and children, Tom got permission from the sheriff's wife to bury Ester on the edge of the field. After digging a grave they wrapped her in a blanket and placed her in it. David said a few words from the bible and after filling the grave, they continued on their journey.

***

Two days later they arrived in Biloxi.

"Master David. Where we gonna stay?" Solomon asked.

"I'll see if I can make arrangements for you to stay in a warehouse until the next ship comes in, bound for New Orleans."

After finding them temporary quarters, they waited the two days before Captain Jarvis' ship came to port.

Solomon and the rest were standing on the dock when the ship docked and heard a familiar voice, "Hey ya'll down there! What you be doin' away from Cliveden?"

Looking up they saw Adam. He came running down the gangway shaking hands with Sam, Solomon and the others, being patted on the back by people who knew him. He had been at Cliveden and Five Oaks years ago, and they still remembered him.

"What ya'll be doin' here?" he asked.

"Master Henry died and Master Tom was told to sell the place and gives the money to Mrs. Henry and Miss Anne, 'dat be Master Beau's wife. Master David didn't think it was a good idea we stay on, so's we packed up and left. He be takin' us to New Orleans to stay or go on to 'dat place he dun talked about... 'dat place he called Cuba." Solomon said.

"Well, he owns a plantation there, and Master Tom's goin' to buy one of his own. You be gonna work there?" Adam asked.

"We don't know nothin' bout 'dat place, or New Orleans either. What it be like there?" Sam asked.

"New Orleans be just like the town with the cotton dock, only bigger. They don't be treatin' people bad like there. It be like Cliveden. Only you gets paid for workin'."

"For sure enough! Gets money?" Sam asked.

"Yeah," Adam replied.

Just then a voice came down from the quarter deck, "Adam, get these people on board."

"Yes Sir, Captn'... right away Sir."

"You mean you works on the ship?" Sam asked.

"Yeah, one day when we was going to the auction house, they was a big storm. John, me and two other mens came out of the hold and helps the capt'n. Some of his crew got killed, so he freed us and keeps me on board. I be part of the ship's crew."

"Well, if that don't beat all," Sam replied.

"That ain't everythin', ya'll goin' to New Orleans and gonna see a few more faces you knows."

"Who 'dat be?" Sam asked.

"Miss Elizabeth and Miss Trisha, they got's them a roomin' house, and a seafood place."

"I guess they be doin' right good. I sure hope's we can say the same," Sam said.

Captain Jarvis yelled down once again, "Come on Adam. What's the hold up?"

"Nothin' Captn'... Come on ya'll. I got's to get you on board."

After getting them situated in the hold the ship departed.

Realizing they were nervous in unfamiliar surroundings and facing a three day sea voyage Tom went below to speak to them.

When Captain Jarvis saw David he asked, "Where's Tom? Who are all these people? Where's Simon?"

"Tom's in the hold talking to Solomon, Sam and the others. He wants to reassure them there's nothing to fear. They were people he owned at Cliveden and some of the others are from Five Oaks," David replied.

"Five Oaks! That's Simon's place isn't it?" Captain Jarvis asked.

"Yes. Simon's dead. He died of a heart attack over a week ago. We buried him at his plantation. Before he died he gave Tom power of attorney and told him to sell the place. His last request was to make sure his wife and Anne get the proceeds. The people below were at Five Oaks for years and Simon asked if we would give them a chance to go elsewhere. It's become too dangerous around there."

"I'd hate to be the one breaking the news to Simon's wife. Losing a son then a husband within several months will be devastating," Captain Jarvis said.

"I know. I'm not looking forward to it."

"When you said it became too dangerous around there, what did you mean?" Captain Jarvis asked.

"Several of them got beat up pretty bad and they hung one for not having a pass. If there isn't a white person on the place it's kind of dangerous. Some of them want to go to Cuba and I thought it would be a good idea. Quite a few died from yellow fever in Cuba and I already know these people. They'll be good replacements. We know them to be good workers and they trust us."

"Why didn't the new owners take them?" Captain Jarvis asked.

Tom was just stepping into the cabin, and overhearing his question replied, "We didn't trust the bastards that bought the places to do right by them. They've been with us for years and not running off when they had the opportunity has something to say about their loyalty."

"Then the same person bought both places?" Jarvis asked inquisitively.

"Yes. They stole them for that price but it was the only thing we could do," Tom replied.

"That pretty much explains it, now how about dinner?" Tom asked.

"I'll tell Ming to set the table. From the smell of food coming from the galley I think dinners about ready," Captain Jarvis said.

"Captain Jarvis, can Adam bring food down to the people below decks? He knows them from Cliveden and Five Oaks. I think it might relieve some of their fears seeing a familiar face too," David asked.

"Certainly. I'll see to it," he replied.

"Captain Jarvis. Can I impose on you for another favor?" Tom asked.

"What is it?"

"We're carrying about eighty thousand dollars in gold. I'd like to lock it away."

"Go and get it. We'll do that right now."

Chapter 30

Human Cargo

After putting to sea the human cargo being transported to safety, were allowed to come above deck. Never seeing the ocean before, they looked out on an expanse of water that seemed endless.

Sam remarked, "Look Solomon! Da ain't nary a piece of dry land in sight."

"Yeah, I ain't never seen so much water."

An excited voice rang out from the crow's nest, "Captain! Ship to port! It's closing fast sir."

"Can you make it out?" Captain Jarvis replied reaching for his telescope.

"Yes Sir. It's a Yankee war ship!"

David hearing it, quickly emerged from his cabin and watched as the ship raced toward them.

"Do you think its trouble Captain?" he asked.

"I don't know."

The lookout in the crow's nest yelled, "Captain! A puff of white smoke... they just fired a shot."

Suddenly, a cannon ball ripped through the canvas sail and splashed down in the water twenty five yards past the ship.

"Adam, get these people below deck ...in a hurry!" Captain Jarvis commanded.

Staring wide eyed at the oncoming ship Solomon and the rest scurried to safety below.

"Why they be shootin' at us Adam?" Solomon nervously asked.

"They just wants to know what we be carryin' in the hold. Don't you be fearin' none. Ya'll ain't in no harm."

Captain Jarvis shouted, "Douse the sail! Make ready for boarders."

"Aye, aye, sir!" the chief boatswain replied.

The ship glided to a halt, ready to receive a small rowboat with two officers and several armed men. After the longboat was secured to the side, they boarded. Captain Jarvis, David, and Tom, stood by the rail.

After the boarding party was on deck, they identified themselves, "I'm Captain Smalls, commanding officer of the U.S.S. Franklin. What's your destination and cargo?" he asked.

"I'm Captain Jarvis, and these are my passengers, David, and Tom Stuart. We're bound for New Orleans."

In a gruff manner that let Captain Jarvis know he was up against stiff opposition, Captain Smalls said, "You didn't answer my question Captain. What's your cargo?"

The armed soldiers hearing the second command put their weapons at the ready. Seeing that they weren't taking any nonsense, Captain Jarvis replied, "We're carrying some cotton and general freight."

"Well. Let's just take a look. Open this cargo hatch," Captain Smalls commanded.

Captain Jarvis had two crew members do as he asked.

After opening it, Captain Smalls looked down on over twenty five men, women and children wide-eyed, staring up at him.

Looking down on them he remarked sarcastically, "Captain Jarvis, is this the cotton you're carrying or the machinery?"

"These people are being taken to New Orleans to safety. The plantations they were on shut down. They have nowhere else to go."

"You sure you're not running slaves? That's been outlawed years ago you know." Looking down at the group, Captain Smalls pointed, "Hey you down there!" he said, pointing at Solomon, "You! The big fella, get up here."

Solomon quickly climbed the ladder to the deck and nervously said, "Yes Sir."

"Is the Captain telling the truth?" Captain Smalls asked.

"Yes. Sir. We be afraid stayin' 'round Cliveden. They beat us terrible when we don't have a pass or we don't be with the white folk."

"Some of them are from my plantation and some are from a neighboring plantation. We're carrying them to safety," Tom said.

One of the officer's who boarded along with Captain Smalls looked around at the vessel and said, "Captain, this ship would make a nice addition to the blockade. Are we going to confiscate it?"

David and Tom looking at each other, held their breath waiting for Captain Smalls to respond. After a long pause he replied, "Ordinarily I would, but with this cargo of darkies, we'd have a two day trip to get them back to port. I don't want to leave our assigned area; we might miss someone carrying war supplies." Turning to Captain Jarvis he said, "Captain, have your first mate escort my lieutenant around. Let's take a look at the rest of your cargo," turning around he said, "Lieutenant, go with the first mate."

While they were in the cargo hold, the second lieutenant asked the first mate, "What's in these cotton bales with the red marks?"

Not certain how to respond he tried to mask his nervousness with a quick answer. "They've been marked to identify them as damaged."

Taking out his sword the lieutenant ran it through the bale several times. Satisfied, they returned to the quarter deck.

After a long pause, the Lieutenant said, "Captain, it seems to be in order. I didn't see any contraband."

"Okay men, get back in the longboat." Turning to Captain Jarvis he said, "Captain Jarvis, you can continue."

"Thank you."

After the longboat pulled away from the ships side, Captain Jarvis commanded, "Release the top sail. Unfurl the gallants!"

With the ship underway again, there was a more relaxed feeling.

"I'm sure glad these darkies were aboard. That's the only thing that saved us from being confiscated," Captain Jarvis said.

"Yes, that was fortunate. I was afraid they were still going to take it when that lieutenant took so long answering," David said.

"Gentleman, let's resume our dinner, it must be pretty cold by now. I'll have Ming reheat it."

***

The rest of the voyage went without incident, and in two days they entered port.

Being met by Charles he asked, "Captain, how was your voyage?"

"We were boarded by a Captain Smalls and his Lieutenant from a Yankee ship called The Franklin. The First Lieutenant was a bit of a hard ass. If it wasn't for the darkies on board, the ship would have probably been confiscated."

"Well, there's been an Admiral coming and going in civilian clothes for the last few weeks. He's taking collections for giving the right course to sail to avoid detection."

David looked at Captain Jarvis reassuringly, "The Senator and

Congressman must have completed their plan by now. I wonder why an admiral's collecting, that wasn't the arrangement?" David asked.

"What are you talking about?" Charles replied.

"Keep this under your hat, we have a deal going. He's probably the point man for them. What does he look like?" David asked.

"He's very distinguished looking. Slim, about six feet tall with graying hair. He travels with someone that's a little shorter but looks just as distinguished. They both have a deep southern accent. They were just here the other day looking for you David," Charles said.

"Did they say when they would return?"

"He said in a few days. That was the day before yesterday."

"I don't want to leave for Cuba until I speak with him. It's desperately important." David said.

"When I see him, should I send him to Brenda's -I mean your home?"

"Yes."

"What are you going to do with all these people? Where are we going to house them?" Charles inquired.

"They can be quartered temporarily in the warehouse. They'll probably want to look around. Some of them probably had enough adventure and just might want to remain here. Some said they wanted to continue to Cuba to work the sugar plantation. We're leaving that up to them. Now, can we get transportation?"

"My carriage is at the end of the dock. My man will take you home."

After a rejuvenating bath, Tom and David retired to the study.

"David, I thought the money was to be exchanged in Havana through Frank?"

"I know. That makes me suspicious. I think they might be trying to cut out Frank. I don't quite understand why. We'll just have to wait and see."

Later that evening there was a knock at the door and two men were admitted. They were escorted to the study where David and Tom were waiting, and the door was closed behind them.

"Which one of you is David Stewart?" the taller one asked.

"I am, and this is my brother Tom, Tom Stuart. Who might you be?"

Extending his hand he said, "I'm Admiral Stark and this is Captain Dillard. We represent the interest of Senator Thompson, and Congressman Lewis."

"Sit down gentlemen. We have a lot to discuss. Can I offer you a brandy?" David asked.

"Yes, thank you," Admiral Stark replied.

"Your accent Admiral, it's quite southern. If you don't mind me asking, where might you be from?" David asked.

Captain Dillard looked on cautiously, as Admiral Stark replied, "That's not important." He was about to continue, when David said "I didn't mean to pry; just curious." Noticing a little hostility David cautiously continued, "I thought monies were to be exchanged in Cuba?"

"They are. I was told by Senator Thompson to get an advance payment, sort of a bonus to begin the deal. After this, everything else is supposed to be as it was set up."

"Okay. We were boarded in our voyage coming here. They were kind of demanding," Tom said.

Captain Dillard remarked, "We know you were..." He was cut short with his statement by an annoying look from Admiral Stark. David looked at Tom thinking, *that's why we were boarded. It was to let us know without directly saying it... who was really in control of the illicit trade.*

Captain Stark took an envelope from his pocket, and laid it on the table. "Here's the schedule you want with all the names and captains of the vessels you'll encounter. They're all aware of what's going on and will try to avoid being in the area your sailing through."

Looking curious, David asked, "How much does the Senator want as a down payment?"

"Personally, he wants fifteen thousand dollars," Admiral Stark replied.

With his response, David went to the safe and withdrew a sack of gold coins bringing it to the table. He reached for the envelope and as he did, Admiral Stark quickly drew it back. David, surprised by his action quickly asked, "What's wrong?"

Admiral Stark hesitated. Examining the surprised reaction on David's face he said, "Senator Thompson wants fifteen thousand. Captain Dillard and I on the other hand aren't that greedy. We'll take say... two thousand dollars apiece to start the deal, and one thousand dollars for each shipment."

David raised his eyebrows at the Admiral's boldness but quickly replied, "Okay, Admiral." Then went to the safe to get more money. After handing it to him, David reached across the table for the envelope. Picking it up he asked, "Is there anything else I can do for you gentleman?"

"You do realize an occupation of New Orleans is going to happen. When it does, we'll have total control over the port inspections. We'll require the same amount for each ship that comes in." Admiral Stark replied.

David rose from his chair and walked over to the liquor cabinet. Carefully selecting his words, he paused with his back toward Admiral Stark tactfully asking, "Then, will that give us the opportunity to bring in more goods?"

"Yes, as long as it's not war supplies." Captain Dillard quickly replied.

Not wanting to show his immediate frustration with the way the meeting was turning out, David asked, "Would you gentleman like another brandy?"

"Yes, that sounds good," Admiral Stark replied.

After pouring them, Tom remained silent during the meeting, but when it was over, raised his glass saying, "Well gentlemen, here's to a successful enterprise."

After toasting, David and Tom escorted them to the front door. Bidding them goodnight, they watched until they were in their carriage, and drove away.

"David. Did you hear that? That's an extra two thousand dollars for each ship. Senator Thompson said the payment he receives would take care of everyone. I wonder if they're charging the other dock owners too?"

"I don't know Tom. This evening was a real surprise. We'll have to speak to Captain Jarvis in the morning. I'm tired -I'm going to bed."

After breakfast, they headed for the dock to meet with Captain Jarvis. Seeing them arrive he waved them and Charles aboard. Directing them to his cabin, he remarked, "I thought the both of you had things to do today. Why are you back so soon?"

After David and Tom looked at each other, David said, "We had a couple of visitors last night."

"Who were they, the one's I told you about?" Charles asked.

"Yes. The people that you told me were on the dock looking for me. One's an admiral, and the other's a captain. They wanted fifteen thousand dollars to initiate the deal for Senator Thompson and an extra one thousand dollars a ship for each of them."

"There wasn't anything said about an amount to start the deal, or the extra money per ship. How the hell did that come about?" Captain Jarvis annoyingly asked.

"The Admiral said that the fifteen thousand dollars was for Senator Thompson to start the deal... that I understand. Senator Thompson may have miscalculated on what he needed to begin. What annoyed me was Admiral Stark saying, 'He wasn't that greedy. He and Captain Dillard only wanted one thousand dollars apiece for each vessel with contraband.' He held back the list of ships and the specific areas they patrolled until I agreed. There's a positive side though..."

"What's that?" Charles asked, disgustingly shrugging his shoulders.

"He said he wouldn't restrict us to a few crates as long as it wasn't war supplies."

Captain Jarvis tapping his fingers on his desk appeared to be in deep thought.

"What's on your mind, Captain? You seem to be troubled." David asked.

"I'm beginning to get a picture I don't particularly like," Captain Jarvis said getting up from his desk.

"What's that?" David asked.

"When that war ship stopped us, it wasn't by accident he was in that area. He was told by someone the route we were taking."

"How would he know that?" Tom asked.

"I'm not quite sure, but the captain of the ship wouldn't have been in the boarding party. He would have sent his second or third officer. Making the excuse for not confiscating the ship didn't sound right. I think he was letting us know he could have. Someone wanted us to know they play a bigger part in this trade, and I think it may be the Admiral and the Captain that visited you last evening."

"What can we do about it?" Tom asked.

"We'll have to see if Frank can handle that without stepping on too many toes. Charles, when will the ship finish being loaded? I'd like to get out of here as soon as possible," Captain Jarvis said.

Leaving the cabin he looked over his shoulder replying, "As soon as we get the rest of the cargo that's supposed to come tomorrow."

Coming down the gangway Tom saw Solomon and a few gathered outside the warehouse. Solomon asked, "Master Tom, when we gettin' ready to leave?"

"Tomorrow evening. Has everyone made up their minds whether they want to stay or go?"

"Last night, Adam dun' took us on over to Elizabeth's. She dun' told us she be doin' right fine. Sure was good to see a familiar face. She dun' told us they be so many people lookin' for work, they just ain't any jobs. Since my poor Ester been kilt, I'm by myself. I thinks I'm gonna stay. Maybe I can makes a go of it. I gots two youngin's to be thinkin' 'bout. Miss Elizabeth, she say she could use a hand too. I thinks most of the others will go. 'Dat is, the ones 'dat don't be scared on all 'dat water."

"I think that's a wise idea Solomon," Tom replied, patting him on the shoulder.

"Master Tom, do you wants me to get them on the ship?" Solomon asked.

"Not yet. Not until tomorrow. Tell Adam to make sure all of you get fed."

"I surely will Master Tom."

Late afternoon the following day, they said goodbye to Elizabeth, Trisha, and Solomon who came to see them off. Waving goodbye the ship quietly slid away from the dock, heading out on the river.

Chapter 31
Trouble in the Gulf

The second day out, they encountered another sail on the horizon. The lookout in the crow's nest shouted, "Captain, Yankee naval ship to starboard. He's signaling for us to stop," immediately continuing, "Captain, white smoke! He just fired a shot."

If it was meant to be a warning shot, the cannon ball fell short of its target to cross the bow and struck the side rail. With the explosion it sent large chunks of wood flying in every direction. Several sailors in the immediate area screamed in pain and one had his leg completely severed at the knee, the detached part going over the side.

Captain Jarvis quickly commanded, "Douse the damn top sail!"

David's full attention was on the movement of the naval ship's action. When he turned to speak to Tom he saw him lying on the deck with several other members of the crew that were wounded. Tom was unconscious from a head wound and bleeding profusely from a gaping hole on his side and his left leg.

"Tom! Tom!" slapping him hard on the face trying to revive him, "Wake up!" David said, applying pressure to the wound.

Tom came to asking, "What happened?"

"That damned ship fired a warning shot that fell short. There are two killed and several others wounded," David replied frantically trying to stop the bleeding from Tom's leg.

Tom nervously remarked, "David, I don't have any feeling in my left leg. How bad is it?"

Tearing open Tom's trousers it exposed more of his injury. There was splintered wood in the wound from the ships rail and a fair size piece of flesh was missing. Cut to the bone Tom was quickly losing a lot of blood. Getting paler by the minute he relapsed into unconsciousness again. David kept pressure on the wound until one of the ship's crew helped apply a tourniquet.

After the longboat from the naval ship was fastened to the ship's side, Captain Smalls climbed the ladder to the main deck. After seeing the carnage he inflicted he immediately ordered the long boat back to the ship to bring aboard The Franklin's doctor.

Captain Jarvis shouted not being able to contain his rage, "Why did you fire on the ship so quickly after giving the command to stop? We didn't have time to douse the damn sails."

"Captain Jarvis, you're forgetting who's in command here. I just may confiscate this ship," Captain Smalls replied.

Knowing Captain Smalls was in total command of the situation Captain Jarvis chose not to throw out a hard rebuttal. He tactfully wanted to throw out names but not to the point of intimidating him, instead he replied in a stern voice, "I dined last evening with Admiral Stark and Captain Dillard. They as much as told me I would have unhampered passage taking these people to Cuba."

"Did you say Admiral Stark?" Captain Smalls asked.

"Yes. He told me New Orleans will eventually be under his control and all shipping will be controlled by his second in command -Captain Dillard who dined with us too."

When he mentioned Admiral Stark it obviously struck a familiar tone with Captain Smalls from perhaps a confrontation in the past. Whatever it was Captain Smalls became less hostile in manner.

After the ship's doctor came aboard, he examined the wounded, and Captain Small's asked, "Doctor, how bad are the wounded?"

"There are two dead and three injured. Tom Stewart will lose his leg for sure if not his life. He's lost quite a bit of blood already."

"Well, if you did all you can, return to the longboat. We're going back to the Franklin."

David replied angrily, "What about my brother? You can't just leave him here if he's that bad. You're a doctor. You could at least take him aboard the Franklin, and see that it he gets proper treatment."

Captain Smalls, realizing the potential problem he made for himself replied, "Carry him to the long boat." Then they departed.

After they were gone, Captain Jarvis gave the command, "Aloft. Set full sail."

"David, you're carrying grim news to your sister-in-law and Mrs. Henry. I don't think I'd want to be in your shoes when we reach Havana."

"No, it's not going to be pleasant. I just hope Tom's alright. He lost a lot of blood. If he loses his leg and lives, it will be devastating to him. How long do you think it will take to get to Havana?"

Looking up at the clear sky Captain Jarvis replied, "With any luck, and the weather holding the way it is, I think in four days we'll be in port."

Deeply filled with worry David stood by the ship's rail watching the Franklin disappear over the horizon.

**

As Captain Jarvis predicted the afternoon of the forth day they made port.

"Captain, would it be alright if Adam gets these people situated while I go to the hotel and deliver the bad news?"

"Certainly. Try to get back as quickly as possible. I want both of us to tell Frank what happened."

"As soon as I'm finished, I'll be right back," David replied.

Getting to the hotel, David waited outside for a few minutes gathering the courage before going in. Entering the lobby alone, Sharon immediately suspected there had been trouble. Coming from behind the service desk she focused on David nervously asking, "Where's Tom?"

"Sharon, there's been an accident but Tom's still alive."

Having a premonition she cried out, "I knew it. I had a feeling something went wrong. What happened?"

Mrs. Henry excitedly asked, "Was Simon injured too? Where is he?"

"No, Mrs. Henry... Simon's dead. He had a heart attack on the way back to Five Oaks. The doctor thinks he was just under a terrible amount of strain. Before he died Simon gave Tom power of attorney and asked him to sell Five Oaks. He also had one more request. He wanted to be buried on the family plot. There were a few people that attended the services. I think that's the way you would have wanted it had you been there."

Tears began to flow as she turned away and Anne embraced her.

"Thank you David. I know you did the right thing. If everyone doesn't mind I think I'll retire to my room."

"I'll go with you." Anne added.

"No Anne. I'd rather be alone for awhile."

Sharon, not finished questioning David, asked, "Now, what happened to Tom?

"There was an incident on the way back. A blockade ship prematurely fired a warning shot. The cannon ball fell short and struck the side rail of the ship. Several crew members were killed and three were injured, including Tom. He was standing at the side rail and received a severe wound to his left leg."

"David, don't keep me in suspense. How bad is it?" she excitedly asked while wringing her hands together.

"Sharon, I won't lie to you. He's going to lose it. They took him aboard the navy ship where he could get better medical treatment."

"Are they bringing him here to a hospital?" she asked.

"With all the excitement I assume so. But that's a question I didn't ask. I know they have a medical unit on board the Franklin, where we only had a doctor."

Stunned at David's words she repeated, "I had a bad feeling something was going to happen. I just knew it. Anne, if you don't need me I'd like to be with Roselyn the rest of the afternoon."

"That's alright Sharon. I'll be fine by myself at the desk."

"Anne, I have to leave for awhile. I must get back to Captain Jarvis. We have to see Frank about what happened."

"Do what you have to do. Compton and I will be fine," she replied.

After kissing her lightly on the cheek he said, "Thank you sister. Bringing all this bad news wasn't easy. You're small and fragile but strong willed. I'm glad I can count on you."

"Someone has to be strong. Mrs. Henry not only lost her son but her husband too. She's going to need all the support I can give her," Anne said walking him to the front door.

Smiling at her words, David left to return to the ship.

Arriving he asked, "Captain Jarvis are you ready to go?"

"Frank came by when you were at the hotel. He saw the damage to the ship and asked what happened. I told him it would be better if we both spoke to him. I did tell him that Tom was injured. Let's go. He's waiting for us."

The door was open at Frank's shack and they both entered.

"Now, what the hell happened?" Frank annoyingly asked in a loud voice.

"Frank, we were boarded en route to New Orleans from Biloxi by a Captain Smalls. He commands the U.S.S. Benjamin Franklin. He threatened to confiscate the ship but after a little hub-bub, he let us go. When we got to New Orleans, David's partner told us a few men in civilian

clothes were looking for him. You better take it from here David,"
Captain Jarvis said.

David continued, "It was an Admiral Stark, and a Captain Dillard.
They visited me that evening. They said they represented Senator
Thompson and wanted fifteen thousand dollars to initiate the deal. Stark
also said, 'He was going to be in charge after they take over the shipping
in New Orleans, and Captain Dillard will head up all the port inspection
teams.' They want two thousand dollars from each ship that comes to
port with contraband. He said they wouldn't restrict the amount of illicit
cargo we bring in."

Enraged, Frank picked up a shot glass from the table hurling it across
the room. David had never seen Frank angry and realized the consequences to Captain Smalls would be retribution for what he did. David's
thoughts were affirmed by Queenie standing up. With her tail between
her legs she exited the shack.

"Those bastards! I told you David you can't trust politicians," Frank
shouted.

David waited for Frank to settle down before continuing, "That's not
all. After the meeting I thought the threat of being confiscated was to
let us know they were really in charge. Apparently I was wrong. On the
way back, Captain Smalls fired on us." David was suddenly cut short by
Captain Jarvis.

"That bastard gave a signal to halt but within two minutes he fired a
warning shot. The damn thing fell short and struck the ships rail, killing
two of my crew and injuring three others. It also hit David's brother
Tom. He'll definitely lose his leg if not his life. That's according to the
doctor from The Franklin. What can we do about this?"

"First thing we can do is use our heads. If they want to play that
game, we'll just have to take the chance and do what they're doing in the
Atlantic."

"What's that Frank?" David asked.

"We'll have to try and find desolate landing spots along the shore
line. That is, until I can get word to the Senator about what's happening
down here; he's invested in it and I don't think he's going to like his
profits being skimmed."

"How can you get word to him?" David asked.

"There are British ships going to New York from Jamaica weekly. I can write out what we request and have John hand deliver it to one of the captain's heading there. As far as Captain Smalls ...he's insignificant. We can get him replaced with someone willing to go along."

"What about Tom?" David asked.

"I think they'll just drop him off here or a hospital in Santiago. We'll find out."

Leaving the meeting David said to Captain Jarvis, "It sounds like Frank is going to be able to handle it."

"It certainly seems like it. What are you going to do with the darkies?" Captain Jarvis asked.

"I was going to see they get transported to my plantation. Sam's with them. He's a good man; he'll get them settled."

"Yes, he seems like he's pretty dependable," Captain Jarvis replied.

Looking out in the bay Captain Jarvis remarked, "There's the Franklin. They have a longboat in the water. They must be bringing Tom ashore."

Hurrying down the line of docks to where the longboat was heading they got there just before it landed. David turned suddenly and saw Frank behind them.

David said, "Captain Jarvis, I don't see Tom. It's only the rowing crew and the ship's doctor."

Frank remarked, "Yeah, and that ass Captain Smalls. His last name must be describing his brain size."

Once they were tied to the dock the ship's doctor and Captain Smalls climbed the stairs to where the three of them were standing.

David excitedly asked, "Where's Tom?"

Captain Smalls and the ship's doctor looked at each other then the doctor replied, "David, we're awfully sorry to say, your brother didn't make it. There was too much blood loss. He's in the ships hold. We'll leave his body with you if you like, or sparing any added grief of a funeral for his missus. we could take him out to sea and give him a Christian burial."

"That's a tough decision to make," Pausing for a moment, David replied, "Maybe you should just leave him here."

"If you'll have a hearse here within the next hour I'll see he's brought ashore."

"Thank you doctor," David sorrowfully replied.

"David, I should share in some of the blame. I should have been quicker to douse the sail," Captain Jarvis said.

"Don't put any added burden on yourself. I was there, Smalls fired too soon. He should have put the shot well ahead of the bow. Do you remember when he stopped us before? The first shot went through the damn sail."

Listening to their conversation Frank said, "Sounds like he enjoys being aggressive."

"Gentleman if you'll excuse me. I have to acquire a hearse," David said.

Walking off the dock, he saw Sam and the other people who were to be transported to the plantation.

"Sam, I have to acquire a hearse; Tom's dead."

"Dat be a damn shame Master David. He be a fine man."

"Thank you Sam. I'll see to it you have transportation to the plantation. I won't be going out with you, but when you get there, Andrew is the name of the person in charge. Tell him what happened, and why I'm staying here for a few days. He'll know what to do. Think you can remember all that?"

Looking at the ground, Sam sadly replied, "Yes Sir! Master David –I remember."

After acquiring the hearse, David watched as they brought Tom's body ashore wrapped in a shroud.

"David, is there anything I can do?" Frank asked.

"I don't think so. Oh wait, when will the next ship leave?"

"These crates right here, are the ones that have to be loaded as soon as John's freight get's here from Jamaica. Captain Taylor will be sailing tonight. Have you ever met him?"

"I seem to think I have, why?"

"He's the one I want to see Senator Thompson, but I have to have a meeting with him before he sails. I want to warn him what he's up against. John isn't aware of what happened, but he trusts me to do the right thing. I'll tell Captain Taylor where he can unload his cargo.... before heading north to New York. There are a few secret places along the South Carolina and Georgia Coast. I'll tell him where they are and how to signal the people ashore. I'll also tell him the return signal if the coast is clear."

"Why isn't my ship getting loaded?" Captain Jarvis asked.

"There's another ship coming in from France. I want you to take the New Orleans route and see what kind of problems you'll encounter. When you get to New Orleans get a hold of this Admiral Stark. Show him the damage to your ship and tell him what happened. Maybe we can get rid of this Captain Smalls."

"Ok Frank. Now I understand."

Getting back to the hotel David asked, "Anne, where's Sharon?"

"She's still in her room. Why, what's happened?"

"Tom died. They couldn't save him."

"Oh my God! She's going to be totally devastated. What have they done with his body?"

"I sent it to the same undertaker that took care of Beau. I'll go up and tell her."

"No. You stay here. I'll do it," Anne replied.

It was a task he wasn't looking forward to but after getting behind the desk he heard a crash. Running up the stairs he burst into the room and saw Anne trying to revive Sharon. She had passed out hearing the news and knocked over a wash stand. After reviving her she trembled uncontrollably with anguish. After a few minutes she began to get over the initial shock and asked, "David, what happened? How did it happen? How did Tom die?"

"I only told you he may lose his leg. I didn't mention to you he lost a terrible amount of blood. The doctor confirmed to me that's what he died from, too much blood loss."

"Then he didn't suffer?" she asked looking for some solace. "No, Tom didn't suffer. He just went unconscious. I've made arrangements with the funeral director that held Beau's funeral. That's where his body is now. We could have his funeral tomorrow if you feel strong enough. I wouldn't wait more than one day. It's been a few days since it happened."

"Whatever you think is best David. I'll be strong enough to handle it. I have my Roselyn to think about."

"That's fine. Where do you think you'll want him interred?"

"I think the cemetery where Beau was buried would be appropriate," she replied.

"That's fine. I'll let the funeral director know."

Leaving Brenda in Anne's care, David went to the lobby.

"Compton, it looks like you're going to be running the hotel for the next few days."

"It won't be a problem. I was use to it when Mr. Garfield was taking care of his wife after she became ill."

"Thank you Compton. I have to go to the funeral parlor and make arrangements. Miss Sharon would like it to be held tomorrow."

"It sure is a shame for the family. So much death in such a short period of time... so much death," Compton said, as he turned to walk away shaking his head.

"Yes it is. But knowing we have someone like you we can rely on makes a terrible situation a lot easier to handle."

"Thank you Sir. I'll do my best."

"I know you will," David replied as he walked away to make the funeral arrangements.

Dawn broke with a cloud cover over the harbor and within a half hour, Mrs. Henry, Brenda, Sharon, little Roselyn, and Anne were getting ready for what would be a traumatic day. They also planned a small remembrance service for Simon at the same time. David knew the events of this morning would linger for quite awhile and realized there was only one positive thought and that was their shared mutual grief. That alone would be self supportive.

During the graveside service a misty rain began to fall making it humid. With the stress it became too much for Sharon and she became unsteady on her feet. Not being able to stay through the service she had to be helped to the carriage. Anne held little Roselyn's hand until it was over then joined her.

"I'm so sorry Anne. I just felt like I was going to pass out. I didn't want to disrupt the service," Sharon said.

"No need to apologize. Here, take Roselyn," Anne placing her in the carriage.

The services being over, they returned to the hotel. Anne asked, "David, when are you going out to the plantation?"

"I sent Sam and the rest of the people that came from Cliveden and Five Oaks yesterday. I gave Sam instructions to give to Andrew for settling them in until I get there."

Brenda asked, "When you leave, I'd like to go with you. I just want to remain here with Sharon for a few days. Do you think you can wait that long?"

"I don't see any problem with that... certainly dear!"

Chapter 32
Finding a Resolve

When Captain Taylor reached his destinations along the Georgia and North Carolina shore line, he successfully offloaded his contraband cargo. After several more days of sailing he made port in New York.

While his remaining cargo was being off-loaded, he asked the dock foreman, "Where can I find the harbormaster?"

The dock foreman replied, pointing to a small house at the end of the pier, "That's where Mister Briggs lives. You can find him there most of the time."

Captain Taylor watched his cargo being unloaded for a short time then left the ship.

Knocking on the harbormaster's door, Captain Taylor was greeted by a short, thin man in his mid 40's, bald, and wearing wire rim glasses. He asked, "Can I help you Captain?"

"Perhaps, I'm looking for Mr. Briggs, the harbormaster."

"That's me. Come in. What can I help you with?"

"It's important that I meet with Senator Thompson. I understand he resides here in the city. Could you direct me to his home?"

"I notice you have a British accent. Is it something I can deal with?" he asked.

"No. I must speak with the Senator myself."

"I don't know whether he's here or in Washington, but I know where he lives. I'll take you there."

"That would be greatly appreciated," Captain Taylor replied.

Getting to the Senator's door Mr. Briggs knocked. When the butler answered he said, "Mr. Briggs, what brings you here this evening?"

"It's nothing urgent on my behalf William, but this captain would like to see Senator Thompson."

"If you gentleman will kindly follow me to the living room I'll let the Senator know you're here."

Captain Taylor wondered why Mr. Briggs was eager to volunteer his services bringing him here personally, and the thought crossed his mind. *There might be some connection to Mr. Briggs, and the Senator bringing in untaxed cargo from Europe to New York*, but dismissed it from his mind as Senator Thompson entered the room.

"Hello Briggs! What can I do for you?" Senator Thompson asked.

"It's not me Senator, I just brought this gentleman. He was inquiring as to where you lived."

Looking at Captain Taylor, Senator Thompson asked, "Can I help you Captain?"

"Senator, we have a mutual friend who wants me to deliver a personal message. His name is David Stewart."

"Oh! I see," Senator Thompson replied.

Escorting Mr. Briggs to the front door, Senator Thompson said, "Mr. Briggs, I don't think you'll be needed. I'll see that the Captain gets back to his ship."

Looking dejected at the gesture of no longer being needed, Briggs left.

After closing the door the Senator said, "Now, Captain Taylor, come into the parlor. Can I get you a drink of Brandy, or French Cognac?"

"Cognac will be fine Senator."

Walking slowly to the liquor cabinet Senator Thompson remarked, "Why don't we leave out the formalities Captain Taylor, call me Harold... and you're?"

"James Taylor Senator," he replied.

After sipping his drink Captain Taylor said, "Harold, this is excellent cognac."

"I know. It's part of a shipment from Europe." Anxious to hear what Captain Taylor had to say he asked, "What's the message from our friend David?"

Carefully not wanting to offend him Captain Taylor came right to the point, "His brother Tom was killed by a cannon shot from one of your naval vessels. He and David were returning to Havana after conducting business in New Orleans when it happened. There were also several crew members killed, and three badly wounded. Captain Jarvis said they fired too quickly after giving the warning signal to stop and was never given time to heed the command."

Looking annoyed Senator Thompson asked, "What ship, and who was the captain, did he know?"

"Yes. It was the war ship the Benjamin Franklin. The captain's name is Captain Smalls."

Opening his writing desk Senator Thompson said as he pulled back his chair to sit down, "Let me jot that name down."

Captain Taylor continued, "He also wanted to relay another message to you."

"What's that?" Senator Thompson said as he looked up from the note he was writing.

"There's an Admiral Stark and Captain Dillard that want two thousand dollars for every ship that comes to port in New Orleans with contraband," he said tactfully not mentioning the extra fifteen thousand dollars the Senator wanted to begin the deal.

Looking bewildered, Senator Thompson remarked, "Well, we'll have to see about that. The next time I'm in Washington I'll speak to the Secretary of War. He may have some input there."

Captain Taylor realized he did the right thing by not mentioning the initiation cost. It seemed that there were more than a dozen people in government involved and realized David might have been right. The extra initiation fee was only to cover an underestimate on the Senator's part.

"Senator: to avoid any further calamities, when will you be going to Washington?"

"I wasn't going to go until the end of the week but this has become rather an emergency. Tell David and Tom's wife how deeply sorry I am the whole thing happened. Also, let David know that Admiral Stark will get a complete dressing down for having Captain Smalls under his command."

"Thank you Senator. Could you see to it I get a ride back to my ship? I'm sailing in the morning."

"Back to England?" Senator Thompson asked.

"No. I'm heading south to Jamaica; Kingston, Jamaica to be precise. But first I want to stop in Havana and fill Frank in on the details of our conversation."

Senator Thompson finished his note and handing it to Taylor said, "Thank you. One more favor you can do for me if you will. If Briggs asked what our meeting was about don't divulge any of it. I think with your English accent and the look on his face as he was leaving he thinks he's missing out on something."

"I won't, and thank you Senator," Captain Taylor replied.

Getting ready to leave, he realized his thought about the connection between Briggs and Thompson was accurate. They must have been in the business of untaxed goods from Europe also. As Captain Taylor was about to leave, Senator Thompson said, "Captain Taylor. One moment! I was just thinking. If you're going back to Jamaica could you use another passenger? If you could wait let's say until tomorrow evening to sail I could go with you and get to Washington much sooner."

"Senator, I'll await your arrival," Captain Taylor said as he departed.

Late the following day Senator Thompson and Congressman Lewis came aboard the vessel. After boarding Captain Taylor immediately set sail.

With a favorable wind they were anchored in the Chesapeake Bay in two days.

"Senator, I'll have a longboat take you and the Congressman ashore," Captain Taylor said.

"Thank you Captain. If you could possibly wait until this afternoon before leaving we may just have something more to relay to Frank."

"I'll wait. The cargo I picked up in New York isn't as important as our arrangements."

Departing the ship, Senator Thompson and Congressman Lewis went straight away to the War Department. Halted at the door by uniformed soldiers they identified themselves.

"I'm Senator Harold Thompson and this is Congressman James Lewis. It's most urgent that we see Secretary Warren."

"One moment gentleman, I'll see if Secretary Warren knows you're here," the sentry replied.

"He doesn't expect us. This business is of the utmost urgency. Please let him know we're waiting," Senator Thompson said.

"Yes Sir."

A few minutes later they were admitted.

"Harold, James, what brings you here so urgently?" Secretary Warren said.

"Donald, we've run into a few problems in the Gulf. I'm sure it's something you can straighten out. One of the ships out of New Orleans was fired upon. It killed the brother of a very influential person we're involved with."

"I sent Admiral Stark there to prevent this kind of thing. What the hell happened?" Secretary Warren angrily said.

"Well, it may just have been bad timing. I think it happened between the time you ordered them there to oversee things, and the time it took before he could get the right people in place. I know you could straighten out any problems that would arise, so I came here posthaste. Another thing, my informant tells me. Admiral Stark and Captain Dillard are trying to extract their own levy on each ship that gets to port. What can we do about that?" Senator Thompson asked.

"How long are you going to be in Washington?" Secretary Warren replied.

"We never thought we'd have to be here at all. The captain of the vessel we came here on is from England. He carries goods from Europe to Jamaica and is the one that told us about the problem. He brought that message straight from Frank."

As Secretary Warren sat down at his desk to retrieve writing paper, he paused for a moment. Tapping his finger to his chin he looked up at them. "Wait! I'll do better than that. I'll send an attaché personally. Is this Captain Taylor heading back to Frank in Havana?" Secretary Warren asked.

"I guess he could sail to New Orleans so your emissary can speak with Admiral Stark first," Senator Thompson replied.

"Good! My attaché will wear civilian clothes. I don't want anyone to know who he represents."

"I'm sure the Captain will wait until he gets aboard," Senator Thompson replied.

Walking them to the door, Secretary Warren said, "Thank you Senator, Congressman; let me know if I can be of any further assistance."

After leaving they retired to their secondary residents in Washington. Shortly after they arrived they received Secretary Warren's attaché, who identified himself, "Gentleman, my name's Christopher Phillips." He was a tall, slim, middle aged man, with signs of graying hair at his temples. He was dressed in a gray suit which looked tailor made, and after being admitted, he began, "I've been sent by Secretary Warren to handle anything you may need done."

After taking seats in the parlor Senator Thompson filled him in on the details. After they finished, Mr. Phillips left for Captain Taylor's awaiting ship.

***

The voyage to New Orleans took just under a week and Admiral Stark was surprised by the attachés arrival.

"Admiral, I'm Christopher Phillips. I was sent by the Secretary of War Donald Warren. I'd like to meet this evening with you and Captain Dillard. Would six o'clock be convenient? There are several things he wants me to discuss with you."

Hearing it was from the Secretary of War Admiral Stark nervously replied, "Yes, Mr. Phillips, six o'clock at my office will be fine."

After he left the room Admiral Stark asked Captain Dillard, "I wonder what this is about?"

"I think it might have something to do with that fool Captain Smalls. He should have never fired on that ship. I told you that he should have been relieved of his command," Captain Dillard replied.

At six o'clock sharp Mr. Phillips arrived.

"Admiral, I'll be quite blunt. Higher ups in the government; people that I'm not at liberty to divulge are very dissatisfied with what's going on here. There was a person of influence killed by Captain Smalls from the Franklin when he fired on a ship prematurely. The first order is to remove Smalls as Captain of the Franklin."

Admiral Stark began to reply, "I was..." He was abruptly interrupted by a stern look from Mr. Phillips. "Please! Let me finish. The second order is to be careful of adding tariffs of your own to the incoming ships. I was told to remind you that your current compensation can also be curtailed by being removed from your responsibilities here. That's something only you can control. The parties that sent me wanted to make that perfectly clear. They, as myself, hope there won't be a need to repeat my journey."

"Mr. Phillips, let whomever you represent know everything will be complied with."

"Thank you gentleman. Now, can you see that I get transportation back to Washington by one of the warships?"

"Certainly Sir. When would you like to leave?"

"As soon as possible. I thought the weather in Washington was humid. This by far is a lot worse."

"I'll get word out to the Franklin to return to port. That will be the ship that takes you back."

"Thank you, Admiral. Now, can you let me know where I can dine?

"Mr. Phillips the best restaurant in New Orleans is Antwonett's."

"It's in the French Quarter," Captain Dillard suggested.

"Then will you gentleman care to join me?" Phillips asked.

After the dressing down they received they never expected an invitation and quickly replied, "Yes, we would."

After dinner and a light repast at Café Durmontee' they parted company for the evening.

***

That same night, word was sent out on the fastest ship to make contact with Captain Smalls aboard the Franklin. Within two days of being notified, he made port. Before the ship was fastened securely to the dock Admiral Stark was already going up the gangway. Met by the officer of the deck he was escorted to Captain Small's cabin.

"Captain Smalls, you fired on a ship several weeks ago that killed someone of influence from Havana. Why didn't you include it in your report?"

Embarrassed and utterly speechless he had no immediate response.

"I take it Admiral I'm being relieved?" Smalls asked.

"Yes. I see no other recourse. You're being transferred to shore duty in Philadelphia. Get your things in order and come ashore."

"Who's taking command, Admiral? Or aren't I at liberty to ask?"

"Captain Dillard for the immediate time, he's taking an attaché back to Washington."

"When will I be leaving?" Smalls asked.

"You'll leave on the next ship available, probably the day after tomorrow. We're expecting a shipment of ammunition from Philadelphia. After it's unloaded it will be going back to the Frankford arsenal in Philadelphia."

"Aye, Aye, Sir!" Smalls said as he stood up to salute the admiral.

After leaving the ship Admiral Stark returned to meet Mr. Phillips.

"Mr. Phillips, the Franklin is in port. It's awaiting your arrival. I'll see that your baggage is put aboard. I also relieved Captain Smalls of command."

"Thank you. What was his reply to being relieved?"

"I think he expected it after the incident but was shocked about being transferred to Philadelphia."

"That's fine Admiral. It seems like you have everything under control. I'll report my findings."

"Thank you Mr. Phillips."

A carriage pulled up to the front of the hotel and both men got in. Admiral Stark rode with Mr. Phillips to the dock where Mr. Phillips boarded The Franklin. After welcoming him aboard, Captain Dillard commanded the ship to set sail.

Admiral Stark watched as the ship slowly moved away from the dock and thought, *I wonder just how far up the chain of command his orders came from?* Dismissing it not wanting to walk on tender ground he left the pier.

Chapter 33
Returning to Havana

The following morning Captain Taylor left the harbor setting his compass heading for Havana. Under fair winds and a calm sea it was the perfect combination for a favorable and speedy voyage.

***

Docking in Havana the ship was met by Frank, "Captain Taylor, I'd like to arrange a meeting tonight at the Havana Hotel. It'll be you, David Stewart, Captain Jarvis, John, and me. I'd like everyone present so we can all get the same information at the same time," Frank said.

"Is John here from Jamaica?" Captain Taylor asked.

"He never went back after you left. He's been bunking with me."

Chuckling Taylor replied as only an Englishman would, "I say! That must be some marriage.... mess and messier."

Frank laughed replying, "That pretty much describes it to a 'T'."

"What time Frank?" Captain Taylor asked.

Walking away Frank looked over his shoulder, "Be there around nine o'clock. Most of the people should be out of the dining room by then. I'm going there now to speak to David."

At eight thirty, everyone started gathering for the meeting. Talking with one another they carefully avoided any conversation about the resolve until everyone was present. At nine o'clock Frank and John walked in the front door entering the lobby.

Frank may have had an unkempt disorganized life, but business appointments were his strong points. He frowned on lateness.

"Hello, Anne. Where's David?" he asked.

"He's in the dining room with the others. Shall I show you in?"

"No thanks. Have you ever met my partner John? He's from Jamaica?" Frank said.

"No, I don't think I have," she replied extending her hand to shake John's.

"My pleasure Miss Anne, from what Frank's told me you've sure had your share of troubles over the last several months. You have my deepest sympathy."

"Thank you, John. Your concern is greatly appreciated."

Frank anxiously said, "Come on John. Let's get this meeting going."

Walking through the swinging louvered doors into the dining room, they joined the others.

Frank, in a low voice said, "Captain Taylor, suppose you start the meeting by telling us what went on in New York."

"First, I want to tell you about the drop off points along the Georgia and North Carolina shore. Georgia was a little tricky. I thought we'd been discovered so I had to quickly jettison one of the crates and prepare to make a run for the safety of the fog bank. As it turned out it was only a young girl with a lantern walking along the shoreline looking for one of her father's cows."

"What was in the crate?" David asked.

"Fortunately it was bottles of French wine. The water isn't that deep so they're retrievable. The North Carolina coast was a lot easier."

Frank appeared to be annoyed with Captain Taylor talking about something so trivial. When the Captain didn't get to the point about what happened in New York Frank frustratingly demanded, "Well, what happened in New York?"

Startled with his outburst, he said, "I met Senator Thompson at his home and told him what was taking place. He was very upset with Tom getting killed and sends his condolences to you David and to his wife. He began to write a letter for me to convey to someone in Washington but after a few minutes of thought he decided to go there in person with Congressman Lewis."

"Who did they meet with?" John asked.

"I don't know but whoever it was felt it necessary to send an attaché instead of a letter. I assume he represented someone very high up in government. He came in civilian clothes and avoided any conversation about his purpose."

Frank asked, "Did he meet with Admiral Stark and Captain Dillard?"

"Yes. From what I understand Admiral Stark relieved Captain Smalls immediately after he returned to port, and Captain Dillard was given command of the Franklin. I had a meeting with Admiral Stark and he told me to convey a message to you Frank, everything will be complied with. As I was leaving he handed me this envelope to deliver to you."

Handing the envelope to Frank he opened it. Captain Jarvis asked,

"Captain Taylor, what did they do with Captain Smalls?"

"They reassigned him to Philadelphia. Captain Dillard took the attaché back to Washington."

A broad smile crossed Frank's face after reading the envelopes contents. John asked, "Well, Frank, what's in the letter?"

"Gentleman, it sounds like the problem is resolved. Here is the revised schedule of the blockade ships and how to avoid them."

"Can we be sure this is the end of the trouble?" David asked.

"The only way to be sure is to test it," Captain Jarvis replied.

"Captain Taylor, would you commit yourself to another run to New Orleans?" John asked.

"I won't take that commitment until I consult the ship's owners in Jamaica."

"That shouldn't be a problem as long as we take care of the governor," John replied.

It was agreed the next shipment would be from Jamaica and the meeting adjourned.

As they walked through the lobby David asked, "Frank, I heard you were purchasing a house here in Havana? Is that true?"

"Yes. That's true. I thought it was about time I decided to clean up my act." Laughing he added, "I couldn't wait any longer for the woman to show up with the mop and broom. Bunking with John the last several weeks in my shack confirmed its necessity. I think Queenie even likes the idea."

David laughed. Surprisingly, Anne hearing the remark laughed too. It was the first time since Beau died that she had, and David realized being busy with the hotel helped her out of her depression.

"Which house did you purchase Frank?" Anne asked.

"I haven't finalized the purchase yet, but it's the Kingsberry Estate."

"Wow! That's not just a house. It's a mansion! You'll have to have a few servants to run it," Anne said.

"I know. Getting the right help will be a problem," Frank replied.

Anne thinking for a moment said, "If I'm not being too forward and David doesn't mind I'd like to ask if Thelma could possibly fill that void."

"Who's Thelma?" Frank asked.

"Frank, she was the one that kept order in my home in Biloxi," David replied. Turning to Anne, he continued, "Sister: that may be a good idea if she's willing to come. I'll ask her on the next trip to New Orleans. I'm going with Captain Jarvis when he leaves day after tomorrow."

***

Setting sail they tested the schedule Captain Taylor had given to Frank. Following the usual precaution of a darkened ship at night and the specific time and navigation instructions they arrived in New Orleans on schedule. Admiral Stark met the ship personally and went aboard.

"Captain Jarvis, I'm terribly sorry for the actions of Captain Small and his overzealousness. David, you have my condolences too, you and Tom's wife."

"Your apology is welcomed but it can never bring back my brother. I heard Captain Smalls was relieved of command," David asked.

"Yes, he was. Captain Dillard will be in command of the Franklin for now until we can hand pick a replacement. We've been selective as to which ships can get through the blockade but you won't have any further need to worry. We've straightened everything out."

"I notice there's quite a lot more troops occupying New Orleans since the last time I was here," Captain Jarvis said.

"Yes, there is. But their main concern is the ships that try to navigate further north than New Orleans where they don't have control of what's being delivered to the Southern Army. You shouldn't have any problem with ships docking here. We're the ones inspecting the cargo."

There was no mention of the added charge and David was relieved in his mind things were finally resolved.

"Admiral Stark, if you'll excuse me, I'd like to return to my home," David said.

"Are you returning for good?" He asked.

"No, I have to return when Captain Jarvis sets sail again."

"I hope I see you again before you do," Admiral Stark replied.

"Maybe.... we'll see," David answered.

Walking off the dock David saw his former partner, "Hello Charles. How has the occupation affected your trade business?"

"It hasn't been good since our agreement but I'm managing finically to stay above water. I heard about Tom. I'm terribly sorry."

"Yes, the whole episode was unfortunate. Sharon's taking it very hard but I think with Roselyn, Anne, and Beau's mother she'll be alright."

"I heard Admiral Stark was trying to extract funds from you bringing in goods. Is that true?" Charles asked.

"Yes, it was, but it's since been resolved. Why do you ask?"

"He's trying to tariff exporting goods. Not that it's going to make much difference. I hear they're going to shut down all trade. Did you hear anything?"

"No, I haven't but with all the extra troops I've seen I wouldn't doubt it. I thought they probably want to at least have some direct control rather than spreading themselves thin watching the coast. I'll see what I can do about it," David said.

He returned to the ship where Admiral Stark was still in conference with Captain Jarvis.

"Admiral, I was to understand that I wouldn't be interfered with. I just found out from my partner that this dock is open to scrutiny. Is that so?"

Looking embarrassed, he replied, "I didn't know you were part owner of this dock. I'll see that it's corrected."

"Thank you, Admiral," David replied.

Leaving the ship, David saw Charles, "It's all straightened out Charles. You won't be bothered any longer," he said.

"That was fast. How did you do it?"

"You wouldn't believe by their appearance but the characters involved, have so much influence both North and South, it's nothing less than remarkable. Brenda's father was right. Mr. Atchison told me the money invested here by northerners would make a difference with how we're governed. Now if I can borrow the use of your carriage, I'd like to go to Brenda's. I mean our house."

"My carriage is at the end of the dock. I'll see you later won't I?" Charles asked.

"Yes. Why don't you stop for dinner around six? Captain Jarvis will be there too."

"I'll see you then," Charles replied.

During dinner they discussed the problems and how they were amicably resolved. Captain Jarvis remarked, "Money talks the loudest, whether there's a war on or not."

"Well, I'm just as glad it's settled. It's a shame it had to take Tom's life to accomplish it. He would have enjoyed being a part of what's happening,"

David said.

At that moment Thelma entered the room, "Master David, is they anything else you be needin? Me and Sarah wants to visit with Elizabeth and Trisha."

"No, I don't think so." Pausing for a moment, he said, "Oh wait! There is one other thing. Would you consider going to Havana when I leave day after tomorrow? There's a great position opening and I think you'll enjoy being there. The house is larger than this so there will be more staff to control. Miss Anne recommended you for the job."

"Can I thinks about it? I'm still not sure 'bout all that water."

"I'm leaving day after tomorrow. Whatever you decide will be fine."

"I'd sure like to see Miss Anne again. That be the only reason I would go."

"I'm sure you'd be a welcomed sight and a big surprise too."

On the morning of their departure Thelma was reluctantly ready for the long sea voyage. Getting aboard was a little hectic but after settling into her cabin she felt more relaxed.

To reassure her of the safety of the trip David knocked at her cabin door and asked. "Thelma, is everything okay?"

"Yes Master David. But we ain't left the dock yet. Ask me tomorrow morning when I can't see no land."

Smiling he replied, "If you need anything let the ship's steward or me know."

"Yes Sir. I surely will do that."

***

During the several days at sea Thelma scarcely left her cabin. Every time she went out on deck she marveled at the vastness of the ocean. Seeing Adam she asked, "Adam, how do the captain knows where he's goin'? They ain't nothin' to steer to."

"He be usin' his compass, and the stars at night to guide the way," Adam replied.

"Well supposin' it's cloudy and he can't see the stars?" she asked.

"Then he uses just the compass."

"I sure hopes that compass tells him the sure enough truth," Thelma replied before going back to her cabin.

***

Four days later they tied up to port in Havana.

"Now, Thelma that wasn't that bad was it?" David asked.

"No Sir. I'm sure glad that compass told the captain the truth. Now, how do we find Miss Anne?"

"Just a moment, I'll get you transportation. I just want to check in with someone that lives at the end of the dock. He's the one you'll be working for."

Walking to the end of the pier David opened the door of Frank's shack. For the exception of the ropes pulleys and other nautical necessities it was empty.

"Do you want me to wait on you, Master David?" Thelma asked.

Chuckling to himself he looked at the empty room replying, "No Thelma. I'm ready now," then closed the door.

After the short ride to the hotel they were greeted by Anne, Brenda, and Beau's mother. Anne came running down the few steps of the Hotel, "Thelma! Thelma! It's so good to see you here!" She exclaimed embracing her tightly.

Thelma looked up at the hotel with approval, "You surely have a pretty place here Miss Anne and all these beautiful flowers. It's like a garden from heaven."

Grabbing Thelma by the arm she said, "Come in! Come in! I want to show you the place."

"Lord child! I'm here now. Don't be in such a rush."

Anne took up most of the greeting then rushed Thelma inside. Brenda remained on the porch giving her full attention to welcoming David.

"Hello my dear. I'm sorry for being absent for so long but there was just so much to do," he said.

"That's alright. You're home now and that's all that matters. How are things in New Orleans?"

"If you're referring to our home it's just fine. I think, or rather I know we made the right move keeping it. From a business standpoint we're fine that way too. How's Sharon holding up?" he asked.

"She's been keeping busy with helping Anne and taking care of Roselyn. She really hasn't had time to dwell on Tom. I do hear her at times in her room at night quietly crying."

Embracing David's arm firmly they entered the hotel.

"I looked in Frank's shack at the dock. I didn't see him there. In fact his bed and personal belongings are gone too," David said.

"He finalized the purchase of the Kingsberry Estate while you were gone. He came by after the paperwork was signed and took us to see it. It's very impressive," Anne replied.

"It must be. I've heard several people tell me it's quite grand. I'll have to visit it one day. Have you seen him lately?" David asked.

"The last time I saw him was the day he took us there. That was almost 2 weeks ago if I'm not mistaken. Yes. I'm sure of it. It was Tuesday, two weeks ago."

"Anne, if you feel you can get along without Brenda, I'd like her to return to the plantation with me in the morning. I imagine being absent for so long Andrew must think I abandoned him."

"I'll be fine. I have Mrs. Henry here and with Compton keeping an eye on how we're doing things we'll be fine. You must be famished. Why don't you go into the dining room and we'll all have lunch together," she said.

"That sounds like a good idea," he replied.

Sitting at the table David glanced up to see Frank coming into the dining room. He was hardly recognizable. His thick black hair was cut clean and combed, something that was foreign to his appearance most of the time David met him. He had on a fresh tropical patterned shirt with pressed trousers.

"I saw Captain Jarvis at the dock. He pretty much filled me in on the trip," Frank said.

"I knew if you saw him he would. I went to your shack and saw you no longer reside there. I hear congratulations are in order on the purchase of Kingsberry. I'll have to make it a point to see it," David said.

Smiling Frank replied, "I thought I better clean up my act. I finally took stock in myself when I passed in front of the mirror here in the lobby. I didn't realize the guy I was looking at was me."

The remark registering true and brought a round of smiles from everyone seated.

"Care for some lunch?" David asked.

"No. I have to get back to Kingsberry. Miss Anne, did the woman you told me about who can run the place arrive?"

"Yes. She's upstairs. Wait just one moment. I'll call her."

"That's okay, don't bother yourself right now. I have to go to the dock. There's a ship coming from Jamaica. I think my partner John is aboard. I want to speak with him. If you don't mind I'll stop by later and pick her up. I'm anxious to have some organization at Kingsberry."

"She's the right person for it. I'll let her know." David replied.

"David, are you going to stay in town long?" Frank asked.

"No. Tomorrow morning Brenda and I are going to the plantation. I haven't been there in quite awhile."

Frank paused as though he was thinking whether or not he should speak. Finally he said, "David, could you do me a great favor?"

"Certainly Frank. What is it?"

"Did you know your overseer Andrew is my half brother?"

"Yes I did. He told me that when he wanted to invest a little money in our adventure," tactfully avoiding knowing why they were estranged.

"Well, when you see him could you let him know I'd like him to visit me at Kingsberry?"

"I'll do that Frank. Now, if you'll excuse me I have a few letters to catch up on."

Early next morning David and Brenda were on their way to the plantation. Upon their arrival they were greeted by Eva.

"Senor, Senorita. Are you here to stay for awhile?" she asked.

"Yes Eva. I believe we are. Is Andrew about?" David asked.

"I see him early this morning. I think maybe he's at the stable now."

"Brenda, you don't mind if I go and speak to him do you?"

"No. I'll be fine. Eva will help me unpack."

After a light peck on her cheek he left for the stable.

"Andrew I'm glad I caught up with you before you headed for the cane field. How's Sam and the rest of the people I brought from Cliveden, and Five Oaks working out?"

"First of all, I was sorry to hear about Tom. It came as a complete shock. As far as the people from Cliveden and Five Oaks they're good workers. We were able to begin planting tobacco with their knowledge of how to get the field ready. I didn't know much about tobacco so they were more or less in charge. We have to build extra quarters for them though. There were just too many of them to settle in the houses we already have. The houses are almost finished and most of the people are settled. You'll be seeing a few bills from the local lumber mill," Andrew said.

"I'm not worried about that." Pausing for a moment David said, "I have a message for you. Frank asked me to let you know he would like you to visit him at Kingsberry."

"Kingsberry!" Andrew replied.

"Yes. He purchased it. It appears he's cleaned up his life style quite a bit too."

Sitting back in the saddle then raising the brim of his hat Andrew said, "Are you sure it was the same Frank I'm related to?"

"Yes, and if you wanted to go within the next few days I wouldn't mind. Sam can keep things going until you return. When will the cane be ready for harvest?"

"The new fields won't be for a few months since we had to burn most of them off. It's actually the in between time anyway."

David remarked pointing at one of the men from Cliveden, "There's Ezra. He knows what has to be done until you return. He's worked tobacco fields before. By the way, I have money for you from your investment."

"Thank you David for allowing me to take part in it," Pausing briefly he continued, "This trip to Kingsberry should be interesting." After settling his hat forward again he said, "I don't want to be too forward but the plantation next to yours is still available. If I can borrow money from Frank would you consider a partnership?"

"That's something to think about when you return. For now just concentrate on getting to Kingsberry."

"I'll leave in the morning," Andrew replied.

Chapter 34

A Relationship Renewed

Leaving the following morning Andrew arrived in Havana that afternoon. The slow ride up the hill to Kingsberry where he would meet the half brother he never really knew, was filled with suspicion and anxiety. Not knowing what to say he thought, *How will I react? Should I let him make the first overt gesture? Well, I can't worry about that now, it will have to wait till we come face to face.*

Pausing at the front door he grabbed the large brass doorknocker then tapped. A tall, light skinned butler named Jacob answered the door.

"Can I help you sir?" he asked.

"Yes, I'm Frank's half brother. He wanted to see me."

"Right this way please. He's been anticipating your arrival for the last few days. He's on the veranda."

Looking around as he passed through the house the furnishings were impressive. The Persian carpeted floors were like a royal greeting to any visitor.

Stepping out on the veranda he could see over the short stone wall. The view of the valley with the harbor in the background was magnificent. Tropical plants such as hibiscus and gardenia obviously maintained by a professional gardener richly adorned the garden.

Seeing Andrew, Frank immediately rose to his feet.

Silently looking at one another for a few moments Frank said, "I don't quite know how to start this conversation Andrew so you'll have to help me."

They let the past remain just that.... the past, and reached out in a heartfelt embrace of each other, as though nothing preceded that moment. After what seemed like an eternity, they looked at each other again embracing once more.

"Andrew, I want to tell you how sorry I was for the neglect I've shown you over the years. I have a lot to atone for."

"Frank it's a new beginning. Let's start over."

"Sit down. We'll talk about the future. Care for something? A drink or lunch?" Frank asked.

"Lunch would be great. I haven't eaten since breakfast," Andrew replied.

Picking up a small bell on the table Frank rang for the servant, "Thelma, this is my brother Andrew. Tell the cook we'll have lunch now out here on the veranda."

"Pleased to meet you Master Andrew, I'll tell the cook Master Frank."

"Thank you Thelma."

"Frank, your house is very impressive. It's a big improvement from living on the dock."

"Yes, I thought it was about time I straightened out my life. I even cut back on my drinking binges. I have something I want to give you. I've had it for awhile. Come with me."

Wondering what it could be, Andrew curiously followed him into the living room. He watched as Frank swung away a large painting to reveal a wall safe. Carefully turning the dial he opened it. Looking over Frank's shoulder Andrew could see several sacks of money. Taking a few out Frank handed it to him.

Looking confused Andrew asked, "What's this for?"

"Its money you earned with the investment Edward Atchison made in your name."

Andrew replied surprised, "I never realized he did that."

"I know. You thought Edward was giving you the share of what you allowed him to invest. In part that may have been true but he took it upon himself to invest more on your behalf. He may have never mentioned it but he thought very highly of you. I just thought it was about time you got the rest of your share. I hear the plantation next to David's is for sale. Are you interested in buying it?" Frank asked.

"How did you know?"

"Tom told me he was thinking about buying it. Since his death I thought you might like to own it."

"Frank, it's strange how things worked out. I just spoke to David about him helping finance me to do just that. Now I won't have to."

"Well, we'll talk about it later. With the war going on I'm not sure how long we'll be able to continue shipping to New Orleans. If you and David have the sugar and tobacco trade going, it will insure a steady flow of profit.

"You know, David told me Mr. Atchison advised him to do that. I think Brenda also mentioned it. Will you get involved?" Andrew asked.

"I don't think so. I have too many irons in the fire as it is. With the money I already have and the contacts I'll continue to keep it will keep me busy enough to coast me into retirement."

"Ever think about marrying?" Andrew asked.

"With the way I was living in a shack and all, I don't think any woman would have been up to the challenge. That's why I bought Kingsberry. It's sort of the beginning of a normal life."

Andrew leaned back in his chair. Smiling, he looked around at the elaborate estate, "I see you didn't just take it a little step at a time. This is elegant. It must have cost a pretty penny."

"That's an understatement but I really had no choice. I always admired the place when I came here on business. I never expected it to go up for sale but when it did, I couldn't resist buying it."

"It's going to take a good home organizer to keep it all running properly," Andrew said.

"Miss Anne told me about Thelma. She was the woman that was just here. She was the house maid to David and Anne in Biloxi. She was like a foster mother to Anne and been a part of their family for years. When David mentioned how efficient she was I just couldn't resist those credentials. I'm sure she'll know how to keep it running smoothly. Enough about me, is there anyone in your future?"

"Not really. I just haven't had time to dwell on it other than a trip weekly to the local tavern. Like you that only satisfies the immediate urge."

After lunch Andrew said, "Frank, I hate to cut this visit short but I really should be starting back. I'd like to begin the paperwork to buy the plantation." Holding the bag of coins securely Andrew patted the bottom of the sack and said, "Thanks to you now I'll be able to do it."

"That's alright Andrew I understand. We'll have plenty of opportunity to get together in the future."

Walking him to the front door Frank watched from the porch as Andrew secured the money in his saddle bags. After mounting his horse he said goodbye. After giving Frank a short wave he started down the hill. Frank stood watching until he was down the road and out of sight. Feeling a lot better than he had for a long time he went back in the house.

Returning to David's, Andrew dismounted and went inside.

"Well Andrew how did the meeting go?" David asked.

With an approving grin he replied, "Very well! He gave me some money." Taking it from his saddle bag, he held it up to show him, "Quite a bit I might add. He said it was the profit Edward invested for me. Why he waited so long to give it to me I don't really know. At any rate I wanted to ask you about buying the plantation for sale adjacent to yours. I know Tom was interested in it but now that he's gone, I wondered if you have any objection."

"No. I certainly wouldn't mind."

"You know David, I mentioned it before. Maybe we could form a partnership and join the properties together. They're about the same size and it would make a much stronger reason to refine our own sugarcane. Between that and the tobacco we could just sit out the rest of our lives shipping those two commodities."

"That sounds like a promising enterprise. We'll talk more about it over dinner. You'll stay won't you?" David asked.

"Yes. I just want to go to the tobacco field and speak with Sam then freshen up a bit."

"That's fine. I'll see you in a little while."

After he pulled the servants cord, Eva entered the room.

"Eva, Andrew will be joining us for dinner. Will you please see to it there's another place set for him?"

"Se' Senor, I tell the cook to prepare more food."

"Thank you."

After Andrew left, Brenda entered the room. "Who was that you were speaking to?" she asked.

"That was Andrew. He renewed his relationship with his half brother Frank. He wants to buy the plantation next to ours and become partners. He said with that much sugarcane we should start thinking about processing our own." Looking in the desk for a blank sheet of paper he continued, "Maybe that's a good idea."

"What was your reply to that?" Brenda asked.

"He's coming to dinner and I think your input would be most helpful."

Giving him a peck on the cheek she replied, "Darling, thanks for your vote of confidence."

Within the hour Andrew returned and entered the dining room. Seated at the table Brenda spoke first, "Andrew, David tells me you want him to join in a partnership?"

"Yes. What are your thoughts on that?" he asked.

Looking at Andrew then back at David with a smile she replied, "It seems as though both of you have no inhibition allowing me to express my opinion."

Andrew replied, "If your father taught you to express yourself as he valued your mother's opinion I have no fear of it."

"Yes Andrew. I learned that early on in our relationship. Edward told me she was instrumental with helping him. She not only controlled things in New Orleans during his six-month absences but paperwork for this plantation also," David said.

Brenda, happy to be able to partake in the conversation said, "I believe you're both on the right path. This war is well into its third year with no immediate end in sight. It will pay to have the alternative to process it here. Once you set up refining, it will probably be a lot more profit on a steady basis. Number one, you won't have to worry about crop failure or labor, and number two, you won't have to worry about shipping destinations. Everyone wants both commodities."

Impressed by her input Andrew remarked, "It's almost as if I was hearing an echo. Your words describe the conversation I had with Frank four hours ago."

"Andrew, what's our first step in this enterprise?" David asked.

"If we want to process the cane into raw sugar the next step would be building a refinery to separate the syrup. Next is the drying process, and finally separating the different size granules. I don't know what the whole process will cost but if we start processing it for all the other plantations it could be quite profitable. I think Frank might even want to invest in it too."

Brenda replied, "We should hire someone that can engineer the project that's familiar with the processing plant. That would save on any miscalculations we run into trying to do it on our own. Father once said, 'It's easier and less costly to correct a mistake with a pencil than with a hammer.'

"Andrew, how many more people will we need to run this processing facility?"

"That's something I don't know. We'll have to rely on whomever we get to engineer it to tell us these things. It won't be difficult hiring anyone as long as the government doesn't interfere with their slave law. The Spanish government can be a little sensitive especially after the slave revolts in 1848."

"What was that all about?" David asked.

"Pretty much like the slave revolts in the southern states of the U.S. Only here, the government shut it down with a mass slaughter of a few thousand. Unlike the United States where they could run north and seek refuge this is an island with nowhere to run. I think most plantations here will eventually be forced to submit and set them free."

Disgustedly Brenda said, "I remember Papa telling my mother about that revolt. The government wanted to make a strong statement and weren't particular who they killed: men, women or children. I remember it set my mother to tears hearing it."

David said, "Andrew, I'll start inquiries tomorrow for someone to take on our project. I guess you'll be busy the next few days buying the property?" Glancing at Brenda he asked, "You seem to have something on your mind, what is it dear?"

"Yes David, as a matter of fact I do. Why don't you try to secure a property for the refinery near the ocean? This way the processing will take place where it will be shipped. You could control all ends: growing, refining and shipping."

Andrew remarked, "Excuse me for saying it but earlier Frank asked why I wasn't married. I told him, 'I hadn't met the woman I could settle down with.' David, you're a lucky man. It seems you've already conquered that challenge."

Brenda blushed with his statement. Holding David's arm she replied, "When you meet her Andrew, you'll know."

Walking him to the door he departed. After closing the door Brenda said, "David, you made me feel that my opinion was so important tonight. It was very gratifying."

"My dear, your opinion always has and always will mean the world to me."

Retiring to bed, they filled the few waking moments talking about their future. It seemed like the troubles they've been through the last few months had finally been set aside. Brenda contemplated, "With the two plantations together, maybe they should have a name."

"Did Edward have a name for this plantation?" David asked.

"I don't think so. He always referred to it as his and mother's plantation. Why do you ask?"

"I was just thinking how much Tom was anxious to have the place next to ours. If we have to name it let's try thinking of a proper name. Andrew might have some input. I'll ask him about it tomorrow. Now rest your head on my arm dear," he said. After kissing her gently on the forehead they drifted off to sleep.

Early next morning Andrew knocked at the door and was promptly greeted by David. "Good morning Andrew. Care for some breakfast? Brenda's still asleep. I'm dining alone."

"Thank you."

"Eva, set out another plate please."

"Se' Senor."

Hesitating, not wanting to speak prematurely David asked, "Andrew if we're going to incorporate, maybe we should give the plantation a name. From what I understand it never really had one."

"That's true. I've only ever heard Edward refer to it as the plantation or the place. We should give it a dignified name," he said. Pausing for a moment he continued. "If you wouldn't mind David, or Miss Sharon wouldn't mind, I'd like to call it The Franklin Sugar Corporation."

"I assume you have a reason for that name," Andrew asked.

"Yes, it was The Franklin that took Tom's life. He wanted so badly to buy the property I'm buying I thought you wouldn't mind."

"I appreciate the thought. I have no problem with the name. However, I think you should consult Tom's wife before we do it. We're going to Havana today. We could ask then."

Both men stood up as Brenda entered the room.

"Good morning, my dear. We were just discussing the name we should give the corporation."

"Good morning, David. Andrew, what brings you here so early?" she asked.

"We're going to Havana to settle the purchase and begin paperwork on the corporation.

Looking surprised she said, "I only mentioned it last night David. I didn't think you would act on it so soon."

"I only casually mentioned it. Andrew must have been considering it for awhile. He immediately agreed that we should name it after the ship that took Tom's life, The Franklin Sugar Company. Do you like the idea?" Pausing, he said, "Of course I'd like to consult Sharon first to seek her permission."

"I'm sure Sharon won't mind. If you're going to town, I'd like to go with you and spend a few days," Brenda asked.

"Certainly dear. It will probably take two days to get all the legal work completed. We'll be leaving directly."

"I only have to pack a few items. That's the other reason I had for going besides seeing Anne and Sharon. I'd like to go shopping."

With smiles both men rose from the table when she left.

"Andrew if you don't mind me asking, how is it you never married?"

"It seems like I haven't found the right person. It's difficult being so far away from town. I did have a short relationship with a woman from a nearby plantation. She was the daughter of the mayor of Havana, but opted to go back to Spain after the slave revolt. I can't say as I blame her. It was a scary time for people that lived on plantations. After the troops arrived they quelled it pretty quickly. We never had a problem because Edward had slaves that weren't abused."

Upon Brenda reentering the room David took her overnight bag and they departed.

Going down the road, they passed Sam in the field with some of the other men David brought from Cliveden and Five Oaks.

"Driver, pull up. I'd like to have a few words with Sam." Calling him to the coach Sam said, "Good morning Miss Brenda, Master David, Master Andrew. Sure is a fine mornin'. Master Andrew what you want us to do after we hoe up this tobacco?"

"After you finished, take these men to the saw mill and pick up the lumber I ordered."

"Yes Sir." Hesitating he said, "Master David, I was just thinkin'. If we had our own saw mill like we did at Cliveden, it might save a powerful amount of money."

Standing up in the coach surveying the area Sam was referring to David replied, "Sam, that's a great idea. Where do you suggest we build it?"

Pointing to the wooded area he replied, "Over yonder. We might be able to use some of those trees right there."

"That's fine. Then you should start clearing the area. We'll need about five acres. We're going into Havana today. I'll look into buying a steam driven saw. I'll probably have to import one and that will take a few weeks."

"Thank you Master David. I best be getin' back to work, fo' it gets too hot."

Continuing to Havana, they were there within several hours. Pulling up to the hotel they were greeted by Compton.

"Good afternoon Master David, Miss Brenda. Miss Anne is in the dining room with Miss Sharon and Mrs. Henry. I'll tell them you're here."

"That's alright Compton, we want to surprise them. Oh by the way, this is my overseer at the plantation, his name is Andrew."

David saw the look of suspicion on Compton's face after learning Andrew was an overseer and said. "Compton you don't have to worry about Andrew. He's not the kind of overseer you had in mind. Perhaps overseer is the wrong term used. I should have said working foreman."

Relieved at the milder description Compton replied, "Pleased to meet you Master Andrew."

Escorting them to the dining room, Anne, Sharon and Mrs. Henry rose to their feet.

Roselyn ran to Brenda, "Auntie Brenda! Auntie Brenda! I have a cat. Mommy gave it to me," she said.

David asked picking her up, "Don't you have a big kiss for Uncle David?"

Shying away as any four-year-old would, he smiled then put her down. Running behind her mother she peeked out from behind her dress not being sure of Andrew.

"You don't have to be afraid of me," Andrew said, "I like cats. Can I see yours?"

Feeling better about his request she went in search of her pet.

"Anne, you wouldn't mind a few boarders for two days, would you?" David said.

"No! I'm more than delighted. Hello Andrew. I don't think you ever met Beau's mother. This is Mrs. Henry."

Bowing slightly he said, "I'm pleased to make your acquaintance,

Mrs. Henry. I was very sorry to hear about your husband Simon. I know he must have been a good person to work for. Everyone that came from Five Oaks speaks well of you both."

Looking solemn as if he had reopened the door to sorrow she replied, "Thank you, and thank the people from Five Oaks when you return home."

"I will."

"Anne, which room do you want me to take?"

"Compton will show you. After you put your things away come down for lunch. We were about to order when you arrived."

After lunch Andrew and David set out for the lawyer's office. En route they ran into Frank on his way to the dock.

"Hello Andrew, David, where are you two heading?" he asked.

"We're heading for the lawyer's office to secure the purchase of the property next to mine. We've decided to make it a partnership, and merge the two plantations. We also talked about building a sugarcane refinery right here to process not only our own, but everyone from the surrounding area. After we set it up, all we have to do is ship it for them to wherever it's to be warehoused. We'll in essence control most of the process. Until now all of us had to ship the cane somewhere else to be refined. Here we can handle the whole process and control the shipping as well."

"That sounds like an excellent idea. Would you mind if I get in on the investment?" Frank asked.

Andrew replied without hesitation, "No. We'd be more than glad to have you join us."

David looked with approval at his immediate response realizing they had truly mended fences and said, "I'm glad you two are on speaking terms again. If Tom's death means anything, it makes me realize how short life is and brothers shouldn't be estranged from one another."

"You're right David. I'm glad it's settled. When can we get together to talk about getting in? If you wouldn't mind I think John might want a piece of the action too," he said.

Andrew and David looked at each other then replied, "I guess it could be as early as tomorrow or the next day. How long would it take you to get John here?"

"I wouldn't have to have him here for his permission. We trust one another that way. How about a meeting tomorrow evening at my place? Bring the ladies too. They can give me advice about décor."

"What time Frank?" David asked.

"Why don't we make it for six o'clock?"

"That's fine. We'll see you then."

Continuing to the lawyers Andrew asked, "David, with the extra money they're investing, we wouldn't have to borrow anything. We could even expand the facility."

"Whoa! Whoa! Not so fast. We haven't even signed for the partnership yet," David said with a smile.

Both laughing they continued on their way.

After finishing the purchase it was time to discuss the partnership to incorporate. All the details were laid out and an appointment was set for a formal signing of the papers.

"Andrew, now we can go back and tell the girls about our arrangement for Frank's tomorrow evening. I'm sure they're anxious to take another look at the place."

"I think you're right," he replied.

Back at the hotel, they delivered the news of Frank's invitation.

Anne remarked, "I'll be so glad to see how Thelma's getting along."

Andrew said, "According to Frank she's every bit of what you say she is efficiency wise. He said she just took over as if she'd been running the place for years."

The following day they were anxious to make the dinner engagement at Kingsberry. Pulling up to the front door, they were promptly greeted by Frank.

"I'm glad you could all make it. This will be the first formal dinner I have here."

"Thank you for inviting us for a second tour," Anne said, "Well, I have to confess, I intend to get retribution from you ladies after dinner."

Anne not understanding his meaning, replied, "Whatever for?"

"I need you to tell me what the place lacks if anything at all."

Sharon looking around replied, "By the appearance it doesn't look like it lacks anything."

"Well after dinner I'll put everyone's opinion to the test. Andrew,

David, come into the study for a moment. I'd like a word in private before dinner."

They all went into the library and Frank closed the door behind them.

"What's so important that we have to leave the ladies so soon?" David asked.

"It concerns the refinery we intend to build. The governor will have to be cut in on the project."

Andrew quickly remarked, "Already! We haven't even finished signing the papers for the partnership."

"I know but after I left you yesterday, I made some inquires just testing the water. It pays to look before you leap."

"And what's the share for his cooperation?" Andrew asked.

"I think we can get by with only about three percent, which is a bargain."

A light tapping on the door Thelma quietly opened it announcing, "Master Frank dinner's ready."

"Is Captain Jarvis here yet?" he asked.

"Yes Sir. He just came in with Master John."

"Good! Thank you Thelma."

"You didn't mention John or Captain Jarvis coming," David said.

"No, but I thought it wise to include them if they were able to make it. Let's get to the dining room."

Getting to the table they seated themselves in no special order. David stood and began with a toast. "Frank: a toast to you and your beautiful home. We sincerely hope you have many wonderful days enjoying it."

John quietly remarked, "Yes, and it makes me ashamed enough that I'll have to change my lifestyle."

A muted laughter came from everyone again.

"John, I was telling David and Andrew the governor is already demanding his pound of flesh. He's asking for three percent before the project gets underway. He's worse than the politicians in the states."

John replied, "Well, he's the governor. It's really his domain. Where were you thinking about building the refinery?"

"My Brenda suggested we build it near where we can have direct docking ocean access," David said.

Everyone turned in Brenda's direction, "David, you embarrass me," she said.

Captain Jarvis replied, "On the contrary I think that's the best idea. I know a spot that's deep enough to allow shipping ports. It's not far from your plantation. All you would have to do is secure the land and that shouldn't be too hard to do. When do you intend to begin?"

David said, "As soon as we find someone who knows how to design a refinery. They'll have to design the machinery to operate it too. With the war we won't be able to get that kind of equipment from the states. All their manufacturing is going toward war supplies."

Captain Jarvis said, "We'll have to seek it abroad, possibly Germany or England. I'll check the next time I get a chance to speak with Captain Taylor. He ports in England. He could find out where we could get the machinery manufactured."

Sharon looking up from her dinner said, "Can we please forego the talk of business while we're eating?"

"You're quite right. We can save it for desert in the library," John said as everyone responded with a light chuckle.

Captain Jarvis said, "Oh Miss Sharon, I almost forgot. I have a few letters here for you from a place called Belmont. They were forwarded from Cliveden."

He was cut short... "Belmont! That's my parent's plantation."

Taking them from his pocket, Jarvis handed them across the table.

"I haven't heard from them for a long time. I sent them a letter telling them about Tom. This must be their response. If you'll excuse me I can't wait till after dinner to read them." Excusing herself, she left the table. As she did the men rose to acknowledge her exit.

"Gentleman, you'll have to excuse Sharon. She's been waiting for word from her family outside of Charleston for some time," David said.

Looking at one another with suspicion as to what kind of state Charleston may be in from the war they fell silent.

Anne spoke to break the silence, "Frank, from what I hear Thelma is doing a good job for you?"

"Yes, she is. She's really efficient. I want to thank you for telling me about her."

David, noticing Mrs. Henry looked to be in discomfort asked, "Mrs. Henry, are you feeling quite alright?"

Everyone looked in her direction and noticed she was suddenly very pale.

"I don't know David. All of a sudden there seems to be numbness in my left arm."

"Perhaps you should go in the parlor and lie down. Here, I'll help you," he said.

Frank immediately rang for the butler. When he and Thelma entered the room, he said, "Tell my driver to bring the doctor at once. Here David. I'll help you," Frank said.

Everyone rose from the table assisting in any way they could. Temporary confusion, gave way to apologies by Mrs. Henry, "Don't make a fuss over me. Go back and enjoy your dinner," she said.

"Nonsense! We were almost through. You just lie still for awhile. Frank sent for the doctor. Thelma will stay by your side in case you need anything," David said.

"Thank you. I'm sure I'll be fine."

Getting back to the dining room, Sharon rejoined them. She held the letter she received in her hand and had a blank look on her face.

Anne excitedly asked, "Sharon, what's wrong... what happened?"

"My brother Franklin's dead. He was killed in the war. Momma died too. Father's no longer at Belmont. He had to close the place with no one left to run it," Suddenly dropping the letter to the floor she threw her hands to her face and began to cry. Roslyn ran to her mother grasping her leg, "Mommy, Mommy, Mommy, don't cry, please don't cry!"

Anne took Roselyn to another room and in a few moments Thelma came in. She said, "Here Miss Anne, I takes her in the kitchen."

"Thank you Thelma. Has the doctor arrived?"

"No, not just yet, Miss Brenda's in with Mrs. Henry. Mrs. Henry's lookin' mighty poorly."

Anne joined Brenda just in time to see Mrs. Henry grasp her chest, obviously in pain.

"Anne, come here. I'd like to tell you something," Mrs. Henry said.

"Yes, what is it?"

Clutching Anne's hand she said, "I'd like to thank you for making my son happy even for the short time you were together. Go on and live your dream that both of you so much desired." With a sigh she let Anne's hand go lapsing into unconsciousness.

Just then, the doctor hurriedly walked in escorted by Frank and David. Taking out his stethoscope he placed it over her heart and several places on her chest. Standing up he removed them from his ears placing them back in his bag.

"I'm sorry. She's gone," he said.

Anne broke down crying, and with Brenda comforting her, she led her from the room.

Frank remarked, "I think we all had enough emotional chaos this evening. We can talk about our plans at another time. David, if there's anything I can do to help let me know."

"I will Frank. If it's not too late in the evening I'll stop by the undertaker on the way back to the hotel. I'll let him know he can pick up Mrs. Henry. I don't know how late he'll be able to come but will someone be available if he can do it this evening?"

"Yes. That's not a problem."

Captain Jarvis said, "David, John and I will stop on the way back to the ship. We'll take care of it. You see the ladies back to the hotel."

"Thanks Captain," he replied.

Captain Jarvis looked back at Mrs. Henry once more before leaving the room, and Frank closed the door.

"I had better get the ladies back home Frank. We'll get together after the funeral," David said.

"Fine, David. I'll see you then."

Escorting them to the carriage they said their goodbyes and started down to town. Getting to the hotel they went directly to their rooms retiring for the night.

The next morning Andrew and David met for the appointment to sign the papers for the partnership, and after completing them, they stopped by the funeral parlor to finalize the arrangements.

"Andrew, I'll have to stay for at least two days until everything here is settled. Would you mind going back on your own?"

"No, I understand. Take as long as you have to."

Walking him to the door David said goodbye.

The funeral was held the following day in a misty rain. Sharon, still overwrought from the letter she received, didn't attend. So much tragedy had befallen her in such a short time it became burdensome. If it wasn't for Roselyn, she probably wouldn't have been able to stand up under the pressure.

The next day Brenda and David bid them farewell, then headed home.

Chapter 35
Building a Legacy

After clearing the land for the sawmill and successfully acquiring a steam driven saw, work was set upon to manufacture the needed lumber for the project. The expertise Sam and the others acquired at Cliveden was instrumental to its success.

Captain Taylor, after arriving in England, set out in search for someone that could help design the sugar refinery.

Entering the office of Mr. Wickingham the owner of the shipping company for whom he was bringing in cargo, Mr. Wickingham looked up from his ledger acknowledging Captain Taylor's entry. He asked, "Captain, how was your voyage?"

Mr. Wickingham was a short, thin man in his early 60's. He had gray hair and wore a visor type head piece, often used by office workers.

"Aside from a few days of rough weather Mr. Wickingham, the voyage was uneventful," Captain Taylor replied.

"That's good to hear. Then my cargo I take it is being unloaded as we speak?"

"Yes, it is."

Pausing for a moment Captain Taylor said, "I have a question you may be able to help me with."

Putting down his pencil Mr. Wickingham said, "If I can, what is your question?"

"A few people in Cuba are in need of an engineer... someone who can design a sugar refinery for processing sugarcane. The people will also require a company to manufacture the necessary parts as well. Would you happen to know of anyone capable of taking on the task?"

Tapping his desk with his pencil he replied, "Yes, as a matter of fact I do. It sounds like the project you're asking about would be lengthy. Whether or not they want to take on such a project in Cuba would be a question you would have to ask. They're here designing a piece of equipment for a customer of mine who owns a fabric mill. The engineers are from Germany."

"You said, 'engineers.' That implies more than one. Is it a team effort?" Captain Taylor asked.

"No, from what I understand it's a man with his daughter. I've been told she possesses almost an equal skill as her father and was very instrumental in redesigning the steam engine for the Trans Atlantic shipping trade. Quite remarkable, I'd say."

"Do you know their names and where I can find them?"

"I don't remember their names, but as I recall they were very Germanic. My friend Henry Connifer is the person who contracted them. He can be found at his mill called Eight Bell's. It's in the White Chapel District. He may know where they're staying."

"Thank you, Mr. Wickingham. My first officer is seeing to the ship being off loaded. If you'll excuse me I'm going to see if I can find them."

"Good luck in your quest Captain," Mr. Wickingham said returning to his ledger.

After securing a Hansom-Cab Captain Taylor hurriedly set off to Eight Bell's. Upon arriving he knocked at the door of the company's owner.

"Come in," a voice from the inner office announced.

After entering the room Captain Taylor asked, "Excuse me is Mr. Conifer available?"

Looking up from his paperwork surprised to see a ship's captain standing in the doorway he quickly replied, "I'm Mr. Conifer," *the first thought entering his mind was, having possibly lost a cargo of goods he shipped.* Seeing the look of extreme concern on his face, Captain Taylor quickly reassured him by saying, "Mr. Conifer, my visit isn't ominous. I've been instructed by Mr. Wickingham, the owner of the shipping company I sometimes sail for, you may have knowledge of the whereabouts of the engineer that recently worked for you."

"Yes, he and his daughter are staying at my home in the Kings Cross section of London until the assembly of a new loom is complete. The address is 18 Kent Square."

"Could you tell me their names? I have a few people in Cuba who are in dire need of their services."

"His name is Hugo Shimmel, and his daughter's name is Katrina."

"Thank you. If I may take my leave, I must speak with them and return to my ship before nightfall."

After arriving at the house and stating the reason for his visit, Captain Taylor was escorted to the library. A drawing board and a few stools comprised one corner where the engineers were working. Clearing his throat to get their attention, they looked up from what appeared to be a discussion about a specification. Mr. Shimmel asked in a somewhat heavy German accent, "Can I help you?"

He was a short thin man in his late 50's with a gray receding hair line, and pencil-thin mustache. He was in a discussion with who apparently was his daughter Katrina, a very attractive woman that appeared to be in her mid-twenties with a fair complexion and long blond curly hair.

Bowing slightly at the waist he said, "Mr. Shimmel, Katrina. I'm Captain Taylor of the ship Verna. I sail to the Americas for Mr. Wickingham, a friend of Mr. Connifer. He told me you've designed and are overseeing a project for him. I've been sent by people in Cuba to seek out an engineer who would take on the project of designing a sugar processing refinery for them. Would you be interested in such a task? If you weren't, maybe you could tell me someone who's qualified to take on such a job?"

Hugo and Katrina, surprised at the request, looked at one another. After a few moments of thought and a nod from Katrina, Mr. Shimmel remarked, "This comes as a surprise. May we think about it?"

"Yes, by all means. The parties I'm inquiring for realize it's quite an undertaking. If you agree to it, I have monies for you to begin your project. I also have a set of drawings that can be the base of your design. It's a processing plant that's already in operation in the north. It's their hopes you can improve on the design for their facility if you choose to accept the challenge. I'm sailing the day after tomorrow so if you could have an answer by then I'll relay the news upon my return."

"Thank you for the opportunity, Captain Taylor. I'm sure we'll discuss it and have an answer before you sail."

Taking his leave, he returned to the ship.

Late the following day Hugo and his daughter arrived and went directly to Captain Taylor's Cabin. They knocked on the door then entered.

"Captain Taylor, we've discussed it and decided to undertake your project. Mr. Connifer offered us the use of our current space to work on the drawings and lodging until your return. Tell your people we already see on the drawings you gave us that we can improve on the facility and begin giving the specifications to the manufacturer for the necessary parts. We'll use the same manufacturer we used to build the parts for Mr.

Connifer. They're quite capable of doing this."

Taking a bag of funds for the initial cost from his safe, he handed it to them. After shaking hands the agreement was written out and signed by both parties.

"Mr. Shimmel, upon my return to Cuba, I'll let the interested parties know I secured the people they wanted. If I may ask... could you give me an approximate time it would take to complete a project of this magnitude?"

"My daughter and I will begin immediately at the conclusion of Mr. Connifer's project. That shouldn't take more than another few days. Then we'll begin the sugar refinery drawings."

"One more question Mr. Shimmel. If they should need you at the site to supervise the construction, would you do it?"

"I think we should be there to see to its construction."

After shaking hands again they departed.

***

Several weeks later Captain Taylor arrived in Havana. At Kingsberry, he delivered the good news to Frank.

"When are you returning to England, Captain?" Frank asked.

"I'll sail day after tomorrow after I get re-supplied and John's cargo is aboard in Jamaica."

"That's great. I'll let David and Andrew know what you've accomplished. Can we expect any of the parts on your return trip?"

"It's been several weeks since I left. I imagine they have already started the process of manufacturing the first few parts. I guess I'll know better when I return."

After the Jamaica trade goods arrived, Captain Taylor hastily set sail north-northeast to England. Arriving in Portsmouth he secured a ride to Mr. Connifer's residence. After knocking he was once again ushered into the library where Hugo and Katrina were busily working.

"Hugo, how are the plans taking shape?" he asked.

Surprised at him entering the room, Hugo looked up removing his glasses. "We have a large part completed and most of the basic designed parts are already manufactured. When are you going back to Cuba?" Hugo asked.

"I'll leave as soon as you think we have enough parts to begin. The acreage is already cleared for its construction. All that's necessary is the parts and you and Katrina to supervise the project being put together properly."

"Then we'll be ready to go when the parts are aboard. I'll have the manufacturer ship them to the dock and the rest when they're completed."

***

Several days later, with the equipment loaded, they departed.

The voyage was without incident and they arrived in Havana the middle of the third week. After docking Captain Taylor took them to Hotel Havana to be temporarily quartered until other arrangements could be made.

"Hello Captain Taylor, how was your voyage?" Anne asked.

"Fine, Anne. I'd like to introduce you to Hugo Shimmel and his daughter Katrina. They're both engineers for the project."

"It's a pleasure to meet you both. Katrina if you have spare time while you're here, we could take a day to shop."

Hugo quickly remarked in his heavy Germanic accent, "Nein, not till we finish the project."

Captain Taylor asked, "Have you seen Frank?"

"Frank's in the dining room with David and Andrew. They're discussing plans for the refinery."

"Good!" Captain Taylor replied.

Entering the dining room Frank, David and Andrew rose from their chairs. Introductions were made and they marveled at a woman so young and beautiful, having the credentials of being an engineer. After ordering dinner they sat down to discussing the project.

After dinner David asked, "Mr. Shimmel when can we get started?"

"Call me Hugo. We can start as soon as the equipment arrives on site."

"Where's the piece of land located where you're going to construct it David?" Captain Taylor asked.

"We secured a piece of waterfront property a mile from here and already built the necessary docks for it."

"It sounds as though you haven't been idle these last seven or eight weeks. I like having access to the site close as possible. We'll have to find a place where we can work in relative quiet," Katrina said.

"I could put you up here in the hotel," Anne replied.

"Thank you Anne. That's very considerate of you," Frank said.

David noticed Anne returning a smile at his compliment said, "That's settled then. I'll have your luggage transferred from the ship."

"Katrina I think you're going to like the shops here. I'm sure Miss Anne and Miss Brenda will be more than happy to show you around," Andrew said.

"I think you're right. I've already been extended the invitation," she said; a light laughter by everyone seated confirmed Andrew's comment.

Hugo taking on a more serious look remarked again, "Only after we've completed our work, there's plenty to do," he said, and with a light laughter, they rose from the table.

Hugo remained seated having more questions and seemed annoyed everyone thought the meeting was at an end. Seeing the serious look he gave them they sat back down.

"Gentleman this is quite an undertaking. There are many things to discuss. I'd like first to know who will be in charge of the labor force that's needed to build it?"

Looking at each other they realized the meeting was definitely adjourning too soon.

"I think Andrew would be the most qualified in that department. He knows the people who would best fit each individual job," David said.

"I think you're right David. He also knows how to contact any one of us if Hugo needs anything. But who will run your plantation while he's gone?" Frank asked.

Andrew replied, "Carlos could do it. He's been there the longest. He knows almost everything that has to be done in the fields. If he has a question he could ask you David."

Hugo, satisfied with the answers, rose from his chair, "Now gentleman... the meeting is over. We start in the morning."

Leaving the dining room, Frank approached the desk to say a few parting words to Anne. David bid farewell to everyone and left for the plantation, and Andrew became involved in a conversation with Katrina about the project.

The following morning Andrew looked as Hugo and Katrina came down the stairs. She was dressed in loose fitting khaki pants and shirt just as Hugo. Wearing a red kerchief around her forehead it accented her long blonde hair. Even dressed in work clothes she looked quite stunning. After coffee, he drove them to the construction site.

Hugo, impressed with the progress already made, asked, "Andrew could we have a small shack erected on site? Someplace where we can work without being in the way of the construction?"

"Yes. I'll see to it right away," he replied.

When the machinery arrived that afternoon they began work getting it assembled and by the second week the structure began to take shape.

***

There was little time for socializing but Andrew looked forward to working with Katrina each day and driving them to and from the hotel. Each day he also enjoyed their company at dinner particularly interested in Katrina's input discussing the project. He thought on more than one occasion, *This is the kind of person I never dreamed would come into my life. She's someone David was lucky enough to find with Brenda."*

***

A month passed as they patiently waited for the rest of the parts from England. There was a lapse of work for several days and that gave Andrew the opportunity to ask Katrina to dinner away from the hotel. Interested in the arrangement she was looking forward to it.

Having seen her most of the time with work clothes, or on occasion with a casual dress, Andrew wasn't prepared to see her coming down the stairs in an emerald colored gown with a necklace to match. Anne was at the desk and several guests from the hotel were seated in the lounge as she entered the room.

"Katrina you look absolutely stunning," Andrew said.

Anne also commenting, "Katrina, you look elegant."

Hugo, sitting in the lounge reading the newspaper, heard the comments and looked up. He had become accustomed to seeing his daughter dressed in either field clothing, or every day dresses. The comments he heard were quite right. She was elegant. Putting the newspaper down, he went to her. Reaching out he held her arms and looked into her eyes, "Jawohl- Ipsh! Beautiful, that she is, he said," kissing her lightly on the forehead he said, "Have a wonderful time."

"Danka Schoen Papa," she replied.

Going up the stairs to his room, Hugo paused looking down from the open hallway at Katrina and Andrew standing at the hotel desk talking to Anne. He suddenly realized how their work took them to so many parts of Germany and other countries. She never had the opportunity to have a relationship, and he suddenly felt guilty. He married late in life and his wife passed away ten years ago. He thought, *We only have a home in Munich and with no living relatives maybe it's time we started looking for something permanent.* Getting to his room, he walked out on the balcony. Scanning the harbor he thought, *Maybe we should seriously look into making this our home?*

Looking down on the street below he saw Andrew and Katrina laughing as their coach was leaving, he thought, *"Yes. Maybe that's the right thing to do."* Just then, he heard a voice from the street below, "Hello Hugo. Enjoying the sunset?"

Looking down he replied, "Yes, Frank. I thought I would turn in early."

"I was just coming to speak to you," he said.

"Wait one moment, I'll come back down."

Entering the hotel, Queenie was about to follow until Frank commanded, "Stay Queenie."

Hearing him, Anne said, "No Frank. Let her come in."

Somehow Queenie understood her remark and disobeyed Frank's command. Coming from behind the counter Anne bent down to pet her, "There. She's a good dog. She won't cause any problem," Anne said, as Queenie wagged her tail enjoying the attention she was getting.

"What brings you here tonight Frank?" Anne asked.

"I just wanted to tell Hugo the parts he was waiting for just arrived."

Hugo, approaching the desk heard him, "That's good news Frank, much sooner than I expected." Turning to Anne, Hugo asked, "If you're still at the desk when Andrew and Katrina return please inform them we'll be going to the site early."

"I'll still be here Mr. Shimmel. I'll tell them."

With her reply, Hugo excused himself and went back upstairs.

Frank said, "Goodnight, Hugo." Turning to Anne he said, "I just saw Andrew and Katrina leaving. Where are they going?"

"Andrew wanted to take Katrina to dinner away from the hotel. I think they're very much interested in one another."

"Yes, Katrina looked elegant. Anne, I don't want you to think I'm too forward but it's been a little more than seven months since Beau passed away. I don't know whether you think that's an appropriate amount of time since his passing, but I was thinking you may want to enjoy an evening just as Katrina and Andrew."

Blushing she replied, "Frank, I guess I've been so busy with running the hotel, I haven't given it much thought."

He began to apologize when she said, "Maybe you're right. That would be enjoyable."

"That's good. Can we make it for next Friday?" he asked.

"Yes, that will be fine."

The following morning, Hugo was in the dining room as Katrina entered.

"Good morning Katrina. How was your dinner engagement?" he asked.

"Very fine, Papa, I was told the rest of the parts are going to be delivered this morning."

"Yes. We should get to the refinery as soon as you've finished breakfast."

Just then, Andrew entered the room to transport them. He was early and it was obvious to Hugo the two of them had formed a relationship working together. Getting a cup of coffee Andrew sat down.

"Hugo, when do you think the refinery will be completed?" he asked.

"It will be finished by the end of the month. Why?"

Looking as though he may have waited too long to make his interest known to Katrina. He wondered if there would be enough social life between them to keep her in his company. Hugo sensing it said, "Andrew the look on your face tells me you're not looking forward to our departure in three weeks."

Katrina, looking at Andrew, smiled at his disappointing facial expression hearing those words. She sensed it seemed to be an expression of wanting to say his true intentions but wasn't sure how it would be received.

After a few moments of silence Hugo said, "Katrina, I was thinking just last night that we never had a real place to call home. Selfishly without realizing it you were deprived of a place where you could have made a relationship." Pausing for a moment staring at the hibiscus on the table he continued, "I was thinking. I'm getting along in years and don't really care to travel all over Europe with our work. Would it be agreeable to make this our home?"

Andrew looked at her anxiously waiting for a response. His facial expression changed from concern to optimistic when she replied with a smile, "Yes, Papa, I'd like that very much!"

"Good, then when we complete the project we can look for a house. We'll talk more about it later. Now we should be getting to work."

On the way to the carriage they passed Anne at the desk.

Andrew more confident of his future said enthusiastically, "Anne, Hugo and Katrina decided to make Cuba their home."

"That's wonderful news. We'll look forward to their company many times in the future."

"Thank you Anne," Katrina replied.

***

Within three weeks the project was completed and the refinery was set in motion. The completion coincided with the harvesting of sugarcane, and aside from a few problems that arose with its initial startup, everything worked out well. The profits that came in not only from David and Andrew's company, but the surrounding plantations as well, more than justified the cost of building it. Frank suggested a meeting at the hotel to toast its success.

During the first month of operation Andrew was able to spend more time with Katrina and they made a mild commitment to each other, something Hugo was happy with. He purchased a small house on the outskirts of Havana, and seemed to enjoy his semiretirement.

One day when Frank was standing at the hotel desk in conversation with Anne, David and Brenda unexpectedly paid a visit.

"Hello David. You're not here on business are you?" Frank asked.

"No, Frank. Brenda wanted to visit Anne for awhile. I think she has an urge to go shopping," then laughed.

"David, I was just thinking. Why don't we have a celebration to the success of the refinery?" Anne said.

"We could have it at Kingsberry," Frank quickly replied.

"That's a great idea Frank. Let's have it when John and Captain Jarvis are here. Do you know when Captain Jarvis arrives?" David asked.

"He's expected next Friday. We could arrange it for Saturday evening."

"Saturday it is. I'll notify the Shimmel's," Anne said.

***

On Friday, the day before the big celebration, Frank returned to Kingsberry. While having breakfast he heard voices coming from the library. As he entered the room he noticed Anne on a ladder adjusting some books and Thelma at the bottom of the ladder, scolding her for doing it. Surprised to see her he thought, *How pretty she looks with her long brown hair flowing down her petite form.*

Surprised by his entrance Anne suddenly turned losing her balance. Frank ran over in time to catch her thinking, *"How light she is. How good it feels holding her in my arms."* In a semi-scolding tone he agreed with Thelma saying, "Anne you shouldn't be on a ladder. You could hurt yourself."

Thelma added, "I dun' told her she was gonna fall. I just kept tellin' her and tellin' her. She just don't pay me no mind. I should just go on back to New Orleans and leave her be." Continuing in a lower tone as she left the room, "If it wasn't for all that water I have to cross, I surely would."

"Frank, I was just trying to help Thelma with the preparations for the big event."

"Well, she's right. You shouldn't be doing it. They're enough people here who can."

The next day everyone gathered at Kingsberry, and as Captain Jarvis came in, David greeted him, "Hello Captain. I haven't seen you in quite awhile."

"Yes, David. I've been busy making as many trips as I could to New Orleans. I know you must be aware of it from the proceeds of the contraband."

"Yes, I was. It helped tremendously with the construction of the refinery. Have you any news to tell us about the war?"

"Last month, the Union Army captured Fort Fisher in Wilmington, North Carolina. That's the last port of the confederacy on the east coast. With everything else closed, and Sherman extracting revenge on the South, I don't see the war lasting very much longer."

"Well, that's a good cause to celebrate both: our refinery, and the end of that horrible war."

With everyone seated at the dinner table, David tapped the side of his glass to get everyone's attention. "Ladies and gentleman I have some good news I'd like to announce."

Looking at Brenda he continued, "I'm happy to say Brenda will be having a baby in about six months." Looking at Anne he continued, "Although I don't approve of her and Anne using the excuse of going shopping to mask Brenda seeing the doctor, I can't express my happiness enough at the event."

Anne and Brenda blushed realizing he figured out their secret.

Andrew rose to his feet. "Well, I might just as well add a little more wood to the fire of this happy occasion. Miss Katrina and I became engaged last evening."

After another round of congratulations, they enjoyed a great dinner with enjoyable conversation.

After dinner they adjourned to the parlor where Anne, Sharon, and Brenda cornered Katrina looking at her engagement ring, asking about her impending wedding day.

"We've decided to have it in June. Anne would you be willing to be my maid of honor?" she asked.

"I'd be more than happy," Anne replied.

As the evening came to a close, Frank thinking about Anne and the previous day asked, "David, Anne came with you. Would it be okay if I drove her back to the hotel?"

"That's fine Frank. I'm sure she wouldn't mind."

***

Several months later, Captain Taylor came to port again. He just arrived from New Orleans bearing good news. The Civil War was over and hurried to the hotel to tell Frank and David.

"David, now that the war has ended do you have any plans to return to New Orleans?" Frank asked.

"Yes Frank. After the baby comes I'd like to go back and see how Charles weathered the last year and a half of the war."

"I think Captain Jarvis will return from Marseille by then. Now that the war is ended, all we have to worry about is paying the port inspectors again. I'm sure everyone enjoyed the profits we made," Frank said.

"Yes, the Franklin Sugar Company's doing so well. We've decided to set up another processing plant in Philadelphia. When Captain Taylor arrives I'm sending Andrew and Katrina there to find a port site along the Delaware River. It's a large hub of manufacturing and we won't have to rely on a company in England to make the necessary parts. They'll be made right there."

"Do you think Andrew and Katrina would mind relocating to Philadelphia?" Frank asked.

"I've already discussed it with them and they're in full agreement. One thing I realize, Edward was absolutely right about Andrew, he's a person you can count on."

"Yes, Edward was right about quite a few things. He said trade would continue no matter what the war was doing."

For that moment, David contemplated the conversation with Edward about New Orleans. He remembered him saying, *'All wars are fought over economics of one sort or another. There are people up North that are heavily invested in New Orleans. They're not going to want to lose money, no matter how the war ends.'*

The End

The author writes in several genre, murder mysteries and paranormals.

Other publications are:

Veronica – a fiction murder mystery which takes place on Long Beach Island, N.J.

New Hope – another fiction murder mystery which takes place in a Theatre in New Hope, Pa.

Mystery of the Windowed Closet – a paranormal with a haunting and an angry spirit.

Mist in the Blue Bottle – a sequel to Mystery of the Windowed Closet. The bottle used for the séance, has far more powers beyond the psychics ability to control.

Crossing the Blue Line – a police murder mystery.

Facebook R. J. Bonett